USA Today Bestse...

DALE MAYER

A Psychic Visions Novel

INKED FOREVER

INSANITY
Beverly Dale Mayer
Valley Publishing Ltd.

Copyright © 2023

All rights reserved. Except for use in any review, the reproduction or utilization of this work in whole or in part by any electronic, mechanical, or other means, now known or hereafter invented—including xerography, photocopying, and recording, or in any information storage or retrieval system—is forbidden, without the written permission of the publisher.

This is a work of fiction. Names, characters, places, brands, media, and incidents are either the product of the author's imagination or are used fictitiously. Any resemblance to actual events, locales, or persons, living or dead, is entirely coincidental.

ISBN-13: 978-1-773367-19-4
Print Edition

Books in This Series:

Tuesday's Child
Hide 'n Go Seek
Maddy's Floor
Garden of Sorrow
Knock Knock…
Rare Find
Eyes to the Soul
Now You See Her
Shattered
Into the Abyss
Seeds of Malice
Eye of the Falcon
Itsy-Bitsy Spider
Unmasked
Deep Beneath
From the Ashes
Stroke of Death
Ice Maiden
Snap, Crackle…
What If…
Talking Bones
String of Tears
Inked Forever
Insanity
Psychic Visions Books 1–3
Psychic Visions Books 4–6
Psychic Visions Books 7–9

About This Book

Tasmin's business isn't for everyone. Yet she recognizes the value she offers for grieving families. Still, the subject isn't something most people are willing to talk about. However, over time, her business has grown through word of mouth—much to the horror of her family.

Until a detective walks in, inquiring about a piece that had been stolen overnight. This is the first inkling she has that someone is out to destroy her business. Unfortunately it won't be the last …

Detective Hanson MacGyver isn't sure what to make of Tasmin, yet he understands the need for licensed morticians. However, how she got into the process of preserving tattoos for grieving family and friends is something he has never seen before and isn't comfortable with. Live and let live works for him as a motto, but, when her works in progress start showing up in public locations and not in a good way, he knows they have someone who hates what she is doing … or hates the owners of the tattoos.

Something's *off* about the whole mess. And that's just on the surface. When both Tasmin and Hanson dig deeper, a whole lot more is going on underneath. And none of it is normal or nice …

Sign up to be notified of all Dale's releases here!
https://geni.us/DaleNews

CHAPTER 1

Tasmin Baker opened up the shop door, twisting the sign to Open. Then she propped the door wide open to let out some of the formaldehyde fumes, turned on the lights and headed to the back room, where she put on the coffeepot. When she turned back again, a man, a huge presence, filled the room. Yet she felt no fear.

He stared at her and asked, "Tasmin Baker?"

"Yes, that's me." She walked toward him with a cup in her hand. "What can I do for you?"

"I understand you run a very unique business."

She snorted at that. "Yeah, something I fell into."

He hesitated and then asked, "I don't suppose you'd care to tell me how?"

"No, not really. What are you, a reporter?" Such disgust filled her voice that she immediately tried to change her tone. "Sorry, I didn't mean it quite that way."

"I'm not a reporter. I'm a cop."

At that, she froze, looked up at him, and frowned. "I have a business license, and everything is in order. Even my taxes are paid."

He held up a hand. "That's not why I'm here."

"*Sure*," she quipped. "In my experience, cops don't usually come by for any good reasons."

He relaxed slightly. "That may be, but I'm not trying to

make your life more difficult. However, I do have a few questions for you."

"Yeah, about what?"

He hesitated and then added, "One of the pieces that you're preserving."

She groaned. "Look. A licensed doctor did the cuttings. I have all the paperwork, including the legal stuff," she stated. "Man, I have more paperwork than you can shake a stick at," she declared, her tone somewhere between mildly irritated and pissed. "It's all legal, I assure you. Who is it you're talking about?" She looked around. "I have quite a few cuttings here. As I told you, I keep a lawyer on tap to help me with this."

"I get that," he replied, then looked at one of the framed pieces. "That's your uncle, isn't it?"

"I hate the way you say that," she admitted. "That is a piece of my uncle's artwork, yes," she stated cautiously.

"Right." The cop turned and looked at a couple others on the wall. "Have you ever had any bad press over this?"

"Lots," she answered succinctly. "People don't want to see tattoo preservation as an art form."

"It is very personal," he noted, looking at her, "and it crosses all kinds of boundaries that make people uneasy."

"Yes, I get that, but what does that have to do with you?" He hesitated. She wrapped one arm around her ribs then took a sip of her coffee, her eyes watchful.

"Has anybody tried to stop you from doing this?"

She shrugged. "Not really. Most people don't know all the details, except for those interested in having their ink preserved."

He nodded. "So there have been no attacks on your shop or anything like that?"

"No. Why?" she asked curiously. She looked around and frowned. "I mean, everything seemed normal when I opened this morning, but I haven't really had a chance to get started. This my first cup of coffee since I was a little late coming in, but now you've got me worried."

"Could you take a look around, please?"

She stared at him for a moment, then slowly nodded. "I gather you won't tell me anything until we get that far."

"No, it would be nice if I could clear something up first."

She put down her coffee cup and glared at him but walked around, checking to make sure everything was as it should be. Then she headed to the back room, to her workshop.

When she got into the workshop, she flicked on all the lights, looked around, and said, "It looks okay in here."

"What about artwork?" he asked.

"I've got four pieces in progress right now," she stated, as she turned to look at the pieces she had saved. "I've got two that are here." She pointed them out. "Then I've got another one in the drying room."

She walked into the drying room, frowned, and looked back at him. "That one's missing."

"Missing?"

"Yes," she cried out. "Oh my God, it's missing-missing." She frantically went through the shop. Then she turned slowly, looked at him, and asked, "You knew it wouldn't be here, didn't you?"

He hesitated.

"Stop," she cried out. "I don't know what's going on, and I don't know what this has to do with you. I don't know anything about it, but I'm missing a piece that matters a lot to somebody, and I will wind up in a shitstorm if I don't find it."

"I think I can help you with finding it," he said, "but it might have been damaged."

She stared at him, then he pulled out his phone and showed her an image of a beautiful tattoo.

She nodded. "Yes, that's it," she cried out in relief. Then she looked at him in shock. "What do you mean, damaged? How did you get it?"

"It was found in one of the fountains downtown," he explained, "stretched out and nailed into the bottom of the fountain."

She stared across the room, her bottom lip trembling, her gut twisting at the image. Ever-so-slowly afraid she'd break and rage at him, she whispered, "What?"

He nodded slowly. "Somebody decided that preserving the art was the right thing to do, but private it was not," he noted, "and he put it out for public display. Do you want to tell me who this artwork belongs to?"

She swallowed hard. "A model, a beautiful model who ended up with cancer and died twelve days ago. I got the legalities taken care of on behalf of her family, with all the paperwork, and the surgeon cut the tattoo off her back, and it was sent to me to preserve for her family."

He nodded. "So, do you have any explanation as to how it went from your shop to a fountain where this model's tattoo is now on display for the rest of the world to see?"

To say she didn't have an answer was one thing, but, as she stared at the craggy features in front of her, she realized he wasn't really looking for those kinds of answers. She took a second, then spoke. "I don't know what to say."

He produced his business card, as a way to formally introduce himself. Then he continued with his questions. "Do you have a security system?"

She nodded. "An alarm, and it was on when I opened up this morning," she said cautiously.

At that, his gaze narrowed. "And you got here to Inked Forever at what time?" He pulled out a notebook and started to ask her questions.

She knew she had to answer but didn't have much to give him. She provided as many details as she could. "I came in at eight a.m., unlocked the door, and disarmed the system. I put on coffee and came back out to find you had walked in," she said quietly.

"Who knows the security code?"

"Lorelei, who's my sister, and my mother, who both come in to cover for me every once in a while. I've had others but no one recently."

She pondered the question for a moment. "Obviously the security company has access to it—through their system, I would think—but other than that, I'm not sure," she said. "I did have a repairman in last week though." She considered that for a moment and shuddered. "I didn't honestly think very much about it."

"Do you know what company it was?"

"Not offhand, but I do have an invoice," she said, walking to the back.

He followed behind, stopped at the threshold to her small back room, her workshop so to speak, and studied the surroundings.

"I'm not sure what you're looking for," she said, as she glanced up from her paperwork, "but I really don't do much of the work here."

At that, his gaze zinged back toward her. "Are you the

one who actually does the preserving?"

"I work with a mortician." She stopped and said, "Look. Just in case you didn't know this, I'm also a licensed mortician myself. It's just not the field I prefer to work in. My family owns a funeral home, and, once I started doing this preservation work, it became my passion. I don't do anything else at the funeral home unless, … unless I get called in because they're really short-handed, but it's not my preferred line of work."

"Yet you went into it as a career."

She gave him a ghost of a smile. "For a lot of reasons that I won't bore you with," she said, "but I will state that there can be an awful lot of family pressure sometimes."

His lips twitched at that. "I'll give you that. I can't imagine, particularly in this field, that bucking the family business would be easy."

"Well, this field isn't any different than any other, and, no matter the career, there's always been that expectation to take over the family industry."

"And what about your sister?"

"My sister *did* take over the family industry," Tasmin confirmed, with half a smile. "My parents have no sons, which is where the expectation would hopefully land. As such, my father still works there with Lorelei, and my mother runs the storefront and the office work side of it."

"And you're the one who walked away?"

"I'm the one who walked away," she said, with a slightly darker tone.

"Any problems over that?"

She pondered that question before answering. "I'm sure my family felt a degree of disappointment, even some aggravation, but this was something I needed to do."

"And how do they feel about your chosen field now?"

"Well, one is disgusted by it, and the other understands—or at least she says she does. Then there is my father. He won't step foot in my store. He is extremely religious, and, in his mind, when a body is dead and gone, it's dead and gone and meant to be returned to the ground," she said quietly. "To him, my preservation business is on the edge of sacrilegious."

He studied her for a moment in surprise.

She shrugged. "There's just no understanding sometimes, even among family members."

"No, I imagine there isn't. I guess I'm wondering if anybody here in your world would actively be trying to set you up."

She stared at him in surprise and then immediately shook her head. "I can't imagine why, or who, but just because I can't imagine it doesn't mean it can't exist as a possibility," she said. "It would be extremely disappointing if that's what happened, but … I suppose it's possible."

She was quiet for a moment. "There was some outcry when an article was done on my business last year, yet an awful lot of people were fascinated by the process, and some were just curious. I did refuse any and all follow-up interviews, mostly because I didn't have time and just didn't want to fuel the fire and deal with the fallout again."

"What kind of fallout was it, and who did the interview?"

"It was just the local paper, but the online version went viral, so it kicked up quite a fuss," she muttered.

"And I presume it wasn't in a good way."

"Well, I'm not sure there is a good way when it comes to a fuss of that nature. Most people would say that any publicity is good publicity, but I'm here to tell you that it's not quite true."

He nodded. "Particularly in something so controversial."

"Exactly, but I'm also an artist, so a part of me really understands why somebody would want to keep their ink forever."

"Sure," the cop agreed. "I guess I can understand why the actual owner might want his ink to last forever, but why would somebody other than the person who was wearing it want someone else's ink to last forever?"

At that, she smiled up at him. "Because a lot of people do even weirder things when it comes to losing their loved ones," she said. "There are people and stories that would make your skin crawl about what people are willing to do to preserve a part of their loved ones," she said. "We get all kinds of requests."

"Such as?"

She stared at him for a moment. "As long as you aren't going to ask for names or details, I can tell you that we've had people requesting that body ornaments be removed or wanted special things added to body ornaments. One woman wanted a special note added to her husband's cock ring. Another gentleman, who absolutely loved his wife's ears, wanted the ear lobes taken off and preserved, so he could have them for himself. Really no way to know how people feel about various aspects of their personal relationships."

He stared at her in shock.

She shrugged. "Nothing stranger in fiction than the actual truth itself."

"Yeah, and who said that, some famous poet or something?" he asked, with a note of disgust in his voice.

"No," she said. "It was me. And, as an artist, I understand and would like to have things I create survive beyond my life, as a gift to humanity, if anybody saw it that way. But I paint on canvas, not skin, and I paint for the ages. I don't paint for today." She could tell that he didn't quite understand that.

He gave her a headshake. "I guess there's no figuring out humans, is there?"

"No, there sure isn't," she said succinctly.

"Why did you leave the funeral home industry?" he asked, his tone piercing and more abrupt than before.

She glared at him. "It has nothing to do with this."

He shrugged. "Maybe not, but I'm curious, and, if it's related, I need to know."

"I just said it's not related."

"But it's you, and something is going on here that I don't quite understand, so I'm not exactly sure I believe you."

She shrugged. "You're a cop. I'm sure you've checked the files, but I don't know if you've run my name," she murmured. "If you do, I'm sure you'll have all the answers you want."

His eyebrows rose ever-so-slowly, as he stared at her. "And you'd rather I go check it out for myself first."

"Absolutely, and preferably not come back," she said, her tone harsher than she intended.

He nodded. "Fine, I'll do that. And, if I need to come back, I will. You can count on that."

And she had absolutely no doubt that he would.

"So, the next question is, if you do all this work at your family's workplace, when did you last see that stolen piece?"

"I brought it here from the funeral home yesterday and was all set to frame it today."

"And what would that entail?"

She looked at him in surprise. "After preservation, these pieces are almost like parchment paper. They're a lot more durable and could handle the water in the fountain just fine probably, at least I hope so," she said, with a wince, as she glanced at him. "How badly damaged is it?"

"It's got extra holes along the perimeter. But, outside of the fact that I know what it is, it is a beautiful piece of artwork."

"It *is* her," Tasmin said gently. "And most of that artwork was done as part of her journey through this process of trying to fight the cancer that ate away at her body. I wasn't sure that I could even preserve it."

"Why?" he asked curiously.

"Because cancer, the treatments, the medications, just the disease, it ravages our body in such a way that people rarely think about how damaged the skin itself can become. Every thirty days your body produces a new skin, and, every thirty days, when you've been struggling with cancer for a couple years, that skin is no longer as perfect as it once was. Therefore, the artwork attached to that damaged skin is no longer in prime condition either."

With that, she knew she'd touched a nerve in a different way. She studied him for a long moment but immediately saw flashes of a woman dying in his arms, somebody he cared about, from the expression on his face. "I'm sorry," she whispered. "Apparently all this touches a nerve."

"It would touch a nerve for anybody who's lost somebody they cared about," he said quietly.

She nodded and busied herself at the copier, giving him time to compose himself. "Apparently it was something like cancer?"

"It was," he said, his voice stronger, as he regained control.

Then, in a casual tone of voice, he put the conversation back on professional footing. "You can't have it back yet."

"I understand, but can I at least see it, so I can assess the damage, since I'll have to try and fix it?"

"You can come to the morgue tomorrow," he said.

She looked up at him and nodded. "Is Dr. Kreimer still there?" The detective nodded in surprise. She smiled. "Because of the industry that I've always worked in, I do know some of the people involved."

"Right," he said. "I hadn't considered that."

"I'm sure some of them can give me a good reference, though whether they would choose to is a whole different story." At that, his gaze sharpened, and she waved a hand. "You'll have to go back to that search of my history."

"Okay, seems I will, as soon as I get back to the office."

"You do that, but, in the meantime, I have no idea how somebody turned off the alarm, stole that artwork, that memorial art piece, or whatever you want to call it. I'm still trying to come up with proper words that don't upset people and don't bring on the tears, you know? Anyway, I'll plan to head down to the morgue tomorrow morning."

"Good enough." He slowly retreated. "I also need to know what security company you had in to fix your system."

She nodded and asked, "What's your email?"

He gave it to her, and she fired off a scanned copy of the invoice. "I've just sent you a copy of it. The repairman was here for … I think maybe an hour, but I don't really know."

"Was anybody else working with you that day?"

"I wasn't working here that day. My sister was filling in for me. My mother comes in occasionally to help me out too, if my storefront is really busy or if I've got lots of customer appointments. They can be time-consuming."

At that, he raised his brows.

She smiled. "Just think about the subject matter," she said gently. "And how emotional people get over a loss like that."

"Right. So you do one-on-one appointments with people?"

"Something like that," she said. "I mean, sometimes it's handled over the phone, and sometimes, if they're local or want to see my work and to decide whether it's something they really want hanging on their wall, they come in and take a look."

"And these are all samples?"

"Yes. They are samples." She looked up at the closest one. "And, yes, that is my uncle's piece up there," she said, "but it's hardly my uncle."

"And yet it's a piece of him."

"Yes, and I, for one, am quite happy to have him up there. He was a good friend of mine, and we were very close."

"I'm sorry," he said. "That must have been difficult."

"Very, and that's also what started my passion for this. He was very proud of his artwork, and he definitely didn't want to die knowing that it was disappearing with him. And there was no need for it."

"Still, I'm sure a lot of people would think otherwise."

"Oh, a lot of people did, a lot of people still do, but it's becoming a little more common. I'm not the only one in the world who does this, you know? Some of these preservation elements—the whole system, the thought process—are thousands of years old. Go do a Google search of some of the

Japanese specialists who worked in this field. Some were better than others, and also check out the multiple collections of tattoos that have been stored in formaldehyde in jars. Of course that's not as pretty and looks much more like a chunk of a person, especially when compared to the pieces that I have."

She pointed out the beautiful guitar, done in multiple shades of black and white and grays, hanging on the wall. "That was a friend of mine," she said. "He was killed in a motorcycle accident, and I did that for his family. Unfortunately his mother was absolutely tormented by it, and I ended up agreeing to take it back. He was my friend, and I'm more than happy to be reminded of him in that piece of artwork up there that he did himself."

As she watched, the cop walked closer and looked at it. "It's really hard to tell it was part of a person."

"That's actually from his thigh," she said, coming up to stand beside him. "As I said, by the time we're done, the preservation looks more like parchment paper."

He nodded. "I did see that with the piece found in the fountain. It's pretty amazing what people can do these days."

"Well, I mean, between cryonics and somebody in Germany trying to do a head transplant," she said, with a note of laughter, "I don't think many boundaries exist where people aren't willing to cross them to do what they want to do with their own bodies. We have body art. We have science. We have bodies flayed into one million tiny slices and put on display, traveling around the world. This is really no different. Somebody made a beautiful art piece, and either the owner or the artist or a family member wanted it preserved as a memento. Considering that I agree with them, I really don't have a problem trying to make their wishes happen," she said. "So I don't know who did such a terrible thing to this poor woman and her family, but I hope, for their sake, you find out. And I really need that piece back. In their minds, it's all they have."

"You mean, for your sake."

"No. I mean for the family's peace of mind," she said. "Will my business take a hit over this? Quite possibly, and I obviously don't need that. This is a very private process, very special, so to have people feel like they cannot put their trust in me to keep the piece safe and the whole thing private, is another headache I don't need to deal with. Therefore, anything you can do to wrap this up quickly would be appreciated."

The cop just nodded.

~

FOR HANSON MACGYVER, this was one of the most bizarre scenarios he'd seen in his work so far. Yet, on the other side of his life, it was just an extension of the craziness he was still learning to control. He could not have imagined before he got up today how his day would begin. But here he was, going down that rabbit hole of craziness right off the bat.

He'd seen the fountain and seen the beautiful piece of artwork spread out and pinned down. He'd originally thought it had been stretched, but, when the forensics team got it out of the fountain, Hanson noted that somebody had tried to stretch it but found that it was already as stretched as it would get. That's when they realized it was a preserved tattoo.

Hanson had thought for sure they had some weird serial killer on their plate, but, as it turned out, this was a professionally preserved piece. He had looked into Tasmin's qualifications before coming here, but he hadn't looked into her history, as far as past cases of just her past. But then this wasn't exactly the type of job he was accustomed to doing or had expected to be assigned to.

He was new to the town, new to the department, and apparently this crime was something perfect for the rookie. He had skills; he had a lot of skills, in fact, but the ones that he really needed for this were those he was not polished at. He knew it would be a challenge whether to stay neutral or to access any of the energy that went into this. Of course it was something he didn't dare talk about to the others.

He studied the woman in front of him, who was trying hard to turn her attention back to her work and to ignore him, but he wasn't letting her.

She finally looked up at him and asked, "Is there anything else I can do for you?"

Her tone was polite, but Tasmin's words and body language conveyed a very clear message. Pretty much that she was busy, that he was in the way, and that he needed to shove off, so to speak.

"I'll be back," he said abruptly. Then he turned and left the building.

Hanson felt Tasmin's gaze boring deep into his back, but he ignored that too. One of the things he often had seen before, both with and without his multiple extrasensory skills and without them, was that putting somebody on the spot, just standing there and staring at them, often made them jump into a conversation. Uncomfortable with something going on in their world, often they would blurt out helpful things.

In her case that didn't happen, which he also found interesting. However, he noted, with a sense of irritation, that she'd experienced way too much in the years that she'd been doing this for anything to really get to her. Yet her gaze was guarded, as if he was an unknown, which he was, but he didn't intend to stay that way. Something was going on at her place that he needed to figure out, not just for his sake but also for his sanity.

As he walked out of the store, he looked around, checking out the neighborhood, trying to take a calm, slow deep breath, backing away from the conversation that had set him off so badly.

He had, indeed, experienced the loss of somebody close. His best friend, his soul mate, the woman he'd loved since middle school, had died of breast cancer in his arms. It had destroyed him for so long. It had been a lot of years ago, but it still had the pain and the power to destroy him in a heartbeat. Tasmin hadn't done it on purpose, but just the memory of such a devastating loss, the way Tasmin spoke about it, was something Hanson could relate to very quickly, and that had been just as hard on him.

He gave a quick mental shake and turned to look back at Tasmin's shop, studying the energy around it, wondering just what was bothering him. He didn't have much in the way of dependable psychic skills yet, since he was something called a shadow seer. At least that's what the person he had been working with had said.

It didn't make a whole lot of sense to Hanson at first, since what was the point of seeing shadows? But, if his mentor had been standing here, she would have reminded him that the shadows were what told you about everybody else. That people had shadows for a reason. That a lot of people kept things in the shadows that they didn't want others to see.

So sometimes in the shadows you saw way more than you wanted to, and that was his gift, seeing the shadow person. Hanson had thought he had gone crazy for the longest time and had taken time away from his job, while he tried to figure out what was going on. He finally realized that what he was seeing was stuff that other people saw, although not many, according to his mentor.

Apparently it was normal and natural for anybody with this kind of ability, though it had taken Hanson a long time to adjust and an even longer time to be comfortable with his *gift*. But he'd managed, and now he was leading somewhat of a normal life again.

Until this job had come up. He was new to Texas, new to the Houston area, and much preferred being here in the small town outside of the big city. He hadn't really cared where he wound up, and this was as good a place as any.

He remained on the block, studying the area for a bit, and he saw no shadows on any level of existence, as far as he could see with his special sight. After a short walk back to his car, he got in and headed to his office. He had to check in on a few things, like the security company that had worked on Tasmin's system. Plus, Hanson needed to confirm with the sister how many other people may have had access to the place. Then frowned at a forgotten question.

He quickly dialed her number. When Tasmin answered, he explained who he was and said, "I forgot to ask if you had cameras."

"I do." Then with a note of frustration, she added, "Unfortunately they aren't working today. After you left, I went and checked them myself, but they're black."

"So, back to the security company, *huh?*" he asked in a mocking tone.

"Unless you have a better idea, yes," she snapped.

"No, not necessarily. I'll get back to you." And, with that, he hung up again.

It was all just a little too convenient—a little too convenient that her cameras weren't working and a little too convenient that she didn't have any answers. She was looking pretty darn good for this. But was that fair? It could also be a setup. An awful lot was going on here, and the last thing she would want to do was bring unwelcome attention to her specialized work.

Then he remembered her comment about the saying that any attention was good promotion and how she didn't agree with that. *Playing devil's advocate,* he whispered to himself, "Is that actually the truth, or were you just saying that?" Because Hanson knew people would say anything when they were under pressure.

Back at the office, he headed to his desk.

Mark, one of the other two guys he worked with, looked up at him and asked, "Did you get anywhere with her?"

"Not very far," he said.

"Yeah, we didn't expect you would."

"And that's why you sent me, right?" he asked in a neutral tone.

Mark laughed. "Yeah, it sure is. She's one weird chick."

Hanson pondered that for a few minutes, as Mark got up to refill his coffee. Was it just him? Hanson hadn't noticed anything weird about Tasmin at all. When Mark came back by Hanson's desk with his coffee in hand, Hanson continued the conversation. "Weird in what way?"

"You saw her," Mark explained. "I mean, she digs dead bodies and preserves chunks of flesh. That's like beyond weird."

"Right," he said, "I guess it's definitely different."

"You guess?" Mark said, with a laugh. "But, hey, you seem to be pretty stone-cold yourself, so maybe she's the kind of chick for you."

He shrugged. "Not my style. I like them warm and willing."

At that, Mark laughed and sat back down at his desk.

"Still doesn't change the fact that we've got somebody out there who put that tattoo on display," Hanson reminded Mark.

"Yeah, but it's not as if he killed anybody," Mark argued. "Whoever it came from was already dead. The thief just broke into this woman's shop and stole it."

Hanson nodded. "Yet her security was on, and there's no sign of any break-in. And that particular piece is the only one missing."

"Well, that's kind of spooky, isn't it?" Mark asked sarcastically, smirking at Hanson.

Hanson shrugged. Mark was a standard, nine-to-five, black-and-white kind of cop, and any of this spooky stuff just wouldn't cut it with him. "So, in other words, she's the one who did it, and she's really crappy at hiding her tracks? I don't know if that's a good assessment either," Hanson stated, looking around at his coworker. "If you think about it, it doesn't do her any good to have her shop vandalized like that."

"Well, you know what they say," Mark added. "Any publicity is good publicity."

"Yet now some people won't trust her security on something like this because it was broken into."

"And yet you also know that anybody's business can get broken into. It's just the luck of the draw," Mark said. "You mark my words. It'll be her. You might as well write up the file now."

"And if she didn't do it?"

Mark shrugged. "Can't say I really care either way. Yet she's looking awfully good for it to me. It's not our job to be the judge and jury about what she did. It's just our job to catch them."

"Regardless of whether they actually did it or not?" Hanson asked, with a note of humor.

"Well, preferably we have evidence that proves they did it," he said in exasperation, "but really I don't give a shit either way. We have cases to close, and, if we don't close them, we're in trouble. I'd just as soon close them and not be in trouble. So get at it."

"Right," Hanson replied, then sat back and wondered again for the umpteenth time what he was doing in this field.

CHAPTER 2

Tasmin worked away in her shop for the morning, trying hard to keep her nervousness at bay. She'd talked to the family involved, explaining that there'd been a break-in at the store and that she was heading to the morgue in the morning and would let them know the condition of the tattoo and that she had been told that it wasn't terribly damaged, but she didn't know for certain what that would mean.

Of course the family wasn't happy and had been less than pleased that her shop had been broken into, but even more so that it had been their daughter's tattoo that had ended up being stolen. Tasmin had done everything she could to make them feel better, but, of course, not a whole lot anybody could do with this right now.

It just rubbed the family raw to know that somebody would violate a piece that they held special, and it was also something that the family did not want to be made public. And Tasmin agreed with that; the family had every right to privacy. As Tasmin got up and measured off the frame again, wondering how she could have gotten such a simple thing wrong, she took the frame back over to the piece she was working on, when the front door to her shop opened.

Her sister called out, "Hey, Tasmin, are you here?"

"I'm in the back," she said.

Lorelei stepped through into the back workroom and sighed. "You could try lights, you know?" She flipped on the overhead lights.

Tasmin sat back and blinked several times at the change in light. "Yeah, *thanks*," she muttered in disgust. "You know I do my best work in the dark."

Her sister stared at her. "You're just getting weirder, you know that?"

Exasperated, Tasmin stood and glared at sister, her hands on her hips. "It's not really a great day. Did you have a reason for stopping by?"

Her sister glared right back. "Yeah, I need you to work again. Plus, you ordered supplies. Here are the invoices," she stated, passing them over.

Tasmin looked down at them and sighed. "And I told you that I'd pay them as soon as the pieces were picked up."

"That doesn't cover my bills though," Lorelei snapped in frustration. "We're both trying to run businesses here, but, in order to make that happen, we both have to pay our bills."

There was definitely some truth to the matter. "Sorry about that," Tasmin replied. "How about we renegotiate my use of the facilities?"

"How about you come work for me part-time as your payment for using the facilities," her sister suggested, for the umpteenth time. "You know I need help."

"You do," Tasmin agreed, "but it won't do your business reputation any good if people know I'm back there again."

"So, they don't find out," she muttered. "We'll keep you in the background."

"You mean, tucked away in the basement, doing all the lovely Dracula things, so nobody knows?"

"Hey, don't put it that way," Lorelei argued, again glaring at her sister. "Respect and all that."

"Right, I got it. ... Did you ever wonder where our lives might have been if we weren't born into a family of morticians?"

"Yeah, all the time," Lorelei declared in disgust. "Do you know how long it took to get a boyfriend who would go out with me because it was me and not on a dare to go out with the spooky chick whose parents dealt with all the dead bodies in town?"

"Since I had the same problem, yeah, I get it," she said. Then the two of them smiled at each other.

"Still," Lorelei grumbled, "it's the life we have and apparently is what we're supposed to do. It's not as if we can turn around and change it now."

"I know, but sometimes I wonder if we shouldn't have though," Tasmin noted, her tone serious.

Lorelei stared at her and nodded. "It's not the first time you've mentioned that—though, in your case, things went a little sideways for a while."

"Ya think?" Tasmin quipped. "A *mental breakdown* is how Mom put it, as I recall."

"What did you expect her to say? That you'd started seeing and having conversations with dead people? You know that wouldn't go over well."

"Even though I *was* talking to the dead people?"

"Sure, that's what you say, but nobody else is talking to them. So no one believed you."

"And why would you even think I would lie about that?" Tasmin asked, staring at her sister, and angry all over again.

"Look. I'm not here to argue with you," Lorelei replied. "I'm just here to remind you that you have unpaid bills. The bottom line is that I need them paid, and, if you can't pay them, I expect you to show up and to work them off."

"*Great.* Thanks a lot."

"You need use of the facilities, and I need the help," she stated. "So you know it's a good solution."

"Maybe," Tasmin muttered, "but then I'd end up working twenty-four hours a day, trying to do that work and mine."

"You're the one who wanted to go off and have your own business, doing *this*," she argued, with a wave of her hand at the workshop. "It's all Dad can even do to let you in the house now."

"Do you think I don't know that?" Tasmin replied, staring at her sister. "It's okay for him to be handling dead bodies, but it's not okay for me to be handling dead body parts? I don't get it."

Her sister winced at that. "Okay, I get it. It doesn't make a whole lot of sense, but it's still him. And again, we don't have any choice in it. This is how it is."

Tasmin sighed, put down her screwdriver, then stood and faced her sister. "I shouldn't get angry at you," she muttered. "I'm just frustrated. I had the police here this morning about a break-in, and I needed that like a hole in the head."

"What do you mean, a break-in?" Lorelei asked, looking around. "What was taken?"

"One of my pieces and, worse yet, it was put on display down on the Old Fountain Square."

Lorelei turned and looked at her in horror.

Tasmin nodded.

"Oh my God. They took one of your tattoos and put it on display?"

"Yes. I don't know whether it was a joke or something

more sinister, but, of course, that made for a great morning," she shared. "I've got the jobs to pay those invoices. I just need to get the work done."

"I'd rather you came and worked for me anyway," Lorelei admitted. "I'm getting pretty burnt out."

"You and me both," Tasmin agreed sadly. "We're both in an industry with very little forgiveness and way-too-much work."

"Since the damn pandemic came through, we have an awful lot more in the way of bodies," Lorelei explained. "We're really strapped. Dad's working full-time, even though he's retired. Mom's been in the office every day, and here they had hoped to be off traveling and doing fun stuff at this stage of their life."

"I think we all thought we'd be doing fun stuff, regardless of the stage of life," Tasmin noted indignantly. "Instead we're both running businesses and just trying to stay afloat."

Her sister stopped and frowned at her. "Are you not doing this because you want to?"

Tasmin now frowned and stared at her shop. "I guess I'm doing this because I feel compelled to," she muttered.

"I'm not sure that's a good answer," Lorelei replied, still frowning.

"No, maybe not, but why are you doing what you're doing?"

Her sister glared at her. "Simple. Because you won't."

Tasmin laughed. "Not to mention the fact that having me around there wasn't doing the business any good."

"No, it wasn't," Lorelei admitted sadly. "Ever since it got out that you were talking to the corpses, it started freaking people out."

"Sorry about that," Tasmin said, "yet it just happens to

be true."

"See? And that's how we end up in trouble." Her sister didn't seem to know what to say. "Why can't you just keep your mouth shut, if that's the case?"

"It'd be easier if the dead wouldn't talk to me, but they insist on it, so what am I supposed to do? Ignore them?"

"Absolutely you're supposed to ignore them," Lorelei cried out. "Everybody else would. I don't know why the heck they would talk to you and nobody else."

"*Uh*, maybe because I talk back to them," Tasmin replied.

"Yeah, but it's not as if you can do anything helpful. I mean, we've had murder victims in, and you're not talking to them."

"I've talked to some of them. The trouble is, you guys want me to give answers to the cops that I can't get because the dead don't have any answers to give me."

"And how does that work? They can give you all kinds of shit, but they can't give you anything helpful?"

"Yeah, that's about it." Tasmin grew weary of this same conversation that they'd had time and time again. Nobody seemed to understand—or to even give a crap—and it was wearing her down. "Look. I can come tonight and help out, if that's of any benefit."

"Yeah, it's a benefit," Lorelei muttered, almost absentmindedly. "Anything is a benefit. I'll see you at six p.m." And, with that, her sister turned and left.

If it weren't for the ongoing family dynamic, Tasmin would have laughed at the exchange, but it was something that was constant, never-ending. Every time she tried to get further away from the family business, they ended up in trouble and dragged her back in again. Sure, she could say no, but she really did need to use their facilities for her work.

Hearing the front door for a second time, she got up, plastered a smile on her face, headed out to greet the first customer of the day.

∼

FOLLOW-UP PHONE CALLS hadn't provided any enlightenment to speak of. Hanson checked with the security company, and, yes, they showed that the cameras were out this morning, but they had no information as to when it happened. They were checking their systems and would get back to him. Also, despite the invoice, they had no record of a technician going to her place last week. Pondering that, Hanson studied the invoice, picked up the phone, and called her.

"According to the security company," he began, without preamble, "they didn't send anybody last week."

She sucked in her breath. "Well," she said slowly, "somebody came, so what the hell did they want?"

"Presumably to find out how to get into your place."

"*Great*," she muttered.

"What about the cameras?" he asked again.

"I told you that they were out."

"Yes, and what about last week when he was there?"

"It overwrites every seven days, I believe."

"Of course, and he was there eight days ago, I gather."

She winced. "Yes, that's exactly when he was here."

"So that was also on purpose."

"Yes, I guess so."

"Do you remember anything about him?"

"I wasn't even here at the time. Remember? My sister was working for me."

"What happened? Why were you not there?"

"I was a couple states over, doing a talk to a group of morticians."

"Interesting. About tattoos?"

"Yes, about that, about preserving skin, about maintaining ethical boundaries, that sort of thing," she muttered. "I lecture on it quite regularly, but I do try to stick to just my group of people in the industry, instead of trying to get new people on board."

"Of course. That would be a less contentious position for you."

"Denial is one thing, but giving these talks to people who aren't believers in the first place is a whole different story. I also talk directly to tattoo artists and at several of the art shows."

"Of course. I'm sure that is something you have to develop from the ground up."

"Exactly. Look. I can give my sister a call and see if she remembers anything about the technician."

"I still have to call her anyway," he said, "so I'll do that." With that, he hung up and quickly dialed the number Tasmin had provided. "I'm looking for Lorelei Baker."

"You got her," she replied, her tone cross. "What's up?"

He immediately identified himself. "I'm Hanson MacGyver, a detective for the local police department. I'm investigating the break-in at your sister's place."

"*Great*, what's that got to do with me?"

"Some days you work there, I hear?"

"I wouldn't say I *work* there. I occasionally fill in when she has to be away, just as she fills in here when we're trying hard to stay afloat."

"Right. Well, a week ago a technician came in to work

on the security system, and you were filling in for her that day."

"Maybe, but it's not like I noticed. It was really quiet, so I was doing a bunch of my own paperwork. I just have to be a warm body there. It's not as if I do any of her work."

"And yet you could, couldn't you?"

"Sure, I could. I mean, we're in the same industry, whether people want to think of it that way or not. But I don't, as it's her job, and I have plenty of my own headaches here."

"How is business?"

"Crazy," she muttered. "In fact, my sister will be working at the mortuary tonight because we're getting behind."

"Right," he muttered. "So you don't remember anything about the technician?"

"No, I remember he was there, but I don't remember anything about him. He had a uniform. He had an ID, a business card that he left behind, and he told me that he thought he had it fixed. I just nodded. He left the invoice, and I carried on."

"Of course. Thank you for your time."

"Do you really think this is targeting her or is it targeting the person who had the tattoo?"

"I have no idea. We're in the very initial stages of our investigation."

"*Great*, the last thing she needs is to have everything torn apart again."

Hesitating, Hanson added, "I haven't pulled all the details on what happened."

"Oh, that'll be fun for you then. There are plenty of details. It'll take you a while."

"Do you want to give me the gist of it?"

She frowned. "All I can give you is the company line, which is basically the family line. She was overworked and had a bit of a break."

"What kind of a break?"

"I don't know what you call it. She supposedly started talking to dead people in front of a family who was there to pick out a coffin. Tasmin had just come up from downstairs, as they were pulling out a coffin. They were trying to choose which one. The father wanted to go with one, while the mother wanted to go with another, and my lovely and helpful sister spoke up and declared that their daughter wanted the pink one."

He froze. "Did she say the daughter was talking to her?"

"Oh, yeah, are you kidding? It ended up being quite a dramatic scenario. It was all we could do to separate her from them. At the time, the decedent's family was both intrigued and upset, wanting to know if Tasmin was for real because some of the things she had said had been right on point.

"However, nobody in our family really wanted it to be for real because that's not the reputation we want as a business. Yet the grieving family wanted to come back the next day and talk to Tasmin about their daughter. She had died from leukemia, and some of the things Tasmin shared with them were so consistent with their daughter that they wanted a chance to touch base again."

"Of course that's a real problem for anybody who can talk to the dead," Hanson stated matter-of-factly.

Silence followed on the other end for a moment. "You're not thinking Tasmin was serious, are you?" Lorelei asked in disbelief.

"I'm just saying that we've seen cases like this before. Time and time again actually."

"Yeah, of course you have, especially on full moons and Halloween."

He asked a few more questions and then one more. "Is that when she started her own business?"

"No, we sent her off on a holiday and thought she would rest, but instead she just got weird for a while. So we kept her away from the business. With her out of the picture, the hubbub faded, and we got the business back on track. Eventually she came back but worked in the evenings, when nobody was around. She didn't have anything to do with the public, so we could keep things calm and quiet.

"Then, out of the blue, she started talking about setting this up. As I'm sure you can understand, my parents were horrified, but my father especially. It's not the kind of thing that goes along well in this area, where most of the people have a staid background and traditional Catholic beliefs."

"And yet the people are already dead, so it's not as if Tasmin's torturing them or anything."

"No, but an awful lot of religions require that you *must* have all the body at the same time for a proper burial. Otherwise, for them, it's not complete, and so this just goes against their beliefs."

"Sure, but that's not everybody, and those people won't be the ones who want something preserved, right?"

"Maybe. Look. I'm not here to justify what Tasmin is or isn't doing. You asked me questions. I gave you the answers. Now I need to get back to work." And, with that, she hung up on him.

He stared down at the phone in surprise. Something about this family continually surprised him, as if they didn't seem to think they had to answer the questions he was asking. And maybe the questions were unusual, but the problems he had were unusual, as was the crime. He shook his head and got up to grab a cup of coffee, when he noted his coworkers, Mark and John, stood nearby, talking.

Hanson walked over and asked, "Anything new?"

Both men turned to him and shrugged. "Not on your case," Mark replied, "but we've got a grave that's been disturbed over on Main Street."

"At the big cemetery?" Hanson asked.

Mark nodded. "Yeah."

"Any idea what's up with that?"

"No, we'll go take a look. We thought we'd leave you to handle this one."

"*Great*, thanks," Hanson muttered. "Hell, you never know. Maybe your disturbed grave is part of my case."

At that, they gave him shared solemn looks and shook their heads. "It better not be."

"I know, right? And we're not even living in New Orleans."

"You used to work there, didn't you?"

"I did, and sometimes I think I should go back."

They nodded. "If you want to, whatever."

That just reinforced the idea that Hanson wasn't welcome here or in New Orleans either. But then Hanson shouldn't be upset by that; it had been a long time since he'd felt welcome anywhere.

Ignoring them, he headed back to his desk and sat down to see what else he could dredge up on this case. Chances were, there wouldn't be anything, not until he saw her at the morgue tomorrow morning. He double-checked to make sure that was set up, and it was, so it was good to go.

With that, he headed back to his email and the never-ending work in front of him.

CHAPTER 3

THE NEXT MORNING Tasmin headed to the shop. Her mother had agreed to step in and would be a warm body in the front, if anybody came in while Tasmin was gone. Otherwise she would have to just leave it closed, with a sign saying she would be back in a bit. But, as long as her mother was still prepared to come, Tasmin would leave as soon as her mother appeared. Tasmin was ready to head out and impatiently waited for her mother to arrive, when Tasmin's phone rang.

With a sinking heart, Tasmin answered and guessed, "You can't come, I suppose."

"I can't. I'm so sorry," her mother confirmed. "We're just swamped here."

"That's fine. I'll just put a notice on the door," she muttered. Not giving her mother a chance to say more, Tasmin quickly put up a sign and added, "I have to go," and hung up.

It would have been nice if her mother had said something earlier, when Tasmin still had a chance to get out on time. Now she would be late for the morgue too. That didn't bother her nearly as much as knowing that she had to see this Hanson guy again.

As she walked toward the hospital and headed to the morgue area, she looked up to see Charlie, who smiled at her.

"Now there's a person I haven't seen in a long time."

She smiled at him. "How're you doing, Charlie?"

"I'm doing fine," he replied, smacking her gently on the shoulder. "I thought you weren't in the business anymore."

"Oh, I am, just not with my family full-time. I still work a lot of evenings for them."

He nodded. "I guess ever since …"

"Yeah, ever since I went bonkers, things have been a little dicey." And then she laughed. "Of course I haven't gone bonkers. That's just the gossip."

"I know. It's just so weird, and I've heard so many strange things."

"Yeah, apparently I started talking in tongues or something."

"I don't know, but sometimes I think they all made it up. Never underestimate what overwork can do to you though," he noted, his tone serious.

"I've definitely been working too hard," she admitted, with a laugh. "I've got an appointment here in regard to the piece found in the fountain."

"Oh, right." He looked down at his schedule and nodded. "I do have you down here. Funny, I didn't think it was you who was coming." He frowned at her. "Are you really preserving these?"

She nodded. "I'm preserving tattoos for family members who want to keep them as memories." When he shuddered delicately, she smiled. "It's not for everybody, but you know what it's like when you have loved ones and their peculiar requests."

"Sure, but you would think that would be a one-off deal, not a case of everybody wanting it to the point that you have a business for it."

"I planned to just add it to the business with the funeral home, but my father was against that idea."

"Yeah, no wonder. Big John is quite a force on his own. Can't say I'm surprised."

"He is, indeed. So, can I see the piece?"

"Yeah, I've got a note here though that I'm supposed to wait for the detective."

"That's fine, as long as the detective gets here soon. I'm running very short on time." She looked at her watch, just as the door opened behind her, and she knew—without even looking—that it would be him.

"Oh good, you're on time," Hanson noted behind her.

"I am." She turned to look at him. "Too bad you aren't." He glared at that, and she smiled suddenly.

"Come on. I'm only a moment late," Hanson pointed out. "You can't possibly get me in trouble for that."

"I wasn't planning on getting you into trouble for anything. You've been out of school for a while now."

"And yet somehow it seems like yesterday."

Surprised, she watched him as he nodded at Charlie.

"Hey, Charlie, can we take a look?"

"Absolutely." Charlie walked over to the drawer, pulled it out, and lifted a cloth off the piece lying there.

She walked over and studied it, then nodded. "Do you mind if I touch it?" she asked, looking up at Charlie.

"You do you. You're the one who preserved this skin. I understand you wanted to assess the damage."

"Yes, and, while it's definitely damaged, I'm not sure it's damaged to the extent that I need to be worried about it." She picked up the piece, noting how supple it was, checking to see if she saw any actual disfiguration on the tattoo itself.

"It seems there was no damage to the design. That's a huge relief."

"It's still weird to think that somebody would want this preserved," Charlie added.

"Not really. If you set aside that aspect and just look at it, you can appreciate that it's an absolutely gorgeous piece of artwork."

"Sure, it's artwork," Charlie muttered, "but it's on somebody's body."

"It *was* on somebody's body, but that somebody is no longer with us," she murmured softly.

He didn't say anything more, but she sensed his curiosity and the very thinly veiled disapproval. Charlie was normally fairly open-minded, but, as she'd come to find out, this subject brought people to two very different sides of the divide, often with surprising results.

She checked it over once more, looked up at Charlie, and asked, "When can I have it back?"

He frowned and shook his head. "I don't know." He looked over at Hanson. "What about you? Do you still need it?"

"I don't need it," Hanson stated, "but we do need to have it well documented, since it is part of a theft."

"However, we do have rightful property owners who have the paperwork to claim it," she added, turning to look back at him.

"Let me talk to the coroner and see what he's got to say about it," Charlie said.

She nodded. "I can give you until tomorrow, but I really need it after that in order to continue with the process."

"But it's already preserved now, right? Won't deteriorate, will it?" Charlie asked.

"It shouldn't, but I've never had a case where I had one sit in water. So, while I want to say it's okay, I can't be positive just yet."

"Right, so the answer really falls into the realm of *who knows*, I gather."

"Exactly," she replied. "What I really want to know is who did this and why." Looking up at Hanson, she continued. "Did you get anywhere with your inquiries?"

He shook his head. "No, not yet. Your sister doesn't remember anything on the day that she was at your shop either."

"No, I'm sure she doesn't, and I'm not surprised. She usually brings in a pile of her own paperwork and tries to get that done, while she's holding down the fort at my place."

"So who is there right now?" Hanson asked her.

"Nobody. My mother was supposed to be, but she bailed on me this morning."

"*Uh-oh*. Does that happen often?"

"Yes, in a way it does, but that's what I have to deal with. I don't have anybody who comes in as an assistant or anything at this point."

"Right. It sounds as if you need to get some hired help," Hanson noted.

"You have to make money before you get hired help," she explained, with a laugh. She looked down at the beautiful artwork in front of her, and her face softened. "She struggled so hard to fight that cancer," she murmured, reaching out a hand and gently stroking the beautiful stylized female face. "Her artist really captured the essence of her in this."

"Do you think that's why the family wants it preserved?" Charlie asked, coming around to look at it. "It is a woman's face, after all."

"It's not just *a* woman's face. It's *her* face. It's a portrait she had done when she was dying, hoping against hope that it wouldn't be the only thing that was left for people to remember her by. But, when they realized that's how it *would* work out, that's when they started discussions about trying to preserve her artwork. And it's not a creepy counterculture memento intended to freak people out. It's something that her parents can hold dear."

Charlie shrugged. "I guess that makes more sense than anything I've heard up until now."

She smiled at him. "People will do anything for their loved ones sometimes," she replied. "It's our job to understand and to be compassionate enough to see where they're coming from."

"Not my job," Charlie said. "My job is to keep track of the bodies, until they head off to you guys. Beyond that I don't have anything to do with them."

She chuckled. "Good enough." She looked back at Hanson. "Thank you for arranging this. It was very helpful. I'll wait to hear from you. Just please remember that there is a potential timing issue here."

He nodded. "I can understand timing issues, but that doesn't change the fact that my hands are tied sometimes, and certain things are beyond my control."

"Got it," she muttered. "In that case, I'll let the family know. Maybe they can help move things along."

"And what good will that do?" Hanson asked.

"They're bigwigs in town, and, since this is clearly a property investigation involving a theft, and we have the stolen property right here in front of us, there's no valid reason for it not to be returned. But that's not my problem.

That will be up to their legal team." And, with that, Tasmin stepped back, smiled down at the beautiful tattoo in front of her, and added, "I'm really happy it didn't sustain any critical damage." With a glance back up at Charlie, she smiled. "Take good care of it for me, Charlie." Then she walked toward the door.

"Hey, hang on a minute," Hanson called out.

She turned and looked back at him. "What?" she asked, as she pushed the door open to step out of the room.

"You're really comfortable in there, aren't you?" he asked curiously.

She frowned at him. "Any reason I wouldn't be? I've worked in the industry for a lot of years, so this isn't exactly a place I'm unfamiliar with."

He sighed, then nodded. "I did look you up."

"Oh, that must have been fun," she quipped, with an eye roll. "All you had to do was ask my sister. She would have given you a mouthful, I'm sure."

"I did actually. She mentioned something about a breakdown."

"Right. Don't you love that simple euphemism for *overworked and burned-out?* It sure makes everybody happy to have that as an answer, doesn't it?"

"It certainly made sense to them, I think," he offered cautiously.

"Yep."

"But not to you, I suppose."

"No, not to me. But nobody ever cares to hear what I have to say."

"What is it that you would say if somebody did care?"

She looked at him in surprise and laughed. "Oh no you don't. I've spent too many years with people like you, black-

and-white, nothing in between. I'm not going there. Listen. I have a job to do, and I really can't afford to start all over again because I say or do something that goes sideways and costs me my business," she declared. "So, if you've got any questions, feel free to ask them, but keep them to the case at hand, please."

He stared at her, then nodded. "Just because you talk to the dead doesn't mean that something's wrong with you. You do know that, right?"

She froze, then slowly turned to look at him. "You would be the only person I know who would say that." She frowned. "And I can't imagine why you would." Her gaze was intense, as she searched his face, seeing something behind the flat black stare. "Unless you're somebody who sees similar stuff." And then she laughed. "But, even then, you'd never admit it because none of us can, can we?" she asked almost hysterically. "We'd get crucified for being something completely abnormal to the rest of the world, and that is hard to live with long-term."

"It is hard to live with," he agreed, "long-term or short-term. Nothing about it is easy."

"No, I guess there isn't, but I did my time. I learned my lesson and all that garbage." She shook her head. "I'm not going there again."

"Even though the ghosts talk to you?"

"I'd be a fool to admit they did," she stated, looking up at him with a smile. "So, this conversation never happened." With that, she gave him a clipped nod and a wave. "Have a good day." Then she stepped outside.

Inside the morgue though, she had heard the voices of the dead bodies in there. She stared down at her hands that she had held clenched in fists so tight that her nails had cut into her palms. She didn't know whether he'd seen it or if he had just guessed, but all those bodies in there, every single one, had sat up and looked at her. Several of them had cried out to her, some pleading, others just delighted that she was there and that she could see them.

Some were terrified and scared because they didn't know what had happened and were asking for her help, for clarity if nothing else. Her refusal to communicate with them was difficult but necessary, since the last time she had, her whole world had come apart and had changed forever. She couldn't afford to let that happen again, especially not now that she was finally getting her life back together.

Her progress had been slow, but she was making it, so to go back to where she'd been before, that would just not happen. Ever.

∼

HANSON WATCHED TASMIN. She walked back to her vehicle and hadn't turned to look at him at all. Yet he saw the shadows all around her. This was not what he'd expected, neither were the words that she had shared. She had mentioned one thing, but her energy said another. Not that he was very good at reading that particular energy, but what she was saying was not the truth. Yet she expected him to believe it blindly. It was as if he wanted to believe something, and he would, and, given what she'd relayed, chances are that's how her family had treated it as well. He pondered that as he made his way back to the office.

When he walked in and sat down at his desk, Mark and John stepped over, looking at him expectantly. "And?"

Hanson shrugged. "And what?"

"Did she recognize it?"

"Sure, but that was no surprise."

"Of course." Mark and John shared knowing glances and mutual smirks.

Hanson frowned. "Somebody still broke into her place."

"But the captain also says we don't have time to spend on this one because we've got a double homicide downtown."

Hanson frowned at his coworkers, then stood and asked, "Why didn't you say something?"

"We were just waiting for you to get back."

He didn't say anything but found their attitude typical of the rest of the team. Everybody just waited until somebody else took action. He shook his head. "Let's go." And, with that, he headed outside.

They were taking two separate vehicles apparently; nobody ever seemed to want to share a ride with Hanson. Not that he wasn't used to it; he was. He wasn't at all sure why, but he'd heard stories from his last precinct, where several people declared that Hanson was spooky when it came to driving, and they didn't want anything to do with it. He wasn't sure what was so spooky about it, but whatever. He was okay with it at this point.

He'd long determined that whatever this was going on with him and his *gift*, it separated him from everyone else, and he could either deal with it or not, but it wouldn't change anything either way. So, he was attempting to deal with it. The separation gave him an odd feeling though, that sense of being different, unique, but not in a good way. Nobody wanted to see him be anything other than what they were, and that was the challenge.

But still, this was the job, and, unless Hanson came up with something different that he wanted to do with his life, this was what he would do.

As he drove to the crime scene, he pulled off to the side, seeing the crowds contained by crime scene tape and several other black-and-whites parked off to the side. He hopped out, walked over, and stood at the yellow tape. He could certainly go in, being a detective himself, but it was more a case of standing here and watching everything around him for a moment.

He studied the sea of faces around him, then caught the coroner straightening up from the body. With a wave of his hand, Hanson ducked under the yellow tape and headed toward him.

The coroner looked around and asked, "Where's the rest of your team?"

"They're on the way," Hanson replied briefly.

The coroner didn't say anything, just gave a brief acknowledging nod.

"What have you got?" Hanson asked.

"This isn't so bad," he stated, "and it's certainly easier than the one that I'm heading to next."

Hanson frowned. "Is it connected?"

"I don't know," he said. "That's your job to find out."

He nodded. "Fine."

The coroner then gave him the details he had. "Two victims, both shot in the chest, walking on the sidewalk from the looks of it. Both male and both young. I'd say early twenties. Both have ID."

"Let's get them photographed here, so we can get these bodies moved."

With that, they turned the scene over to the forensics team. who quickly laid out the IDs, took photos of them, and finished documenting the rest of the scene. When they were finished, the coroner directed the orderlies to remove the bodies. With that, he looked back at Hanson and said, "I'm pretty backed up, but I'll try to have some early results for you tomorrow."

Hanson nodded. "At least we have ID, and I'd say the cause of death is pretty clear."

"And the time of death," the coroner noted. "Lots of witnesses."

"And I'll be on them next," Hanson stated, waiting until the bodies were loaded up and the vehicle was moving away, before he turned to canvass the crowd. He specifically needed everybody to stay until they provided a statement and was happy to see several of the cops already out there taking statements. By the time Hanson was done, four hours had passed.

He walked over to where a few cops stood, drinking coffee, and asked them, "Where the hell did you get the coffee from?"

One guy looked at him, grinned, and pointed toward a coffee shop around the corner.

Hanson nodded. "I'll head there next. What do we know about cameras around here? Did anybody get a look at the vehicle?"

"I've got two different eyewitness statements on a vehicle, a light gray car, one of the smaller models, but we don't have a make and model yet."

"Nobody has any pictures?"

"In this day and age the younger crowd always seems to have pictures of shit going on," noted another cop.

"One guy took a video, and, as he went to show it to us, managed to erase it."

Hanson stared at him. "What?"

"Yeah, exactly," he muttered. "The little bit I caught had his thumb across the front of it anyway, so I'm not sure it would have been of any value."

"We did get a partial license plate number from two people I interviewed," one of the other cops shared. "I'm putting all this into my report, and we'll start a run on this stuff."

Hanson nodded. "That's good. I've got a small car, but I don't have a year," he told them. "But, so far, that information jives with the rest. What doesn't jive is that he didn't just do a drive-by. He got out and walked right up to the two men, shot them both, then ran back to the vehicle and hopped in." He looked up at the others. "Agreed? Did anyone hear a different version?"

The group of cops nodded in unison.

Hanson added, "That's what my witnesses say too. As far as a description on the shooter, I've got short, somewhere around five-five, baseball cap, sneakers, jeans, jeans jacket, and no discerning marks." He looked up to confirm with the others.

"That's what I've got too," one cop stated.

Hanson nodded. "So, he wasn't trying to hide, outside of the fact that he was wearing a baseball cap, and these people were targeted. Why they were targeted is a different story."

"You don't think it's because he knew them?"

"No, not necessarily," Hanson replied. "It could just as easily be because they either fit a profile or they looked like somebody he might have known or somebody he had a grudge against."

"Bad enough that he shot two of them and killed them both but to do it in broad daylight? That's pretty brazen."

"Broad daylight and didn't give a shit from the looks of it," Hanson added, as he gazed around at the streets.

A few people still hung around, as if wondering if there was still more to see, but Hanson knew that they would disappear pretty quickly, then come back with their neighbors and friends to show them all the excitement. Hanson sighed. "Okay, I'm heading down to the coffee shop right now."

"What, you don't like the coffee at the station?" one of them joked.

He smiled. "I'll check and see if the owner's got any cameras up. We'll need to check on street cams too."

At that, the cops nodded, but their radios went off just then. "We're heading to a multi-car collision up ahead," one said, as they walked back to their vehicles. And, with a wave goodbye, they headed off.

But Hanson hadn't gotten the call, and traffic accidents weren't part of his caseload, so he headed to the coffee shop. He walked in to find the place completely empty of customers. Wandering over to the counter, he ordered a coffee and asked the employee about cameras.

"Yep, we have cameras," the man confirmed. "You must be asking because of the trouble up the street, *huh*?"

"I am. We could use some video footage to help pinpoint the vehicle and the shooter."

The guy nodded. "Okay, give me a minute." He disappeared into the back, and, when he returned, he had a video playing on his phone. "Is this what you're looking for?"

At that, Hanson studied it and watched as the same gray car drove up and parked, but not off the side of the road—right in the middle of the road, just enough to block both ways—and the guy hopped out with a small handgun and fired into the two men. Oddly he didn't run back to the car, which Hanson thought was interesting, but walked back at a good clip, then hopped into the car and took off again. He'd also been wearing a large coat and a baseball cap. "Yeah, that's exactly what I'm looking for," he said. "Can you email that to me?"

With that done, he paid for his coffee and stepped outside, then stood for a moment, before wandering the block for a bit. Not a whole lot else to be gotten from here, since nobody had recognized the driver or the vehicle. The question was whether there was any connection between the two dead men and their killer or this was a random shooting. But it wasn't random in the sense that somebody started firing. It was possible that these victims were chosen at random, which was a whole different story than a targeted shooting.

With that still to be determined, Hanson headed back to the station. When he arrived, he found his work area empty.

The captain walked out, looked around, and asked, "Where is everybody?"

Hanson shrugged. "I don't know. I just came in from the double homicide downtown."

"*Great*, a shooting, right?"

Hanson nodded. "Yeah."

"Did you get anything?"

"We've got it on video, with the vehicle and a rough description of the shooter. Both young men were shot point-blank in the chest, one bullet each, and then the gunman walked back to his car, hopped in, and left."

The captain shook his head at that. "Good God, you work on that. I don't know where the hell the rest of them are." He frowned, as he looked around, his hands on his hips, then his gaze turned back to Hanson. "Did you go to the crime scene alone?"

"I thought Mark and John were coming too, but I didn't see them there," he noted in a noncommittal voice.

The captain frowned at that but completely ignored him.

If the captain expected dirt from Hanson, that wouldn't happen.

"How are you settling in?" the captain asked.

"I'm settling in," he replied. "It takes time."

"Yeah, it does unfortunately," he muttered. And, with that, looking frustrated, the captain turned, spun on his heels, and walked out again.

Hanson looked up to see the captain's retreating back, recognizing the temper in it, but unsure whether it was directed at him or at the rest of the team. He presumed the other detectives had good reasons for not being around right now, but it wasn't Hanson's business to give a crap. He would do what he needed to do and would carry on from there. The problem was, when teams didn't get along well, or when it took them time to blend, it was difficult to get cohesive information flowing.

It's not as if Hanson wanted it to be this way, but he wasn't sure what to do about it. He was here. He showed up for work every day and did his job, and, so far, that's all it was. He'd only been here a couple weeks, and it would take a hell of a lot longer than that to be a part of this team, obviously. He just hoped it wouldn't take too long. But, if anybody had done any background work and had found out why Hanson had changed departments, he would be in for a rough time no matter what.

CHAPTER 4

TASMIN WALKED INTO her office area, turned on the lights, and sat down on her bench with a hard *thump*, as she stared at the pieces she had to work on. Almost instantly a spirit spoke up.

"You lied, didn't you?"

She stiffened and glared at the room in general. "I didn't lie," she muttered. "As a matter of fact, I told him way more than I expected to. More than I wanted to, in fact."

"Oh, that's interesting."

"Oh, stop it," Tasmin said. "You don't know anything."

"How can I?" the spirit asked, presenting as a weird preamble of a disembodied vision. "You haven't told me anything."

"I'm not going to either," Tasmin muttered. "It's bad enough that I'm dealing with all this, without adding you to the mix."

"As soon as you figure out where I belong, then I'll be happy enough to get out of your hair," the spirit stated cheerfully.

"Yeah, well, I don't know how to do that," she muttered.

"Then I guess I'm stuck here for a while, so you better get used to it."

"I don't want to get used to it," Tasmin snapped.

When someone called out in the shop, Tasmin groaned and whispered, "Good Lord, give me patience." But she hopped up and walked out to see her mother standing in the doorway.

"Who are you talking to?" she asked suspiciously.

"I was on the phone, Mother," she replied, with a weary sigh, watching the relief cross her mother's face. "It's fine, you know. I'm not going crazy."

She flushed. "You know how it looks to everybody else."

"I really don't care about everybody else at this point. I'm just trying to maintain some semblance of a normal life, and having you constantly question me at every turn is not helping."

At that, her mom flushed again.

"Look, Mom. I'm sorry. It's been a rough day. Did you come for a reason?"

Her mom hesitated. "Your sister told me that the cops were here."

"Of course the cops were here. I had a break-in, though I'm not sure how, since my security was on when I arrived that morning. So, somebody came in, disconnected my security, took what they wanted, reset the system, and left." She glanced around the shop, adding, "Whoever thought that breaking and entering would be done in such a conscientious way? Not even a broken window or anything."

"That's bizarre," her mom said, staring at her in worry. "Are you all right?"

"Sure, why not?" she asked. "It's not as if they were after me."

At that, her mom gasped. "You shouldn't even joke about such things," she scolded.

"Maybe not," Tasmin muttered, "but sometimes the rest

of it is just a little too much to deal with." She wandered behind the register and pulled out a notepad, while she turned to her mom. "So, what's up?"

Her mom shrugged. "I was just coming to check on you."

"Because of what Lorelei said?"

"Sure, that's as good a reason as any, isn't it?" Her mother gave Tasmin a wan smile. "I mean, you're always in the back of my mind. You're my daughter. I love you, and you've been through a tough time. Plus, I felt badly for not being here to cover for you earlier."

"I'm not going mental. I'm fine," she murmured. Stepping out from behind the counter, she walked over and gave her mom a hug. "I'll be fine."

Her mom just nodded nervously. "Have you heard any more of those weird noises?"

"Do you mean *those voices*?" she corrected in a low tone. "Don't worry about it."

At that, visible shock whispered across her mother's face. "You have, haven't you?"

"Does it matter?" she asked, with a groan. "I wouldn't say so if I had."

"No, of course not," she agreed. "It really freaks out your father."

"Yeah, but that's not my problem, remember?" She reiterated the point for the umpteenth time. "That's Dad's problem."

Her mom just stared at her worriedly.

"I'm fine, Mom. No need to be worried."

"But you had a break-in and now you're hearing voices again."

"I didn't say I'm hearing voices again. *You* did," she declared. "I didn't clarify what I'm hearing because I don't know what I'm hearing. For all I know it's just noises rambling around in the back of my head. Who knows. Maybe it happens to all of you, and I just never realized that it's normal."

"It's not normal," her mom stated instantly, staring at her, her fingers rattling against the doorknob.

"You're making me nervous, so either come in and sit down or leave."

"I can't stay," she said immediately.

At that, hating the sigh of relief in her own mind, Tasmin replied, "Then go and just calm down. I'm fine." But her mom clearly didn't want to calm down, and *fine* wasn't an answer that appeared to mean anything to her. "Honestly, Mom."

"Honestly, Mom, what?" she asked, raising her hands. "It's pretty unnerving to know that this is happening."

"And yet it's not happening to you."

The look her mother gave her wasn't hard to decipher. Something akin to a *Get real, I'm your mother* type thing.

"Didn't you tell me Grammie used to have problems?" Tasmin asked, with a broad smile.

"She was schizophrenic, and she heard voices all the time."

At that, Tasmin snorted. "Yeah. I wonder why? She was *not* schizophrenic. Of course she heard voices, she probably had to, so she had somebody to talk to."

"There was some talk about that in the last ten years of her life, but she didn't associate well with people."

"And how much of that was because of the treatment she received?" Tasmin asked caustically. "Look. Nothing is wrong with me."

Her mom shot her a thinly veiled glance again.

"I mean it. It's all fine." Then she looked down at her watch. "You mentioned how you can't stay, so you'd better not be late for whatever it is you're heading out for."

"I've got to do a bunch of errands," she noted. "I've got the dry cleaning to pick up and to order supplies for your father."

"*Great*," Tasmin said, with an eye roll.

"How's business?" her mother asked.

"Crazy busy, but what can we expect? It's a strange time of life that we're all going through right now."

"I won't argue with that," her mother replied. "And, in our case, it's a business that picks up when tragedy strikes."

"Unfortunately," Tasmin agreed, with a soft sigh. "Are you ever sorry you married into the industry?"

She looked at her daughter in surprise. "I won't say I'm sorry, though it's not been easy. However, I knew that ahead of time."

"Sure, but did you really know how anal Dad can be?"

She flushed at that. "Don't say anything mean about your father," she cautioned.

"I wasn't going to," Tasmin noted gently, "but I'm also not blind to his faults."

"Nobody can be expected to accept a daughter who is hearing voices. It literally scares the crap out of him. You know that."

"He's a whole different story than just about accepting things," Tasmin murmured. "He doesn't even want to be around me anymore."

"It makes him uncomfortable," she rushed to say, "but he still loves you."

At that, Tasmin laughed. "Look, Mom. Go off and do

the things you need to do. The fact that you're trying to convince me that my father loves me, even though he can't stand to be in the same room with me, really won't wash. So let's just stop this conversation right there."

"But he does let you use the facilities."

"Because I pay," she stated in exasperation. "And I'm not even sure that he knows that I use them. I'm sure Lorelei takes the credit for the hours I put in, so he doesn't know that I'm there."

Her mom immediately flushed at that too.

Tasmin nodded. "Just as I thought. He doesn't even know, does he?"

"It's just hard for him, and he doesn't want anything to damage the reputation of his company."

"*His* company, right? Not *our* company, not *the family* business? It's *his* company, and it always will be."

At that, her mom looked at her crossly. "Let's not start down that road."

"I didn't want to go down any of these roads," Tasmin pointed out. "They all have pitfalls."

"No, you're right," her mom agreed absentmindedly. She stared around the room. "Everything looks to be fine here."

"I know that," Tasmin said. "The police have been here. They wrote up an incident report. They're looking into it."

Seeing the relief on her mom's face, Tasmin walked over, gave her another hug, and nudged her out the door. "Go on now. I have work to do."

She waited inside by the front door, until her mom got into her vehicle and drove off. As soon as she was gone, Tasmin bowed her head and immediately cleansed the room of all the negativity, fear, and doubt that her mother inevitably brought into Tasmin's world. She could do very little to control a lot of this that went on, but one of the things she could do was control her reaction after her mother left.

As soon as she managed that, she returned to her back room and sat down again. Almost instantly the same spirit popped up.

"And you lied to her too."

Tasmin stiffened and glared around the room. "I didn't lie to her."

"You did." And then the spirit laughed and laughed and laughed.

The laughter echoed around the room, making Tasmin tense. Irritated, she got up and walked to the back counter, where she put on a pot of coffee.

"Just what you need, more caffeine," the spirit said in a mocking tone.

"Go away," Tasmin muttered.

"Nope, not going to. You have a job to do. Find out where I belong, and then maybe I will," the spirit suggested. "Until then, I'm sticking around."

"Why?" she asked, spinning around and glaring at the empty room. "Why? You're doing nothing but tormenting me."

"I know, and a part of me says that I should be sorry about that, but another part is damn glad you can even hear me," the spirit muttered. "You may not be happy about it, but I am. You know what it's like to be in this state and to not have anybody to talk to you? To know that you're stuck here, trying to talk to everybody, and they're not responding?"

"They're not responding because they can't," Tasmin

cried out. "I've explained that to you."

"I know that," the spirit stated calmly. "And I get it. I really do. They can't hear me, but you can, and that means I'm stuck with you. You're the only person I have to talk to, so you're it. You don't like it? Solve the problem of where I belong."

"You belong in a grave," Tasmin snapped. "You're dead. You're gone, and it's not my problem."

"Until you can put me back together again with whatever part is left of me, then it is your problem."

"And, for all I know, you were cremated."

"Then you can cremate the rest of me too," the spirit snapped. "Don't think I don't understand. But I was raised to believe that the whole body had to be kept together."

"And now your beliefs have changed," Tasmin muttered. "If anybody had reason to change their beliefs, it would be you because you're sitting here completely dissociated from the rest of your body, and that's not my problem."

"Nope, but the fact that you can talk to me is," the spirit declared, and, with that, the spirit blinked out.

Tasmin pinched the bridge of her nose. To even argue with a spirit was beyond crazy, but, if her mom heard Tasmin, if any of her family overheard Tasmin, they would try hard to get her committed. She knew it. It was something that struck terror in her heart, and she was afraid to even contemplate that it could happen.

Plus, she also knew that her father would be leading the charge. In his mind it was way better to have that happen than to acknowledge that there might be something paranormal about this crazy world he was involved in. He wouldn't even acknowledge that it had something to do with the work he did or with the fact that they'd been exposed to all these bodies.

She could hardly blame him; it was the family business, and it was a business that somebody had to do, and he, as a caretaker, was very good at it. He was a funeral home director, and they had done very well off the business. He'd raised his family off the income from that business, but apparently finding out that his daughter could talk to some of these people after they had died sent him over the edge, and he would do anything to make sure none of that information got out.

And she knew that, if anybody heard her having a conversation, such as she just had, she would be in deep trouble. And yet, somehow, she couldn't seem to shut up when this particular spirit started to harass her. And that's exactly what the spirit was doing. Tasmin figured the spirit couldn't have been very nice when alive because the spirit was definitely an asshole now. And yet, could she blame the spirit for being belligerent about these circumstances?

She had met other ghosts who didn't understand and had desperately tried to contact their families, and yet, when nobody in the family could talk to them, they felt absolutely abandoned and horrified. These empty ghost shells clung to these live people, who were desperately dealing with their own grief but not seeing the spirit right beside them the whole time.

These stories just broke Tasmin, and yet what was she supposed to do about any of it? She didn't have anything to do with them if she could. However, when she didn't have a choice, all she tried to do was talk to them and help them to see the light. Of course even saying that to her family sent off all kinds of alarm bells, and she knew where she would end up if she didn't shut her mouth.

She quickly poured herself a cup of coffee and walked back out to the front of the store. She had put jingle bells up in case the door ever opened, just in case she was busy talking to somebody ghostly. It served as her warning that she wasn't alone, but even now she sensed that eeriness, that creepy feeling of being watched, being heard.

Tasmin knew that, at some point in time, those bells wouldn't be enough. Somehow, she had to keep her sanity long enough to find another place to live or another way to make a living. She had to do something to get out of this. She didn't want to spend the rest of her life locked up in a padded cell, and unfortunately that's where her father figured she belonged.

∽

HANSON WALKED BACK into Inked Forever, hearing the bell jangle as he entered. Almost immediately Tasmin came out with a smile on her face, only to have that smile fall away as she glared at him. He slowly raised an eyebrow. "I don't generally get that kind of a greeting when I walk into a store."

She shrugged. "Give it time. I'm sure you'll get more of it."

"Is it because it's me or because I'm a cop?" he asked. And genuine curiosity filled his voice.

She shrugged. "I'm not sure how to answer that," she muttered. "I can't say I enjoy being disturbed, and you're bringing back memories I don't really want to deal with."

"You mean, the break-in?"

"What else would I mean?" she asked in exasperation. He knew she was wishing he wouldn't walk through the opening she'd given him.

He just stared at her steadily, making her uncomfortable.

She shifted her weight on her feet and stared back. "You're back again, so what does that mean?"

"It means you are now cleared to bring the art piece back here again."

"Good," she said in delight. "And did you bring me paperwork that clears it?"

"Yes. I was going to bring the piece myself, but then I thought maybe you would need something to preserve it on the journey."

"I shouldn't need to, but I will run out right now and get it."

"Who'll look after the shop?"

"I'll just lock it up," she said. "I need to get that piece back. The family is absolutely beside themselves."

He suggested, "I can stay and wait, if you want."

She looked at him and then slowly shook her head. "No, that's okay. You're a cop. You have other things to do."

And he did at that, and he honestly had no idea why he had offered, particularly when he hadn't planned on saying that. He nodded. "I am and I do. I guess I just thought it wouldn't take you very long, and maybe you needed to keep the store open for business."

"Most of my business is through online connections, and I very rarely get walk-ins," she explained. "I don't have any appointments this afternoon either."

"Ah, so in other words, you don't need me to stay." And what the heck was that forlornness in his heart about her rejection? It wasn't a rejection of him, although he was darn sure it would be if he pushed it. Yet, at this point, it was more of a rejection that he didn't understand.

She smiled. "It'll be fine." She looked down at her

watch. "Besides, it's almost two-thirty anyway."

"And what does that mean?"

"I close at three-thirty generally. Although, if I'm working in the back, I often forget and leave the doors unlocked and open until five o'clock, if not six."

He stared at her.

She shrugged. "It's an unconventional business, and I'm not used to having office hours here. Typically it depends on my schedule and when I have to go help at the mortuary."

"Right. You go help out at the family business, don't you?"

"Yes, and I have to tonight too," she said, with a groan. "I'd forgotten about that, but my sister is in need of assistance."

"I'm sure it's handy for them to call on you."

"It is and it isn't," she replied. "It's more a case of I need to go and help them or I don't get to use the facilities for some of my work."

"Right, and are you involved in cutting away the actual tattoos?"

"It depends," she said. "We have coroners, doctors, who frequently do that job, depending on where it comes from. But trying to get the pieces here so I can work on them and get them preserved is a different story altogether. Formaldehyde preserves it, but then it makes the long-term preservation process very difficult. So I try to avoid it when I can. The tattoos are generally transported much like live organs, but, of course, they're not live."

"No, of course not." He stared at her curiously.

She frowned. "I really do need to go."

He nodded, then stepped back out of the doorway. "Sorry."

"Hey, no, I didn't mean it that way." She stopped, took a deep breath. "You've been very kind, and I appreciate it."

He laughed. "All I've done is tell you that you can go pick up the piece you're waiting for. Not a whole lot of kindness in that."

"You also haven't mocked me or done anything else to make me feel bad," she noted. "So, in my book, that makes you one of the good guys."

"I am one of the good guys," he agreed. "Yet, surprisingly enough, being a good guy doesn't necessarily do it for people."

She stopped, studied him, and slowly nodded. "I would agree with that. I would have said I was a good guy too. Yet, so far, it's not winning me brownie points."

And, on that cryptic note, she ran into the back of her office, grabbed her keys and her jacket, and proceeded to follow him outside. She locked the door and walked over to her car, parked just a few cars down the block.

Looking at him, she added, "I really do appreciate you letting me know. The sooner I can get that back into my hands, I can get to work on it and see what I can do about the damage."

"Got it, and you're welcome." He stayed where he was, watching as she hopped into her car and took off.

Turning, he looked back at the store and the weird shadows that he saw all around it. It wasn't a popular street. It was more of a side street, but, then again, it was a business that didn't really require walk-in traffic. According to Tasmin most of her contacts were made online, which made sense.

Her specialty service was not exactly something that most people even knew was possible, so her store would probably be found through a Google search, as much as anything. That's how Hanson had found what he had on her, so it was no surprise that's where the bulk of her business came from.

He was loathe to leave though. Something was odd about the shop; something was odd about the energy around it, not to mention that shadow hanging off to the side. He tried to look at it from a side view to get a better grasp of what was going on, but it wasn't showing up well.

He sighed at that. "Don't know what you want and why you're here, but surely she doesn't have anything of interest."

A soft faint voice replied in the background, "You don't know that."

He froze, turned, then looked around again and whispered, "Who said that?"

Part of the shadow detached from the wall of the store and slowly dissolved into the sidewalk in front of him. He felt the shadow going up and down his back, as Hanson once again saw something that made no sense in his world but would have made sense if he just accepted it. There was no such thing as complete explanations in his world. He just didn't want to end up imagining something far worse than what he could tell was going on.

As the talking shadow dissipated into the sidewalk, Hanson no longer saw any clue as to who and what it was. He called out gently, his voice soft, as he glanced around to make sure he was alone. "If there's a problem, you need to tell me."

"Oh, there's a problem all right, lots of problems. Stick around the store, and you'll find out more." Then came a weird laugh, and suddenly the shadow was gone.

He frowned at that and stared at the store, even looking

in the window, but he couldn't see anything else and couldn't see any more shadows. So, he didn't know if that was a spirit, an energy, or some conversation on the other side. It was another one of those things that he sometimes got caught up in without realizing it.

Finally he shrugged. "Whatever." And, with that, he turned and headed back the way he'd come.

CHAPTER 5

AS SOON AS she got to the morgue, she walked down to see Jim, another old friend she knew.

He looked up at her and smiled. "Hey, I heard that they'd released this piece for you."

"Yeah, I think it's more about what it is than anything else," she muttered. "I think in a robbery, they typically don't return the stolen property quite that fast."

He shrugged. "They do in lots of cases. It's not as if the actual pieces themselves hold the keys, particularly once they're released from forensics."

"I guess," she muttered. "For me, I'm just grateful because the family is more than a little worried about the whole thing."

He nodded. "Personally I think what you do is cool. It's not something that most of us think about, but, as soon as you do give it some thought, it really is pretty easy to understand."

She smiled up at him. "I'm really glad to hear you say that, because believe me, an awful lot of people don't feel that way about it."

He winced. "No, and there'll always be people who are stick-in-the-muds, who believe, once you're dead, you're dead, and it should stay that way."

"That's true enough, and I'm certainly not somebody

who'll get into an argument about the rights and wrongs of it, considering what I was doing before, except this just follows right into that same ideology."

He nodded. "Your piece is over here. Is it okay if it's in a box? We happened to have something the right size, and it had a lid as well."

"No, that's perfect, thank you." She picked it up quickly checking it over.

"Wait, one second, I still need you to sign for it."

"Right." She sighed, put the box down again, and quickly filled out the papers as best she could. It was hard to figure out what to put down in some of these cases. This situation didn't quite fit the standard forms.

Paperwork completed, she picked up the box, gave him a wave, and said, "Thanks, it was good to see you." And, with that, she raced out.

She placed the box carefully on the passenger seat of her car and then slowly drove back to her store. She didn't know why she was anxious about the detective still hanging around her store, but she had to admit that she was quite relieved to find he had left. She unlocked the door, turning off the security alarm as soon as she got inside again, and headed into the back room.

Once she laid the box down, she went back out and locked up the front door, then returned to her workshop. She sat down and carefully explored the piece. Outside of a few holes, where it seemed somebody had tried to nail it to the fountain, it didn't appear to have been damaged. The preservation process made it quite durable, and that was the saving grace in this case.

With it back in her possession again, she quickly worked on getting the piece finished. When her phone rang, and she checked the clock, noting it was ten minutes to five, she wasn't at all surprised when she saw that the caller ID showed the mother, calling about the piece Tasmin was currently working on. She answered it immediately.

"Did you get it back?" she asked anxiously.

"I have it," Tasmin said gently. "And I'm almost done with the framing."

"Oh, thank heavens," she said. "Will you have it done today?"

"No, I have to go work somewhere else for the next little bit."

"Oh. Oh."

And such a well of disappointment filled the mother's voice that it caused Tasmin to reconsider.

"Look. I still have about an hour, and I don't need too much time to finish it. Do you think you could come and pick it up?"

"Oh, absolutely," she said in a rush.

"You'll have to be close to six p.m.," Tasmin explained, "as I'll need every bit of that time in order to get it finished."

"No, that's fine. We'll be there." With that, she hung up.

Tasmin was really pissed at herself for agreeing, but she also didn't want to have the piece hanging around. There had been so much trouble with it already that she wanted this beautiful woman to have the final resting place she deserved. Plus, her parents were rather desperate to get it, particularly after having come so close to losing it to whatever idiot had tried to take it.

Actually they'd done more than try. They'd succeeded, and that was something she was trying not to even think about. Shaking off all those feelings, she buckled down and set to work, determined to get it finished before the parents arrived. Finally, with fifteen minutes to spare, Tasmin sat back with a happy sigh. "It's perfect," she murmured.

When her phone rang, she looked down to realize that the parents were waiting outside her store. She bolted to her feet, raced out, and unlocked the front door. "Hey, I'm so glad you made it on time. Sorry about the locked door, but it's the only way I can make sure I get any work done."

It was a bit of a lie but, hey, it was one that most people would accept. The couple moved into the store, both older, rotund, with tears in their eyes, and she realized just how much this would mean to them.

"Hang on. I'll bring it out." And, with that, she went into the back room, picked up the beautiful piece of artwork, and brought it out.

They gasped, both of the mother's hands going to her mouth as she stared at it, wordless.

Tasmin waited until she thought they could speak and then asked, "Are you happy with it?"

"Oh my, yes," the mother whispered. "I know that, for some people, this may seem ghoulish, and they think it's not right. But, for us, it's like having a piece of her back again."

"It absolutely is, and you know that this is a piece that she loved."

"Yes, of course it is," the mother agreed.

With that, the husband took it quietly, and Tasmin could see the tears in the corners of his eyes.

He looked over at his wife and whispered, "I'll take this outside."

"Do you want something to wrap it up in?" Tasmin asked.

He shook his head. "No, I'll put it right on the back

seat, and we're taking it straight home."

"Good," Tasmin murmured. She headed over to the till and rang up the purchase. It was a fairly pricey piece, being the size it was, but the mother paid without a qualm.

As she walked over to the front door to lock it behind them, the mother gave her a quick hug and whispered, "Thank you." And, with that, they were gone.

The whole exchange was once again a reminder that the reasons people had for doing things were not for others to judge, and, as long as it meant something to the people involved, Tasmin was happy to do this work.

She gave them a quick wave as they took off, then, feeling some of the stress roll off her shoulders, she turned around, looked at her shop, and said, "Everything else will just have to wait until tomorrow. I wasn't planning on completing that tonight, but, hey, at least it's done."

With that, she quickly reset the alarm, snatched her purse and her jacket, and once again headed outside. Only this time, *yay, her*, she got to go work at the funeral home. Once she drove there, she went in, much to her sister's obvious delight.

Tasmin glared at her. "I told you that I'd come."

She shrugged. "I know, but you know when we're overworked like this, it's always a joy to realize that somebody means what they say and that they'll show up."

"Since when haven't I shown up?" Tasmin scoffed. "It seems all I do is come and bail you guys out."

"And it's appreciated," her sister stated firmly. "But, if you hadn't walked away, I wouldn't be having this problem to begin with."

"And yet it's your business," she reminded her sister. "Dad has never left any doubt about that."

Her sister stopped and stared at her. "That really stings, doesn't it?"

"If the shoe had been on the other foot, what would it be like for you?"

Her sister winced. "Thankfully it's not, and I don't have to consider that. He told me that he would give you money in compensation though."

"Yeah, well, nowadays he'll just put me in a padded room and pay those bills," she muttered.

Her sister froze and looked over at her. "Did you hear them talking about it?" she asked.

Tasmin stared at her in shock and then saw the knowingness in the back of her sister's eyes. "I didn't have to hear them," Tasmin stated. "It's an ever-present undercurrent in every conversation I ever have with Mom these days. Believe me. It's always right there. And you telling her that I had a break-in at the store didn't exactly help."

"And yet the break-in had nothing to do with any of the conversations in your head." And then she stopped and looked up at her. "Or did it?"

"Of course not," she said in exasperation. "Thank you very much for that vote of confidence, by the way."

"Just think, if they lock you up, I really don't have to worry about sharing, do I?"

"Neither would you get any extra help, and I'm certain it's very expensive to replace me," she snapped. "Any more comments like that, and believe me. I'll be more than happy to turn around and to go home. It's already been a very long day."

Her sister held up a hand. "Hey, you know I was joking."

"No, I don't," she declared grimly. "You say things like

that all the time, and they're hardly jokes to me. Not when I know Dad is sitting there, looking for any excuse to have me committed."

At that, her sister slowly put down the paperwork she was holding. "Do you really think he would?"

"Yes, I really think he would," she snapped. "And so do you. But you're not bothered by it because it's not about you."

Her sister swallowed hard. "I hope you don't really believe that. … We're sisters, and I know that he's given me the business, and, to you, that probably doesn't seem very fair, but I honestly don't think he did it to upset you."

At that, Tasmin turned and stared at her. "So tell me then, why did he do it?"

"Because he thought I was the better person to carry on the family business."

"And why did he think that?"

Her sister flushed. "Okay, it's because of the episodes you've had. I'm pretty sure he had that decided a long time ago and only thought that he would ever change it if and when I proved not to be a better choice than you," she admitted, staring at her sister.

"And that was never likely to happen because I've never been the favorite."

Her sister snapped down the clipboard and glared at her. "We're not going back to that too, are we?"

"Nope," Tasmin declared. "Look. I came here to work, so, if you've got something for me to do, let me at it. Otherwise I'm out of here."

"No, please don't leave," Lorelei wailed in a beseeching tone. "Seriously, we're swamped."

At that, they headed downstairs to the embalming

rooms. "Fine. How many do I have to do?"

"How many can you get done?" she asked, only half joking.

Tasmin turned and glared at her sister. "How many are you lined up with?"

"Six."

"Jesus," she muttered. She waved at her sister and said, "Put on a pot of coffee and leave me alone. And you're paying overtime for this too."

"Hey, you haven't put in eight hours."

"I was here last night too," she muttered. "And the night before that and the night before that. I can't keep doing this. I can't run on empty and run your business in the dark without Dad knowing and still run my own place, which is supposed to be showing a profit. Otherwise, hey, it's not proving that I'm doing anything."

At that, her sister turned and headed upstairs again.

Tasmin called out, "Don't forget the damn coffee."

"You drink too much of that stuff," her sister called back.

"Yeah, but it's what keeps me working. So, if you shut down the flow, I'll shut down with it."

"That's a guarantee of getting the coffee if there ever was one," Lorelei replied, with a note of humor. And with that her sister disappeared up the stairs.

Tasmin took one look at the clipboard and the row of bodies she had to deal with and groaned. It would be a very long night. One of the reasons her father had always struggled with her at work was because she took her time and made sure that each of these people were well taken care of and looked after. It's not that her sister didn't do the same, but Tasmin talked to them as she worked, and that's where the problem had started. It was fine until she was fourteen, and suddenly they started talking back.

With that, she looked around at the room, then walked over and closed the door, so her sister couldn't come barging in unexpectedly, and announced, "Fine, who's first?"

She reached for the clipboard, but the first body that rose, the sheet coming up off the bed, was an older man.

He looked at her, smiled, and said, "Me please, if you don't mind. I'd very much want to be first."

She looked down at the paperwork and nodded. "Roscoe, John Roscoe, age ninety-two, you died of heart failure."

"Yes, yes, I did," he confirmed. "And honestly, I'm quite happy to go."

She looked over at him and smiled. "In that case, let's deal with you first." And, with that, she brought the gurney to the sink and got started.

∽

LATER THAT NIGHT, Hanson found himself wondering whether or not the parents had managed to pick up the piece successfully from Tasmin. He made a quick phone call to her, knowing she was still up, and confirmed it was gone. With a nod of satisfaction and happy that she'd at least managed to get that much done, he got back to work.

CHAPTER 6

BY THE TIME she was finished with her night's work, Tasmin was dragging her sorry butt around the funeral home. She locked up downstairs, headed upstairs, and let herself out to the cool morning air. It was coming on 5:00 a.m. She'd hoped to be done a lot sooner than that, but it didn't happen. Yet she'd done what she could, and the day shift would just take over when they got there.

She slowly rotated her head and her neck, looking around at the parking lot. This was the place that she'd hated the absolute most in the world for the longest time because it seemed, as the bodies arrived, the souls parked themselves out here and waited. That made no sense to her, until she realized that she was seeing them in the parking lot right from the get-go. She just hadn't made the connection that they weren't living people and family. They were souls waiting for their bodies to be unloaded into the back room. That realization had changed her view of parking lots.

Now she had visions of heaven being this one long hallway from a parking lot, where they were all standing and waiting to come inside. She had absolutely no confirmation from anybody that there even was a heaven. She wanted to believe in such a thing, but just because she wanted to believe it didn't mean she could. Not when she saw what she saw on a regular basis.

However, right now she was too damn tired to deal with any of it. She would be late opening her shop again, which just added to the pain. Every time she tried hard to make a go of her business, the guilt reared up since she couldn't even get her doors opened in a timely fashion. But, as she had told both her mother and the detective, she didn't need to be there.

What she really should do is have a bed at her place. She contemplated that for a moment. She did have a couple blankets there and a chair, and maybe what she should do is just fix that up and have a few hours of sleep, something to give her enough energy to get through the day. She refused to work for her sister tonight. Tasmin was too exhausted, and her sister needed to understand that, at some point in time, Tasmin had to start looking after herself.

Of course she hadn't managed to make that clear so far, and her sister wasn't interested in listening anyway. Tasmin got into her vehicle, and, driving very carefully, thankful that the roads were completely empty, she headed to her shop. As she got there, she unlocked and then relocked the door, reset the alarm, but with her inside, and headed to the back room. She'd had so much coffee that she was swimming in it at this point and dare not have any more.

She washed up in the small bathroom, then grabbing the blankets, she looked at the chair, which now seemed much less appealing. So back to sleeping on the floor, and that's what she did. It worked well enough, especially when she was dog tired. Her bed on the floor included a strip of foam that she often used. Satisfied, she curled up on the floor and closed her eyes.

She didn't know how long it was before she heard voices, but, when she did, she bolted to her feet and froze. Although the voices were clear and crisp as day, they were inside the shop. She got up slowly and looked into the storefront, but nobody was there. She searched around the back of her shop and then realized that the voices were discombobulated, as in they came without bodies.

She groaned. "Anybody who wakes me up will get in deep trouble," she muttered.

"It's too late for that, isn't it?" a woman noted softly. "You're already awake."

"And why am I awake?" Tasmin asked, glaring at the vision in front of her.

"I am sorry. I didn't know there were rules to this."

"Would you wake somebody up if you were still alive?"

"Yes, if it's something I wanted," she stated immediately.

At that, Tasmin groaned. "Of course. Now I must have a smart-ass for a ghost too."

"I'm not trying to be a smart-ass," she replied. "I'm still trying to figure out who you are and why it is I can talk to you."

"You mean, when nobody else will?"

"Yes, exactly," she said eagerly, then looked around. "It did take me a while to figure out I was dead, but why am I here?"

"I don't know. If I was mean, I'd probably say that you are not going to heaven or hell, and you're probably stuck somewhere in between. But usually, when I try to explain these things to people, they freak."

The other woman stared at her in shock. "Is that *in-between* place even a thing?"

"I don't know," Tasmin admitted, "but here you are, so I'll say, yes."

She watched as the energy shivered in front of her.

"Look. I'm not trying to be rude, but you woke me up, and I'm desperately in need of sleep."

"Then go back to sleep," she replied in a whispery voice.

"Yeah, and then you'll just wake me up when you don't like something else."

"Besides, I heard another voice."

"Who was that?"

"I don't know," she said, "but I thought I heard somebody here, so I was trying to talk to them, but they weren't talking to me."

"You thought you heard somebody else?" she asked, looking at her. She got up slowly and walked through her shop. "Where was this other person?"

"At the front, at the door, he was trying to get in."

"And did he recognize you?"

The woman stared at her. "I didn't know him, so I don't know how he would have recognized me."

Tasmin groaned. "You realize you have no body, right?"

The woman looked down, then at her. "That's not a nice thing to say."

"Oh, for crying out loud," Tasmin cried out. "I wasn't trying to be mean. I'm just saying that you're a ghost, so he won't recognize you unless he saw you, which would mean he can see ghosts."

The other woman, if she were alive, would probably be screaming right now.

Instead her face had turned huge, bigger than the rest of the wispiness of her. "I don't even know what to say to that," she replied, "but it does make a sick kind of sense."

"It does. Now can we go back to talking about this person?"

"I would say he did not recognize me," she stated immediately. "Or recognize that I … That I don't have a body. She looked around. "So, where is my body, and why am I here?"

"I don't know," Tasmin said, studying her. "Do you know when you died?"

"No, I don't. I didn't even realize I was dead," she replied in a snappy voice. "I was trying to talk to my husband all day, and he wouldn't talk to me."

"No, because he doesn't see ghosts," Tasmin stated. "So, as far as he's concerned, you're dead and gone, and he may or may not be able to talk to you."

"When you say *may or may not* …"

"Talking to ghosts generally isn't something that people accept. Therefore, in his world, it may not be a possibility. And, if it's not a possibility, it's much harder to break through," Tasmin tried to explain. But she'd done this so many times that, by now, the explanations were almost rote, and she acknowledged probably missing important stuff, only because she expected a certain level of understanding— which honestly, most ghosts didn't have. "Look. Is there any chance you can just hold tight and let me get some more sleep?"

"Sure." The woman stared at her, clearly fascinated. Then immediately asked, "How come you can talk to me?"

"Because I can see ghosts," Tasmin replied patiently.

"Lucky me, *huh?*" At that, she laid back down again. "Look. I need at least a power nap for twenty minutes. Otherwise I won't make it through my day."

"Fine, I'll be here when you wake up."

"Yeah, that's what I'm afraid of." Tasmin groaned, but she closed her eyes and immediately crashed. She was so tired that, when she woke up again, she still felt groggy and out of shape. She slowly rose, looked at the clock, and muttered, "at least I got more than twenty minutes."

"You got close to two hours, if that clock is anything to go by," the woman noted.

Tasmin froze, having forgotten about her new visitor. She turned to her. "Hi."

The other woman replied in a much happier tone. "Hi. You have no idea how happy I am to find somebody who can talk to me."

Tasmin nodded. "I hate to say it, but I hear that all the time."

"If this is for real, how come most of us don't know it when we're alive?"

"Because most people can't see the ghosts, and most people, even if they could see ghosts, wouldn't want to. I mean, think about the belief systems that you had." Then Tasmin went on to try and explain it to the woman while she made a pot of coffee, knowing caffeine would be necessary to kickstart her day.

"I mean, most belief systems don't allow for something like this. There is always talk of the afterlife and the supernatural, but not when we talk about ghosts. We talk about resurrection. We talk about salvation. We talk about being in angel form and going to the good Lord above," Tasmin explained. "We don't talk about being stuck in the cosmic plane between here and there."

The other woman nodded, her energy leaving little wispy bits to fly off in all directions. "So I guess the million-dollar question then is, how do I get back?"

"Back where?" Tasmin asked, frowning at her. "Because if you're talking about going back into your body, that's not happening."

A cry came from the newest ghost, and Tasmin nodded.

"Once you've come this far, that is not an option. I get that you're probably really hoping you can find out how to reverse this," Tasmin suggested. "But, if somehow it were reversible, I've never seen it happen, and I wouldn't begin to know how it could."

"But you don't know that it's *not* reversible."

"No, I don't, but where's your body?" she asked pointedly. "Generally, not having a body is a pretty good indication that you're not coming back alive."

The other woman's energy immediately dimmed.

Tasmin nodded. "I know. That makes me the bearer of bad news again."

"Wow, you must really like that part of this."

"No, I sure don't. Nobody likes it when I have to tell them all this stuff."

The other woman started to weep gently. "Do you even understand what we go through?"

"I'm not you, and I haven't been there, so I can't say that I do. Yet I have seen many, many ghosts over the years. I know that, if you're like most cases, you're missing your friends and your loved ones, especially your children, spouses, parents. Sometimes animals," she added, as an afterthought. "And all you want to do is stay with them."

"Exactly," the ghost agreed. "I promised my husband I'd stay with him."

"And that promise is likely what has kept you here in this ethereal form," Tasmin suggested. "Instead of your husband allowing you to go off and to die as you needed to, you made him a promise that you would stick around for him, probably because he couldn't let go."

"Yes, yes, of course. I mean, he's terrified of death. It's

just not his thing."

At that, Tasmin cracked a smile. "Honest to God, it's everybody's thing. We'll all die sometime," she declared. "Outside of taxes, I don't think there's anything else that we can count on in this life."

The other woman's face seemed to pinch, as if she didn't appreciate the humor.

Tasmin scrubbed her face and tried again. "Look. I get it. You loved him, still love him," she immediately corrected, seeing the energy swell, as if to say something against her past tense usage. "All I can tell you is that, when the time comes, you will be there for him on the other side. He'll see you, and you can reach out a hand and help him across. However, you can't do it in the form you're currently in. While you're in this form, not only can you *not* help him but you can't help anybody, and the people who were there to help you are still there waiting to help you. However, they must get to you, so you've got to get yourself to the place where they can find you."

There was dead and complete silence.

"Good Lord, I feel like … Did you ever watch the movie *Matrix*?"

"Yes, and the *Matrix Glitch*," the ghost replied, "absolutely."

Tasmin nodded. "In your case, the matrix glitched, and it's usually because of emotions. You feel bound and connected, probably to your husband."

"And my daughter," she murmured, her voice catching.

"Exactly. And they are now dealing with the loss of not having you around, but they love you, and they need to let you go. More than that, you need to let yourself go."

"But I can't," she cried out softly. "They were everything

to me."

"That's fine. I get it. But guess what? You're not there anymore." And Tasmin winced because, once again, her bluntness wasn't received at the level anybody would want to receive it.

The ghostly woman just stared at her.

Tasmin held up a hand. "I get it. I sound extremely cruel, even though I'm not trying to be." Tasmin sighed. "But I do need to tell you that the only way for you to see them, outside of seeing them such as you are, is to get yourself in your proper place, so that, when they die, they can see you."

"But I don't want them to die," she cried out. "That is not how I want this to go."

Tasmin smiled gently, then reached out a hand so she could touch the energy. "I get that. I do. That's because you love them, and they love you, and you really want them to have a rich, full, happy life. It's just that you didn't expect it to be without you."

The other woman, her features blurring, almost as if tears covered her face, nodded. "You do understand, don't you?"

"Yes, I do."

"Have you ever lost anybody you cared about?"

"I've lost several people I cared about," Tasmin replied, her voice quiet. "And I've dealt with a lot of people who are dealing with loss, the biggest of all being the loss of their own life—the loss of their own hopes, their dreams, their future—not realizing that the loss they saw was not necessarily a loss at all. It was just a change of life, as they move from one existence to the other."

"Are you saying there's life after this?"

It was obvious the other woman needed some time. And

the time was good because Tasmin needed coffee. With a cup in her hand, she headed out to the front and opened up the store, hoping that nobody would come, and realized that was the absolute opposite of what she really needed to happen. She sat down on the front step outside her store and just sipped her coffee and watched the world wake up. It was now 9:00 a.m., but she was on a side street, so there wasn't a whole lot of traffic and not a whole lot of work for her to do. She was totally okay to have a few hours of just waking up.

When her sister phoned, Tasmin groaned but answered it. "What's up?" she asked.

"I hate to ask—"

"No. Don't even," she interrupted. "I'm sitting out here, trying hard to muster enough energy to get through the day. I can't possibly work through the night again too."

Her sister groaned. "I know. You've been working so hard. I guess I hoped you had made it home in time to get some sleep last night."

"At five-fifteen a.m., I made it to the shop, and I slept on the floor," she snapped. "You need to hire more staff."

"Isn't a whole lot of staff to hire."

"Yet you went home at closing time, didn't you?"

"No, I waited for you to show up," Lorelei said in outrage. "I am there doing overtime every night."

"That's a good thing," Tasmin replied, "since it is *your* business. And I get that, in your world, you get to walk away, when it's time to walk away, but, in some people's worlds, that's not an option."

Her sister asked, "Was it okay last night?"

"What do you mean, *was it okay?* Do you mean, was anybody talking to me? No, nobody was talking to me," she responded, a glib lie she had learned to perfect. "Everything was fine. Just a lot of work to be done."

"I know," Lorelei confirmed, "and we have a lot of families who are emotionally overwrought."

"Of course you do, when you have six bodies to deal with and six sets of families to deal with, and all that can be heartbreaking. What about Dad, is he helping?"

"He hasn't been doing very well health-wise," she admitted. "So, I have one person working today, but I could really use two."

"So you were going to ask me to come in and work today too?" Tasmin asked in disbelief.

"I was just checking to see if you've gotten six hours of sleep or not," she said, "but obviously you haven't and obviously you need more."

"Yeah, ya think?" And then Tasmin groaned. "Look. I'm not trying to snap at you, but I'm exhausted."

"Got it. I won't call you for a little while. Try to catch up on some sleep."

"Yeah, I'm working on it," she muttered. She hung up the phone and stared down at it. "It's not your fault. You don't have to deal with this," she muttered.

But when her mother phoned not that long afterward, Tasmin knew it would be the same thing again.

"Your sister needs you."

Tasmin stared at the phone, shook her head, and stated, "I've already worked all night, Mom."

"Your sister needs you. We need you," her mother whined. "The business is really suffering."

Tasmin frowned at that. "The business isn't suffering. You're running a lot of people through there, so there's no way."

"We may not be suffering financially, but we don't have

enough skilled staff."

"Right, but remember that part about I worked all night? I can't work all day too."

Her mother huffed. "There were times when you did a lot of double and triple shifts."

"I've worked five nights in a row without a break, and every day I've also come in and run my own business."

"But you don't really have much business, right? You could just come and work for us for a while instead."

"Really? And what will you tell Dad?" Tasmin was trying hard to not let her tone betray her feelings. "You'll just hide me downstairs and keep him away from the basement?"

Her mother sighed. "I wish you wouldn't treat him quite so harshly."

"You wish *I* wouldn't treat *him* quite so harshly?" she asked in shock.

"Look, Tasmin. It's a problem, but, if you would just not say anything to him, it would be a lot easier."

"Oh Lord," Tasmin replied.

"Look. It's just for right now. We're really, really struggling here."

"Lots of people are struggling right now," she snapped, "and I get it. You need help. But honest to God, I've helped, and I've helped, to the detriment of my own business. Right now I'm exhausted, and I need to look after myself."

Her mother snorted. "Fine. If you won't help, then I'll have to get your father down there again."

If she thought that would be some threat for Tasmin, that was the opposite of a threat. She snapped, "And so you should. It's *his* business, remember? Oh, right. It's not *his* business. It's *Lorelei's* because you guys gave it to her." And then she winced because that was the last thing she'd wanted to bring up.

Her mother wouldn't let it go though. "Of course you would bring that up. You are paid every time you come into work, you know?"

"I am not. I take it on credit for my use of the facilities. If I need to, I can certainly find another site to do what I need to do. It would definitely be better than constantly being hounded by you guys."

"We're not hounding you," her mother argued, trying to stay calm. "Obviously you need to sleep, and I shouldn't have called you. I'll talk to you later." And, with that, she hung up.

Tasmin sat here, sipping her coffee, but it was hard to enjoy it when she realized just what was going on in her sister's world. It was her sister's business, her sister who had phoned in, her sister who was relying on Tasmin to do night duty. But, at some point in time, Tasmin had to step back. Particularly since her father wasn't allowed to know she was working there or to even let him see her. That was a large part of why she was struggling with it so much.

As she sat here, she heard a voice. She looked up, but nothing was there. She looked around and still couldn't see it. She didn't want to call out because talking to someone invisible was the last thing she wanted to do. Therefore, she sat here and waited.

When another voice called out, she spun to look. And there, standing in front of her, was the detective. Hanson, she thought his name was. And then she froze because the detective, if that was him, was in an odd form.

He looked at her, smiled, and said, "Seems your family life is about like mine."

She shook her head slowly, as she got up, backing away

from him.

He frowned. "Problems?"

"Yes. Jesus." She stared at him, shoving her hands into her pockets and glancing around wildly. "What happened?"

"What do you mean, *what happened?*"

She took several long slow deep breaths. "You're a ghost," she pointed out. "Somehow, between talking to me last night and now, you've died, and you've joined my world as a ghost."

∽

HANSON AWOKE AND snapped upright. Frowning, he looked around, but he was in his apartment, on the couch of all things. He was also fully dressed. He vaguely remembered coming home in the early morning hours, after a rough night on the streets, dealing with a couple car crashes—one of which had been a deliberate vehicular homicide and another as a result of a drive-by shooting.

He'd made it as far as the couch, deciding that he'd just sit here for a minute to unwind, but obviously hadn't gotten any farther. What happened after that he didn't know; it was almost as if he heard the woman from the tattoo preservation place talking to him.

He gave a headshake, checked the time, then groaned out loud and whispered, "Damn."

He walked into the bathroom, quickly shucked his clothing, and stepped into a lukewarm shower, scrubbing himself down, while trying to wake up. Once he was done, he quickly dressed in clean clothing, grabbed his keys and wallet, and stepped outside. He hightailed it to his car, hit the first drive-through that he could for coffee, then headed into the office.

He got there just on time. The other detectives looked at him and back at the captain, who stood up front, just about to start the meeting.

The captain looked at him, smiled, and noted, "There is coffee here, you know?"

"Yeah, sometimes there's coffee," Hanson replied, with a ghost of a smile. "This way I make sure there is."

The captain stared at him for a long moment, as if not quite understanding, but the laughter around Hanson indicated that everybody else understood. Taking a spot at the back of the room, Hanson pulled out his notepad and just waited.

The captain quickly began. "Okay, we've had a series of drive-by shootings. These are mounting, and it's definitely a problem." He looked over at John and Mark. "Did you guys come up with anything new?"

John nodded. "We've got a vehicle and a license plate, and we'll track those down today."

"Good. Do we have an update on the victims?"

"Two fatalities," Mark replied.

The captain frowned at that. "Since when did that become our murder of choice around this place?" he muttered. "It doesn't even give the victim a chance."

"And too often they're not targeted either," added Callie, from the other side of the room.

She was also a new hire, but before Hanson came on board. Yet she seemed to bond quite well with Terri, who was the only other female detective on the force. Hanson was the odd man out, mostly because they ran in teams of five, and everybody else had partners when he showed up.

The captain eyed her and asked, "And you've got the vehicular homicide from last night?"

She nodded. "Yes, and that was apparently a husband running over his lover."

"Not the wife?"

"No, not the wife, a lover, who decided that he would never leave his wife, so she broke up with him in a church parking lot."

At that, the captain's eyebrows shot up. "Of course, the church parking lot."

She smiled and nodded. "She was there for choir practice, and he was hoping for a little nookie session afterward," she explained in a droll voice. "Instead she broke up with him. So he got into his vehicle and ran her over, before she ever had a chance to get to her car."

"Have you picked him up?"

"I have, and he's sitting in lockup right now, while I write the reports and get things done."

"Good enough," the captain said. "At least we got something locked down tight." He turned his attention over to Hanson. "And you?"

"Nothing new on the tattoo artist break-in, and I'm following up on the other drive-by shooting," he replied.

The captain frowned, looked at the other two male detectives and back at Hanson. "Hate to say it, but it seems you're all on your own for this one."

Hanson was used to that, and honestly he preferred that.

The captain looked down at the papers in his hand. "Things are heating up around here. I've asked for more budget, but you know how that goes around here."

Groaning murmurs came from around the room, and Hanson just ignored it all. He didn't know a police department yet that didn't have budget constraints, where every one of the officers and detectives were hollering for overtime approval or additional staffing because it was needed to solve the cases. All across the country, departments were short-staffed and underfunded. It was the same old, same old; sitting here, groaning about yet another department which couldn't change anything.

As soon as the captain got up and walked out, Hanson turned on his computer, ready to get some real work done. He turned his attention to the double shooting from the day before.

As the two male detectives walked by his desk, they looked over at him. "Yeah, sorry we didn't get to the crime scene yesterday."

He looked up in complete disinterest. "That's fine. I was there."

"We knew you would be," John said, with a laugh. "Besides, we had a funeral to go to."

Hanson turned to face them. "I'm sorry. Was it a coworker or family?"

"Neither. It was a snitch, somebody we worked with for a long time," John offered, with a heavy sigh. "We were wondering if somebody at the funeral would give us some information, but … almost nobody showed up."

"Whoever would show up would be immediately suspect," Hanson noted.

"We didn't say it was an accidental death or a murder," John argued, looking at him.

"No, maybe not, but, if anybody knew he was a snitch, then it would have made things complicated for anybody who showed up."

"Nobody showed up, so it's not an issue."

"What'd he die from?"

"Cirrhosis of the liver."

"Ah, that'll get you too, I guess." Hanson returned to his paperwork, not sure why they bothered to explain, when, so far, they'd been pretty blunt and mostly ignored him.

"The captain talked to us this morning," John shared, still standing in front of Hanson's desk. "He was pissed that nobody was here last night, but, of course, Goody Two-Shoes, you were here."

"I was here because I'd just come back from the crime scene," Hanson snapped. "Wasn't anything Goody Two-Shoes about it, but whatever. Think what you like."

At that, John let out an exaggerated sigh.

Mark added, "We're just trying to get along."

At that, Hanson looked up at him. "Seriously? That's your line?"

Apparently unbothered, Mark just shrugged.

"Look," Hanson said. "I'm here to do a job. And, if you guys don't want to work with me, that's fine. Tell the captain. Otherwise leave me alone, and I'll get my stuff done, even if it's separate from yours."

"He doesn't want that. The captain doesn't want any lone ranger stuff."

"Then, somewhere along the line, something has to change," he stated coolly, as he stood. "I've only been here a couple weeks, not long enough to figure out the ins and outs. I don't know what the hell's going on or why everybody hates my guts, but you can bet that I really don't need this shit."

At that, Mark lowered his voice. "Somebody found out why you left your last job."

Hanson frowned at that. "Ah, that's great, isn't it, since that thing is supposed to be confidential."

"Nothing's really confidential in our world. You know

that."

"So, what then? Everybody's waiting to see if I crack under pressure? What are you thinking, that I'll start speaking in tongues, whatever the hell that even means?"

"Kind of," Mark said cheerfully. "And, if you are, you want to give us a heads-up, so we can get it on tape? That would be great for everybody." And, with that, he headed over to his desk.

"You know it's catching, right?" Hanson replied, satisfied to get two looks of horror from his coworkers. Trying to ignore the ribbing, yet reminding himself that he'd known all along that somebody would find out about his medical history, it was still pretty annoying that it had happened so fast. The fact that it was supposed to have been confidential just irked him all the more.

But when something was confidential and people knew, it just made them want to dig deeper to find out. So, no doubt they'd used all kinds of excuses for why they didn't want him on their team. Hanson could imagine the list, starting with the fact they couldn't count on him, couldn't trust him, he wouldn't have their back, et cetera, et cetera.

He'd heard it all before and had hoped that it wouldn't happen here, but, of course, it would. They didn't want anybody new; they didn't want anybody different; they didn't want change. And whatever the hell was going on in their world, they just wanted the status quo to continue. Well, Hanson wasn't here to change the status quo, but he was here to do a job, and he sure as hell wouldn't let them stop him. He had a job, and that's what he would focus on.

Hanson opened up his notes on Tasmin's case. Something was just so strange about her. And waking up this morning, as if talking to her in some sort of dream state, was beyond weird. But, as he brought up his email account, he saw one from her. He quickly clicked on it, opened it up, and found it was a formal note, thanking him for facilitating the release of the tattoo piece. Sure, he'd done something to help it move along, but mostly because he also knew it was biodegradable, plus a family was waiting.

At least he thought it was biodegradable, but she hadn't really explained the process, but then, as an embalmer, she probably knew all kinds of tricks of the trade. But still he pondered that, as he stared around the room. Bodies still decomposed over time, even in coffins, so maybe it was something to do with the way they were sealed in the picture frame under glass.

He responded with the obligatory reply and didn't say anything more than *You're welcome*. He was surprised when a response came back almost immediately. He opened it and saw that she was asking him to call. Frowning, he pulled out his cell phone and called her right away. "What's the matter?"

There was silence on the other end for a long moment. "I guess nothing," she muttered, confused and puzzled.

"Is something going on?" he asked impatiently.

"There could have been, yes, but maybe not," she muttered. "Anyway, sorry to bother you." And, with that, she quickly hung up.

He didn't know what to make of that call, but he quickly made a notation about it in his file and copied over the contents of the email as well. Something weird was going on there with her. But, hey, a lot of weird was going on in his world too. As it was, she was one of the most interesting women he'd met in a very long time, and, since everybody here thought she was spooky as hell, but not him, that would just accent how different he was from the rest of them.

Both John and Mark soon got up and left.

Terri walked over, Callie with her, and asked, "Hey, do you need a hand with your cases? We're supposed to be a team around here."

"We're *supposed* to be a team," he repeated, with a ghost of a smile. "It's always a problem being the new guy."

Callie smiled up at him. "Isn't that the truth," she confirmed. "Now that you're the new guy, I'm no longer the new one. Still, a team of five shouldn't mean two pairs and one off on his own."

"If you've got anything to offer on my cases, I'd be happy to have fresh eyes and would always offer the same for yours. I need to run down and collate all these witness statements, but, so far, we haven't got a whole lot, though I do have part of a license plate."

"Oh, good. Run that, and, if you run into dead-ends on the rest of it, give us a shout."

"Will do. I'll also hit the city cameras to see what I can come up with. We do have a bit of video, although it's not as clear as I would like."

"Seems you've got more than we do," Callie admitted, with a laugh.

He shrugged. "Some days are better than others, aren't they?"

"And some witnesses better than others," she replied, with a nod.

As Hanson sat here, working on his notes, he set up a run on the license plate. Unfortunately far too many popped up with those last few numbers. But narrowing it down to the vehicle and color brought it down to fifteen. As soon as he ran through each of them, he sat back and finished off his coffee, which had now gone cold, then tossed the cup in the garbage.

When his computer flashed, he leaned over and swore.

Terri looked over at him. "That doesn't sound good."

"The gray vehicle used in the drive-by was reported as stolen last night and has just been found abandoned on a dirt road outside of town."

"Of course it was," she muttered. "At least you have it, so you can get forensics, if there is anything."

He nodded. "I'll head out there to take a look at where it was and call out forensics for it."

"Or you can get it towed back to the impound yard and have forensics go over it there," she suggested. "It's a little easier on the budget."

He pondered that and then nodded. "Okay, that's a good call. I'll do that as soon as I get there."

"Yeah, nothing quite like looking at the scene with your own eyes, is there?"

He smiled in understanding. "I've always found it helpful." He snagged his coat and his keys and headed out.

As Hanson left, John and Mark were coming back in. They looked at him in surprise. He just ignored them and walked over to his car. If they wanted to talk to him, that was fine; if they didn't want to, so be it.

It took Hanson twenty minutes to get to where the vehicle was, and the tow truck was already there, waiting for instructions. He talked to the man for a few minutes, realized the presence of the vehicle had been called in by a neighbor. Once it was determined to be stolen, the tow truck had been called out.

"Thank you for waiting," Hanson added.

"I could have loaded it up, made sure I got my fee out of

it at least, but more and more of these dumped vehicles are just stolen."

At that, Hanson nodded. "You're right. Drive-by shooting, two dead."

The tow truck driver winced. "In my day there was no such thing. Now all of a sudden, it seems everybody's involved in drive-by shootings."

"Give me a few minutes to go over the car," Hanson said, "and then you can take it to the police impound lot. I'll get forensics to go over it there."

"Will do. I've got coffee, so I'll just wait in my truck." With that, the driver returned to his tow truck, hopped in, and sat with a thermos in his hand.

Meanwhile, Hanson wandered around the vehicle, put gloves on, and took a closer look. He opened it up, looked inside, and checked for anything of interest. He found a discarded coffee cup and fast-food wrappers, which he left in place, not knowing whether they belonged to the owner or to the drive-by shooter. If from the shooter, that was great because maybe they could get some DNA on them. Hanson hadn't noticed on the video if the shooter wore gloves, so Hanson would go back and take another look. He quickly did a thorough search of the stolen vehicle.

Finding nothing else of interest, he motioned to the tow truck driver, who hopped out and started loading up the vehicle. For himself, Hanson stood back and studied the area. He was looking for anything, shadows, something that would say why it was dumped in this area.

And then he halted the tow truck driver, as Hanson reached in and started the engine on the stolen gray car, just to check the fuel level. He shut it off, hopped out, and said, "He ran it out of gas."

The tow truck driver looked at him in surprise. "For twenty bucks worth of cash, he could have gone two states over."

"Yeah, so the question is, why didn't he, and how did he take off from here?"

The driver shrugged and didn't have anything more to say, anxious to get on to other jobs, so it took him only fifteen minutes before he had it loaded and was already driving away.

Hanson waited until the tow truck was out of sight, then turned and took another close look at the road around him. He took photos of the tire tracks, noting that a second vehicle had come up close behind the abandoned one. He wondered whether the shooter had just flagged someone down for a ride, saying he was out of gas, or he had a partner.

Both were viable options.

CHAPTER 7

TASMIN KEPT STARING back at her phone throughout the rest of the morning. Twice, she'd gone outside to take a look around, right where she had seen what she thought was Hanson's ghost. Obviously it wasn't his ghost, and that concerned her more than anything. She knew she was exhausted, and that was a concern because, anytime she got too tired like this, whatever she saw morphed—and morphed into something that wasn't terribly comfortable.

She didn't know what to do with these things when they happened, and, so far, she'd kept it all under wraps. However, if she was starting to lose it, her father would only have that much more ammunition to get her locked up. She didn't know what his problem was, or why he couldn't just be supportive of whatever she was going through, but it seemed to bring out the fear in the worst way for him, and he just didn't want anything to do with her.

To be honest, that's why she was only asked to work nights because he worked days, and the family did everything they could to keep him away from her. He would lose it as soon as he saw her, then start calling her a liar and a cheat and a devil spawn, even though she came from his own loins.

Then she stopped and frowned, wondering whether she had come from his seed or not.

"I'm losing it," she muttered to herself.

Another spirit voice, the same woman as before, said, "I guess this must be hard for you."

"Very hard," Tasmin muttered.

She returned her attention to the framing that she had to do. She used low-E glass and a special gas on the inside to hold back any deterioration, but the truth was that these things were almost like parchment paper at this point, only more durable. She could roll it, could basically try to rip it, but it didn't rip; it was much tougher than that. Several other people had started this process. Then Tasmin had added a few of her own tweaks over time, as she got more experience. She couldn't guarantee a lifetime without degradation, but she could certainly count on at least twenty years.

For most people that was enough, and Tasmin didn't know whether it would be a lifetime or more than that. She could only explain that it was a new science, and, as such, they didn't have any long-term research for it. Most of the time the people who wanted this really wanted it. There were no ifs, ands, or buts about it; they wanted it, and they were prepared to do it, no matter the risk or guarantee.

She'd talked a lot to people before she went down this pathway, and most decided a picture of the tattoos would serve them just fine. They didn't want to have a piece of Uncle Joe hanging on the wall or a piece of Aunt Mary's butt sitting in a picture frame. That was just beyond what they could even contemplate. Of course they were thinking of it from that point of view, instead of somebody who was now missing someone they cared about and couldn't get back again.

Often the tattoos that people chose to have her preserve were beyond things such as a simple rose on Aunt Mary's butt. They were something much more incredible, artistic, and special. In those instances, Tasmin certainly understood how that artistic expression had every right to be preserved, no matter what the format was.

Not a popular opinion, she knew, and, of course for her father, what she was doing was even more sacrilegious because, as far as he was concerned, dead was dead. He did his job as best he could to make the dead look good for the living, but, once they went into the casket, he didn't want anything to do with them.

It was absolutely flabbergasting to her that he went into this field, but it was a family business, so maybe that explained everything. She didn't know. At this point in time it was much better if the two of them didn't show up in the same room. But it hurt, it hurt terribly. Her father had always been her idol, and she'd always planned on taking over his business, but, when they'd turned around and given it to her sister without a word to Tasmin, it had been absolutely shocking.

Of course, at that time she had just come from a bout of seeing things, things that the family were not comfortable with her seeing. But they didn't give her a chance to "recover" from this so-called illness; they'd just decided that she would not be good enough to handle the business. Her sister hadn't even mentioned anything to Tasmin and had just accepted that's the way it was, and life had moved on. But, for Tasmin, it was hard to move on.

It was a betrayal, where she had long been promised something and had always accepted that as inevitable. She'd always assumed that she and her sister would potentially run the business together, and she would have been okay with that. But to have been completely cut out without a word, yet continually asked back to pinch hit for them, when they couldn't handle it all, just added insult to injury.

Of course there was no shortage of insults anyway, provided by her father any time her name came up. Her sister often filled in Tasmin on his latest and greatest insults, which always came around to the topic of her being a devil spawn, without the same right to life as everybody else because of it. Some of that talk actually terrified Tasmin, but her sister seemed to think it was funny.

When Lorelei had mentioned that it sounded like Dad was the one losing his grip on reality, Tasmin had stared at her sister. "I wouldn't be at all surprised, but don't ever let Mom hear you say that—and especially not Dad. You'll be locked up faster than you can shake a stick at. And yet it sounds like maybe he should get locked up," Tasmin noted.

Lorelei nodded soberly. "He does act like a fanatic sometimes," she muttered, "and that's a bit scary."

"A bit?" Tasmin asked, eyeing her sister. "So, you're okay with all this, *huh*?"

"No, I'm not," Lorelei stated. "I don't know what to think about you," she added briskly. "But you work hard, and I need the help. You were raised in this business, and you certainly know how to make everything run. I don't know what to say about what they did to you, but, as the beneficiary of that decision, I'm not sure what I'm supposed to say anyway. *Sorry* sounds pretty trite."

"Maybe so, but it would be a start," Tasmin snapped.

"I'm not really sorry though," Lorelei admitted, looking at her sister. "I mean, why would I be? Look what I got out of the deal." Then she laughed. "I'm not trying to be mean or anything, but I was raised with the knowledge that you would always get the business. Then, all of a sudden, things changed, and they'd already signed it over to me. So from having nothing to getting the keys to the castle was pretty cool."

"Sure it is," Tasmin agreed, her voice soft. "For you."

"Right, but, for you, it's such a betrayal, isn't it?"

"Ya think?" she replied in a sarcastic tone.

"But it's really your own fault. I mean, even if you are seeing things—and I'm not saying you are—but you sure as hell shouldn't have opened your mouth about it. You know how Dad is."

Trouble was, Tasmin hadn't really realized that her father was that scared or that full of hypocrisy. Because there had been more than enough instances at the funeral home that she had asked him about, but he had been pretty much silent on the subject, saying there were things they didn't talk about, and these souls needed to be buried so they could rest. That had been a weak explanation at best, but it was probably all that her father could do for her.

As such, it had ended up raising more questions than answers and had hardly helped in any way. And when she tried to ask him later, after she started seeing things, he wouldn't even talk to her, probably afraid that he had put it all into her imagination somehow. He told her once that her imagination was way too strong and had run amok, and he didn't want it to go anywhere else.

Of course that wasn't true. Her imagination had nothing to do with this. If it had, she would write books and could make a million on horror stories, but it wasn't that at all. She'd been seeing these things for a very long time; she'd just never brought it up, not until she got a little older. And, even then, she somehow instinctively knew it was something to stay quiet about and still rued the day she'd opened her mouth and had said something to her father because she had endured all kinds of hell ever since.

But her demise had come when she brought it up again and then once more. Now, realizing she would never be accepted where she was, even after all the psych testing and the work testing she'd been put through, her family would only ever acknowledge an illness. So Tasmin would never have a chance for a normal life, as far as her family was concerned.

Not a whole lot she could do about it.

She knew perfectly well where she stood, which was outside the family, outside the family business, and on the off side of normal. And quite possibly one step away from being locked up. That fear kept her awake at night, worry that her father would have her committed, regardless of what he said or did right now to the rest of them.

Her mom laughed at her and told her it would never happen, yet then pushed more buttons by saying, "Besides, if you've got some weird connection with the undead, surely you would find out about it before it happened anyway." As if not realizing that this was a fear she would never overcome, particularly since she had already been locked away for far too long, before the medical profession proclaimed absolutely nothing was wrong with her but an overwrought imagination.

She had worked very hard to give that appearance too. Her father somehow seemed to know she had finagled the doctors into believing her, and that had made him even more distrustful. There was really no good answer for this untenable situation, and she'd often contemplated moving out of state, just to get away. She still contemplated it with some regularity, but she had made herself a business and a home here, making it that much harder to consider moving away completely.

Although, the more she realized her sister didn't really appear to give a crap, Tasmin realized that leaving her sister wouldn't be all that hard either. No, that's not true. Leaving them would be hard, but they probably wouldn't really care, with the exception of all the work she did at the "family" business.

With all that rambling through her head, while ignoring the newbie ghost at her side, Tasmin quickly buried herself in her work. When her stomach started rumbling, she groaned, stepped back, and looked around. She hadn't brought any food here either.

Rubbing her face, she knew she needed sustenance and an early bedtime tonight.

There wasn't enough work here to keep her late. She even contemplated going to bed early and just eating there too, but she still had a lot of paperwork to deal with. Picking up her phone, she ordered from her favorite pizza joint and asked for it to be delivered.

As soon as she hung up the phone, her grandmotherly ghost, who questioned everything Tasmin ate, spoke up. "That's not very nice, dear. You should be eating a home-cooked meal."

"Yeah, maybe that's what I need, a wife," she said, with a snort, "but, in the meantime, pizza it is."

A hard sniff came from her food-monitoring ghost, not appreciating being mocked, so Tasmin turned and smiled. "Sorry, times have changed a bit."

"Not if you got married. You could stay home and do the cooking, and he could go to work."

At that, Tasmin rolled her eyes. "As I mentioned already,

times have changed, and, even if I did get married, chances are I'd have to work anyway. Besides, I want to work."

"This is no work for a lady," the grandmotherly ghost stated primly.

"Right, well, working in the funeral home as an embalmer wasn't exactly work for a lady either, but nobody seemed to give a crap back then."

Thankfully, at that, the woman stayed silent.

Later on, when Tasmin heard the bells on the door, she raced out to the front, with a big smile for the pizza delivery guy. "Oh thank God, I'm starving."

"No problem," he said, "here you go."

She gave him a decent tip and waited until he was gone before taking the pizza to the countertop behind where the cash register was. She pulled up the one and only stool, sat down, and, tearing open the box, picked up a piece and took a big bite.

Closing her eyes in relief, she felt a sense of satisfaction, responding both emotionally and physically to the food after going far too long without anything. When the bell rang again, she opened her eyes to see the detective standing in front of her, an odd look on his face.

She frowned at him, and he mimicked her frown immediately.

She sighed and asked, "What's the matter?"

"You had an interesting look on your face when I walked in," he noted cautiously.

She shrugged. "I just took a bite of pizza, and it's the first thing I've had in"—she stopped, pondered—"at least twenty-four hours, probably more."

He stared at her.

She nodded. "Things have been a little crazy."

"Problem crazy?"

"No, just incredibly busy," she said.

He glanced around the shop, puzzled.

She shrugged again. "I know. It never looks like I have much work here, but I do, all right? And, besides, my family is really struggling with the workload at the funeral home, so I've been going there every night and pulling a night shift to help them out."

He shook his head immediately.

"I know. I know. You don't have to tell me. I'm burning the candle at both ends, *blah-blah-blah*."

He walked closer and stared down at the pizza, an odd look in his eye.

She moaned. "Ah, jeez, are you going to make me be polite?"

"If that means offering me a piece of pizza, yes, please, that would really be great." Without hesitation, he reached over and grabbed a piece.

"When did you last have your meal?" she asked him.

He stopped, looked at her, and frowned. "I don't remember."

She winced. "Our lifestyles suck."

He cracked a smile and nodded. "You could be right, but I haven't found a satisfactory way out of it, have you?"

"No, I sure haven't, and, as long as my family keeps hounding me, it doesn't look like I'll catch a break anytime soon."

"Why don't they just hire more staff?"

"They tell me that nobody is qualified."

"Do you believe them?"

She pondered that for a moment as she ate, then she shrugged. "I don't think they're trying very hard, perhaps because I'm too convenient."

"It's your funeral home too, isn't it? The family business and all."

"No, it's my sister's," she replied stiffly. "They gave it to her."

"Interesting," he murmured, his gaze locked on her face. No judgment, just an intensity that made her feel odd, almost hollow, as if he could see right through her.

She glared at him, then shrugged. "Hey, it happens."

"Oh, absolutely it does," he agreed, "although, it seems like that is a place you were very at home at."

"Very at home," she muttered, with a nod.

"Particularly since you can see things."

She winced. "Yeah, I can see things all right. I can see that you came here for a reason, and I hope it's not just to sit there and eat my pizza."

"If I'd known you had pizza, I would have come earlier."

"It's a good thing you didn't. Plus, the pizza just arrived anyway," she said grudgingly, as she snatched a second piece.

"You ordered a large, so you must have been really hungry."

She looked down at it and sighed. "Honestly, I didn't really think about it. It's probably what I had last time, and I just hit Reorder because I was past caring."

He nodded, as if fully understanding.

When she saw the weariness on his face and his own exhaustion, she admitted, "You don't look like you got much sleep either."

"Oh, I was out on a case last night, and I ended up crashed on the couch. I thought I would just relax there for a minute when I first got home, then woke up on the couch this morning, still fully dressed."

"Oh, I hate that," she muttered. "Nothing like sleeping in your clothes to make you feel like you didn't get any rest."

"I should be used to it by now," he said.

They ate quietly for a few minutes. When she snatched up a third piece, she looked at him, then nudged the box closer to him. He nodded and accepted another piece himself.

"I guess there is enough, isn't there? Thank you."

"There is," she said, feeling better now that her stomach had food in it. "I can always get something for dinner later on."

"But will you?" he asked, with half a smile. "Or will I come around tomorrow and find you in the same boat."

"It's not that bad," she protested.

He just stared at her steadily.

She frowned. "Okay, so maybe it is." Shaking her head, she admitted, "I slept on the floor in here for a few hours very early this morning, when I got through at the mortuary."

He just nodded, as if he already knew that.

She sighed. "Okay, so both of us suck, and both of us either need to tell our bosses to back off or need to find other ways to make a living."

"Or, in your case, maybe you need to just stick to the one job, the way you've chosen to earn your living."

"Yeah, well, I flat-out told them I wouldn't work tonight. I've worked five nights in a row for them and still have worked in my own shop for five days, but apparently that's not enough because they are still hounding me today."

He stopped eating to study her, yet didn't say anything.

"Right, I know. It's my fault. Too much of a pushover."

He cracked a smile. "Sometimes with family it's hard.

Particularly if you're looking for acceptance."

She stiffened in outrage at first, then heard his words and the intent behind them. Her shoulders sagged. "I guess that is what I'm doing, isn't it?" She chewed fiercely, as she contemplated his words. "That really sucks," she snapped. "The last thing I want to do is work this hard just to gain acceptance … from my own damn family. The very same family who basically kicked me out. If they don't want me in the family all the way, then I don't want to be in it at all."

"So, why are you doing so much work for them then?"

"I would have said because they needed the help, and earning the credit for the time served is also helpful for my business, since I do a lot of my work there."

"And yet …"

"And yet, in reality, I've already banked up enough hours to the point that I would be hard-pressed to use them for my business in the next six months, which means, in the end, I've probably been working for free."

He cracked just the barest of a smile.

"You're right. Damn it. I sure didn't want it to be about acceptance."

"Why'd they kick you out in the first place?"

She looked over at him and blew out a big sigh. "Oh, you know, … all those rumors and things."

He didn't say anything, just finished a piece of pizza and stared down at another.

She nudged it toward him. "Go ahead. It seems we're both exhausted and starving."

"And you wouldn't want to see anybody suffer, I suppose."

"Not particularly, no," she agreed, with a smile. "No need for everyone to suffer. I don't know about you, but, for me, these last few weeks haven't been easy."

"When did they give the business to your sister?"

"About, oh, let's see, four days after I was released, after going through an in-patient psych eval," she stated, her tone harsh. "They didn't like what the doctor reported, which is that I had an overactive imagination, and they figured that I had somehow conned the doctors into giving a diagnosis less gloomy than what they thought."

"You mean, like, either a psychotic episode or that you're completely delusional?"

She stared at him, her hand slowly lowering, the pizza in it almost forgotten. "You sound like you may know what that's all about."

"Been there, done that," he declared. He took a deep breath. "Because I see things too."

∽

HANSON HADN'T MEANT to say anything, but it had just slipped out. And, from the look on her face, she wasn't all that surprised.

"So, tell me something," she began. "What were you doing this morning at about"—she pondered it for a moment—"about nine forty-five?"

"Sleeping," he stated succinctly. "On the couch. And trying to avoid being late for a ten-thirty meeting at the office."

"And did you make it?" she asked curiously.

"I did but barely."

"You were sleeping, *huh*?"

"Why?"

"Because I swear to God that I saw you outside," she shared. "That's why I sent you that email."

"What good would the email do?" he asked.

"Maybe nothing, maybe everything. I don't know. But when I said that I *saw* you, I meant—"

"Meant what?"

"I meant, I saw you in a ghostly form."

His jaw dropped. "What?"

"Yeah, I know. So, we're back to that very vivid imagination I have."

His eyebrows shot up. "That's beyond imagination."

She winced. "So, I'd really appreciate it if you don't tell my father any of that because it will just give him more grounds to have me committed."

He stared at her in surprise. "I won't say anything to your father about it. Having already been through psych evals myself and knowing how strange the outcome of that can be, I totally understand. Plus, it is so hard to prevent something like that from being a black mark on you that somehow impacts your life forever."

"It does, doesn't it?" she agreed.

"Yes. For example, I was cleared, yet what was supposed to be confidential information was leaked out to the rest of my team. Even here, after I'd moved to get a fresh start. But, once they found out, nobody wants to work with me." With a ghost of a smile, he added, "Of course I'm totally okay with that."

"Yeah, I would be too," she agreed. "I much prefer to work alone. I would have preferred that nobody knew about the whole thing either, but my sister, no doubt enjoying being deemed the favored child, made a point of telling several of my friends what happened."

He stared at her. "And are they still your friends?" he asked, his tone overly polite.

She shook her head. "Not a one."

He nodded. "In which case they weren't really your friends to begin with."

She snorted at that. "Easy to say, just not all that easy to accept."

"So presumably, you're truly alone then."

"Yeah, but isn't that what happens? What about you?"

He lifted his chin in a clipped nod. "Yeah, that's exactly what happens. Everybody you know, everything you knew, it all changes."

"And why does that have to be?" she asked softly, staring at him, her eyes wide. "I don't understand."

"Fear," he replied succinctly. "Fear that whatever we're dealing with will rub off on them somehow. Fear that we'll find out something they don't want us to know. Fear that we touch a level of evil that everybody is always so terrified about, but I don't even think exists," he explained.

She hesitated at that. "You don't think evil exists?"

He raised his eyebrows and then replied, "Obviously you have a different opinion."

"It's not that I have a different opinion," she noted cautiously. "I've just seen some things."

"And seeing things is a great prelude to sorting this out," he stated. "I don't think it's evil as much as I think it's *man*. I think man—humanity as a whole—is capable of doing many things that are evil, but I don't think we get to give them a pass and call it this nefarious evil entity out there, somehow forcing them to do it."

"Oh, I agree with that," she said instantly. "My father doesn't though. He believes in the devil and hell to the max. I'm certain that he thinks that's where I'm going and wants to keep his distance, so he doesn't get caught in the undertow."

"Considering the environment in which you were raised, a lot of people might say he's equally responsible for the condition you're in because of the work you did."

She laughed. "People might want to think that, but it's really not the truth."

"No, but we won't let them think anything different, will we?" he asked, with a smile. "Because there's very little available to us to fight these accusations that keep coming our way."

"How do people keep quiet about it? Or do they?" She frowned, looking at him. "And believe me. I never expected to be having *this* conversation over breakfast."

He looked down at the pizza and repeated, "Breakfast?"

"Lunch," she corrected, with a wave of her hand. "Or dinner. I don't care what we call it. I'm just saying, this day isn't turning out the way I expected when I got up this morning. Of course I got up off the floor of my shop after working all night for my sister, so what did I expect, right?"

"But you did get up, and something is going on in your world," he pointed out. "What I want to know is whether it's connected to the tattoo that ended up in the fountain."

She slowly lowered the last bit of pizza and stared at him in shock. "Good Lord, I hope not." Then she shook her head. "There's no way."

"No way? How or why?" he asked her curiously.

She frowned. "How would that work? How could anybody?"

"I don't know. Does somebody know what you do, and would they have felt what you were doing was something that needed to be put on display, for example?"

The look on her face made him wince.

"Look. I'm just bringing up something to contemplate."

"Meaning, you have absolutely no idea where to go with this, so you're going to the dark side." She stared at him, and he knew that she saw the glint of humor in his gaze, but he was pretty sure there was an answering glint in hers.

"Maybe."

"So, when you see things," she whispered, looking around, "do you see anything here?"

"Shadows."

She stiffened. "What kind of shadows?"

"There's one beside you."

She looked, and there was the older ghost, intent on nagging Tasmin about her eating habits, now staring at her pizza. "That's Nanny," Tasmin said. "I've been trying to get her to go home for a long time, but she doesn't know where home is anymore. She had Alzheimer's when she died, and now she's lost in this world too."

He stared at Tasmin. "I hadn't considered that such a condition would carry through."

"I don't think it's supposed to," she noted, with a shrug of her shoulders. "But I think, when she ended up with Alzheimer's, her worry and fear for her loved ones carried through to the point that she was medicated for being upset all the time. Mostly I think because she was so upset that she was looking out for her daughter in some way or other. Therefore, when she passed, she was still upset and still searching for answers."

"That is a thought I didn't want to contemplate."

"And when you say, *shadows*, what exactly do you see?"

"Darkness," he stated. "Some of it's a lighter gray. Some of it is jet-black."

"Any emotions attached?" she asked curiously.

He shook his head. "I rarely get any emotions attached." Then he stared at her and asked, "You?"

"Absolutely. Sometimes way too many emotions, including tears and breakdowns. Everybody is loved and lost. They want to go back to their loved ones, and they can't, or they want to be anywhere but here, and I can't help them. That kind of thing."

"I don't see any of that," he murmured, "but then I also don't usually communicate with them."

She frowned at that, stared down at her crust, and proceeded to toss it into the box. "*Usually?*"

He nodded. "It's uncomfortable to talk about, isn't it?"

"Yeah, it is," she agreed. "Nobody understands."

"I do."

At that, she nodded but stared down at the cardboard box.

He didn't know how to break through her guards. They were having a conversation that he had hoped he would have with other people many times, but, when it never happened, he figured that nobody out there saw what he saw. But Tasmin did, or at least she saw a variation of what he saw. "Do you know anybody else in this field?" he asked her.

She immediately shook her head. "Not in my world. There are some pretty well-known psychics out there, and a couple have worked with the police. Maybe that's one of the reasons why, when this happened to me, I understood a little more, and I just kind of shut down. Why did it happen to you?"

"Who knows?" After hesitating for a moment, Hanson shared, "I was shot on the job, and I almost died. Maybe I did die. I don't know. When I came back, I brought some things with me." Her eyes widened, and he winced. "I guess that sounds pretty rough, especially when I say it that way."

She immediately nodded. "Yeah, it sure does. What do you mean, *you brought some things with you?*"

"People, bits of people," he replied. "People who were stuck on the other side, who recognized I was dying and sent me back, but I don't think that they were completely on the other side themselves."

She just stared at him and blinked, then blinked again.

He sighed. "See? Even though you see things, and you talk to people, and ghosts are in your world, it all just seems a bridge too far, even for you."

"No, it's not," she argued cautiously, "but it's definitely different. I mean, it's not a conversation I would ever want my father to hear, for example."

"Or my police captain," he added, with a wry look in her direction.

She shuddered at that. "Oh, God no. And, if they already knew you had a psych eval …" She stopped, letting her thought linger.

"Obviously I passed the evaluation, but it does make it a little hard to gain the trust of the other team members, and, when they won't give you a chance, that's even worse. They figure that I was one of those necessary budget additions, even though I come with some baggage. They had no money, no time, and not nearly enough man-hours to solve their cases, and it was getting them all into trouble. I guess, from their perspective, a warm body is better than nothing, even though I'm not necessarily sane."

"And that's just wrong," she cried out softly.

He shrugged. "Yeah, it is, but I've been trying to control it."

The words came out so abruptly and so harsh that it

took her a moment to fully recognize what he had just said. "Control what?"

"Who I see, when I see, how I see," he replied. "But, to be honest, it's come with mixed results. Some good and some not so good."

"I never tried to control it," she admitted. "I don't know. I've always been a free spirit and have always seen them. I just wasn't smart enough to keep my mouth shut. Well, I was for a long time because my grandmother told me not to let anybody know, so I didn't. However, when she passed a few years ago, I guess I forgot. I was too emotionally overwrought at seeing her again, and, when I started to talk to her, so excited because she was there, but my father flipped."

"Oh, yeah, that would do it," he said, with half a laugh. "Is she still around?"

"No, I convinced her to leave, although at times I wish I hadn't. It's damn lonely in this world sometimes."

At that, he nodded again. "Yeah, I would agree with that."

She frowned at him. "You don't really think that anything that you and I see is connected to this case, do you?"

"I don't know. This is still pretty new to me. I did reach out to somebody that my previous police force used on the sly every once in a while. Again, nobody particularly liked it when he was called, but he was always very respectful and didn't put on any kind of shenanigans. He only came for the worst-of-the-worst cases. Plus, the accuracy of his information was uncanny."

She stared at him. "That has to be Stefan Kronos."

His eyebrows shot up, he nodded slowly. "Yeah, do you know him?"

"No, but I've read a couple online articles about him," she noted. "You know it's always that conundrum, do I call him or do I not? But what would I say if I did call him? It's not as if he gives a crap about me anyway. He doesn't know me or anything about me."

"Exactly. I've been wondering about contacting him too and haven't for the very same reasons," he admitted, with a ghost of a smile. "Besides, what do we say? *Hey, we've got this problem that's not necessarily a problem for us, but, for other people, it's a big one. So, what are we supposed to do about it?*"

"Stefan would probably laugh," she guessed, with a smirk, "and tell us to deal with it the way he did, by gaining acceptance of your own abilities, then letting the rest of it slide because people will always be people."

∽

"THAT WOULD BE a really good way to look at it," Stefan agreed, slowly appearing in the room, between the two of them. "You should also be aware that I monitor the ethers and always find conversations such as this to be fascinating."

He waited for a moment, recognizing the shock on both their faces, only to realize that they had both heard something. Whether it was his words or something else, he didn't know. Part of his ongoing challenge was recognizing new talents out in the ethers, people who needed help, before, as Tasmin had mentioned, they were committed and locked up in padded rooms.

"If you would phone me that would make my life easier right now. Talking to two newbies at once this way is a bit hard." At that, he picked up the pencil beside the cash register and wrote out his phone number. "Give me a call." With that and a chuckle, he left. He didn't normally do things like that, but, hey, it sounded as if they were both struggling.

When Stefan opened his eyes, his beautiful wife was smiling down at him.

"So, did you contact them?"

"I did, but whether they'll follow through and call me back, I don't know. They were pretty freaked out when I showed up."

She snorted. "And why wouldn't they be? It's not as if it's something they could have expected."

"No, it wouldn't be," Stefan confirmed.

He slowly rotated his neck, feeling the tension and the strain in his back. He'd injured it the other day and was continuously running healing energy through it, but he'd woken up with the stiffness again this morning.

"You should get Maddy to look at that."

"Maddy has real issues to deal with," he told his wife, with a smile. "A stiff neck is hardly anything to be concerned about."

"I guess I was wondering if it was something else," she suggested.

"What do you mean by *something else?*"

She shrugged. "You're the pro at this, not me, but it seems to me that, whenever you get a stiff neck, something is happening out on the ethers that isn't necessarily good."

He stared at her and was instantly tossed into an image that he had absolutely no grounding for. A murder was happening—a man, a young woman, and something they were fighting over. Something that was important to the young woman, yet also important to the man, but for the opposite reason. He wanted to destroy it, and she wanted to save it.

Stefan shuddered and came back to reality, when his phone rang.

As he turned to pick up the phone, he asked his wife, "How about some tea, if you don't mind? This could be a long call."

When he answered the phone, he greeted them with "Put it on Speaker, Tasmin, so I can talk to Hanson too."

CHAPTER 8

Tasmin stared at the number and then at Hanson. "Surely we shouldn't be calling him." But, even as she spoke, her fingers were dialing. Very quickly, Stefan was on the other end of the phone. At least she assumed it was Stefan, and he was calling them by their names. "How do you know us?" she asked instantly.

"Because, like you, I see things, and maybe or maybe not like you, I hear things," he replied. "And I feel things. So I keep a sort of antenna out for when people in my field are in trouble. Because there really is nobody out there you can talk to."

"Yeah, you're not kidding," Hanson agreed.

"And you're a cop?"

"Detective, actually," he corrected. "And we've got an odd case here, which brought the two of us into contact."

At that, Stefan replied, "And, Tasmin, you've already been committed once?"

"I was held for psychiatric evaluation," she clarified cautiously. "I wasn't actually committed at the time."

"Good," Stefan said. "So, have you learned enough to keep all this away from the people who are afraid of you? Because they are the ones you must worry about."

"I got that," she declared, "but, in my case, my family poses the most danger to me. My father in particular."

After a moment of silence on the other end, she looked over at Hanson. He just raised an eyebrow, as he stared at the phone.

"I would agree with you there," Stefan stated, "but there's also another entity around you."

She gasped and looked around, and, of course, several ghosts were in attendance.

"Several entities are here," she replied cautiously. "I see them on a regular basis."

"Yes, of course. And what is it that you do for a living?"

She laughed at that. "I was raised at a funeral home. I'm a licensed embalmer, and now I have my own shop where I preserve tattoos from the dead."

Another moment of silence passed on the other end, and then he laughed. "Of course you do. That's one hell of a sideways step out of the normal boundaries of what society will accept."

"Most of the time they don't," Tasmin replied, "but I don't do work for them. I do this work for the people who are desperate to preserve the historical value of the tattoos in question. For example, I have one Asian family as clients, and I have preserved tattoos from twelve members to date. Those tattoos have become something akin to a living history of their family."

"Oh, I like that," Stefan replied.

"You might like it, but having full skin suits preserved under glass as wall art is not everybody's idea of normal." Even at that, she looked over to see Hanson staring at her, his gaze wide. "Hanson didn't know about that family either," she noted, with a smile.

"No," Stefan confirmed, "but many years ago, one researcher was collecting and cataloging similar things. He kept an archive of all the tattoos done in a certain way. Unfortunately he lost all his samples and photographs in the Second World War."

She nodded. "Yes, there have been several of those that I have read about. There's one collection from a Russian prison, where they kept all the tattoos in formaldehyde and glass," she shared. "That's very different from the way I'm preserving them, but, as long as it works, we're not 100 percent crazy."

Stefan laughed through the phone. "Look. Both of you were in circumstances that resulted in opening yourselves up. In your case, Tasmin, because of the way that you were raised. You were obviously a sensitive, and, once you realized spirits were out there, you became more and more aware of them."

"Honestly, I saw them from when I first started working in the funeral home," she admitted. "It didn't take long because I spent a lot of time with my grandmother, who also worked there. She saw them as well, and she very quickly told me not to say anything."

"Good," Stefan said briskly. "And, Hanson, did you say you had an accident?"

"Yes, not so much an accident, but I was shot in the line of duty. Apparently I died on the operating table, and, when I came back, … I tend to think of it as if I came back with some extra pieces."

Stefan went silent again on the other side. "Serious injuries and experiences, such as dying on the medical table, can often open up abilities that we didn't have before," Stefan noted. "But the fact that you came back *with something* is also very strange."

"I know," Hanson agreed, "and I don't really know any

other way to describe it."

"Can you try? What is it you think you came back with?"

"Don't you mean you came back with an ability?" Tasmin asked, looking at him. "How else would you bring something back?"

"It feels like energy. Such as I spoke to somebody while I was dead, and he came back with me."

Stefan sucked in his breath at that. "Have you spoken to this entity since you returned?"

"Every once in a while. He's very scared."

"Scared of what?"

"The world he finds himself in," Hanson replied carefully. "He has proven to be quite invaluable, as twice, when I was in danger, he warned me."

"That's lovely," Tasmin cried out. "Like a guardian angel. None of my spirits do that."

At that, Nanny at her side sighed. "What do you mean? I've tried to warn you about the ills of pizza every time you have it."

A shocked silence filled the room. She looked over at Hanson to see if he had heard it. Since he had a perplexed, almost confounded look on his face, she assumed that he did. She assumed that Stefan didn't, but soon realized he hadn't said anything because he was laughing so hard. "Did you hear that?" she asked the detective.

Hanson nodded. "Yes, but why? Why did I hear that?"

Stefan's laughter grew louder and louder. "You have to love ghosts," he said, with unmistakable mirth in his voice. "Every once in a while, you get one with a sense of humor. Or one who just can't stop mothering you or telling you off or something. Most of the time they're just sad souls, lost and looking for a way forward, either to stay connected to the people who they still love so much or for a way to get to the other side," he explained calmly. "We do have people who work with both groups."

"I don't even know what to think about that," Hanson admitted, staring down at the phone. "I mean, I did plenty of research, when I recovered enough to think straight. I guess I must have talked to the wrong people though because I was immediately sent for a psych eval at the police department."

"You do have to watch who you speak to," Stefan stated. "In my case, I now work with the police, and I have a reputation for the type of work that I do, but I can't even begin to tell people about a fraction of what I can do."

"Does it change?" she asked abruptly.

"You mean, your abilities? Yes, absolutely. Your abilities change over time, particularly as you use them." Hesitating, he then continued. "In addition, hanging out with other people with abilities will also cause your own to grow."

"*Great*," she muttered, shooting Hanson a wide-eyed look. "So because Hanson and I have connected, we'll see our abilities change?"

"It's possible," Stefan confirmed, with good cheer, "but it's not something to be afraid of."

"Both of us have come very close to losing the world as we know it, so we may be a little gun-shy."

Stefan's voice softened as he said, "I know. One of the things that I do on a regular basis is work with people in psychiatric hospitals to see if we can help some get back to a level of capability that would suggest they could handle what's going on in their world. Sometimes yes, sometimes no. Unfortunately psychiatric institutes are full of people like us who just can't handle these abilities," Stefan explained, "so it's really important that you don't go too far or too fast … or deal with something too strange."

"I see shadows," Hanson said abruptly.

Stefan didn't say anything for a long moment. "Do you see anything in the shadows?"

"Sometimes I see visions, but they're never very nice."

"But then you're a detective, right?"

"Yes, homicide and the like."

"So, whatever is in those shadows is probably connected to crime scenes."

"That's what I was thinking, since they are rather recent. I've just moved to a new police department in a new city, and they've started to come on more and more."

"Don't let anybody know what you're seeing," Stefan warned, "but write down those visions. Start taking notes, and you'll probably match it up with the culprits pretty quickly."

"That would be nice, since it would help me get some cases closed. At the moment, it doesn't seem I'm getting very far on the couple cases I do have," he admitted, "but unfortunately I'm not sure these visions are connected to cases even close to me."

"That would be another issue, wouldn't it?" Stefan noted. "The other thing, not that I want to scare you, but it's also possible that these incidents haven't happened yet, but they will. In that case, you would be seeing precog visions."

Tasmin winced at that. "Isn't it enough that we see some of this stuff without knowing we may be seeing stuff that hasn't happened yet?" she muttered.

"It doesn't matter how or what it is that you're seeing," Stefan explained. "What you need to understand and accept is that what you're seeing is what you're seeing. Don't try to push it off or have it be anything other than that. Trust the process, maybe take some notes, and hold tight to who you talk to. Now that you've each found each other, I would recommend that you meet at least once a week in private, where you can't be overheard and where you're free to dissect everything that's gone on," he suggested. "I can't speak on the phone for long, but I'll contact you again in a bit," he added. "There's something about that tattoo, something strange. Be on the lookout because something weird is going on, and it could be connected to this case." He paused. "The tattoo from your shop, was the person murdered?"

"No, she died of leukemia. She was a model. The tattoo was removed, and thankfully I had already preserved it. It was ready to frame when it was stolen from my shop. Oddly enough, my shop was locked, and the security system was on," she shared with Stefan. "Hanson here was on the case, and we have no idea what happened."

"Oh," Stefan replied, his voice getting soft and deep, with a bit of a hard edge to it. "I might, but I'll have to look into it a little deeper. Until later." And, with that, he hung up.

CHAPTER 9

TASMIN HAD JUST picked up lunch, dinner, whatever she should call it, and had gotten back to the shop later that afternoon. As she turned the front door sign back to Open, she watched as Puggs walked toward her. She opened the door for him and smiled. "Hey, Puggs, I haven't seen you in a while."

He shrugged and gave her a bashful grin. "The boss sent me over to make an inquiry."

"Yeah, what about?"

"One of his tattoo clients is not doing so good, so she was asking about preserving her tatts afterward."

"Yes, of course," she said. "Does he want me to talk to her?"

Puggs nodded immediately. "If you wouldn't mind. It's still not a subject a lot of people are comfortable with."

"But you are," she noted, looking at him curiously. "And I know you are because we've talked about it."

"Sure, but I'm in the background of the business," he stated, with a wave of his hand. "I run the supplies, keep the store going, clean the floors, you know? I don't do too much with the customers."

"Maybe you should start," she suggested immediately. "You have a generous soul."

He looked at her, somewhat startled, and then laughed.

"I don't think anybody else would agree with you," he stated, still chuckling. "My mug isn't exactly anything the customers want to see. That might tend to scare off more people than anything else."

"You're too hard on yourself," she said, with utmost sincerity. "You've just got some scars from your boxing days."

"They're mostly from my street days," he clarified. "I had most of these before I ever hit a boxing ring."

She chuckled. "So, that's where you honed your skills, before you entered the ring?"

"Sure, but I never got good enough to do anything with it," he shared, with a shrug.

"Hey, not everybody is meant to shine in a ring," she said gently. "As long as you're happy where you are, I don't think anything else really matters."

He cocked his head at her and spoke with a gentle smile. "I forgot how nice you are."

She winced at that. "Being called nice isn't exactly something people like to hear these days."

"That's a shame," Puggs replied. "We need more *nice* in this world that's gone to hell in a handbasket, and I just see more and more of that hell every day."

"I agree with you there," she stated, with a nod. "Sometimes I wonder how society will ever survive."

"I'm not sure it will," he said.

They exchanged a knowing smile, understanding they both had similar viewpoints. "Here's the lady's name." He held out a piece of paper. "Pinch told her that you'd probably give her a shout in the next little while, but we couldn't guarantee when."

"Oh, that's good," Tasmin replied. "Life is kind of busy at my end too."

Puggs, who was on his way out the door again, turned back and looked at her. "Is it?"

"Absolutely it is," she confirmed. "A couple articles ran on the West Coast, and that's really helped business."

He stared at her. "So you fly out there?"

"I do sometimes, if it's a complicated art piece," she replied. "If it's not too-too bad, then I'll get a funeral home close by to do the job, if they have anybody skilled enough. Otherwise we get a doctor to do it."

"Right, but I guess if you put that kind of money into tattoos …"

She nodded. "As you well know, some people put an incredible amount of money into their tattoos, and, for some family members, they want that reminder."

"I'm still kind of tossed up over it myself," Puggs shared thoughtfully. "A part of me says it's freaking awesome, and another part of me says it's freaking gross."

She burst out laughing. "The good news—for me at least—is that enough people are on the positive side to keep me somewhat in business."

At the *somewhat*, he rolled his eyes. "Yeah, I know all about that *somewhat* thing. It means that you somewhat get food and you somewhat get your rent paid, but generally you need something a little more reliable than *somewhat*."

She was laughing as he exited the door with a big grin on his homely face. He was a good soul, a wonderful person, and she'd known him a good dozen years by now. She had known Pinch, the tattoo artist Puggs worked for, almost as long. Now that she was doing this work, they had just that many more reasons to communicate.

Of course Tasmin also had a tattoo that Pinch had done, something she had gotten in memory of her grandmother when she passed. Tasmin hadn't bothered to tell her family because she knew what kind of reaction she'd get. It was one thing for them to deal with the body piercings, tattoos, and other modifications on the bodies that came through the funeral home, but it was another thing entirely for them to have any association with it on a personal level.

Her father's religious beliefs had gotten more and more extreme, and now he even fancied himself a preacher and was trying to build himself a church. She had often wondered how they could go through life with such a rigidly black-and-white attitude, but gradually she had come to realize that her family was more prejudiced and judgmental than most.

At least she hoped it was more than most or else the world really was going to hell in a handbasket, as Puggs had just pointed out. She looked down at the name on the card he had given her. The woman's name was Joy. Tasmin fingered the name and sighed. "Well, Joy, it seems not a whole lot of joy is in your life right now."

Tasmin hesitated about calling her too quickly, not wanting to appear as if she were way too eager for the business. Although a contact call wouldn't necessarily give her the business, as people often needed time to think about it. And, in some cases, they had just enough time to think themselves out of doing it.

Tasmin had just as many cancellations after people had a chance to talk to friends and family as she did signups. She wasn't trying to push anybody and had only started doing this for a couple friends of hers, who had been rather desperate to save some beautiful artwork that had been done on a friend of theirs killed in a car accident. Tasmin had really scrambled to get things in place for that case, and, once she had gone through the process, it just seemed like another service she could offer, ideally through the funeral home.

Unfortunately her father was horrified at the thought, and her family had kind of blown up around her. Once that had happened, she needed to promote the work in her fledgling business in order to earn a living. It had made sense at one point to work at the funeral home in exchange for the use of the facility to do her projects, but that had morphed into what was now working at the funeral home on the sly, under the cover of darkness to keep her father from finding out.

At this point, she was giving far more than she was getting out of the arrangement. She didn't feel it was fair at all and that didn't make her feel very good either. What had been her father's business, was her sister Lorelei's now, and they needed to run it however they needed to, but that didn't mean that Tasmin had to be locked in the basement in the dark of night, doing all the work for them. Without getting any of the recognition or even a paycheck at this point.

Hanson had been right when he pointed out that she was seeking acceptance. She still felt a mix of emotions as she tried to work her way through some of that, only to immediately discard it, realizing she didn't have to work through any of it. It was all too confusing and something she would probably never make sense of. She needed to let it go.

Turning her attention to the work she was more passionate about, she picked up one of her pieces that was almost ready to go. A bit later, as she sat back and smiled down at the beautifully finished piece, she picked up the phone and called the customer. As soon as they answered, Tasmin identified herself and in a gentle voice said, "It's ready."

The woman on the other end gasped, and there was a hint of tears in her voice as she whispered, "Thank you."

"No problem," Tasmin said. "Come on down whenever you're ready." With that, she hung up, then picked up the phone again and dialed the number on the card from Puggs.

When Joy answered the other end, Tasmin identified herself. "I was told you spoke to Pinch today about the possibility of preserving your tattoos."

The other woman sighed. "Yes," Joy said. "I will still do my best to try and preserve them on live flesh as long I get to live and breathe tomorrow and the days that follow, but apparently that plan may not work for too long."

"I'm sorry," Tasmin murmured. "It's the downside of living."

"What's that?" the other woman asked curiously.

"Dying," Tasmin said simply. "And when we have assets we want to preserve, it becomes something we must deal with legally and aboveboard, before our Maker knocks on the door."

"*Assets*," Joy repeated, rolling that around on her tongue. "I kind of agree with that. So many people I have mentioned it to are so against the idea of preserving my tattoos, but I've spent a fortune on them. Not only that but the artist who did a good share of them is no longer living, and I wanted her amazing work to be preserved as well," Joy explained, with a noticeable catch in her voice.

Almost instantly Tasmin realized that the artist was someone Joy had loved dearly. "If she has passed to the great beyond, I'm sure you know that she's probably over there, waiting for you to join her."

"That's one of the reasons I'm not as torn up about dying as I had expected to be," Joy shared, her voice getting stronger. "There's a certain amount of relief in knowing that I'll see her again. But I don't want her work and the work that Pinch has done to finish what she had started to die with me."

"No, and that's exactly why I do what I do," Tasmin stated. "Nothing is easy about making that decision though, and I'm not here to push for or against it. If you like, I can send you an email showing some of the work I've done, so you can see what it means to have artwork preserved for life. Of course it's confidential, and I don't use any names of the donor or the artist."

"Yes, and I would appreciate that anonymity myself, if you were to ever use any photos of me in your advertising." And then she burst out laughing. "On the other hand, I'm really not likely to care, am I?"

"I hope not, but I don't know for certain," Tasmin replied gently, "though I haven't had anybody come back to complain."

Joy burst out laughing at that. "Can you imagine?"

"Considering that I'm doing this at the request of my clients, if they do come back, I would hope they would come back happy to see the job that was done as they wanted."

"It's a new science, I presume," Joy noted. "Honestly I don't even know quite how the process works."

"As an embalmer, and a licensed one at that," Tasmin shared, "it's taken me years to perfect a process and to adapt it to each situation to get the best and the easiest results, with the least amount of decay. … That's why the photos will help you to see what I mean and to show you how the tattoo will look at the end of the day. Of course, at some point, I would also need to see the tattoo itself, either in person or in photographs, so I have a better idea of what I can do. Also the location matters."

"Does it?" Joy asked curiously.

"Some skin is tougher. Some skin is thinner," she said. "So, depending on exactly where you've got the tattoos that you want to preserve, it makes a difference as to what kind of a job I can do for them."

"And will you try for it no matter what?"

"Yes, absolutely," Tasmin confirmed. "But you have to understand that certain places, such as sexual organs for example, are a little more difficult. So, as much as I would do my best to preserve it, I can't guarantee it will come out as good as it is now."

"Do they potentially come close?" she asked.

"Oh, yes, most are very close. As a matter of fact, for some people it's startlingly close, and, for others, it's almost too close."

The woman continued. "So, I gather I would pay for this ahead of time."

"Yes, but more to the point is establishing who you want to look after your tattoos upon your death."

"Right, there's that. Is there a place where I can donate them?"

"There is. I am doing a book, and one of the local hospitals here is doing a scientific show on some of it, but we don't want this to go the way of medical science. A book is one thing, but I don't have a museum or something like that. There are a few scattered around the world, but they have very specific themes, and I don't think yours would fit into it."

"No, I don't imagine it would. I'll have to talk to my daughter about it," Joy said. "We spoke about it briefly, and she thought it was a cool idea at the time, but that doesn't mean she'll want to lug around a picture frame for the rest of her life."

"No, but you don't know that either, not until you ask," Tasmin pointed out. "Maybe it would be her joy to know that she has a part of her mother with her always."

"Ah," Joy said, then a sob broke free. "You do know how to put it gently."

"It's a tough subject no matter what," Tasmin noted. "I'm certainly not trying to convince you either way. If you want to give me your email address, I'll send you some information, and you can go from there."

"That would be lovely, thank you."

With that done, Tasmin got off the phone, sat down at her computer, and opened up a new email, attaching a few of the promotional files she had created for just these occasions. So many people were exploring the idea, but that didn't mean they were anywhere close to making a commitment to this. Plus the person involved in making a commitment was a totally different story than getting the family on board as well.

Often Tasmin got the commitment from the family who hadn't even spoken to the people while they were alive, which caused her all kinds of hell. If they were willing to donate their body for medical science, then she was okay to continue on with her preservation process because then the family members were not hung up on the actual physical body itself.

But she'd had to go to court twice already—not her favorite experience—but it was part of the business as far as she was concerned. She'd had to go to court in her role as an embalmer as well. Having a funeral director business did have certain legal ramifications, when the grieving families got upset about the process involved.

With the email to Joy sent off, Tasmin was ready to turn her attention elsewhere. As she stood, she felt an icy wave fill the room. She froze and slowly turned to look around. She couldn't see anything, but she had no doubts about what she had felt. "Hello?" she called out cautiously.

She heard nothing in reply, none of the giggling or smart-aleck ghosts, no anti-pizza ghost, nothing except a weird ugly chill. Frowning, she stepped toward the front of her store, unsure of what she was supposed to do, when there was a weird, not musical, but almost a weird cry in the background. She froze. "Hello?" she called out cautiously. "Anybody here?"

There was a whisper, just the faintest whisper, and it came through as clear as a bell.

"Help me, please. Dear God, help me." And then it was gone.

She froze and then reached for her phone once again, only this time she found herself dialing Hanson's number. She didn't even know why, except that maybe it was Stefan's call that had gotten her to put Hanson on the same level as a helpline.

Whatever it was, she didn't think Hanson would appreciate it, but, when he answered the phone, he immediately asked, "Are you okay?" His tone was harsh, as if he already knew.

"What just happened?" she asked him, her tone sharp.

He said, "I'm not sure."

"And yet you were expecting my call, weren't you?"

"Maybe," he replied softly. "I just had an eerie feeling of something wrong."

"Yeah, something was wrong," she agreed, and she

quickly explained.

"*Huh*, well, I don't know what to say," he murmured. "That is not what I was expecting."

"I don't know what to expect right now either," she agreed, "but whatever this is, it really can stop anytime."

At that, he burst out laughing. "I'm not sure we're involved in something that'll allow for stopping."

"Why not?" she asked, pouting. "I'm not finding this a whole lot of fun."

"No? I'm sure Stefan would probably tell you to just stay safe."

"How?" she asked. "It's not as if I can have a conversation with this entity. It was very much a case of spookiness going on in the background."

"But you're used to spookiness," he reminded her gently, then his voice shifted. "Yeah, I'll be right there," he called out to someone.

"Sorry," she said, immediately wincing. "You're at work."

"I am, but I'll stop by afterward, okay? Will you be there?"

"I will be today," she noted, "but, after that, I probably have to go back and help out my family."

"Or you could tell them to stuff it," he declared, "because you're wearing yourself down to the bone."

"It's not the first time, and probably won't be the last."

"Maybe not, but did you ever consider that it may be your level of exhaustion that's letting all these people into your space? If you took better care of yourself, maybe you'd be stronger, and they'd stop." And, with that, he quickly hung up, leaving her staring at the phone in shock.

"How many pieces have you done so far?" Hanson asked, as he accepted a cup of coffee from her, while he wandered her shop.

"You mean, in this preserving business?" He nodded. She pondered that. "I think it's about seventy or so at this point. ... I do have records."

"Seventy? Interesting," he replied.

"Why? What's interesting about it? I mean, it's nowhere near the numbers another shop I know of does, but, hey, it's certainly something for me."

"And this other shop, is it close by?"

"It's in California," she noted. "And I really wouldn't want to give you their name if I didn't have to."

"Why?" he asked. "I highly doubt it's top secret. They must have some level of public approval in order to stay in business."

"They work along with another funeral home because it's easier. Plus, in this case, they also have a problem with negative publicity. So, short of somebody asking specifically for a referral to someone they could work with in another area, personally it's not something I really want to share, not without talking to them."

"And yet I'm a cop," he said in a dry tone. "Remember that."

"Yeah, you are." Tasmin stared at him. "That's not always a good thing."

"It is if they're operating aboveboard."

"It's the whole industry," she explained. "It has a bad name."

"You mean, tattooing."

"That's not what I meant, but, yeah, that too. It doesn't need to be that way, but certainly a lot of people have the wrong impression of what goes on in a legit tattoo parlor," she noted, with an eye roll.

"And of course you would know."

She stiffened slightly, then relaxed. "Yes, I would. Not that it's any of your business."

His eyes widened, and she watched him studying her, trying to figure out if she'd gotten a tattoo herself and, if so, where it might be.

She smiled at him. "Now, how about my break-in case? Did you come up with anything as to who might have stolen the tattooing?"

"I did not," he replied.

Before she could question Hanson further, her phone rang. She looked down at it. "Hey, Pinch. What's up?"

"Hey, did you ever talk to that woman I referred to you via Puggs?"

"I did, thank you. Why did you send him over instead of calling me, by the way?"

"I don't know. It just felt better in the moment. It was kind of weird, but Puggs was heading out anyway, so I just figured, whatever, he could stop by and say hello and see how things are going. I heard about what happened to that one piece."

"Yeah, it turned out all right though. I got it back again, and it's already safely gone to the owner."

"Oh, good," Pinch said. "I wasn't sure what the cops would do with it."

"It was missing property, stolen property," she explained. "It's hard to attach any life status to something already dead and gone."

"Oh, ouch," he replied.

She nodded. "It does help to put it into those terms for

people though."

"Not me, you know that. I'm totally open to this. Anyway, Joy seemed to be pretty interested in the idea when she was here, so I gave you a plug about it anyway."

"Good, I appreciate that very much. Do you find very many people in your business are talking about it? The break-in, I mean."

"A lot of people, particularly since the piece was found in the fountain. It's caused a bit of a buzz about the whole topic, and a lot of people are talking to me about it when I'm working on them—you know, asking what the options are and if it's really that popular. I was wondering about having you come do a talk or something because I've got quite a group who is interested."

"Sure, why not."

He laughed. "Right? It is becoming part of the industry."

"It is, and we've got to drum up business wherever we can, right?"

"There you go. That's the commercial attitude I was looking for," Pinch confirmed. "So maybe what, next Monday, Tuesday? Can you handle something like that?"

"Sure, morning or daytime?"

"How about two*ish* in the afternoon? I can bring in a few people to talk to you."

"Okay, and, if you want to cancel or if nobody shows, just let me know, and I won't come over."

"Or you come over anyway, and, if nobody shows, you can walk back to your shop. It's not as if you're far away."

"True enough. How's your sister doing, Pinch?"

"Ah, Rose, she's doing okay," he replied. "She's working on writing up the family memoir and doing a history on my work. That seems to be giving her a certain amount of peace, like a sense of, I don't know, connectedness maybe?"

"Good," Tasmin said. "She's really had a rough go since the accident."

"You're not kidding," he murmured. "Trying to keep her busy and feeling like she's a part of the world around her? Well, … it's hard. Anyway, we'll see you next week." And, with that, Pinch signed off.

She pocketed her phone and caught Hanson staring at her.

"Pinch?"

She smiled. "Yeah, he's a local tattoo artist. He sent his assistant over with a referral for someone possibly interested in getting some preservation work done."

"That's interesting," Hanson noted. "I guess it does makes sense that you guys would work together."

"It's his art that would be preserved, and, in this case, he's finishing off a piece that Joy's beloved partner had started, who then passed on rather unexpectedly. Now Joy is trying to figure out whether she could preserve her tattoo art, which would then also preserve some of her partner's work.

"She was hoping for some museum or something, but I don't really know of anything like that right now. I only know about the stuff that I'm dealing with. I think, over time, there will be more options. Yet, in many ways, the vast number of pieces that could be donated would be huge and would create a logistical problem.

"Plus, even though we preserve them, and there's some space saving to be had, since it's just the tattoo, it will still require a lot of selection decisions, as in, why this piece over that, you know? And then an awful lot of issues over the legalities of putting them on display again."

"Yet if they are donated …"

Tasmin nodded. "Exactly, but, even at that, it'll take a lawyer to draw up the paperwork, and that's not something I really have the money for at this point."

"Could you see yourself setting up a museum?"

"I don't know about a museum, and I'm not too bothered about having a historical reference. There have certainly been a lot of doctors over time who have done something similar, but methodologies have improved, so preserving is in a much better place now," she murmured. "But still, there are thousands of people with absolutely stunning tattoos. Which ones do you decide to keep and what do you do with the rest?"

"I hadn't considered that," Hanson murmured, "mostly because I didn't realize it was even a thing."

"That's the problem. Once you do realize it's a thing, then the mind questions all sorts of things, like, if these have been preserved, what about the ones that aren't being preserved just because people don't know about this service? And, if people want to preserve it, what do you do with it? In this case I'm working with loved ones, but, if it's not loved ones, then what? How do we step in to preserve some of this artwork?"

He just shook his head. "I don't have any answers."

"What about you?" she asked him. "Has your day been full of shadows?"

He looked over at her and smiled. "Thankfully not as many as it could be."

"Funny how there are days when we think that's absolutely a gift, isn't it?"

"More often than not," he admitted. "I have no objection to a little company sometimes, but it seems this stuff happens when you're not at all ready for it."

"Yes, or when you have no time for it," she muttered.

At that, her pizza-nagging ghost popped up and snipped, "If you looked after yourself and didn't work so hard, you'd have more time."

She caught sight of Hanson's face and realized he had heard her too. "Do you see her or just hear her?"

"I'm hearing something," he answered cautiously. "I'm not exactly sure what."

At that, she explained about the pizza-condemning ghost.

"Right, that's the one who was here last time."

"Yes, and she has no intention of leaving apparently."

"Have you asked her why?"

"Yes, and she says it's because dementia has her not knowing where she came from and as she can communicate with me, then she'll stay where she is because the rest of the world is dark, lonely, and very scary."

"Oh, now that's not something we want to think about, is it?" he murmured.

"I sure don't, and it's not as if I have a whole lot of choice."

At that, he considered her for a moment. "You really believe that?"

She frowned. "I don't know what to believe. I haven't put any thought into trying to get rid of them. I did speak to my grandmother about it once years ago, and she told me that you had to help them find their way home, but that it takes time, effort, energy, and a willingness of the ghost as well."

"Not something all of them are willing to do, is it?"

"No, definitely not."

"Got it," he said. "In that case I guess you're stuck with

her."

"I am, for the moment anyway, but maybe one day I'll wake up, and she'll have found the light and moved on."

At that came a sound of disgust in her ear, then a snort from the nagging ghost, who Tasmin in her own head called Nanny. "Not happening. If I'm alive, I'll stay alive because this is all there is. I won't become no rot in some wood box."

Tasmin didn't bother translating any of that to Hanson but could tell from the look on his face that he knew something was going on. She sighed. "They just have very strong ideas of what they should be allowed to do and to be."

He smiled. "You get the ghosts. And I just get the shadows—the dark, scary, eerie shadows that tell me that something's wrong, that somebody has done wrong or somebody is doing wrong," he murmured.

She stared at him in surprise. "And what are we talking about here? People who have potentially been murdered?"

He nodded slowly. "Yes, often that is so, and it makes for a hell of an arsenal in my line of work."

She stared. "Wow, I hadn't even considered that, but it would, wouldn't it?"

"The trouble is, nobody wants to believe me if I don't have proof."

"You should become somebody like Stefan," she suggested.

"Sure, wouldn't that be nice. But I'm sure Stefan had a multitude of years where he wasn't believed, listened to, or trusted either," Hanson noted. "I'm not sure I'm up for that."

"Maybe not," she agreed thoughtfully. "On the other hand, I'm not sure that we always get a choice."

When her phone rang again, Tasmin was surprised to see

it was Pinch on the other end. "Hey, Pinch, what did you forget?"

"Forgot to ask you about something," he began. "My sister was wondering if you've got any of my art tattoos that she could put in the book."

"Oh, I'll have to check my records and see. I'm not sure. I haven't done that many pieces overall really," she replied.

"No, I understand." Pinch sounded somewhat relieved. "It's kind of a creepy feeling."

"Creepy for you?" she asked.

"I don't know. I mean, maybe not creepy-creepy but still creepy."

It's not what she would have expected from him, but, hey, people still had the capacity to confuse her, and it happened all the time. "I'll check. I do have a log here. I'm thinking there might have been one, but that's all so far."

"Okay, well, if you do, let me know. Then I'll decide if it's a piece I want in the book," he explained in a joking manner.

"Yeah, good point," she agreed. "Just because people want to have it preserved, that doesn't mean the artists themselves love the piece."

"I know, right? There's a lot of times when it's just a job. There are Monday tattoos and Friday afternoon tattoos, and then there are those tattoos that are the best things you've ever done. Those are the ones you really want to preserve. But, in this business, the people we work on kind of head off into the sunset, and you never, ever see them again."

"Exactly, and that's not really where any of this preservation work comes in anyway. So I'll take a look and get back to you. By the way, how big of a book is this?"

"It depends on how many pieces she can get photographs of."

"As long as it's only photographs of the artwork. Aren't you taking photos of your models?"

"Yeah, but Rose is looking in the past, right? She's looking for models that I've already done, and I can't really contact a bunch of them to ask if I can put them in the book."

"You should probably get an NDA or a consent form now from your clients, just to use your artwork on them for any promotional materials."

"If I'd realized that keeping my sister happy would mean putting her on a project such as this, then I would have," he admitted, "but who knew?"

"No, I get it. Put that in place now as a standard practice and within what, a week or two? You should have tons of material."

"Yeah, although she's looking for a particular kind. I just don't know exactly what that is. She told me that she's not sure either, except to say, she's looking for the perfect pictures."

"Right, well, good luck with that," she teased. "I'll go through my records and take a look." With that, she hung up.

"That's interesting," Hanson said, "but I guess it's a valid point. Just because the person may love their tattoo doesn't mean the artist does."

"And, since Pinch and his other artists do tattoos constantly, that doesn't mean they love the design the client wanted or feel as if they did the best jobs on some of them. Whether you agree with that opinion or not, that's just the way it is."

He didn't say anything at first, but slowly nodded. "So,

what kind of person would want to put this piece on display in the fountain? Maybe the artists themselves?"

She frowned at that. "I don't think that quite fits. These artists do it for the clients. I have yet to meet an artist, a tattoo artist, who would want to have it on display like that. It's not …" She added, "It's not that it's not intended to be on skin and possibly seen by others—it is—but it's not intended to be some ghoulish display, such as in the fountain. … I can envision it being lovely in a tastefully done book, displaying the artistic elements, but in the fountain or any kind of street art setting? I just don't see anybody appreciating that, certainly not the artist."

"Was it an up-and-coming artist?"

"I don't think so." She frowned, as she walked to the back. Moments later, she brought forward a big book and opened it up. "So that tattoo was done quite a few years ago," she murmured, flipping through her book, photos of all the preserved tattoos done by her to date. "I didn't have the artist identified. This photo was taken on the actual canvas, yet the artwork was a hard thing to see." She brought up the photos along with a magnifying glass. "See? You can almost see it here."

He looked at it and nodded. "*Almost* is right. That's not very clear at all." But as he studied the picture, he nodded. "It is a beautiful piece."

"In a way it's a self-portrait, and that's even more important. She drew the picture of herself, and then the tattoo artist put it on her."

"Ah, so that's a whole different type of art then."

"Exactly. It's not necessarily the artist's work in this case."

He nodded, still staring at the picture. "In the form that

it's in right now, it's beautiful."

His words were so simple, yet heartfelt, and she immediately warmed to him. "Right? Not so scary as when it was in the fountain."

"I think it was the surrounding events at the time."

"Right. I understand that," she murmured. "It kind of freaks out a lot of people, but, in this case, I don't want that response to be something that distracts from the absolute beauty behind what was once a fabulous art piece. It's anybody's guess who this tattoo artist was. I thought I had a lead at one point, but, when I talked to him, he said it wasn't his."

"Who was that?"

"Ron Kismet," she replied, surprised at the question. "Who we call Pinch."

"That doesn't resemble his style, at least not what I've seen. But you said that the client, the model, drew her own picture, right? Then someone just copied it."

Tasmin nodded. "That's true, so I don't know what to say. Pinch told me personally that it wasn't his work, so I have to go by that. Do you think the artist is important?"

Hanson shrugged. "I'm not sure that it's important, as much as just going through the steps and tying off loose ends. … In my line of work we do a lot of that."

She smiled up at him. "As long as nobody makes a return trip to steal more of my preserved tattoos, I'm totally okay with that, and you just do you. I really just don't want break-ins to become something I have to live with on a regular basis."

"I would hope not, but honestly your security system is pretty pathetic."

"Thanks for that." She glared at him. "I get that it's a

fairly simple system, but everybody has to start somewhere."

He nodded. "You do, but, at the same time, these pieces really are almost irreplaceable, aren't they?"

"They *are* irreplaceable," she murmured, "and, for some people, that loss would be absolutely devastating."

Just then a courier walked in the door, looked around until he saw her, then smiled. "Hello, have you got a package for me?"

She hurried to the back and snatched the parcel she had just packed up, then returned with it. "Here you go, thanks."

He took the parcel, she signed the forms, and he was gone.

"What was that?" Hanson asked curiously.

"Another piece heading off to a new destination."

He stared at her.

"What's the matter?" she asked.

"I hadn't given it any thought, but I guess you probably have pieces coming and going by courier fairly regularly. The clients don't have to necessarily come and pick up their finished pieces."

"No, they don't have to," she confirmed. "Once it's preserved, it's preserved. I take photos, and sometimes we have people come in and take a look at my wall art too. However, a lot of times, the whole transaction is done online, start to finish."

"Wow. I hate to ask this, but how are the bodies delivered?"

She smiled. "I only need a surgeon—or, in some cases, a skilled worker at a mortuary. Just somebody with a sharp knife who's capable of excising the tattoo. Usually the body art is quite big, and, if so, then I have to go do it myself," she explained. "Of course that increases the cost tremendously.

Most families try to find somebody local who is capable. Someone from a funeral home, the coroner, a local surgeon. It's really not that unusual."

Hanson nodded. "It might not be unusual, I just … I hadn't come across it before."

She smiled. "Stick with me, kid. You'll come across all kinds of stuff."

He laughed. "Seems I already am. … Well, the day is over. I was going to head out for dinner. Do you want to join me?"

She looked up at him in surprise.

He shrugged. "You have to eat before you go to work anyway."

She winced. "Just for a moment there I forgot I had to go to work again," she said crossly.

"Yet you're the one who told them you would."

"I said I would for tonight only."

"And will they believe you?"

"No, they won't, but it'll get me off the hook for another day." She groaned.

"Or maybe you could buy the business from them."

"No way, that's not happening," she stated, her voice sharp and hard. "It was supposed to be my business to begin with, until I ended up in the loony bin. Then Dad decided I was too crazy and would destroy his business. So, just like that, he gave it to my sister, … lock, stock, and barrel."

He frowned. "That's hardly fair."

"Oh yeah? Let's not even talk about fair. It wasn't fair the other way either, I suppose," she noted grudgingly. "From the beginning, I was supposed to get it. It was my grandmother's, but my father wasn't ready to retire at that point in time, even though my grandmother wanted him to.

So, he kept it, and it was willed to me, to follow after him, but then he changed it all, so it doesn't come to me. It went to Lorelei."

"Wow."

"Yeah, don't ... don't get me started," she muttered. "Again that's just bad news all the way around, no matter which way you look at it."

"So, your grandmother bequeathed it to you for after your dad retired, but instead he changed it so you can't have anything to do with it at all."

"He doesn't even know I work there," she stated. "Essentially they lock me up in the basement at night. I do all the work to make them look good, and he doesn't know the difference."

Hanson just shook his head.

"I know. I know. I shouldn't do it, and I should be walking away from this whole nightmare. But I still need to have facilities to do my work. And yet that seems to be more and more pathetic of an excuse."

"And do you do your preserving work there at the mortuary during the night or in the daytime?"

"I have to do that at night, on the evenings I'm not working for them." She rubbed her eyes. "And you're right. I do need food."

"Come on then. Lock up. Let's go get a meal, and then I'll follow you to the funeral home."

"Why is that?" she asked, turning to look at him.

"Just something I need to sort out. And I would like to see the process."

"I'm not working on one of my pieces today," she warned.

"When will you be working on one of your pieces?"

She shrugged. "Tomorrow or the next night probably. It depends on my energy. I have two coming in, but, until they get here, I can't really do much."

"And once they arrive, you have a time element?"

"Yes, but I also have a time element to do the funeral home work."

"What about finding another location?"

"I'm working on that," she admitted. "I haven't said anything to my sister yet."

"If you had another place to do your preservation work, you wouldn't be at their beck and call all the time."

"True. And you're right. I need to stop this. It's just too much."

"It *is* too much," he stated cautiously, "and it's not equitable. Plus I hate to see you as worn out as you are."

She smiled. "Is that because you're afraid I'll end up with too many *ghosties*?"

"You'll definitely have a ton of *ghosties*, as you call them, but that doesn't mean you can't handle it. I'm just concerned."

"Yeah, me too," she muttered, "but one thing at a time."

He nodded. "Food first."

With that, she quickly locked up, and they headed out.

OUTSIDE, AS THEY stood on the sidewalk, Hanson noted, "So, the funeral home isn't very far away. Do you walk?"

"I do when I'm tired, although that probably sounds backward," Tasmin admitted. "The problem with that is that I don't necessarily want to walk home at night, but, by then, I can really use the fresh air."

"Is there a place close to the funeral home where you like

to eat?"

She pondered that and then shrugged. "A good Italian place is there." Looking at her watch, she added, "They're pretty fast too."

Just enough doubt filled her voice that he realized she was already trying to back out of their dinner plans.

"We'll go there," he stated and quickly led the way.

"How do you know where we're going?"

He smiled at her. "Not an issue."

"Are we walking?"

"No, we're driving." He pointed to his car up ahead.

She got in the passenger side of a small black car. "You use your own vehicle for work?"

"I do."

"Why is that?"

"Not everybody is terribly comfortable driving with me. They were short on staff at the time of my hire, and now they're short on budget as well, so there isn't a vehicle. I just use mine and expense it." They got to the restaurant in no time.

She frowned as she got out. "I don't think I've ever made the journey that fast."

He shrugged. "We got lucky with the lights."

She didn't say anything, but, as they walked into the restaurant, she whispered, "Are you lucky with the lights a lot?"

He just gave her a flat stare.

She smiled and nodded. "As it turns out, I am too."

His eyebrows lifted, and he grinned. "Now that … I find fascinating."

"It seems maybe it's a side effect or something."

"Hey, I'm okay with it," he replied. "I can get where I

need to be a whole lot faster these days because of it."

"Do you always want to be there faster though? Sometimes I feel as if I'm rushing toward nothing."

"Rushing toward nothing or rushing to somewhere you don't really want to go?" he asked.

"Same diff in a way."

He didn't say anything to that.

As they were seated, and one of the waitresses came over, he asked, "Since we don't have too much time, is there anything already prepared?"

She smiled. "We have the special ready, … cannelloni. Can I bring you two of those?"

He looked over at Tasmin, and she nodded immediately. "Yes, please, we'll take two."

The waitress quickly disappeared, only to return moments later with coffee and a big basket of sourdough buns. He stared at it and smiled. "Something is so very reassuring about an Italian place that serves fresh bread."

At that, she nodded, as she slathered butter on a bun. "This was a really good idea. Thank you."

"You probably would just ignore your rumbling stomach, keep working, and then head off to the night shift, wouldn't you?"

"Yes. But the more time I spend with you, the more I realize how badly I need to find another location to get my work done."

"Yep, you sure do," he agreed.

"I hate to in some ways though, since that's been my workspace forever."

"I find it fascinating that they still want you to work there, yet they don't want you to work there."

"My sister and my mother want me to do the work," she

clarified, with a half-mocking smile. "My father wouldn't likely survive another heart attack if he found out."

"He had one already?" he questioned.

She nodded. "He did, and, of course, the doctors tell him that he's not allowed to be upset, so he's supposed to stay away from work and all that."

"But I suppose he can't."

"No, he can't. He already had that heart issue before my grandmother died, which is why the business was supposed to go to me in the first place. Of course he's become fanatically religious and considers himself a preacher just to add to the chaos."

Hanson gave her a blank stare and managed the topic. "What's the deal with your sister?"

"My sister didn't want anything to do with the business, until it started to make some money, once I was running it. Then suddenly she was all too interested, except she didn't really want to have anything to do with the actual subject matter."

He stared.

"Yeah, she doesn't really like the fact that she's involved in a funeral home."

"Wow, okay. So, what does she expect? Was everybody to turn around and to give her a different company?"

"Maybe. There was talk of it."

He shook his head. "I don't live in a world where we hand companies down to our kids."

"Maybe not, but a part of me says that it's maybe a possessiveness about it because I've worked there since I was ten. Every day after school that's where you'd find me, working alongside my grandmother, either moving inventory, working in the embalming area, or working on the makeup, trying to make our guests …" She paused, smiling gently at the memory. "Trying to make our guests as pretty as possible for an open-casket viewing. There are all kinds of tricks of the trade that you don't think about, and I was quite happy to be there."

"It seems all these changes in your life were devastating."

"Yeah, that's one word for it," she said, her smile falling away. She waved her hand. "But that's enough depressing conversation. Let's talk about something else."

"Good enough," he agreed.

She looked over at him, then around quickly. Keeping her voice low, she asked, "Do you get into trouble at work?"

He shook his head. "No, but then again I also don't get any support." She frowned at that, and he shrugged. "Once you've had a psych eval, and you've changed departments, people tend to be a little leery. I'm also an outsider here, and they don't take to outsiders well."

She nodded at that. "That's true. This town itself isn't great for accepting newcomers very quickly."

"I've always thought that was a shame," he murmured. "The world is so big, and, when you narrow it down to just those in your own town, it really cuts off a lot of good things in life."

"Maybe so. My grandmother would certainly have agreed with you."

"Sounds like I would have really liked your grandmother," he replied.

"She was a lovely lady," Tasmin said, choking up a bit. "She was full of life, full of joy, and she knew her time was coming well in advance."

"Why is that?"

She looked over at him and gave him a wry smile. "Because she saw things. She talked to the *ghosties* out there. She didn't ever really want to find out exactly when she was going, but, as she started to fail health-wise, she started communicating with the ghosts a bit more. I think that's why my father is so adamant that we don't communicate with spirits because no good comes of it." She chuckled. "But, in my grandmother's case, she started to get messages and have conversations. Such as, *Get prepped. It's time. You're going home soon*, things like that. She used to work with me even longer and harder hours, trying to get me ready for the world out there."

"You mean, for the angry and unpleasant world out there?" he corrected.

"Yeah," she said, her voice soft. "She was the gentlest of souls, and she was in the right place for the work she did. People here loved her. She was compassionate and so caring, both of the dead and of those left behind."

"Have you ..."

The waitress arrived just then with two steaming plates of cannelloni, then promptly left.

Tasmin looked at it, sniffed the plate and the air above, and whispered, "Oh, this looks lovely."

He had to agree. "It is a lot of food."

"Yeah," Tasmin replied, "and that's okay with me. I'll take a doggie bag and have it later tonight."

He winced. "You really do need to get some sleep at some point."

"Yep, I really do, but it's not likely to happen tonight."

"So, you were talking about your grandmother."

She laughed. "Yeah, my grandmother was really a special force. Life just hasn't been the same since she left us."

He asked, "Have you ever talked to her since?"

She looked over at him and slowly shook her head. "Just that once, soon afterward, but never again. Though I've often wondered if it were possible, and, if it's not, why not? Because, if there was ever anyone I thought would come back to talk to me, it would be her. For all the ghosts I have in my world, I was really hoping that she would come back."

"I'm not sure it's something that she can't do, as much as maybe she just hasn't gotten around to it."

"You mean, like her social life is so busy?" she asked, with a giggle. "That may be. I don't know, but it makes sense."

"And maybe she was one of those angels on earth, who went straight to heaven, with no questions asked."

"Oh, that was her all right. She buried far more people than Dad knew about because, even though they couldn't pay, she wanted to give them a proper burial. She kept a certain number of plain and simple caskets, yet she decked them out as nicely as she could for those who couldn't afford anything," Tasmin explained. "You understand respect when you see how many people showed up for her funeral."

"Who looked after her body?"

"I did," Tasmin stated gently. "She wanted to be cremated, so I made all the arrangements. My father was a basket case. I cried throughout the whole process, but, in a way, it was helpful because at least I could do that for her."

He handed her a napkin, and she immediately wiped the tears off her face.

"Good Lord," she muttered, as she struggled to hold back even more tears. "I hadn't realized how emotionally charged that conversation would get."

"I'm sorry. I didn't mean to upset you."

She smiled. "It's not upsetting in the sense of upsetting

me," she explained. "More in the sense that my grandmother is gone and how that profound grief and loss will always be there."

"Understood," he replied.

She looked at him. "Have you ever met any friends on the other side?"

"No. I've seen a few spirits who had been murdered, but they weren't anybody I knew personally."

She stopped, stared, and then nodded. "If anybody else heard this conversation …"

"Exactly why I chose this table at the very far side of the room," he noted, with a smile. "Now, you better eat up, before you're late for your second job."

"Yeah, well, maybe if I'm late, they'll fire me. I think I might be okay with that."

But she tucked into her meal, and that was the end of the conversation.

CHAPTER 10

TASMIN WALKED INTO the funeral home shortly thereafter. Some three hours later, she sat down and pulled the next chart. She'd done two already, and two more were lined up for her. She wasn't sure how much she would even get done. As she looked around the office, she felt a pang, as it was home and yet not home at all. Something she had never thought would happen.

She looked around and called out, "Well, Grandma, this is a hell of a spot for us to be in."

With the file in hand, she got up and walked to the other room. As she did so, a file from the top of the desk slid to the floor with a crash. She stared at it, then walked over, picked it up, and put it back on the desk.

"I don't know what that was," she muttered, then headed back out again.

As she went through the door, another crash came, and she looked back to see that the same file had hit the floor.

Slowly, unsure what was going on, she picked it up again, put it back, looked around, and asked, "Who is it?"

And a voice, soft and gentle, whispered, "That's the right question."

She looked up and, out of the corner of her eye, caught sight of something that made her heart freeze. "Grandma?" she asked in the faintest of whispers. Instead of a response, a verbal response, she experienced a feeling of pure joy washing over her.

She stopped, bowed her head, feeling the tears pricking the back of her eyes, and whispered, "I wondered if you could come."

"I'm here, child. I'm here."

She whispered back, "I was really hoping you would cross over and leave this plane."

"I will when I'm ready and not before," her grandmother stated.

At that, Tasmin chuckled. "Of course. I wouldn't have expected anything else." With tears in her eyes, she felt the sensation slowly drift away.

Carrying the file, she walked to the other room. She looked around, but, of course, no one was here. The room was empty. It was always empty. She smiled, feeling something akin to bliss in her heart, as she realized that her grandmother was here.

Although, when she looked around once more, her grandmother was gone again. That was okay. It didn't matter to her; she wanted her grandmother to move on. Tasmin wanted her grandmother to be happy and at peace. Tasmin would never want her beloved grandmother staying here because of Tasmin's problems.

She got busy on the next case, looking around constantly as she worked, checking to see if her grandmother had returned. Seeing nothing, Tasmin finally relaxed and realized that she might never see her grandmother again. But Tasmin had gotten that confirmation on a soul level that her grandmother was watching over Tasmin, something she had desperately wanted, without realizing how much. But now that she had it, she felt such contentment inside. She plugged away for the next few hours, then made herself a cup of tea.

As she sat back after the second-to-last one, she announced out loud, "Okay, we're down to the final one of the night." Just as she was about to start, her phone rang. She glanced at the screen and realized it was Hanson. "What's up?" she asked.

"Are you still there?" he asked, his voice low but hard.

"Yes, I am. Why?"

He said, "Good. Could you stay there please?"

"Yeah, I'll be here. I've still got one more to go."

"Lovely," he murmured. "Stay there. I'll be there in about twenty minutes."

Not sure what he was up to or how he would get in when he got here, she got to work, prepping. She had to do the makeup for a viewing the next morning. Well, now later this same morning. The problem with that was that some of the makeup wouldn't last all that long, so she preferred to do it just before the viewing. They were asking a lot of this chemical makeup to keep it looking good much longer than it should. And since this body should have been ready and done two days ago, she wasn't at all sure what kind of magic she would even be able to work. But she laid out her tools and got down to it.

When she got a phone call twenty minutes later, he said, "You need to open up."

"Why?" she asked, as she straightened, wincing as her back screamed at her.

"I need to see you. I'm coming up."

"Come around to the back," she said. "I don't want to go to the front."

"I'm already at the back," he replied impatiently.

She walked to the rear door, unlocked it, and, disarming

the security system, she opened the door, and there he was.

"Let me in," he stated, as he brushed past her.

"What's the matter?" she asked, staring at him. "You aren't usually this edgy."

"Maybe not," he agreed, then brought up his phone and showed her a picture. There was another fountain. She looked at the piece in it and groaned. "Please no."

"You did set the alarm at your place, right?"

"Of course I did," she said. "And obviously I'm here, and I have been all night."

"Do you have any proof of that?" he asked cautiously.

"You mean, outside of the fact that you dropped me off here and that I've been here ever since?"

"Did you disarm the security alarm here?"

"Yes, for you," she said, "but that's all."

He nodded. "Go show me."

She immediately walked over to the security system and showed it to him. He nodded and took several photographs, then contacted the security company to get confirmation if it had been on or off during the time that she was here.

"There's really no reason for me to steal one of my own art pieces and put it on public display like that."

"Have you considered that maybe it's not somebody who wants to have the art publicized at all, but instead the goal is to see you publicly maligned and disparaged?"

She stopped and winced, with a big long exhale. "I wouldn't be surprised necessarily, but it certainly wouldn't make me happy either."

"Ya think?" he quipped. "Anyway, the piece has been removed, and it's back in the morgue. I don't know how long it'll take before you can get it back again."

She grimaced and shook her head. "I don't even know

what to say. And that particular piece is caught up in a family feud. This is likely to send it all the way off on the wrong side."

"I'm sure it will," he agreed. "Had you already done the work?"

"I had, and they were supposed to pick it up, but apparently other family members found out, and now there's quite an argument going on. The last I heard, he would pay the bill, but I was to destroy the piece."

"Ouch." Hanson stared at her. "For whoever wanted to have this preserved, that had to be a hard decision."

"It is, but second thoughts do happen," she murmured. She groaned as she looked back at her makeup project. "I've got another hour or so maybe, and then I'm done here. I just want to go home and rest."

"That would be fine," he said. "How about I wait for you?"

At the inflexible note in his tone, she frowned at him. "Meaning?"

"Meaning, I want to be the one who takes you back to your store, so I can see the state of things there."

She closed her eyes and sighed. "Fine. Sit down, make yourself quiet as a mouse, and let me finish."

Then she headed back into the room where she was doing the last of the makeup. When she looked up an hour later and slowly straightened her back, she found him standing there, watching her. She stared back and shrugged. "I didn't even know you were there."

"You get very into your work."

"This should have already been done, and she should have been buried two days ago, but they are behind," she explained. "I wanted her to look as good as possible for the open casket. When things are behind like this, it's much better if there isn't an open casket, but I presume they did their best to persuade the family otherwise and failed. Unfortunately this is as good as I can make it."

He stepped up beside her, looked down at the older woman, and said, "She looks beautiful."

"She was a beautiful woman in life," Tasmin noted gently. "I could do no less than to make her look as close to that as I could."

He reached over and gently rubbed her shoulders.

She gasped at the unexpected pain. "I didn't realize I had been bent over quite so badly."

"Yeah, and for a long time," he replied. "You don't look after yourself."

And his tone was so abrupt that she stared and then laughed. "Yes, *Dad*." He glared at her. She shrugged. "You're right. I probably don't, but I wouldn't be working here all the time if I did."

"No, you sure wouldn't be."

She stepped away. "I've just got to clean up, and then I'll be ready to head home."

"And what about her?" Hanson pointed to the woman's body.

"The viewing is in a few hours, and then she'll be buried today." Tasmin cleaned up and put things away, then stopped for a moment and whispered out to the ethers, "Go with peace and love." Then she turned off all the lights and slowly walked outside with him.

As she got into his car, she said, "This is getting to be a habit."

"I drove you to work, and I'm driving you home," he replied. "Hardly a habit."

"But that means you didn't get any sleep either." She turned to look at him.

"No, I didn't," he murmured. "And I got the call about this and came running."

"Of course, and thank you. Anything that keeps this a bit quieter is good."

"I just don't know what's going on. I can't quite figure it out."

"Neither can I, but again it's just … I mean, it's not just body parts. I get that. But at least nobody's killing these people."

He looked over at her, his frown growing in the darkness.

"What's the matter?" she asked.

"Do you know that for sure?"

"No, I don't know that for sure. What do you mean?"

"I don't know," he replied. "Something just clicked when you mentioned that."

"Good for you." She sighed. "My brain's past clicking, and, if you want any cognizant conversation, you'll have to wait until I get some sleep."

He chuckled. "That's fine. We'll have time to talk tomorrow—which is later today."

"Right, you'll have to interview me about this case, won't you?"

"Yeah, I will. Plus you'll have to pick up the piece again. Forensics is working on it, but they should be done soon enough."

"And they're okay to let me have it?"

"I'm not sure how or why, but apparently everybody seems to think the stolen property can be returned to you. They're just more concerned about why you're doing this."

When he said, *you are doing this*, she stared at him in shock. "They don't really think I'm doing this, do they?"

"Oh, I think some of them absolutely do."

"Good God." She stared at him. "What possible reason would I have?"

"Publicity if nothing else. It's one of the reasons they're okay to shut this down as fast as possible and to let you have your piece and go. But I'm afraid that, at some point in time, they'll consider pressing charges, just for the nuisance value."

"Christ," she muttered, having not considered for a moment it could go that way. "What a mess. That is not something I thought would ever happen."

"It's easier for them to consider that than to consider anything else," he explained.

"Sure," she murmured. "It's just not helpful."

"No, no, it isn't. Let's get you to the shop, make sure that nobody is around there, and then we'll talk."

∽

HE PARKED AND together Hanson and Tasmin walked up and stood in front of the store. "It must be convenient living above the store."

"More like *in* the store these days." And she didn't say anything more.

He shook his head and frowned. "Sounds like there's more to that story than you're letting on."

She shrugged. "The bottom line is that I can't pay rent on both a store and an apartment," she stated baldly. "So, the shop is it, at least for now."

"Oh, crap. You don't have another place?"

"Nope, I sure don't," she murmured. "But that's okay, as I don't have any time to spend somewhere else anyway."

She quickly entered the security code, and, as he watched, he realized the system had been fully armed. "You'll have to change your security codes."

"Yeah, I guess so," she said.

And he watched the fatigue roll through her, as she stepped into her storefront. She immediately headed to the back to a sleeping bag and bedroll. She collapsed on top of it and muttered, "Set the security on your way out. I'm done."

He swore, as he watched her curl up into a ball, pull a blanket over her shoulders, and crash. He wandered the store on his own, trying to figure out what he was supposed to do. She'd literally just gone to bed without another thought, mostly because she was so completely burned out. She had to stop working at both places. He understood her reasons, but it was killing her.

As he stood here, he watched a shadow break free in the distance and drift toward him. He stiffened and watched as it got closer and closer. When it reached him, intending to brush up against him, he flicked at it and sent it tumbling. He wasn't sure who or what it was, but the last thing he wanted was a burn from a ghost. He'd been burned twice, both times because he hadn't pushed them away first. Now he just didn't stick around long enough to get burned.

He put on coffee and went out to the front of the store and sat down in a chair, wondering just what was going on and why. What possible reason could somebody have for doing this? And, yeah, once the cops realized what was happening, they were all of the opinion that it was just a nuisance prank. He certainly needed to check out her security, but it was a pretty simple system.

Hanson realized she had changed the passcode from the last theft, but only one number, as if it were something she was habitually used to doing. That meant that anybody who had access to her security beforehand likely knew her habits in that regard and would easily figure it out. She also didn't have any ongoing monitoring on her security.

At this point in time he figured that somebody knew the security code and came and went at will. He sat here for a good twenty minutes, and, when his phone rang, he looked down to see Stefan's number. "Good morning," Hanson greeted him, somewhat briskly.

"Good morning," Stefan replied. "How is she?"

"Burned out," he said bluntly. "She's burning the candle at both ends and doing way too much."

"Yes, and the ghosts are collecting around her," Stefan stated thoughtfully.

"More and more. Possibly because she's burning out. I don't know. She doesn't want to listen to reason."

At that, Stefan laughed. "I don't know too many of us who do."

Hanson had to smile at that. "No, that's a good point, particularly when we're being told to do something that we don't want to do."

"Exactly," Stefan agreed.

"But are the ghosts a problem?" Hanson asked hesitantly.

"I don't know," Stefan admitted. "It's almost as if somebody is building up to something."

"Somebody?"

"Yes, somebody. I just don't know who or why."

"You make it seem as if this were a human event."

"Very much so," Stefan confirmed. "This has a very human touch. I'm not sure who though at this point. But feels like feminine energy."

CHAPTER 11

TASMIN WOKE WITH more of a groan than a happy sigh. She opened her eyes to see somebody towering over her. She let out a startled squawk and bolted upright.

Immediately Hanson dropped to his heels beside her, his hand on her shoulder, his words calm, relaxing. She felt the energy surging from his hand, running all the way through her system, almost pulling the stuffing out of her. So she dropped in place, but calm, as if it were intended that way.

She stared up at him. "You pack a punch," she murmured, as she tried to reorient herself as to what just happened. When he frowned, she shrugged, then explained, "It's just that you deliberately did something that made me feel that all this was okay, with such an instant calming effect."

He chuckled. "Most people would say I have the opposite effect on them."

She shrugged again and smiled. "Whatever it's worth, that's not how it felt."

"Good to know, because I was trying to calm you down, that's for sure. I didn't want you freaking out when you saw me here."

"And yet why are you here?"

He stared at her. "I brought you back home. Remember?"

She stared at him, her brain slowly processing his words. "Did you stay here the whole time?"

"I did. You desperately needed sleep, and I didn't want anything to keep you from getting that. You also need an actual bed—or at least a cot to get you up off the floor."

"Yeah, well, some things just have to happen the way they happen." Tasmin yawned.

"Is your sister paying you?"

"My funeral home work is supposed to be in exchange for doing my preserving work using the funeral home's facilities," she explained, "but I've been having a hard time getting my other work done, with so much work at Lorelei's place to do. Let's just say, I've built up a sizeable credit."

"And if she were to pay you?"

"Yeah, then I could afford to have a proper place to sleep. I could have paid my rent for example, but she says they don't have the money. So I've got to help get them squared away again, so I can get back to getting money myself."

He shook his head.

She sighed. "It really doesn't do any good to argue, you know? People make arrangements all the time."

"People make arrangements, and sometimes they get screwed over on those arrangements," Hanson snapped. "I don't see your sister sleeping in the shop or working double shifts, do you?"

"Of course not." Tasmin gave a half laugh. "Chances are my parents are giving her the house eventually too." His eyebrows shot up. She nodded. "Yeah, definitely a reversal of fortunes. But, as my sister told me, she had never expected to get anything, just some cash to help her do whatever it was that she would do. Instead she inherited everything."

"And is the money she thought she would get then coming to you at some point?"

"According to my father, I'm heading for the loony bin, so the answer to that is no."

His frown deepened, and she just laughed.

"And again you can say what you want, but I haven't been able to talk to them about it. My mother and my sister are very close. I was very close to my grandmother, and neither my sister nor I were close to my father. So, that leaves us in a bit of a problem right now."

He nodded slowly. "And your grandmother passed away when?"

She frowned. "About a year now." Then she smiled, her whole face crinkling up. "You don't get to tell anybody this, but I talked to her last night."

"Your grandmother was at the funeral home?"

She nodded and chuckled. "Last night, while I was working. It was the best feeling in the world."

He nodded. "I imagine for you that would have been. Did she give you hell?"

"No, not yet, but, if this spirit version is anything like she was in this world, it won't be far behind."

"I gather she was hell on wheels."

"She was absolutely everything she possibly could be in terms of being a good person, but lying, cheating, and stealing were certain things she wouldn't tolerate. Yet, if you needed help, if you didn't have a meal or you needed to bury a loved one, and you didn't have the means, she was there for you."

"Right, so she was one of the good ones."

"Exactly, she was a truly good person and is sadly missed."

"How did she take it when you spoke to her last night?"

Tasmin pondered that. "Grandmother was relaxed and calm about it. Not excited like my other ghosts."

"And maybe she expected you to communicate with her."

"I don't know, maybe. … She mentioned something about me finally asking the right question or something."

He asked, "No offense intended, but is there any chance your father is stealing these art pieces and putting them out in the fountain?"

She stared at him in horror. "You have to understand my father, but, if anybody is heading for the loony bin, it's him. However, he would do anything possible to avoid getting anywhere near my pieces. It's one thing to look after bodies in the morgue or in the funeral home. It's another thing entirely to do something so wrong, in his mind, as to turn them into art pieces and to make a business out of it. My father might hire somebody to steal them, but no way in hell he would ever touch them himself," she murmured. She studied Hanson's features. "Have you looked into that?"

"No, it just occurred to me," he murmured. He helped her up to her feet. "How are you feeling?"

She blinked at him. "Surprisingly good actually." She frowned. "I didn't get that much sleep, but I feel as if I just got eight hours."

He smiled at that. "Good."

She stared at him suspiciously. "Did you do something?"

He smiled at her innocently. "Yeah, like what was I supposed to do? You came in, and you crashed. You literally walked to the bedroll, mumbled something about locking up, then dropped."

She nodded. "Yeah, that's pretty normal for me." She

yawned. "I don't get a whole lot of choice when I'm running on empty."

"So maybe you shouldn't be running on empty," he stated firmly.

"Maybe not," she agreed, "but, until something changes in my world, I don't see an alternative."

"Your family business should not be suffering, not with the number of bodies they're processing."

"You would think so, particularly since they're not paying me." Tasmin frowned.

"So what's the matter then?"

"I don't know. I haven't been able to find any paperwork one way or the other." She walked to the back and put on a fresh pot of coffee. Stepping back into her shop, she scrubbed her face. "I need a shower," she muttered.

"And where do you go for that?"

She stared at him blankly and then smiled. "I have a shower here, up in the loft. If I could ever get it set up properly, I would just sleep up there." She pointed to the stairs.

He took one look at them and asked, "Do you mind?"

She shrugged. "Go for it."

He headed upstairs, while she waited for the coffee down below. She walked out to the front and stared out the windows. It was a beautiful morning out there, but it felt odd, off somehow, like something was stirring. She didn't even know what the hell that meant. But then she remembered her grandmother and hugged the memory close. There had been something so very special about seeing her grandmother again.

When Hanson came back down, he pointed upstairs and said, "You could turn that into a full apartment with living room and a smaller bedroom, with a kitchenette."

"It's close to that now, it just needs some work," she replied cautiously. "It just takes time and money."

He shrugged. "I don't really have anything to do on the weekends, if you wanted a hand."

She stared at him in delight. "Do you know what you're doing though?" she asked, her smile dimming somewhat.

He laughed. "I'm very handy with a hammer and nails."

"In that case, fly at it," she said, "because I'm not. I am good at all kinds of things, but that's not one of them."

"Do you have any plans for it?"

"No. Not only do I not have plans, I don't even really know what to do with the space. But if I could make a living space up there, it would be huge."

"That's where the bathroom is anyway," he noted.

"I know, and that's complicated with staff. If I were living up there, I don't really want to send them up there to my private bathroom, so I've never figured out what to do."

"Mind if I take a look around?"

She nodded, and he quickly walked around the workshop area of the space, which was really the largest portion of the building.

"You could turn a room here into a downstairs bathroom pretty fast, and that's where all the plumbing comes from anyway." When he started into the details, she found herself in the part of this discussion that always made her eyes glaze over.

Finally seeing her bored expression, he stopped and changed gears. "I don't know how much money you might have for materials, but, if you're interested, I wouldn't mind having a project."

She stared at him and asked, "And the money for your

labor?"

He looked at her. "Nothing. I'd do the work for nothing just because I want something to do that's different than my regular job."

She beamed, and then her smile fell away again. "And how about the money for materials?"

He frowned. "I could do up some estimates, take some measurements, and spend some time at the hardware store, figuring out what you'd need. It shouldn't be too bad, but obviously a cost is involved. So, if you don't have the money just now, it's a nonstarter, but we could at least figure out what is possible."

"Yeah, let me think about it."

He nodded slowly. "I think you really could have something nice up there, and it would be way more than you have right now."

"Meaning?"

"Meaning you would have a home."

"Having a home sounds great," she said. "It seems like it's been a long time."

He shook his head. "Is this where you came to after you were released from the psych testing center?"

"When I got out, I went home with my family for a few days, but it wasn't workable because it meant my father couldn't come home because he couldn't stand to be in the same room with me. I tried staying with my sister, but that was pretty difficult as well, since she'd just been handed the entire business, so I didn't feel as if I had any place to go. The rent for this was really cheap, so I locked in a year's lease and came here," she shared. "The bathroom is there, and I do have some furniture at home, but I don't know what it'll take to get it."

"Did you ever have an apartment rented?"

She stared at him and slowly shook her head. "No, I didn't. I told my parents that I did, but how are you supposed to survive and pay all this rent on my shop and a separate apartment, when you're not even getting paid for the funeral home work that you do?"

"That nighttime job needs to stop," he repeated, staring at her.

She looked up at him and nodded. "Yeah, it does. I think that was partly why my grandmother came to visit me in the first place."

"You mean, the visit you had last night?"

She nodded slowly. "There was such a beautiful sense of peace in having her around, but I could also sense the worry in her."

"It's no wonder why. I mean, just think about what she is seeing from her side."

Tasmin smiled at that. "No, you're right." And then she yawned again. "Coffee's ready."

"Good. I don't suppose you have a tape measure do you?"

"Sure." She nodded. "I've got a couple in the shop." She headed into her workshop, and he followed. She had all her framework out on the big workbench, and she picked up a tape measure and tossed it to him. "Here you go. Fly at it, but don't you have a job to go to?"

"Yeah, I do. I'll leave in just a minute, but I meant to tell you that, because I'm primarily a homicide detective, and since this is a burglary, your case has been … well, it's not my case anymore."

"I get that," she muttered. "It's not anybody's case, is it?"

"It's definitely a robbery, but nobody will be doing too

much about it. As I mentioned before, most of them think that it's you doing it for free publicity. So, if it is you, I suggest you stop, and, if it isn't, I sure hope the thefts are done."

"*Great*," she muttered, as he took the tape measure and disappeared back upstairs again. "Even when I'm not responsible, I'm still in trouble."

"I heard that," he called out.

"Good," she muttered. "And, just for the record, I didn't have anything to do with those thefts."

"Oh, I know that," Hanson declared, "because I checked with the security company at the funeral home, and it wasn't accessed at any point in time during the night while you were inside."

"Great, so working for free overtime did pay off."

"Maybe a little but not nearly enough. They're killing you there, Tasmin."

The trouble was, he was right. They really were. And, if they weren't really in financial difficulty and were just taking advantage of her, she would have to put a stop to it. No way she could keep this up, no matter how many dead people she met on the job. An awful lot of things in her life she liked, but, if people, dead people, wanted to talk to her, they didn't have to do it just there at the funeral home.

∽

HANSON RACED INTO his office, energized by the idea of having a renovation project to work on outside of his detective job. He hated the thought that she was staying in her shop, sleeping on a bedroll on the floor, when the family obviously had money and was taking advantage of her. It just felt wrong on so many levels.

When he got to work, he tucked away his notebook that had all the measurements. He'd get to the hardware store later today, if he could. He wasn't looking forward to meetings, follow-ups, phone calls, and a whole pile of other garbage that was really just drone work. But, as it was the only drive-by case they had at the moment, he should be grateful because generally murder didn't take a holiday.

The captain passed by and even noted that too. "Hey, it's pretty light days at the moment, but don't get used to it. It's rarely like this, so don't expect it to stay this way." The captain sent Hanson a glimmer of a smile. "Get current cases closed and fast, while you have the time."

Not long after that, Hanson got a phone call from Dispatch. He groaned.

"Drive-by," the woman said, "two fatalities." And she gave him the address.

He confirmed and headed off immediately. When he arrived at the crime scene, he was happy to see black-and-whites there already, holding back a crowd. He walked over to the two police officers, standing beside the bodies of the victims, and asked, "Any witnesses?"

They pointed to two guys, talking to another cop nearby.

With that, Hanson headed over to talk to the witnesses, and it became very clear that a vehicle, small silver-gray car, drove up and targeted both victims, fired multiple shots, then took off, all in one smooth motion. They didn't catch a license plate, and nobody caught anything more than the fact it was a small silver car. However, since this was now the second drive-by shooting in a small silver-gray car, there was no doubt in Hanson's mind that they were connected.

As he walked over to study the two victims, he found a

middle-aged woman, possibly forty, maybe mid-forties, and the other one appeared to be her daughter. Both had been shot in the chest and another one in the head, both basically peppered where they'd been standing.

As he looked closer, one had a tattoo on her wrist. He pulled her sleeve back and took a photo of it.

When forensics arrived, the coroner walked over, took one look at him, and groused, "I really don't like all these drive-by shootings."

"No, neither do I," Hanson confirmed. Together they pulled out the ID from each of the victims, and, with that photographed, Hanson said, "I'll go do the notifications."

"Good luck with that," the coroner replied. "That's always the worst."

Hanson nodded. "And, in this case, we don't have any idea what's going on."

"I know, and that's a problem too," the coroner added. "I'll have more for you later in the day."

"This one's also got tattoos," Hanson shared.

The coroner shrugged. "We're having a spate of those lately."

"When?" Hanson asked, more alert now.

"It just seems that a lot of our fatalities all of a sudden are pretty heavily into tatts," the coroner explained. "It goes that way. Sometimes a lot. Sometimes none. We'll have none for a few weeks, and then I'll get several who are covered," he muttered, with a shrug. "It's just the random things that I notice, while I try not to be horrified at such blatant disrespect for life." Before long, he and the forensics team had the bodies loaded up.

While Hanson stood here and watched, the last thing on his mind was that this was random. As a matter of fact, it all felt very much the opposite of random.

CHAPTER 12

TASMIN DIDN'T EVEN open her shop today, before she learned she had to fly to California. She had another order. She got the paperwork back almost instantly on the California job, then came a deposit for thousands of dollars, along with a note saying, *Please look after her.* The family had prepaid and wanted only Tasmin to handle a precious daughter gone too soon in a car accident in California. Tasmin quickly booked her flight, made arrangements for the transport, and then phoned the coroner in California and told him what was happening. He was okay with it and confirmed that he would be available during normal working hours. He had the body there now.

She'd had a couple power naps on the plane to get through the morning, but things had been busy. Tasmin did have somebody good there in California, but the family wasn't interested in that. They wanted Tasmin to personally oversee the tattoo removal. And that was fine, and prepaying her costs didn't seem to be a problem.

When she got a phone call later, before flying back home, she smiled at her Caller ID and answered, "Hey, Pinch. We are almost becoming bosom buddies."

"Yeah, but unfortunately this is another case for you."

"In what way?"

"One of my customers was killed in a drive-by shooting

today," he told her sadly. "The family is asking about her tattoos."

"Oh no," Tasmin cried out.

"Yeah, I'm, ... I'm pretty choked about it myself. She was a nice girl and the tatt? It's one of the nicest ones I've ever done. I wouldn't mind in the least if this one was preserved," he murmured.

"I can talk to them, but I can't promise anything."

"I know," he acknowledged. "It just happened today, and obviously they're still pretty raw over the whole thing. I told them that I would talk to you and would put you in touch with them."

"Sure, I can touch base with them. Go ahead with the number."

And, with that, she quickly made more phone calls. After talking to the family and reassuring them about the process, she sent them paperwork to sign. She'd been in this business just long enough to realize that, without signatures, no way she was taking a step down that pathway. Things were bad enough sometimes, but, in the event it got ugly, she had to make sure that she was well protected.

She winced at that thought and then phoned her local city morgue, looking for Pinch's client. When she got the coroner on the end of the line, she explained who she was, and he immediately laughed.

"Hey, Tasmin. This is Gerald."

"Gerald?" she repeated. "Did you get a promotion?"

He laughed. "I sure did. So, if you've got the paperwork for this, you'll be all set. We still have to complete full forensics and autopsy. I'll let you know when you can come up to retrieve the body."

"The sooner, the better," she said. "I'm flying back from

California now."

"Wow, you're really getting busy," he noted. "Why California?"

"I have somebody in California who could handle it," she explained, "but the family wanted me to fly in and take care of it personally."

"Okay, I'll keep you posted then. What time does your return flight arrive?"

When she gave that info to him, he said, "I'm not sure but maybe I can get it for you today. If not, it'll probably be first thing in the morning for you."

She made a mental calculation and replied, "That works."

"Yeah, I'll call to let you know when to come. I think we can manage that. Is that okay for you?"

"Yes, as long as we keep her cold in the meantime."

"Yeah, no problem there," he said. "I'll see you soon."

"Good enough." With that, she hung up, surprised that she suddenly had a double set of clients to work with.

For the first time she realized just how busy and how crazy her life could be, depending on what was going on in the world. But generally that was a good thing for her.

∽

AS SHE RETURNED to her shop, happy to have her business on the right trajectory, she turned around and stopped because there was her grandmother again. Tasmin cried out in delight. Yet the look on her grandmother's face was sorrowful. Tasmin walked forward hesitantly. "Grandma?"

Grandma just gazed at her, gave her the tiniest smile, and then whispered, "This is bad. This is really bad."

"I don't understand. What's bad? Of course I'm not

happy about these deaths, but I can be happy about the business."

But her grandmother shook her head yet again. "No, you can't be happy about this. There's no way. It's bad news, and you're in danger because of it."

"No, no, I'm not," she said, gently reaching out a hand.

But her grandmother's wispy form slowly dissipated in front of her.

Tasmin knew that crying out was hopeless but couldn't resist, and, by the time her grandmother's spirit form slowly faded, tears were once again dripping from the corners of Tasmin's eyes. What did Grandma mean, *This was bad*? Danger? She didn't understand if her grandmother even realized what Tasmin was doing now, and that was a whole different problem.

∽

AROUND NOON, THE captain called out to Hanson, "Come into my office for a few minutes."

With a nod, Hanson got up, grabbed his coffee, and headed toward the captain's office. Once Hanson sat, the captain frowned at him, but Hanson just stared back at him calmly.

"I guess it hasn't been all that easy since somebody found out about your psych eval, *huh*?"

Hanson just shrugged. Absolutely no point in worrying about it, and commenting on it now would only give away feelings he would prefer to remain private.

"I did have an interesting conversation with the rest of the crew, and, so far, nobody has any complaints about your work, though they are a little worried that you tend to be a lone ranger."

Hanson just raised an eyebrow at that.

The captain nodded. "I presume that's because the rest of the team hasn't been so welcoming, is that it?"

"I'm just trying to do my job," he stated.

"Right, got it." The captain tapped his hand on the corner of the desk in irritation. "Look. I'm not trying to make this harder on you," he said. "I was just hoping the team would gel by now."

At that, Hanson shrugged. "It'll gel when it's ready to gel."

The captain smiled at him. "That's the truth, isn't it? I should just stay out of it."

"You should," Hanson agreed. "I'm getting good work done. Just let me go do it."

"How is the case going?"

"Until we got two more drive-by shooting deaths, we were doing better," Hanson replied, "and now we're not doing as well."

"Yeah. Have you run down the first vehicle?"

"I have. It was stolen. The second vehicle as of this morning was another silver-gray car, but since the first one was stolen and abandoned, and we already have it in impound, I presume our shooter is looking for a type."

"Any similarities in the victims?"

"Young," he said. "The ones this morning were female and appeared to be mother and daughter, so I'm not even sure that *young* applies, as I think about it. … The earlier drive-by killed two young men. Now we have a middle-aged woman and a young woman. Multiple gunshots this time, as if maybe the angles weren't right or maybe they didn't drop the way he wanted them to. Or maybe he just wanted to make sure."

"That *making sure* is always a bit of a dodgy thing, isn't it? Targeted?"

"Targeted in the sense that they were likely in the wrong place at the wrong time. But targeted in that he knew them and chose them intentionally?" Hanson shook his head. "That much we haven't confirmed so far."

The captain waved at him and said, "Go on and get to it then. And look. If things get ugly around the office, you just let me know."

"They won't," Hanson replied and then walked out.

The last thing he would ever do was complain to the captain about the treatment from the other cops. That was a good way to get yourself shut out of everything. He planned on doing his job as he always did, and either the others would come around or they wouldn't. But, as he thought about it, he was fine either way.

He also felt a hell of a lot better about being new in town, especially now that he had connected in some way or other with Tasmin. She was fascinating, not just because of the skills that they had in common—or the fact that both of them were relatively untouched by those skills—but also the work that she did, her overall attitude, and the time of life that she was in.

He wondered about the family dynamic that put her in such a difficult situation, but he was determined to get her up off the damn floor and at least get her moved up into the loft. He presumed it was just confusion and stress that had her sleeping on a bedroll on the floor. Did her mom know? Did her mom even care?

He wanted to rattle both the mom and the sister to try and figure out if they were just selfish and looking after their own interests and really didn't care what happened to

Tasmin, or if something else was going on. In the meantime, he needed to figure out what was happening with these shootings.

∽

HANSON TOOK A quick break to grab something for lunch and just to get outside for a bit. As he sat back down at his desk, he got a call from the front desk, saying somebody was here to see him. Frowning at that, he got up and walked out to the front, and there was a young kid, maybe sixteen, standing there nervously. Hanson looked at him and identified himself.

The kid studied him and nodded. "I saw you at the scene this morning."

He nodded slowly in response. "You want to talk?"

"Yeah." But then he looked around. "Is there anywhere private we can go?" he asked in a very low tone.

Hanson led the way to the nearest interview room, opened it, and asked, "Do you want something to drink?"

"Pop if you've got it, a Coke maybe?" Then he walked over and sat down at the table.

Rather than giving him a moment to change his mind, Hanson asked the clerk to go grab that for him. She immediately hopped up and walked away, returning a few minutes later to give it to Hanson, while he stood in the doorway. He handed it off to the kid, then sat down across from him. "So, what brings you in?"

"I might have seen something more," he began nervously.

"Tell me."

He hesitated, and then the words just couldn't be contained anymore. "I was hanging with my friends. We were just standing at the corner, with our skateboards, talking, you know, wasting time."

"And looking to get into trouble."

The kid immediately flushed and glared at him.

Clearly Hanson had displayed more shrewd intuition than the kid had been expecting. He shrugged. "Go on."

"Anyway," he said, staring at him, "we were just standing there, when this small car drove past, eyed us for a minute, and there was this look, an odd look on the guy's face, and then he kept on going. When he turned around, I pointed him out to my buddies, and we shifted a bit so we could watch him, and he went past us again and then disappeared. Didn't think anything of it until I turned around at the noise of the shooting and saw him on the opposite side of the road, and he's firing at these people, these two women on the street," he uttered, his voice raw with shock. "I knew the one girl. She was pretty decent. Her mom was too. She worked at the grocery store." His voice hiccupped. "They didn't deserve that, man. They didn't deserve anything like that."

Hanson nodded slowly, giving the kid a chance to calm down. "Can you describe him?"

The kid frowned at him, seemingly considering the question. "Maybe. I mean, I didn't get a close look at him. He was inside the vehicle," he added cautiously. "And the silver car, it was just one of those little sedans, four doors, those cheap cars that you can buy everywhere. They all look the same, the same look. Now, if it had been a truck, I might have been able to help ID that," the kid said. "I do like trucks. But cars?" He shrugged. "They all look like something my grandma would drive."

It was all Hanson could do to hold back his smile at that

comment. He understood what the kid meant though. "Did you catch a license plate?"

"Oh, yeah, I did," he stated, pulling out his phone. "I didn't get a photo of it. I only caught a few notes as it went by, mostly because I was quite perturbed at what he was doing. I mean, it seemed he was looking for something, and we were kind of close, but we weren't right there or ... I don't know." He stopped, looked over at Hanson, and said, "Please tell me that I'm nuts. Tell me that this guy wasn't just looking for somebody to shoot and thought that we might be the ones."

"I'm afraid that's exactly what he was doing," Hanson confirmed. "So far, we haven't found any rhyme or reason for why or how this guy is choosing his victims. Therefore, if you continue to hang around with your buddies on the streets like that, you might not be so lucky next time."

He shuddered, picked up the can of Coke, slugged back a big gulp, and started coughing. When he cleared his air passages and sat back, he frowned. "God, it was something awful to see."

"I get that," Hanson noted gently. "I'm sorry, but after witnessing this? There's no such thing as innocence when it comes to looking at people driving by."

"No, man, no, there sure isn't," he agreed, his voice raspy. He swallowed hard several times and then added, "There was something odd about his face."

"What about it?"

"Punched in, a bit of a bruiser, but I don't know. It could have just been puffy. He might have taken a beating from somebody recently and was looking for payback. But if that was the case"—he stared at Hanson—"why wouldn't he have beaten that guy up, not those poor women?"

"It's possible he did take a beating," Hanson suggested, looking at the kid. "And it's also possible that he already took care of this other guy, but he's still angry at what happened, or maybe this other person who beat him up is not available, and he can't get to him for payback."

The kid just shrugged, but it was obvious that he didn't like either of those answers. "Man, I don't even want to go outside anymore."

"Considering that this guy might know that you saw something, I would definitely want you to be careful when you're outside," Hanson warned. "We don't have any specific reason to believe he'll come back after you, but, if he thinks you saw him, I don't know what he might do if he came across you again."

At that, the kid stared at him. "Oh, man, my mom'll kill me."

Hanson chuckled. "If you die or get shot because of this, yeah, she might," he shared, with a note of humor. "But, if what you're doing right now keeps you safe, then I'm pretty sure she'll understand."

"Maybe. She keeps telling me to get off the damn street corners as it is, and I just never listened to her. I didn't see any reason to."

"Maybe she has her own good reason for you to do that. Maybe she's seen something in her life too," Hanson suggested. "You become quite wary after witnessing this type of violence."

He just nodded at that. "Man, I don't even know what to think now."

"And what about your friends? Do you think they saw him?"

He shook his head at that. "No, they were arguing about

an exam we had a few days ago," he relayed with disinterest. "To me, the exam was over and done, so who gave a crap, but they were still arguing about one of the questions on it."

"Right. And what about you? Do you think you can give any description on the shooter?"

He shook his head. "Honestly, outside of the fact that he looked like he'd taken a beating, not really." He paused and thought for a moment. "He seemed, maybe he was tall. I couldn't really see his head because of the sun visor."

Hanson contemplated that. "I'll bring in a police sketch artist anyway. So I'll need you to spend an hour or so with him and see what we can come up with."

The kid frowned at him.

Hanson gave him a frown right back and then smiled. "Hey, it would be your good deed for the week."

The kid snorted. "And I figured coming in here was my good deed."

"It is," Hanson declared. "But, if we can get a description, maybe we can catch this guy, before he decides to drive by and shoot somebody else."

That shut up the kid.

Hanson stood and quickly excused himself.

∾

LATER IN THE afternoon, Tasmin sighed, as she put down her things in the shop. She would be lucky to set things to rights before she relaxed for a few minutes and headed for the morgue. Exhausted from the whirlwind trip to California and back, she sighed again, then got busy.

Wishing for a moment to touch base with Hanson—since she hadn't heard from him since dawn—she realized he must be really busy and didn't need interruptions from her.

Maybe she could sit down for a cup of tea before she called him. Just as she reached for the pot, she heard knocking at the front door. Hoping they would see the Closed sign and come back later, she was disappointed when the knocking continued. She walked to the front and pulled open the door, seeing someone who made her blood run cold.

Dr. Bellevue from Bellevue's Sanatorium.

He stared at her and gave her that very special smile, before he said gently, "I see we need to talk, my dear."

∽

BACK AT HIS desk, Hanson arranged to get the sketch artist here as soon as he could. When he walked back toward the interrogation room again, the kid was at the open door, looking to sneak out. Hanson stood in the hallway and shook his head at him. "The artist will be here in about twenty minutes," he told his witness.

The kid's shoulders sagged, and he walked back into the interview room.

Hanson wasn't sure whether he was trying to leave or was just bored and done with the whole thing. Deciding he needed to check it a little further, he headed back inside the interview room and asked, "So, what's the big deal with leaving?"

The kid grimaced. "I really don't want anybody to know I'm here," he confessed nervously. "And it's already past time when I was supposed to meet up with the guys."

"Sure, but don't you think this is a little more important?"

"Yeah, I do, otherwise I wouldn't be here," he snapped, "but the guys don't know I'm here."

"Ah." Hanson realized how important it was to keep

your actions in line with everybody else's. "And you don't think they'd agree."

"Hell no," the kid replied, "so I need to get out of here as soon as possible."

"Have you got a decent excuse to give them?"

He shrugged. "Not really."

"Can't you get grounded, or doesn't your mom need you or something along that line?"

He just stared at him. "Those lame-ass excuses would never work with my friends."

"Right. Well, you've got twenty minutes to think up an excuse, and then the artist will be here."

"And I suppose you'll sit here and watch over me."

"If you hadn't been about to sneak off while I was making arrangements, I wouldn't feel the need to," Hanson stated, his tone clipped. "But I guess my work doesn't get done while I get to sit here and babysit you either."

The kid just glared at him and then slowly shrugged and sat back down again in the chair. "Whatever. Hopefully I can get it done and get out of here fast."

"Let's not just do *fast*," Hanson said. "Let's do *right*. I don't suppose you want to see another two people dropped on the side of the road in front of you."

At that, the kid winced and shook his head. "No, I really don't, but it sucks. I didn't do anything, and now I feel as if I'm being punished."

"By talking to a sketch artist?" Hanson asked.

The kid shrugged. "Okay, so not so much punished but I'm being forced to do something I'm not real comfortable doing."

"You're not real comfortable coming in here, and this is just pushing it one little bit further. However, in this case, it's for a good cause," Hanson reminded the kid gently.

But it was obvious the kid was struggling with the whole concept. Thankfully the sketch artist arrived faster than expected. Hanson looked up to see Brock walking into the room. "Hey, Brock, this is Roy. Roy, this is the sketch artist."

The kid looked up at the sketch artist and said, "You don't look old enough."

Brock laughed. "I'll take that as a compliment, but I've seen the backside of thirty."

"*Hum*," the kid said, looking at him. "You don't look it."

"No, sometimes I don't, but sometimes I look twice this old," Brock stated. "It all depends on how the day goes." He sat down, opened up his laptop, and said, "Okay, let's get started." He looked over at Hanson. "Are you staying?"

"No, not if you're good with him. Roy was having second thoughts, thinking about trying to book it out of here. Therefore, I decided to keep him company, while waiting around for you."

Brock nodded. "We'll be fine. I'll get through this pretty fast."

"You'll do it on a computer?" the kid asked suspiciously.

"Yeah, I can do it by hand too, but a computer is often faster. I'm working on my skills there."

At that, Hanson smiled at the kid's look of disgust and suggested to Roy, "You might want to keep in mind that Brock's skills are way better than almost everybody else's you've ever seen before."

"I don't know," Roy argued. "I'm a pretty good artist myself."

"So, in that case," Brock said, slapping down a piece of

paper in front of the kid, "why don't you give it your best shot, and I'll work alongside you, asking you questions, and maybe between us we'll come up with a good sketch."

Looking mildly curious at the idea, Roy took the pencil in his hand and looked down at the piece of paper. Then he looked up at Hanson. "You can leave anytime," Roy said.

Hanson smiled. "Yeah, I'll be back in a bit to check on you." And, with that, he returned to his desk.

As he got there, Mark looked over at him and asked, "What's with the kid?"

"He saw the drive-by shooter, and we're trying to get a sketch from him."

Mark looked at him with surprise. "You got a witness?"

"Yeah, got a couple of them, but only one's really willing to talk to me," he shared.

"That's pretty normal," Mark murmured. "Everybody here sticks to themselves."

Realizing that dig was as much at Hanson as anybody, he didn't say anything but sat down at his desk, checked his clock, and noted that the day was whipping by. Almost instantly, as he freed his mind to consider what else was on his day, he felt this weird instinct. He bolted to his feet, snatched his wallet and keys, and basically ran from the room. He heard the guys laughing at his exit.

"What the hell did he forget?" one of them joked.

But Hanson couldn't have explained it, even if he'd had the time to stop and chat.

∽

HANSON RACED TOWARD Tasmin's place, and, when he came to a screeching halt in front of her shop, the panic was almost overwhelming. He dashed inside the store and saw her flat against a wall, talking to somebody, but her body language spoke volumes. He raced over beside her. Slipping an arm around her, he tucked her up close and turned to face the man who had terrified her so.

The other guy looked at him in surprise and said, "Hello."

"What's going on here?" Hanson asked.

The other man reluctantly stepped back, as if realizing things were about to change. He looked at Tasmin and said, "I'll be back."

"Don't bother," Hanson declared in a forceful tone. "I'm not sure what your business is with her, but, if your intent is to scare her, you don't need to return."

At his side he felt the trembling rippling through Tasmin's slight frame.

The man looked at him, and then, with a smile that gave him the creeps, he spoke gently. "Oh, I have no intention of scaring her at all. She just must understand how much she needs help." He gave her one of those eerie smiles again and repeated, "I'll be back, dear. Don't you worry. I'll be back, and we'll talk then." And, with that, he walked out the front door.

Hanson waited a moment for him to disappear, and then he turned and looked at her. "Who the hell is that?"

She opened her mouth and then snapped it closed again, as if she didn't dare trust her voice.

He walked over, locked the front door, and was going to turn the sign to Closed when he noticed it already was. Then he returned to her, pulled her into his arms, and just held her.

She protested physically for all of thirty seconds and then collapsed in his arms and buried her face against his neck. The shivers got worse and worse, until he got really worried. Then she suddenly calmed down again and could breathe. She took several long slow deep breaths, as he rubbed her back, easing in as much soothing energy as he could.

Finally she took a step back, looked up at him, and muttered, "I'm not sure what brought you running to my rescue, but your timing was perfect."

"Who was he?" he asked. He let her step back again and regain some semblance of control, but he kept his gaze on her, not willing to let her off the hook yet.

She gave him a bright, cheerful smile that was as fake as the calm soothing smile of the man who had just left. "That was the director of Bellevue Hospital," she replied, her voice stumbling over the words.

His eyebrows shot up. "And that's where you were placed for a psych eval, wasn't it?"

She slowly nodded. "And, if there's ever anything in this world that's guaranteed to terrify me, it's to see that man in my home, in my office, anywhere at all really. If I thought he was ahead of me on the street, I would change my plans and go the other way."

He thought about the man who had just left and nodded. "He was really creepy."

"Right? It's not just me, is it?"

Hanson shook his head. "No, not just you. He's definitely creepy." He nudged her toward the back of the store and said, "I need coffee."

She snorted. "And you're waiting for me to put it on? What's wrong with you?"

"I was trying to be polite," he replied, looking down at her, "but I don't have to be."

"Don't be," she said. "I'm really not sure I can even handle putting on coffee right now."

In the kitchen, he quickly got a pot started, then turned to face her and asked, "Better?"

She nodded slowly. "A bit, yes."

"So, what was he doing here?"

She shook her head. "I have no idea why he would come here at all," she admitted, her gaze wide. "I haven't got an appointment with him, nor do I want one. I would do a hell of a lot to never see that man again. Yet, out of the blue, he showed up. I'll tell you one thing. All the ghosts and nightmares of my world are nothing compared to the night terrors brought on by seeing him again."

Hanson reached out, squeezed her shoulders gently, and asked, "Did somebody send him?"

She frowned at him. "Why would somebody do that?"

He didn't answer, just stared at her for a long moment.

She shuddered. "The only person who would do that is somebody who absolutely hated me. Somebody, anybody who realizes what I've been through, would never do that."

"And yet the creepy guy was here. So how did he get your address? Did you have this place back then?"

"No, no, I didn't." She gasped, looking at him. And then she winced. "It could just as easily have been from the news articles. There's been a lot of media attention," she murmured. "And, if somebody was trying to put me out of business, it's failed. In fact, all it's done is brought me more business. I was down in California this morning, I flew back this afternoon, and now here I am. I just got back."

"California? How did I miss that? Oh, right. I was a little busy myself. Man, the time just flies by when a new case comes in."

She looked down at her watch. "Damn, speaking of time, I've got to get to the morgue right now, so the coffee's all yours."

"Hey, hey, hey, wait a minute. What do you mean, you have to go to the morgue?"

She quickly explained, as he stared at her.

"That's one of my victims," he told her.

She gasped. "No! I was afraid of that but was hoping I had the wrong information."

At that, they both stopped and stared.

She shook her head. "This woman is one of Pinch's clients. They'd just been talking about me earlier, like within the last week or so, and, when this happened, her parents contacted him, and he reached out to me on their behalf. I called them, and here we are."

"And what is it you'll do?"

"I'll remove the tattoo," she stated simply.

He asked, "Can I come?"

She eyed him, then back at the coffeemaker. "Do you have a travel mug with you?"

"I do in the car," he said, with half a smile. "I thought you got the coroner to do it or other doctors."

"If I can, I do, just because of the drag on my time, but the family specifically requested that I do this one," she explained, "which is something that happens a little more often than I like."

"Why does it happen that way?" he asked curiously.

"Because it's their loved ones," she stated simply. "And, in their mind, if I'm the one who's preserving the skin, then they want me to do the job. The whole job."

"Right." It was in the back of his mind to ask her how she felt about skinning all these people, but it was obvious that she wasn't up for it, so asking wouldn't help things. He did say, "I'll be right back. I'll grab my travel mug from the car."

She just nodded.

He dashed out, grabbed the mug, and came back in, just as the coffee had finished dripping. He filled it and then noted another travel mug on a shelf. He asked, "Do you want me to bring one for you too?"

She looked at it and then slowly nodded. "Yeah, ... that would be good."

With both mugs filled, and the coffee pot turned off, he said, "Come on. Let's go."

She took a deep breath. "I'm coming."

"You don't look as if you're in any shape to do this."

"Maybe not, but I have to. It's what I do," she declared. "This family has already been through enough, without my disappointing them on top of it."

"While you do that," he shared, "I'll run a check on that creepy doctor."

She looked at him hopefully. "Please find out he's a wanted murderer, serial killer, or something worse, so you can lock him up in his own bedlam for the next sixty years," she muttered.

He chuckled. "No, I don't think that'll be possible, but I want very much to know why he showed up for a house call and who requested it." He studied her. "Have you talked to your dad lately?"

She winced. "No, I haven't. And you're right. He could have called them, and that would be if he'd heard something from my mom or my sister." Tasmin swore at that. "I should call them and find out."

"Let's go take care of this job of yours first, just in case whatever information you get from them isn't something you can deal with easily."

A little relieved, she settled into her seat, and they quickly headed to the morgue.

CHAPTER 13

TASMIN HATED TO admit it, but she was still overwrought over Dr. Bellevue's visit. He'd backed her into a corner very quickly, telling her that he was there for her, how very much he cared, and how he could see how much she needed his assistance. She kept telling him that she was fine and to leave her alone, even to get out of her shop, but the closer he got, the less her voice seemed to want to operate, and that terrified her more than anything. He seemed to understand that she was struggling, yet, instead of giving her support, he just fed on it. She shuddered at the reminder.

"Hold tight," Hanson said calmly beside her.

She looked over at him. "I just … I don't know what would have happened if you hadn't shown up," she whispered.

He looked at her sharply.

She shrugged. "I told him to leave me alone. I told him to get out of my store. I told him that I wanted nothing to do with him, yet he just kept getting closer and closer," she cried out softly.

At first, he didn't say anything. Then in a low voice, he asked, "Did he touch you?"

She pondered that. "I don't think so."

He turned and looked at her. "No recollection?"

She shrugged. "Honestly I felt everything inside me just freeze, and I couldn't do anything," she explained in a low tone. "That man terrifies me. I'd rather deal with a dozen serial killers any day than have him around."

"He was responsible for your loss of freedom once," Hanson noted. "I imagine anything to do with him is guaranteed to bring all that fear back again."

"Yet, how did he know where I was, unless it really just a fluke from hearing about me through the media?" she asked, her voice gaining in strength. "It had to have been my family." She glared around at her surroundings. "And if they did that ..."

"And when you say *they* ..."

"If it was them, I would prefer to think it was my father because that's the behavior I would expect from him, but I don't know that it was him."

"No, you don't, and you also don't know why he would do that, since you haven't had any contact with him."

"And I keep his damn business running for free," she snapped.

He pondered that. "Which also is a reason for your sister not to report you to the crazy doc because it would mean she could lose a free worker."

"That's true," Tasmin said in shock. "So I can't see it being either of them. I mean ..." And then she sank back again. "I just don't know," she said, her fear evident in her tone. "It's all just too bizarre."

"It might be too bizarre," he agreed, "but it's not so bizarre that it didn't happen. Unless it's just because of the news articles. How much trouble did you have getting loose last time?"

"I had a lot of trouble," she admitted. "It was an enormous hardship to get out of his clutches, but I was suddenly released, after another doctor had been through doing assessments. I can't even remember who it was, but it was a woman."

At that, he froze, glanced over at her, and asked, "Did you ever talk to Stefan about it?"

"No, why?" she asked curiously.

He pulled up in front of the morgue and said, "Let's deal with this now, and then we'll deal with that."

"It would help if you'd tell me what you're talking about," she admitted. "I don't ... I have to go in there, and I have to deal with this, and I will. I want to, but the rest of this is pretty terrifying."

He nodded. "I think we need to talk to Stefan after this."

"Why?" she asked. "What's he got to do with it?"

"Maybe nothing, but, at the same time, I know that he monitors a lot of the mental health clinics and sanatoriums. Plus he also has a female who works with him, Dr. Maddy."

Tasmin gasped. "That's her! That was the woman's name. I had a fascinating talk with her." Tasmin frowned. "Yet I can't remember anything she said. That's weird."

He smiled and nodded. "Look at that. You've been blessed with a second guardian angel."

"How is she a guardian angel?"

"I would bet my last dollar that Dr. Maddy is the reason that you're walking free and clear."

As she got out of the vehicle, Tasmin stared at him and asked, "But wouldn't she have said something to me?"

Almost instantly a voice came in both their heads.

She did, Stefan told them, fatigue rolling through his voice. *And still you guys didn't hear her. I took over monitoring*

Tasmin, knowing that Dr. Bellevue would come back around again. But, hey, you're out, and it's all good at the moment. Now go take care of your stuff, and we'll talk later.

∽

WHILE HANSON WAITED for Tasmin to get her permissions together to get into the morgue and to do what she needed to do, he sent an email off to Stefan. Stefan confirmed that Dr. Maddy had flagged Tasmin's presence in the psych center. It hadn't taken long for them to get Tasmin reassessed and released. But Stefan warned Hanson that Tasmin was on somebody's watch list, and so they both needed to be careful.

Hanson sat here for a long moment, wondering what *needed to be careful* meant. What did any of this mean when it came to somebody put on some watch list like this? He really wanted to phone Stefan and ask him questions, but it wasn't the time and definitely wasn't the location, as he looked around at the various offices in the morgue. He was sitting at a desk just off to the side, while she was in the other room, working.

The coroner was in there, curious, wanting to see what she was doing, yet at the same time leaving it to her. Apparently they already had a decent working relationship, and that was more than Hanson had with the coroner's office, since he was relatively new here.

When they came back out, both animated, Hanson realized they had a lot in common and a friendship—or a budding friendship, at least. Hanson stepped up and shook hands with the coroner, who gave them a nod and turned and left.

Hanson stood and smiled at her. "Feeling better?"

She smiled and nodded. "Yes, and I'm very grateful that we got the piece. It's in perfect condition."

He asked her, "Now where?"

She muttered, "Now we go to the funeral home."

He nodded and led the way outside.

She was carrying the package in a cooler, and he took it from her arms, carried it to his car, and put it in the trunk. "Do they know you're coming?"

"It shouldn't matter if they do or they don't," she stated crossly. "That's why I do all the work I do for them, after all. But considering that my father might be around, it could be an issue."

"Yet that's why you have access, right?"

"Yes," she agreed, with an eyeroll, "in theory."

"Maybe you're right, and it is time for you to find another location."

"Yes, it quite possibly is. We'll see what it's like in there tonight."

While he drove, she phoned her sister, who answered with her tone cross and stressed. "Oh, it's you," she snapped loud enough for Hanson to hear. "What are you doing?"

"I'm on my way in to work downstairs."

"Oh."

"Why? What's *oh*?"

"Dad's here," she added.

"That's fine. I'll be downstairs doing the work that I need to do. I've just come from the morgue with a piece that I need to work on."

Hanson almost heard the distaste in the sister's voice as she replied, "*Great*." With a heavy sigh, she added, "I'll do what I can to get rid of him, but this is really inconvenient."

Tasmin's eyebrows popped up. "It might be inconvenient, but I think it was a whole lot more inconvenient for the poor woman who died."

"You know what I mean," Lorelei snapped. "It's not easy when you don't schedule your time in here."

"*Really?* It's not easy when I get last-minute phone calls from you, saying you need me to come in and to do work all the time either," she muttered.

"I know. I know. Whatever. I mean, I'll deal with it. Just come in the back way and make sure he doesn't see you."

Tasmin disconnected the call, put her phone in her lap, and stared straight ahead.

"That's hardly a comfortable working relationship."

"And yet, for the moment, I'm not sure what else to do about it," she muttered.

"There are other funeral homes."

She smiled. "And I do know several people from those other facilities, and it has certainly crossed my mind. I have an invitation from one of them, if I ever need to use the facilities. One even offered me my own table, my own office. I just didn't have the money to set that up."

"And yet you could work for your sister, get the money from her, and then pay for the rest of this."

"Maybe. … Do you think my sister would pay me?"

Startled, he took his eyes off the road for a split second, looked at her, and frowned. "If she doesn't, you shouldn't be working there. Not only is your time important but you're doing important jobs, jobs that are important to you and to your clients. You need to be compensated for the work that you do for your family."

"I get that I'm *supposed* to be compensated," she admitted. "It's all mixed up in my head with the fact that I used to do all this as part of the family business and never got paid anyway. I've worked there since forever and never got a dime."

He made a startled exclamation.

She looked over at him and smiled. "Family businesses are often like that."

He shook his head. "No, they aren't, Tasmin. You might get paid a lower wage, or maybe not overtime, but you should be compensated for your time in some way."

"I'm pretty sure they would say that my stay in the sanatorium cost them a bundle and that I'm supposed to work that off."

His breath came out in a slow *swoosh*. "Your family's been taking advantage of you for a *very* long time," he declared, his voice harsh. "And it's time we had a talk about that."

She laughed. "Not really a good time, considering where I'm at and what I'm trying to do right now," she noted. "I have this to preserve, and it's not just the memory of the woman but it's the memory of the artist as well. Plus it's the piece that matters to the family, so I'll do an awful lot to make sure that I can get it done."

"And that is also why your family has you over a barrel because you're so determined to get what you need out of it that you're not negotiating your own needs personally. You're negotiating only for the needs of your client, and your family is negotiating for their company, which no longer includes you."

She winced at that, and he nodded.

"I get it," Hanson said, "and that's probably a really harsh way to put it, but I don't know how else to say it, when you're working for them for nothing. You're basically doing a full-time job for your family, so you should be earning a salary of thousands a month. How much do you really think renting access to their space is worth?"

"Thousands a month in theory," she admitted. "Yet it depends again on the arrangements made. It should—" Then she stopped and shook her head. "It doesn't matter what it *should* have been. It is what it is. They don't think that I'm of sound mind. So they believe I'll lose it at any moment. Therefore, they don't want to give me an inch, thinking any investment will just go to waste."

"Seems they're all about themselves," he stated, struggling to not express the degree of horror he felt. "I'm not sure how they can even begin to feel like your family."

"Sometimes I don't feel like I'm family at all," she admitted. "I haven't felt that way for a very long time."

"Since your grandmother passed," he replied in understanding.

"Exactly." Tasmin nodded.

"I guess when she passed, you were really terrorized, weren't you?"

"I don't know. Is *terrorized* the right word?" she asked in confusion. "I mean, I certainly didn't feel loved or cared for anymore."

"Is it your maternal grandmother?"

"No, paternal. She's my father's mother, and they didn't get along either," she shared. "The business was hers, and he was supposed to keep it running smoothly. Then it was to be mine."

"Who else would she have given it to?"

"Me," Tasmin stated bluntly. "The other option was to give it to me directly."

"So two people had it down that you were supposed to receive the business, and your sister would get financial compensation instead. Yet now she's got the business, and you didn't get any financial compensation." He shook his head. "How fair is that?"

"I don't think *fair* comes into it," she said. "All they're concerned about is keeping me away from the business now, so I don't damage all that they worked so hard to build up," she explained bitterly.

"But it wasn't just them who built it up."

She looked over at him and smiled. "No, it wasn't. I worked every day of my life here in this industry with my grandmother from the time I was ten on. I never had another job. I worked here constantly, and I put myself through embalming school from money that my grandfather left."

"Why did your grandmother not see that you got paid then?" Hanson asked, his tone harsh. "I know you loved her and all that, but that doesn't seem right."

"It was supposed to be my own investment into my future," she replied. "You know, skin in the game and all. It was supposed to be so that I did both earn and learn the business. My sister didn't do all those hours. She didn't participate in the business at all, and that's because she wasn't getting the business. She was getting the cash compensation."

"Equal amounts?"

She shook her head. "No, not in equal amounts because I had put in all those years that she hadn't. My grandmother was keeping a tally of it, but somehow, between her death and now, that tally apparently either went missing, never happened, or something else went wrong."

"Okay. So, what are you not saying?"

She groaned and glanced at him, as they drove toward the funeral home, which really wasn't all that far away.

"Basically I don't have any choice in the matter, but it looks to me as if the record of all my work was wiped clean as the cost of their raising me. If anybody ever gave a crap about it, nobody does now. … So, basically all those years I spent were a thank-you for having a home to grow up in."

"And your sister's contribution?"

"Apparently she's coming out of this smelling like a rose. But the really stupid thing is that she hates the industry and hates the business. But you can bet she'll be more than happy to take it because it's a moneymaker."

"Yet how much of a moneymaker is it actually?" he asked, glancing at her as he pulled into the parking lot. "Particularly considering the fact that supposedly they're not paying you because they can't afford to, and so you have to help them get back up and out of trouble before they can pay you."

She stared at him. "All I can say, and I don't have any access to the inner workings and the books anymore," she added, "but, when it was my grandmother's, it was lucrative, very lucrative. It took care of all of us and gave her a pension that she refused to spend. So she had a little nest egg."

"And what happened to the nest egg?"

She shrugged. "I don't know. I don't know what happened to it. My father has it, I would think."

"Was it cash in a bank?"

She pondered that. "I'm not sure. She told me once that she didn't trust my father in many ways, but there were only so many things she could control, and, when she was gone, things would happen."

"If and when you get a chance to talk to her on this side again, you might want to ask her about that."

She snorted. "Doesn't matter. Everything would have

gone to her son, and everything from him goes to my sister, so whatever." At that, she got out and told him, "I don't think they'll let you come in."

He asked, "Because I'm a cop?"

She looked worried for a moment and then she said, "Honestly I'm not sure whether it's because you're a cop or just because you're associated with me, but it could get pretty ugly."

"In that case," he said, getting out of the vehicle, "I'm definitely coming in." Slamming the driver's door hard, he stepped in line behind her.

CHAPTER 14

TASMIN USED HER keys, unlocked the back door, and quickly headed downstairs to the embalming room. Once there, she faced him and asked, "Are you sure you want to stay?"

He shrugged. "I don't want to leave you alone."

She studied him, gave him a glimmer of a smile, and said, "You know they won't attack me or anything, right? This is my family, after all."

He stared at her. "But you were locked up because of them."

Immediately her smile fell away, and she nodded. "Fine, stay then. Just maybe go into the office or something and get some of your work done."

"Will do. Do you have a time frame?"

"I'll need at least an hour for this section," she murmured. Then she immediately dove into her work, barely noticing when he came out and checked on her a couple times, only to go back into the office again. When she heard a different noise, she was just at the point of washing up, when she turned and looked, and there was Grandma. She smiled. "Hey, Grandma. As much as I absolutely love knowing you're here, I would much prefer knowing that you're safe in your own world."

"I'm safe. Don't you worry, dear," she replied. "I just

can't leave you to suffer the consequences."

Tasmin stared at her, her heart sinking. "The consequences of what?"

"Of what's happening," Grandmother said softly. "I don't know how to help though."

Hearing another noise behind her, Tasmin spun to see Hanson standing there, watching her. She spun back, but her grandmother had gone. "That was my grandmother," she stated.

He nodded. "I didn't so much see her as I could sense something."

"A shadow?" she asked sharply.

He contemplated that for a moment. "No, less of a shadow and more of what I would call a disturbance."

Her eyebrows shot up at that. "I'm not sure I would care to have her called a *disturbance*."

He gave her a ghost of a smile. "Are you done here?"

She nodded slowly. "Yes, thankfully." She looked around, brushed a few strands of hair off her face, then smiled at him. "Are you ready to go?"

"I'm ready. *Um*, … I don't know if you've heard, but quite the argument is going on upstairs."

She stared at him and walked closer to the door, cocked her head, and then winced. "Oh, *great*. We're definitely leaving."

"Why?" he asked, as she raced to the back door.

"That's my father, and I heard my name mentioned."

"Are you sure you don't want to find out more?"

"No, I definitely don't want to find out more," she snapped, with an eyeroll. "My father is not somebody I want to spend time with."

"Is he really that scary?"

She took a second before answering. "As a child, I'm sure I didn't see him as scary at all. As an adult who had the power to lock me up, he was terrifying," she murmured. "And I'm still terrified."

"For that reason alone," Hanson stated, "I'd like to meet him."

Just then a door burst open behind them, and a six-foot-four blustery father stood there, glaring at Hanson. "And I'd like to meet you," he snapped, his hands on his hips. He turned and glared at his daughter. "What the hell are you doing here? You'd better not have brought any more of those disgusting things here."

"Hi, Dad. How are you?" It was obvious that he was already on a tirade, and the only way to get out of here was to calm things down enough that she could escape. "Have you talked to Lorelei?"

"Of course I've talked to Lorelei," he snapped. "And your mother. You are not allowed to bring those things here anymore."

"Pretty sure it's not your business anymore, Dad. I mean, it was supposed to be mine, but, hey, apparently you made a lot of changes. I'm not sure some of them are allowed."

"I'm allowed to do anything I want. It's my business," he yelled, stiffly glaring at her. "And you are incompetent. Believe me. I'm working hard to make sure we rectify that."

She stiffened and glared at him. "*Incompetent?* You're really accusing me of that?" He stiffened, and she glared at him. "So I suppose you are behind Dr. Bellevue's visit today?"

He glared at her, and then his face darkened. "Dr. Bellevue knows what's good for you," he snapped. "Obviously you don't."

"If you mean that I am not prepared to deal with the BS you keep spouting about me being incompetent, you're quite right," she argued calmly. "I've never expected to deal with that."

"That's too bad because you'll deal with it, whether you like it or not. At least until we get you certified."

"Certified what?" Hanson stepped forward and faced him. "You're really trying to get your daughter locked up as being psychiatrically unstable, aren't you?" he asked in astonishment. "Why would you do that?"

At that, her father turned and glared at him. "Who are you?" he roared. "And what are you doing down here in my place?"

"I invited him, Dad," Tasmin replied. "He came to help me out."

At that, her father gave a visible shudder. "Did you bring one of those things here?" he roared. But he was already backing up out of the room.

Hanson, as if seeing an obvious advantage, pressed home the fact that it was a possibility. "Of course she brought something here," he declared, with a look over at her. "This is partly her business, is it not?"

"No, it is not," he snapped. "You're mistaken if you think *that* has anything to do with this. This is my business, and I'm leaving it to my daughter."

"*Leaving it?*" Tasmin repeated. "My understanding is that you already left it to her."

He stared at her and shook his head. "No, not yet, the paperwork isn't complete."

She shook her head. "That's not what Lorelei told me."

"I don't care what Lorelei said," he snapped. "I'm not

sure what game you're playing at here, but this is my business until it isn't, and believe me. Until I'm dead and gone, it'll remain my business," he snapped, his fury all-encompassing.

She wasn't even sure what to think about that. "Interesting," she murmured. "That's not what I heard at all."

"I don't care what you were or weren't hearing," he snapped, shaking a fist at her. "What I'm hearing is that you need to be locked up."

She immediately sighed. "Dad, of all of us who may be incompetent around this place, I'm afraid you're the one leading the pack."

Sucking in his breath, he stared at her.

She nodded. "So, maybe it isn't a case of my needing to be locked up, but instead a case of somebody needing to check your meds again."

At that, he seemed to lose it. "There's no way, absolutely no way you'll be allowed in my house again. You're nothing but the devil's spawn."

"So, is she your daughter or not?" Hanson asked, adding insult to injury all over again.

Her father stared at him and started spouting nonsense words, his spittle flying, as he rushed Hanson.

Hanson caught him up, swung him around, and sat him down hard on the stool next to him. "Sit," he ordered, "and I might forget the fact that you just tried to attack me."

Her father looked up at Hanson, his face working. "Who the hell are you, and what are you doing here?"

As it was almost a repeat of the previous question, Hanson studied him carefully. "I'm a cop," he replied, his tone hard. "And your daughter invited me in."

At the word *cop*, his face paled, and he turned and

looked at her. "What have you done now?" he cried out in horror. "What have you done?"

She pulled out her phone and quickly called her sister, who was upstairs.

"You deal with him," Lorelei cried through the phone. "I'm done with dealing with him for today."

"What did you tell him?" Tasmin asked, as she stared at her father, who was struggling to get back out of the chair, but Hanson held him down again. She hit Speakerphone.

"I told him that you were working here. What am I supposed to do? Keep it a secret all the time? You're the only one who knows how this place even functions."

"You'll have to find somebody else to make it function because I'm not dealing with this anymore. He's threatening to have me locked up, when you know perfectly well he's as unstable as they come."

"Trust me. I know he is," her sister roared into the phone.

"Do you hear that, Dad? Everybody thinks you're the one who's unstable around here." Such a hateful look filled his gaze that Tasmin swore and stepped back a bit. "I'm leaving," she told Lorelei, still on the phone. "I don't know what the hell's going on here, and, if you can't keep him out of the business, you won't have one."

"I don't think I even want this damn place anyway."

"According to him, he didn't give it to you. Not yet."

There was silence on the other end and her sister, her voice soft and deadly, asked, "What?"

"According to him, he hasn't legally given it to you," Tasmin pointed out. "So you may want to have that out with him first. But do it when I'm gone, will you? I'm really not up for any more of this fighting with him tonight." And, with that, she snagged her bag, looked over at Hanson, and said, "It's time for us to leave."

He nodded. "I'd say so. It was time to leave a while ago."

She nodded. "That's a hard thing to do when it's your family."

"Yeah, I hear you, but, in this case, it seems you've lost your welcome."

"I'm not sure I ever had it, not since my grandmother died. I was welcome then, but, ever since, not so much." With that she turned to leave.

Just as she turned to close the door again, she saw her father standing there, one of the big knives in his hand.

He looked at her and yelled, "You come back here, you're dead."

She froze in place, as Hanson stepped forward, took the knife from his hand, and laid it down on one of the workbenches. "Is that what you really mean?"

"Yeah, damn right that's what I mean," he bellowed. "She's nothing but the devil's spawn. If she ever comes back here, I'll kill her with my own hands."

And, with that, her father ran out of the room in a fury and tore back up the stairs again.

She sank back down on the stairs leading to the downstairs entrance, the cool night air washing over her, but nothing would wash away the stain of what had happened here. She looked up at Hanson, feeling the tears in the back of her eyes. "Now you know why everybody is so sure I belong in Bellevue."

He stared at her. "You don't belong in Bellevue, but he might."

She winced. "And that is his greatest fear—and my grandmother's. She avoided locking him up but did warn me that he was getting more and more unstable."

"She warned you, but what about your mother?"

"My mother doesn't do anything to upset the applecart," Tasmin said softly. "And, in this instance, she wants the business to run because it's their only source of income."

"But it looks like you're the only one who runs the business."

"Sure, my mother always ran the upstairs, and I would pinch hit when needed. But the real work, the job, is down here, and that's where I was always the most comfortable. That's where I worked with Grandmother all that time, but now I don't even know what to say." She looked up as her sister came through the door. Tasmin asked her, "Can you lock up? I really need to go home and get some sleep."

As she got up and went to head out, she heard a scream of outrage. She stopped, her eyelids closing, as a sinking feeling settled into her heart. She turned to face her sister. "Now what?" she asked, the fatigue rolling off her.

"You have to work tonight," Lorelei cried out. "We're well-past time on some of these."

Tasmin had lost track of when she had come and when she hadn't, who she'd worked on and who she hadn't, so she didn't have any arsenal of responses to fire back at her sister. What she did have was logic. "You know perfectly well that this business needs more than one embalmer, particularly when the one embalmer doesn't actually work here," she snapped. "This isn't my problem. You got the business. It's your problem."

"Oh, so now that you're sitting here and working on your stuff, you're not interested in following up on your obligations, are you?" her sister demanded, now stirred up into a royal fit.

"What are you talking about? I've done nothing but your work for weeks. Now I have some of my own work here, and you couldn't even keep Dad off my back for that time? Funny how you can keep him away for hours and hours while I'm doing your work."

Her sister looked at her and had the grace to look ashamed. "I told you that I would try to keep him out of there, but it's not that easy when he goes on a rampage."

"Of course it's not," Tasmin agreed. "So, where is Mom? Why isn't she helping you?"

At that, her sister looked at her in disgust. "You know what Mom's like when things get tough."

"She's hitting the bottle again?"

"Yeah, big-time," she muttered. "This place is a freaking mess." She shuddered as she looked around the basement. "You know I can't even stand to be down here."

"And yet—"

"Don't say it," her sister snapped, as she turned and looked at her. "Yeah, it's my business. But believe me, as soon as I get it back on its feet again, I'll sell it. No way I'm working with all these dead bodies," she declared. Then she glared at her sister and added, "And you owe me."

"I owe you for what?" she cried out.

"You owe me for letting you work here. You owe me for fighting Dad when he wanted to sign you up for six months in Bellevue," she spat. "You owe me period."

"You mean, I owe you just for being alive and for being your sister. Apparently that comes with a price," Tasmin replied, bitterness in her voice.

Her sister snorted with laughter. "That's almost a good way to look at it. You don't get to leave here tonight until you've done these bodies," she snapped. "At least two have to be done now. We can't hold off any longer."

"Where were you these the last few days?"

"Sitting here waiting for you to show up."

"Yeah, remember that part about having a full-time job? Besides I worked here last night." She snorted, glaring at her sister. "I'm not your slave."

"If you were my slave, I would have kept you locked down here, where you could at least do the damn job. So consider yourself lucky that you aren't my slave." And, with that, Lorelei flounced out and headed upstairs.

∽

"GOOD GOD." HANSON stared at Tasmin. "Surely you're not planning on doing it."

"You know what catches me up wrong?" she said. "It's not my sister. It's not the business. It's the families," she whispered, as she scrubbed her face. "I need about four hours to get this going, but I don't even know if these are open showings or what. It would be a lot easier if I was just dealing with cremation," she muttered, "but presumably, if they're still sitting here, they aren't."

She walked back into the office, and he followed, hating to see the slump in her shoulders and the anguish in her heart, as she realized the impossible position she was in.

"You realize most people would have just told their sister to eff-off and be done with it, right?"

She nodded. "I know. Believe me. My grandmother and my father had quite the bouts at times too, but it was my grandmother who trained me that the families mattered, nothing else. And, if it was my family, I would want to think that somebody gave a damn," she added. "It's also why I'm here at nighttime, working on these tattoos. I don't want them to be thought of as just an art piece but to be treated with the same care and respect as if it were me or my own child," she explained, looking up at him.

"I get it," Hanson told her. "So, you're really staying?"

"I'll grab the files and see what I'm looking at."

"And what about tomorrow night?"

She winced. "I guess what I need to do is give her two weeks' notice and tell her that I'm leaving."

"Yeah, at the same time, you also need to get paid."

She looked up at him and shrugged. "After a lifetime of not getting paid, I've probably already lost any argument I had for not being paid before."

"Yeah, I can see that," he replied. "Don't worry. I don't have a problem asking her to pay you. I'll have a talk with her about labor laws in this state. You go through your files and figure out what you're doing tonight," he suggested. "I'll be back in a minute." And, with that, he bolted up the stairs, leaving Tasmin staring in shock behind him.

∽

HANSON GOT UPSTAIRS to the office, only to find the place seemingly empty. When he walked through to the showroom, the sister stood there, her arms wrapped around her shoulders, staring out into the night.

She turned, glared at him, and asked, "Who the hell are you anyway? What have you got to do with this?"

"You already know I'm a cop, and you already know that I've been dealing with your sister's breaking-and-entering case, but I'm also her friend."

"No, you're not," she argued, with a wave of her hand. "You're too smart to be her friend."

"Wow, you just keep hitting those insults out of the

park, don't you? I'm here to tell you that there are labor laws in this world, particularly in this state. Therefore, if you don't start paying Tasmin for all the work she's done for these last several months, then somebody—and that will be me—will open an inquiry with the state labor authority."

She stared at him and started to laugh. "Oh, wouldn't that be great. Nice to know she's got somebody to stick up for her." Looking around at the office, she said, "Fuck it. I'll take my money and run while I can."

"And what money is it that you think is yours?" he asked, curious.

She glared at him. "Do you know what it's like to be told, from the time that you're born, that your older sister will get everything? Then, all of a sudden, it all turns around, and suddenly you get everything? Then you realize how wrong you were for all this time hating her, all this time thinking she was getting something special. Hell no. She was getting a pig in a poke that not only stunk but dealt with some of the worst atrocities in life. Then you see that you really don't want anything to do with it. All I ever wanted was to get the business to be prosperous, so I could turn around and sell it. Then tonight I find out that my father hasn't even got the paperwork in place to give it to me, and, if he hasn't done it by now, chances are he never will."

Hanson almost felt sorry for her, but that wasn't good enough, not in this instance. Not when she'd done so much to take advantage of her sister. "You do realize that she spent her entire childhood, working here for free, no wages, because it was supposed to be her business, and she was working in advance for that."

She stared at him and laughed. "Yeah, that was my grandmother. You see? She was a user."

Since that was one of the first contrary notes he'd heard about the grandmother, he was interested in hearing more. "Keep talking," he invited.

"She was a user. This was her place, and everything about it was perfect in her mind. Anyone interested in anything else—any hopes or dreams or desires to have anything different, to have any life past this—you were deemed a loser. My grandmother just didn't understand that you could want something other than this."

He nodded. "So I presume you didn't want to work here."

"Oh, God no," she spat, with a shudder. "Can you imagine? You know what it's like to come in here, knowing that your best friend's grandma is downstairs on a cold slab? Or how they felt knowing that Grandma was downstairs on the cold slab? It's not as if we had a regular house to go to. This was where we lived, day in and day out. Pretty sure it's what made my father loco," she declared. "You saw him. He's absolutely petrified over the work Tasmin does. I mean, what's one more dead body and not even a whole body in her case?" Lorelei shook her head. "Everything's so messed up. Ever since Grandma died, it's been messed up. The place needs to be sold, and somebody who gives a damn needs to take it over."

"And yet the person who gave a damn—"

Lorelei held up a hand. "Don't, just don't. I don't know what's happening with my sister. I don't care. I mean, if she needs to go back to Bellevue and get signed in, whatever. That's her deal. I just want to get the hell out of here and have a life. So, go down and help her or don't. I really don't care. Just get the hell off my back."

And, with that, she turned and strode out the front door.

CHAPTER 15

WAKING WITH A start, Tasmin sat up slowly and looked around. She was in a bed, a big wide cozy bed, and yet she was alone. Blinking, struggling to clear her mind from what was obviously something she didn't remember at all, she slowly pulled herself out from under the covers and noted she just wore her underwear, with the rest of her clothing neatly folded on the chair beside her. As she sat here on the edge of the bed, the bedroom door opened, and she watched Hanson step into the room.

He smiled. "Hey, how're you feeling?"

She looked up at him and blinked.

He chuckled. "Obviously it's a bit of a surprise to be here, I bet."

"Ya think? ... I don't even want to think about how long it's been since I slept in a bed this nice." Then she shook her head. "And, no, the beds at Bellevue are as horrible as one might imagine."

He nodded slowly. "There's a shower, if you want."

"Yes, please," she confirmed, her tone formal.

She got up, and he walked over to the bathroom, pulled out a towel for her, and said, "Here you go."

"Where did you sleep?"

"I slept on my couch."

She winced. "You should have put me on the couch. I

would have been fine. Honestly I don't even remember coming here."

"Yeah, I'm sure you don't. You were pretty exhausted after the session at the funeral home last night."

She opened her eyes in remembrance. "Wow, I forgot about that. At least I got the job done."

"Of course you did. I'm sure the families will appreciate it."

"Yeah, but mine won't."

"I'm not sure if your sister will even show up for work today."

She frowned at him.

He said, "Go get your shower. I've got coffee on."

She immediately smiled. "Coffee sounds great." Snatching the towel, she entered the bathroom, closed the door, stripped off the rest of her clothing, and stepped into a hot shower. She just stood here for a long moment, letting the water wash over her, totally in love with the feeling of having this lifestyle again. She didn't realize how far she'd fallen and how bad it must have looked to him when he'd come to her shop to find her bedroll in the back room on the floor. It would look bad to anybody.

She didn't even think her family realized how she was living, not that they would care, although it would just be more evidence that she wasn't fit to be on her own. She groaned, as she scrubbed her head and hair, using his shampoo. She would mention it in case she owed him another bottle or something. She regretfully turned off the water, having enjoyed that more than she thought possible.

She came out of the bathroom, wrapped in a towel, and, grabbing her clothes, quickly redressed. Wouldn't it be lovely if she had clean clothes here too? She yawned and thought about all she had done in the last few weeks and groaned because it really wasn't sustainable.

What was important on her list was that she had to go back to the funeral home to work on the tattoo today as well. It wasn't something that one just started and then could walk away from. It was a process, and it had to be babysat. And she was up for that challenge, but, boy, the last thing she wanted to do was go back to the funeral home.

Dressed, she walked out into the kitchen to find him sitting at his laptop. He hopped up, walked over, and poured her a coffee, then carried it to her. She collapsed on the massive couch. She looked at the couch, smiled, and said, "Okay, this couch makes much more sense."

He chuckled. "I'm a big guy, and I really don't want furniture that makes me feel like I'm sitting in a dollhouse."

"Nope, this is a massive couch." She curled up sideways on it and held the cup of coffee. "I presume I was so exhausted last night that I didn't even notice it."

"Yep, that's about the size of it," he agreed cheerfully. "Yet you do look much better this morning."

She yawned and nodded. "I feel much better too. What time is it anyway?"

"It's just going on eight o'clock now."

She stared at him. "Wow. Okay, so considering I didn't get all that many hours of sleep, I'm feeling better than I deserve to."

"That's probably true," he said. "I have to go to work in another half hour. I would have woken you anyway, but at least this way you're awake and can get some coffee and get your brain warmed up."

"I'll grab a lift to my place, if you don't mind."

He nodded. "I expected that."

She smiled. "Thank you for taking care of me, and, by the way, I used some shampoo."

He chuckled. "Shampoo is really not an issue, and I'm glad you feel better. You do have to come up with a solution to your living arrangements and to your family."

She snorted. "I'm not sure there is a solution to my family."

"Your sister was pretty angry last night. I got the impression she was planning on leaving and never coming back."

She stared at him steadily and nodded. "She's done that a time or two."

"Seriously?"

"Yeah, seriously. The only *normal* in my family was my grandmother."

"So, where's your mother in all this? I saw her when she came to the shop once."

"Yeah, to pressure me to go in and work some more at the funeral home." Tasmin yawned. "When my father is having good days," she said, with an eyeroll, "he goes down and works on the bodies. Yet, for whatever reason, apparently working too much sets his—" She didn't know what to call it but continued on. "It sets his state of mind back, let's put it that way."

He sat down across from her and nodded. "Any chance that he is psychic?"

She stared at him and then started to laugh. "Wouldn't that be something? I mean, to have him blame me for what it is that's ailing him."

"But if your grandmother was, and you are …"

"At times I've wondered. I've just never seen any sign of it."

"Good enough, at least for now," he said.

"I do have to go back to the funeral home today though."

He winced. "Seriously?"

"Yes, and for the next couple days. It's partly why I need access to the facilities."

"And yet maybe it's time to take a serious look at the other offer."

"I think it probably is," she admitted. "I can't keep doing what I'm doing, I'm running on empty."

"Thank you. It makes me feel better to realize that you're at least starting to see how much damage you're causing yourself."

"*Causing* is a hard word for it, but I think we're all still trying to find our place in the world, after my grandmother's passing."

"Sounds as if she's what kept the family together."

Tasmin smiled. "Absolutely, and in many ways my mother. They were very close too."

"I still don't understand how your mom fits into any of this."

"I don't really know either," she admitted, with a wave of her hand. "I haven't seen her in the last few days, so I'm not sure where she's at. She was at my place a few days ago though, so she's around, but she does avoid the funeral home outside of the offices. Plus, she generally sets up appointments and goes in and deals with customers."

"She's okay to deal with that aspect of it?"

"She is, or maybe it's just what she knows," Tasmin suggested. "Once she married into the family, there wasn't a whole lot of options for her either."

"Hard to believe it's going so badly, considering how much your family should be making from this."

"Yeah, that's a conversation that needs to be cleared up, and I really don't know what's happening with that. There should be lots of money, so I'm not sure why there isn't."

"No, I'm not either," Hanson noted, "but that's definitely a concern, particularly when you supposedly can't even get paid because of it."

"I know," she murmured. "Believe me. That's not something I'm particularly happy about, especially right now, when it would be nice if I had some materials to get the loft taken care of at my place."

He slowly nodded.

"Unless you've had second thoughts," Tasmin added.

"About helping? No, not at all," he said instantly. "We do need to get some materials, and there is obviously a cost involved. I'm not sure how much you're making on your business, but obviously not enough to even pay for rent."

"I pay my rent for the store," she corrected, with a wry tone. "I just couldn't pay for rent on an apartment too."

"And yet you're working double-time, right?"

"We're back to that whole family thing again."

"You mean that whole family *abuse* thing?"

She glared at him.

He shrugged. "Let's call it what it is, and then you won't keep fooling yourself. They're taking advantage of you, and ultimately it's your fault because you're letting them."

She stared down at her cup of coffee because his plain speaking, although accurate, just didn't help right now. She sighed, looked at the clock, and said, "We better get on the road, if you plan to drop me off."

He nodded and stood. "I have your travel mug here. You want me to fill it up for you?"

"I can make more at the store," she said, protesting.

"Mine's full too, so it will just go to waste if we don't take it."

It was hard to argue with that, and she was never one to let food go to waste. He packed up both travel mugs, and she headed toward the car, wishing that she had a change of clothes, yet feeling so much better nonetheless. "Thank you for taking care of me last night," she noted formally, when they got to her place. She opened the car door, stepped out, and added, "I really do appreciate it."

"Good, because I'll be back here tonight to make sure that you eat, and then I want to take a bunch of measurements."

"Are you sure?" she asked, frowning at him. "I feel as if I'm taking advantage of you."

"Then remember that, just like you're letting them take advantage of you, I'm letting you take advantage of me. And that's the end of the conversation for the moment," he stated, giving her a glance. "I've got to go to work, and so do you." Then he motioned behind her, and there was Puggs, his back to them, standing in the shadows by the door, waiting to talk to her.

"Interesting," she noted. "Business has certainly been picking up."

"And you've got the one from California to do too, right?"

"Yeah, I do," she confirmed. "That one is a completely different process, but, yeah. I've got to get back to the funeral home and deal with both of them."

"Or do you immediately start an arrangement with another facility?"

"Maybe I'll give them a call later today. Gotta go." With that, she closed the car door and walked over with a smile to

Puggs. "Hey, how's life going?"

He smiled at her. "It's better for you and me than it is for these victims," he said. "I hate to say it, but another client with one of Pinch's designs was killed last night."

She stared at him, her heart sinking. "Seriously?"

He nodded. "I know. None of it makes any sense. Pinch mentioned today that he wondered if he was being targeted."

"Yet, if he were being targeted, he would be the one who's dead, not his customers."

*

HANSON STARED AT his computer screen, pondering the information in front of him. He'd gathered up as much information as he could on Tasmin's father. He had no criminal record, absolutely nothing, not even a parking ticket. Hanson stared at the info in surprise.

John walked over and said, "You look as if whatever you're seeing isn't what you were expecting."

Hanson closed down the window and shrugged. "Just information that never seems to gel."

"Hey, with people around here, nothing ever seems to gel," he muttered. "How're you doing on the drive-by shootings?" he asked.

"We did get a decent-enough sketch," he noted, picking up the image he had just printed off and handed it to him.

"Oh, shit, that *is* pretty decent."

"Of course we don't really know if it's close or not, so that's a whole different story."

"It is, indeed."

"I'm still contemplating the problems with the tattoo pieces."

"That's just a robbery, not our department," John stated,

his voice harder. "We don't have time to waste."

"I know. We don't have time to waste," he repeated, his tone mild. "Yet at the same time it is a curiosity."

"Nothing about it is curious to me," John declared. "It's disgusting, and it's dark shit. I don't like anything about it."

Hanson looked up at him. "That might be, but I can't say it's all that surprising. Every form of art seems to end up being preserved in some way or another."

The detective shuddered. "*Ugh*. Don't even talk to me about that being a preservation thing. No way that's normal or natural."

"Yet, we have medical museums all over the world," Hanson pointed out, "so this is hardly anything different."

"This is abnormal. This is shit people do to themselves, and then, in order to preserve it, we have to cut the bodies up," John detailed. "No, definitely not my bag."

"Good to know," Hanson said.

"Did you hear that night shift caught another one?"

"Another what?"

"Another drive-by shooting."

"No, I didn't get a phone call," he said, frowning.

"It wasn't your call night," John stated. "You need to connect with the team who was out there."

Hanson frowned at that because, in the past, if he was on a case, and it was connected to his, he would have been given a shout-out on it. "Why wasn't I tagged?" he asked in frustration.

John looked at him and said, "I don't know. Maybe somebody didn't want to work with you." And, with that, he turned and walked away.

Swearing under his breath, Hanson quickly brought up the case and contacted the cops involved. He asked for all reports to be directed to him and then realized Mark had caught the case himself. Hanson got up and walked over to where Mark was on the phone.

When Mark got off the phone, Hanson asked him, "So why didn't you tag me on the case?"

"What the hell? It was your night off. No big deal."

"If these cases are potentially connected, I'd like to be kept in the loop."

Mark just gave him a flat stare. "We'd all like shit in our life. Doesn't mean we'll get it." And, with that, he turned, picked up the phone and started dialing again.

Hanson returned to his desk, completely frustrated. The first overt signs of antagonism were impacting his job.

When the captain walked in a bit later, he asked Hanson, "Have you got an update on the drive-by shootings for me?" His tone suggested his frustration had been boiling over the lack of progress.

"I might have," Hanson noted, "but the guys who got called out last night didn't think to tag me on it," he stated, his voice hard. "You'll have to ask Mark about it."

The captain stared at him, then turned and glared at Mark. "What?"

Mark shrugged. "Hey, I was trying to be nice and give him the night off."

"No nights off," the captain roared. "And you know that, Mark. If this has got to do with the fact that he's new, I don't really give a crap. We're short-handed as it is, so we need to get these cases solved. No more shutting him out."

"Hey, I wasn't shutting him out," Mark stated, with a genial smile.

No way anybody would have believed it, and Hanson certainly didn't.

"I sent him my case files already, and, besides, it was just last night."

"And how many hours have already gone by?" Hanson asked, swearing.

"What will you do in the meantime?" Mark asked. "We've got nothing. This time there aren't even witnesses."

He stared at him. "Who were the victims?"

"I'm just tracking them down now."

"So you don't even have an ID for them?"

Mark turned and glared at Hanson. "No, I don't. I've been a little busy."

"Case in point," the captain snapped. "We need these victims ID'd and fast."

Hanson heard his cell phone ringing, saw the call was from Tasmin, and pondered whether he should answer it or not, when it rang again. "What's the matter, Tasmin?" he asked, keeping his voice low.

"Another one of Pinch's customers died in a drive-by last night," she said, her voice hoarse. "Now both Pinch and I are wondering if that's the basis of the targeting."

It struck him odd that Pinch and Tasmin knew the identity of the victim, and yet the cops on the case did not. All business, he pulled a notepad toward him. "Do you have the name?" She gave it to him. Then he asked, "And who was it who told you?" She lowered her voice yet again, and he wasn't sure if somebody was in the room where she was or what.

"Puggs, that's why he was here waiting for me."

"And Puggs is Pinch's assistant, right?"

"Yes," she confirmed.

"Has he left?"

"Yes, of course."

"If you want to send him a text, tell him that I'll be over there in a few minutes."

"You'll come see him?" she asked.

"Yes, of course I will," he stated, with exaggerated patience. "If somebody is being targeted and if this angle could be a lead, we need to see if we can figure out why."

And, with that, he got off the phone. Looking over at Mark, Hanson said, "Looks like we have an ID on that victim."

Mark looked over at him and frowned. "I haven't heard from forensics yet," Mark replied, clicking his email to see if anything was there.

"I'll go down and talk to him, see if we get a match," Hanson stated, "but I have a name." Then he hopped up and walked out.

As soon as he got down to the coroner's office, he passed on the information that he'd received. It didn't take very long to have it confirmed.

With that, he headed back to the office, tossed Mark the name, and stated, "I'll send you the forensics' ID on it, but it's confirmed." And, with that, he snatched his wallet and his keys and headed to the doorway.

"Now where are you going?" Mark cried out, frustration oozing from his voice, probably because he hadn't managed to get an ID on the victim. "If you'd asked for any damn help, it would have been solved a long time ago."

Hanson stopped and turned. "I have a new angle on it. This is the third victim with a tattoo."

"So," Mark said slowly, drawing it out, an incredulous expression on his face, "you're thinking that somebody is targeting people with tattoos?"

"In this case, it's the third customer of a specific tattoo artist. I'll go talk to him." And, with that, he was gone.

CHAPTER 16

Tasmin picked up her cell and dialed. "Hey, Pinch. I heard about the latest customer."

"Jesus, it's bad," he said. "Shit like that gets around, and I may never live it down. I'll be ruined."

"I know. I know," she agreed. "People get really freaky about those things."

"Just something about a lot of this that is getting very bizarre. It's bad enough that people are dying, but, on top of that, I just can't afford to have anything happen to my business."

"I got it," she replied gently. "A detective assigned to these cases will be on his way down to see you this morning," she shared. "He's a friend of mine, and I trust him. If you've got anything to tell him, then tell him. He's a good guy ... really."

Pinch asked, "Are you sure?"

"Yes, I'm sure. You can trust him. This will possibly get ugly for both of us, so we want to make sure we've got the right people in our corner."

"Yeah. So, what about your corner?"

"Ah, you have no idea the shit I'm going through," she replied, with a sigh.

"Bet it's partly that bitch sister of yours."

"And my father and mother to a certain extent," she

muttered. "It just never seems to get any better."

"Sorry, girl. Oh, well, shit. Looks like I got a cop here already."

"Tell him I said hi," Tasmin replied.

"Oh, you really do know him, as in know him, know him?"

"Uh, no, not like that," she corrected, "but he's been bailing me out of trouble lately and with no expectations of paybacks, if you know what I mean."

"That would be unusual in itself," he noted. "I'll at least see what he's got to say."

"More to the point, he needs to hear what you've got to say."

"Right, but I don't even know what to say to that."

Hanging up, she grimaced. She'd already been to the funeral home once, working downstairs in the quiet. She didn't see anyone, and that's just the way she liked it. She'd managed to get out before anybody saw her, and now she was back at her shop again. She'd worked on both projects this morning, and now was taking notes on their condition and the photographs, setting up a chart on both cases. She'd also updated both families as to where she was at on their projects. Now they had to pick out frames and address some issues on shape and definition.

Tasmin had a few suggestions to make and was working that into the emails right now. She couldn't make those kinds of decisions until she saw the condition of the skin, and, from that point on, it became a little easier, where she could involve the families. Not every family wanted to be involved to that degree, but, in this case, they did. So that made it something she was quite used to from the funeral home, where she had to involve people in the decision-making process regarding the caskets and the ceremony, and everything that went along with that.

So this was territory she was well and truly used to. Now, if only she could get a bit more business, she could do this full-time. Both of these cases would bring in several thousand dollars, and that was good because she needed it and gave her a little distance from that poverty edge. Then there was the regular work that she did—and of course her work for her sister. Tasmin winced, deliberately putting that out of her mind.

When the phone rang a little later, it was Lorelei. "Hey," Tasmin said.

"Hey." Her sister's voice was subdued.

"You okay?"

"Yeah, I'm okay. I had a long talk with Mom this morning."

"Oh, that must have been fun."

"No, not really. ... Did you know that Mom and Dad are probably getting a divorce?"

Tasmin thought about it and said, "Mom's finally jumping ship, is she?"

At that, her sister gasped. "Seriously? That's all you have to say about it?"

"It's been a threat she's held over my head for a very long time," Tasmin muttered. "So I can't say I'm very surprised if it's finally come to that point. He's getting quite unmanageable."

"I guess you didn't like what happened yesterday, did you?"

"No, I sure didn't. That was a very ugly session with Dad."

"I think it set off something with Mom too."

"But if anything is seriously wrong with Dad …"

"I know," Lorelei groaned. "We'll have to handle it."

∼

HANSON WALKED INTO Pinch's shop, then stopped in the doorway and took an assessing look. Pinch had several artists with clients, working at stations in various parts of the store. It didn't really surprise Hanson now that he realized it was that busy of a place, versus a one-man operation.

He walked over and introduced himself, and the man at the counter nodded. "I just got off the phone with Tasmin," he said.

At that, Hanson nodded. "She alerted me to the suspicion this morning."

"Yeah, man, it sucks big-time. I don't even want to think about this happening."

Hanson looked around and asked, "Is there any place we can talk privately?"

Pinch nodded. "Come into my office."

He led the way to a small, jam-packed room, barely big enough for a desk and a chair. Pinch brought in a stool with him, plunked it down on the far side of the desk, and said, "You can sit there. Sorry, this is where I do the paperwork, which, as you can tell, doesn't get a whole lot of priority. I have way-too-many clients to be too bothered about paperwork. So, I come in here, do the work, and get out as fast as I can." He grimaced.

"Got it," Hanson noted, as he sat down, surveying the mess. "Do you get anything done in here?"

"I do, but only when I'm forced to." He gave a half laugh.

"Everybody seems to have this thing about paperwork."

"Yeah, it sucks. All of it sucks. I don't like paperwork. I don't like anything about it. I think it's a creation to drive us all mad. I get it done, but then it pretty much just goes in the heap."

At that Hanson burst into laughter. "I don't know about that, but I can see that it's not everybody's thing."

"Definitely not mine," Pinch muttered. Then he looked at Hanson and said, "Look. I don't know what to tell you, but I just know that the last—I don't even know if it's the last three victims, but whatever—the last three of my customers, good customers with beautiful tattoos and more lined up to get done, have all been hit in drive-by shootings."

At that, Hanson felt something inside him start to come alive. "I am really glad to hear you say that," he muttered.

Pinch looked at him in surprise.

"Not that your customers have been victims, but that we're finally getting down to a reason why they might be getting shot."

"I don't understand," Pinch declared, raising his hands in frustration. "I mean, I've never done anything to these people."

"No, I understand," Hanson agreed. "The fact of the matter is, we don't have a motive yet, but we're trying hard to figure out what's going on."

"Motive?" Pinch asked. "What could possibly be a motive? Is it the customers? Is somebody pissed off at me, and they're trying to stop my business from flourishing? I mean, once this gets out, it will be bad news. I might as well just close up shop and go because if somebody's targeting my customers, I won't have any more," he stated flatly. "I might as well head back to where I came from."

"Where was that?"

"California. I had a big shop in San Diego for a good ten years."

"Why did you leave?"

He shrugged and then shared, "Things were getting a bit dicey for me. I had a couple artists, and one was into drugs. Unbeknownst to me, he started selling them out of my shop. I got in trouble with the cops and ended up getting a bunch of fines. Once the fines start hitting, your profits go down, and it got ugly. Let me just say, it was not a good scenario.

"I ended up having a bad fight with a couple of my artists and put them out of my shop. They were pretty pissed off and decided that they would screw me over. I finally decided that I'd had enough of that shit and pulled up stakes and shut down the shop. Well, I meant to shut it down, but I ended up selling it to one of my other artists. So he kept it open, and that was that. It's part of the reason Tasmin has business in California because some of my guys there know her from the work that I've done with her here. Thus they've referred her to some of their clients."

"Interesting," Hanson said.

"When you think about it, tattoo shops are the most likely place for her to get business. That sounds ghoulish maybe because of the mortuary thing, but the tattoo preservation aspect is really a big industry."

"Is it though?" Hanson asked.

"Maybe not yet," Pinch admitted, "but it will be soon. I mean, give that girl a couple years, and she'll be leading a very specialized field that'll keep her busy with enough work for her and several assistants," he muttered. "If I'd thought of it, I would have done it myself. Except I wouldn't have had a clue, but, because of her background, she's uniquely qualified to do it. So I'm totally okay to not get into that side of it. It really pisses me off to know that some of my best pieces aren't preserved because the owners have already died, but who knew such a thing would even be possible? And now it seems in these last few drive-by cases that they may have even been targeted. I mean, what are the odds?"

"It's the targeting that I'm interested in because, if we could figure out why these particular victims were chosen, I would have a much better chance of making sure we don't have any more."

"You guys really don't have much to go on though, do you?"

Hanson stared over at Pinch.

"You haven't stopped it yet," he noted, with a wave of his hands. "So, I just take that to mean you don't have any suspects, or you would have been on them, that's all. No offense intended."

"Ah, no suspects identified so far. Unfortunately they have an MO of stealing a vehicle, hitting certain people we thought were random, and now realize maybe they are *not* so random."

"Yeah, that really sucks," Pinch said. "I mean, when you think about it, you shouldn't be targeted, not for something you're wearing on your skin. That's just disgusting."

"It might be disgusting," Hanson agreed, "but you cannot even begin to really think about all the people in this world and how they view certain aspects, including body modifications, tattoos, any body art. The opinions are all over the map and back, you know?"

"And yet we never really think of it, do we?" Pinch noted sadly. "I only think of doing something that brings a client pleasure and creating a piece of artwork that will last their lifetime. And now with the work Tasmin's doing, it's not even limited to their lifetime. We are doing a piece that could last indefinitely."

"Which is good," Hanson shared. "Believe me. I'm not against this work being done at all. Tasmin seems to be filling a very specific void out there, and obviously there's room for it."

"Oh, she definitely is," Pinch agreed. "It's not something I have really thought about, outside of the certain amount of sadness I've felt that, you know, my pieces die when my clients die. But even that is far better than my clients potentially dying because they're wearing one of my pieces. I can't even wrap my head around that."

Hanson understood. Nothing was easy about any of this, and trying to figure out what was going on when everything was so messed-up made it even more challenging. "How long have you known Tasmin?" Hanson asked curiously.

"Years, likely just over a decade," he replied. "I grew up in this town way back when. She's a good ten years younger than I am, but her family wasn't really one you could ignore. If you ever had a death among your family or friends, that's where you went. Her grandmother was gold, absolutely gold, and we had reason to make use of some of her generosity at one point in time. My dad ended up paying her back every penny, but it took a long time. He gave her ten bucks a week because that's all he could afford.

"She never said a word about only getting ten dollars. She never docked him interest or made him feel bad about it in any way. She just kept updating his account every time he made a payment, and, when he finally paid it off, she looked over at him on that last day and said, 'Nice job.' I don't think he'd ever been prouder of the fact that he had managed to pay that off, but it just became one of those things. So I knew the family, and Tasmin was there at the funeral home.

"As a matter of fact, she was *always* there, always working with her grandmother, always on the floor, down below. I mean, even in school, I know that she had a lot of hardship because of the work that she and her family were involved in. Nobody ever wanted to go over to her place, not that they were ever even invited," he noted in consideration. "Maybe that was just her keeping everybody out because she went through so much, but there was a lot of talk about her being"—he hesitated—"I don't know, ... *weird*."

"Weird how?" Hanson asked.

"Just weird."

At that, there wasn't a whole lot Hanson could say. He nodded and added, "In a way it's a good weird."

"Oh, it's definitely a good weird," Pinch agreed, smiling. "And now I have a chance to work with her on some of my own art pieces, and it's very much appreciated. She's really very talented."

"Good to hear," Hanson murmured. "Now, what can you tell me about each of these victims?"

Pinch winced at the word *victim*. "God, I hate to even think of them like that."

"Maybe, but we don't really have a lot of choice right now," Hanson noted gently. "These people are dead, and they were all killed by a drive-by shooting."

"So, that's two females and one male. I've got Chris and then Angela and ..." Pinch stopped and looked around at the papers on his desktop. "And Lois."

At that, Hanson nodded. "Right."

"One of the reasons why I wondered if my shop, me, my art, or whatever, was being targeted, was that all three of those clients had been here recently."

At that, Hanson brought out a notepad. "Okay, I need more details than that. When were they here? How long were they here for? Why were they here? That sort of thing."

"Whoa, whoa, whoa, they were here because they had a session. In Chris's case, he's been doing a big piece on his back, but there's only so much we can do at a time, so he came in to set up an appointment for his next session."

"Okay, and when was that booked for?"

"Next week." Pinch winced. "Man, this already has impacted my life," he muttered, as he brought up his schedule on the computer. "I had him down for two hours next week. On Tuesday."

"Okay, do you know who might have been here during the time that Chris was here to make that appointment?"

At that, Pinch stared at him and then slowly shook his head. "Oh, God no. … I mean, I could probably look back on the books and figure out who was getting work done and which artists were here, but we also have a lot of walk-ins, a lot of people asking questions, a lot of people coming in to visit our guys who are getting work done. Then they take off again. They come back. They bring coffee, and they, … you know, it's a social thing. So I have an open-door policy," he explained.

"Okay, and who else might have known who would have been here?"

Pinch shook his head. "I'd have to ask everybody."

"That's what we'll do then," Hanson confirmed.

"Everybody?" Pinch asked, looking up at him in horror.

"Everybody. For every one of these victims."

Pinch shrunk in on himself. "Oh God. Even once my staff knows, it'll change everything."

"It will. On the other hand, what we don't want is to

have a fourth customer get taken out in a drive-by," Hanson pointed out.

"God no, no we don't," he murmured. He leaned forward, dropped his elbows on the desk, and then face-palmed onto his hands for a long moment.

Hanson just waited.

Finally Pinch offered, "What I can do is bring up the days, the clients who were with my artists had at that time, and then ask them if they had any idea who else might have been here."

"That would work," Hanson said. "Let's do that now."

At the look of shock on Pinch's face, Hanson realized that Pinch thought he could get rid of Hanson, could sort this out himself, and could have a private talk with his own clients.

Hanson shook his head. "We can't do this on the sly. This has to be done fast, and it has to be done in the open. Otherwise I have to more or less shut you down, while I talk to everybody on a one-on-one basis," he explained. "If we can get through these names and the appointments as quickly as possible, it will have much less impact on your business."

Pinch grimaced. "You don't understand how this will have a major impact on my business."

"I do know," Hanson clarified, "and I can't do anything but apologize upfront. However, it's what has to be. You said it best earlier. *If you keep losing your clients, you won't have any more.*"

"Oh God," Pinch muttered. "Here I was really hoping that I could just talk to you for a few minutes, and you'd go away and solve this."

"Going away and solving this would be one thing," Hanson replied. "Solving it without you or without asking all of your staff who has been here in recent days, that would be a whole different story."

"Shit," he whispered. "Okay, fine, give me a minute."

Hanson just sat here and waited.

Pinch stared at the detective. "I mean, just a couple minutes. I have to cross-reference the schedules."

"Just take pictures of your schedule on the days that you had those three clients in. And were any of them in multiple times in that same week?"

Pinch nodded slowly. "Angela was. First to okay the final picture, and then we got started. Afterward we had a lot more work to do that we continued on with."

"And was that the only tattoo you did for her?"

He shook his head. "No, she's been in here a lot."

"Any chance you had any discussion with her about the preservation that can be done?"

He stared at the detective, frowning. "It's been the talk fairly regularly for the last couple weeks. It came up one day when one of the customers had inquired about it. Then I started telling them about Tasmin and the work she was doing, and, of course, you get the usual group of people, where some think it's disgusting, and others think it's freaking awesome."

"So it's been something that's batted around back and forth quite a bit?"

At that, he just nodded.

"Okay, that's a place to start."

"How is that a place to start?" Pinch asked. "It seems to me that's the place to end."

Hanson smiled at that. "And I get that, but we've got a lot more to do."

CHAPTER 17

TASMIN WAS STILL staring at the order in front of her as she hung up the phone, only to start when the door opened. When Hanson walked in, she flashed him a bright smile. "Hey, how's your day?"

"How do you think it's been?" he grumbled.

She winced. "Given the work you do, probably not great. You saw Pinch, I presume. How's he doing?"

"He's pretty upset at the moment," Hanson shared. "We just met with everybody in his shop."

Her eyebrows shot up. "Why is that?"

"Just to see if anybody remembered who all might have been in the store at certain times, such as the drops-ins. According to Pinch, people come and go on a regular basis. People come to visit clients getting work done. Others come in making inquiries and stuff like that. So the dates that we've determined those three particular customers were in his shop, we needed to line up who all would have known they were there."

"And that's just the people who would have *seen* them there," Tasmin noted. "That doesn't include all the other people who might have known by word of mouth."

He nodded. "I'm heading to the house of this last victim, and we'll cross-reference all the phone numbers."

"Good. I suppose you have to get a different court order."

"Yes, and the families of the second one were being rather difficult and have only just now agreed to let us have the phone number we need."

She stared at him. "Doesn't that make you suspicious when people do that?"

He gave her a fat smile. "Oh, it absolutely does," he confirmed, "but a lot of times people are just more concerned about rights and freedoms, particularly now that the other person is dead, as if to say, *It makes absolutely no difference, so leave it alone.*"

She shook her head. "Yet here I am, trying rather desperately to find peace on a legal level with all this," she shared. "I don't have time for people who want to argue on simple stuff."

"It's not even simple stuff," Hanson clarified. "Yet a lot of people hold very stringent views on what the police should be allowed to access and what we shouldn't."

She shrugged. "Good for them," she muttered. "And, yes, I have to deal with a lot of people like that just because of the funeral home, and I can only deal with so much of it."

He nodded. "Did you ever ask your sister about money?"

"No, not yet. She's pretty upset right now."

He cocked an eyebrow and looked at her, as he pulled up the stool on the other side of the counter and sat down. "Why is she upset?"

"According to her, my mother may have decided she's had enough and may be about to divorce my father."

He stared at her.

"As you saw, my father is quite a handful already, but it's likely to get worse if she leaves."

"I would think so," Hanson agreed.

"I don't know that he's of sound mind right now."

"No, and anybody talking to him will have those same doubts."

"But nothing is in place to let us do anything about it legally," she noted. "So it's likely to get particularly difficult."

"Have you talked to your mother?"

"No, I sure haven't," she stated. "You have to understand. She's been holding that threat over my head all my life. If I didn't behave, didn't do what I needed to do, *blah-blah-blah*, then she wouldn't handle him and would pack up and leave."

"That's an interesting threat to use on a child."

"It's been a long time since I've been a child," she declared, with a hard laugh. "And you grow up quickly in my industry."

"You certainly see the reality of life and death, though I'm not sure how that makes you grow up."

She shrugged. "I don't know either, but it is what it is. I had to grow up fast after my grandmother died, and that's when my father started to really lose it. She was the one who kept him more or less calm and in control."

"Is he really unstable?"

"I don't know. You met him," she reminded Hanson, with a glimmer of a smile. "For a lot of people, my dad might seem perfectly normal. Just because his views are not our views doesn't make him unstable," she noted, with a wave of her hand. "Just think about what you were saying a few minutes ago about the legal advice or even getting phone numbers for the deceased and checking phone calls."

"Yet you'd think that if they had a family member who was murdered—"

Tasmin interrupted him. "Honestly, I can tell you that a

lot of people are very fatalistic about dealing with death, and some are so wrapped up in guilt that you can hardly talk to them. Others just want someone else to deal with anything they don't want to. *Here's a check. Let us know when it's done.* Or *Maybe don't let us know. We just want it to be done today.*"

He shook his head at that.

"In my industry you meet all kinds," she explained. "I've been working on not judging everybody for their different reactions to death."

"I agree with you there," Hanson said. "I've had more than my fair share of dealing with people on the receiving end of that. They don't quite know what they're supposed to say or do. Plus, they're in shock. They want to ask questions, but, at the same time, they don't want anything to do with it. On the whole, I'd say most are good people, and they're just looking out for each other—or, in some cases, maybe themselves."

She laughed at that. "Then there's that whole group of people who bend over backward to try and help everybody. Whether it's out of a sense of guilt or a sense of compassion, I don't know," she added. "But, with my grandmother's death, things didn't go very well."

"How did your grandmother die?"

She sighed. "She had a heart attack. … It was the worst day of my life."

"How did your family react?"

"I wasn't there. When my father found out, he told my mother, who told me, but honestly, I halfway knew."

He looked at her strangely for a moment, then understanding hit his gaze. "Right. That's not always a gift either, is it?"

"No, it sure isn't. I phoned my mom and asked if

Grandma was okay because I just had that feeling, and they were already at the hospital, and Mom said *no*."

"And how did your mother take it?"

"I don't even know what to say to that," Tasmin replied. "I think my mother and my grandmother had this agreement that my grandmother would stay out of their lives as long as everybody minded their *P*s and *Q*s with Grandma. And that also meant taking care of my father and helping him out."

"Has your father ... I don't want to say he's *special needs*, but obviously he's a challenge."

"He's a challenge all right, and no, not special needs. He's just ... does the word *fervent* fit?"

"Yeah, I'd say so," Hanson confirmed in a dry tone. "And not necessarily in a good way."

"We see it over and over again," she noted. "So, what can I say?"

"Do you meet people like that at the funeral home?"

"Oh yes," she stated. "Some people who are absolutely certain their loved ones are in heaven, and they just want ... I've had people ask me to help them join their family members."

He just stared.

She nodded. "Obviously I said no, then sent them home to try and get some sleep, knowing things would look different when they woke up. But, when grief overtakes you, it can be crippling."

He pondered that for a long moment. "So, considering all you know about death and dying," he began, "what is your take on these shootings and the fact that they're somehow potentially connected to Pinch?"

"Believe me. I've sat here thinking about that today," she shared, "at least until I got this very strange phone call that sent me down another rabbit hole. You've got to understand," she explained, as she looked around the shop. "I didn't set out to do this. I mean, I am an artist on my own, although I haven't had much of a chance to do anything with it.

"And I've certainly had some success with framing people's art, a business I started when I was wondering about another future away from the funeral home. My grandmother convinced me that I wouldn't have a future away from there and pushed me to really invest everything into it, but she didn't stop me from framing paintings for friends and for a few of my own pieces.

"Yet there was always that understanding that I would have the funeral home as my priority. When my family took it away from me, and I realized I couldn't trust them, I sat down and started looking at options. So I also frame paintings, photos, and things here. Also, because of my industry, I've been asked to do a few odder things."

He straightened up and looked at her. "Such as what other things?"

"So, one guy was in a car accident and lost two toes. He asked me if I could preserve them. They were still in the cooler at the hospital, and, since the hospital had decided they couldn't reattach them, he would have to do without. Yet he didn't want to do completely without and wanted to know how he could preserve them."

"Interesting." Hanson studied her. "So, did you pickle his toes?"

She winced, and then she laughed. "Yeah, I did," she confessed. "Though I felt weird doing it. At the same time, it's not as if I was hurting anybody. I wasn't doing anything wrong or illegal. I looked at it as a request from somebody trying to deal with the loss of his own personal body parts," she shared, for lack of any better wording.

He let out his breath. "Okay, so a whole lot of craziness is here, more than I thought."

"I don't think any of it's connected to your case," she suggested.

"No, I'm not saying it is, and obviously we've got something going on with the case. But your whole industry is kind of crazy because here I was thinking there was no way you could afford to live off this work, but Pinch assured me that it's a very specialized industry, and, once your name gets out, he doesn't think you'll have any problem at all."

"He's partially responsible for my going into this, for encouraging me. He had some clients back in California who had contacted him, and the guy who bought his shop there asked Pinch if he knew anybody who was doing this kind of thing. And that's how it began. You start with one client and then comes another and another. A lot of the time I only do the finishing—you know, how it's sealed glass on the casing," she stated. "In some instances it's a little more than a framing job, but it's very specialized, and I can charge a bit more for it."

"Yes, I would think so," he muttered. He looked around at the shop and then his gaze was drawn to a piece on the wall. "In a minute I'll walk over there and take a closer look at that piece on the wall, but I'll go really slow to prepare myself."

She burst out laughing. "That was from a friend of mine. She had breast cancer, and she asked me if, in her memory, I would preserve the tattoo that she had designed and had drawn herself. So I did, and I've kept it up here in my shop ever since."

At that, he got up and walked over to take a look at that tattoo. "And where was this on her?"

"Her right shoulder," she murmured, walking up to him. "It's such a beautiful gold dragonfly."

He nodded slowly. "That is beautiful."

"Isn't it? Do you like the title?"

"*In memory of Corinne, may she fly free.*" He nodded slowly. "I see something like this and hear you talk about it, and I can see why people would want to do it."

She smiled. "Thank you for that. That's more acceptance than I get from some people, and I honestly wasn't sure how you felt about it."

"Especially since my first sightings were found in the fountains."

"Oh yeah. No, that's … that's not exactly a good thing to look at," she replied, her voice hardening. "It was pretty traumatic for the families, when they found out what had happened."

"I mean, we need a whole different language to even talk about this," Hanson shared. "You don't want to offend people, but, when you talk about their body parts, do you talk about them as if they're living? I can see how that would insult a lot of people, but then how can you talk about them as being dead when really what you've done is preserve a piece of them?"

"I've preserved a piece of their physical bodies," she clarified. "In most cases I try to reference them as if they have passed on, and this is potentially a way to memorialize them. But it's not easy, and you're right. I think everybody is still trying to find their way with the language of a new industry that nobody really understands quite yet."

He nodded, as he stared at the framed body art. "This is

truly beautiful," he said abruptly.

She smiled. "It is beautiful," she murmured.

Then he turned and looked at the piece beside it. "Is this another one?"

"That is one of my art pieces," she admitted.

He raised his eyebrows as he turned to her, then looked again at the artwork. "Seriously?"

She nodded. "Yeah."

"Who is it?"

"It's my grandmother. I did it before she died."

It was a portrait of an older woman, heavily wrinkled, but the life and the joy in her eyes were absolutely stunning. "You've done a hell of a job with her," he noted.

"I was trying to use it to demonstrate the frames and how I set up pictures. It's not always easy, but I try to do something to accent the image itself," she explained, with quiet pleasure. "Though I don't always succeed."

He shook his head. "It's really beautiful. I haven't seen such work before. … I'm really surprised. Stunned actually. This is pretty spectacular."

She beamed. "Thanks. My grandmother wasn't happy when I did it, but she often would look at it and would say that I was really talented. But then somehow it seemed to make her very sad."

"Maybe because she knew that your talent in art wouldn't flourish, not if she was the one with her foot on the brake, keeping you in the business as an embalmer."

"I certainly went to school and became what she wanted. However, if I had a choice, would I do it differently now? Yeah, probably. But because that experience was so tied into my life with her, I wouldn't change a thing. She was the reason for my getting out of bed in the morning."

"I'm sure she knew that," he said gently.

"I don't know if she did. Toward the end, things had gotten pretty bad between her and my dad. The fighting was out of hand, and things were getting rough," she explained. "It had gotten quite difficult to get up and go into that drama every day, but I did because of her."

"Of course," he agreed. "I suppose that's another reason your mother has been looking at leaving for a long time."

"Probably, and even more so since my grandmother died and now that my father has become even more unstable."

"Seriously now, is he wacky unstable or dangerous unstable?" he asked, turning to look at her.

"You've asked me that before, and I still don't know how to answer that question. I mean, you saw him yourself."

"I did, and nothing was terribly positive about it," he muttered. "He did threaten to kill you, after all."

She stared at him, then shrugged. "Sad to say, I'm used to it. That's who he is. I don't think there's anything sick or really dangerous about him. Yet, at the same time, he and my grandmother used to get into some fights that were pretty bad. Sometimes we weren't exactly sure if everybody would be alive at the end of it. Yes, I've also known people where that dynamic was a normal part of their lifestyle or some people whose family would even get into real physical fights. They were all used to it, as part of their family culture, and nobody really thought anything of it."

"What did you think of it growing up?"

"Oh, I hated it," she said. "Oftentimes my grandmother would pull herself back and would put herself under tighter control because my sister and I were around, and she didn't want us exposed to it. We did talk about it sometimes, and I told her how I hated it. She always apologized, saying it's not how she wanted us to see her. But sometimes Dad would purposely do things that would just enrage her." Tasmin sighed. "The only thing I could think of was that, at times, they were more alike than either one of them would care to admit."

∽

ABOUT AN HOUR later Hanson got up, walked around, and asked, "How late are you staying here?"

Tasmin shrugged. "I don't know. I'm done with my work. I guess I'm half expecting my sister to call, asking me to go to work down there."

He stopped and stared.

She nodded. "I know. I need to get out of here before she does, but it has become my routine, you know?"

"Then her taking advantage of you is also a habit," he declared. "As much as I want to like your grandmother, I don't feel as if she was the best person to look after you."

She frowned at him. "Why would you say that?" she asked, astonished.

"Because she also worked you to the bone, and she instilled this work ethic in you and then let everybody else take advantage of you. You were already primed for that because of her. That's the hardship. I recognize that you were joyous and happy to be there and to help her, and you were doing it because you thought it was your industry, but nothing is stopping you from walking away from it now, … except you."

She winced.

"And you wouldn't even think anything about that, except for the fact that you've been called in so much recently. If they'd even given you a reasonable break or were making some effort to get someone else or to pay you or both, then it might be different."

"I have to go down there anyway to get through the next stage and rinse the preservation pieces I've got there."

"Okay. And what about dinner?"

"What about dinner?" she asked, then looked at the clock and winced.

Hanson snorted. "You mean, the fact that it's well past six p.m., and you still haven't locked your shop door?"

She shrugged. "I don't know. I guess I was thinking that you were still here, so it must still be the workday."

"In the meantime, I've already gone upstairs and taken a bunch of measurements, while you were on the phone. So now I can get some better prices for you. I took a few measurements before to get an idea of the layout but not enough to make an estimate."

"Oh, good." She smiled, as she stared up at the loft. "Then sometimes I think I'd be better off to not stay here."

"Believe me. I've thought about that too," he replied. "But still you lease this place, right?"

She nodded. "I do."

"Maybe these upgrades would save you a rent payment or two. You can check with the owner. Plus, have you ever considered …"

"Considered what?" she asked, looking over at him.

"Have you ever considered just leaving here, like changing states?"

"I've considered it," she admitted, "but this is home. I don't know any other place."

"I get that," he said. "I mean, that's why I came here, just looking for a new beginning."

"And yet that didn't work out all that great for you, did

it?"

He chuckled. "Not as well as I might have hoped, no."

"Are you getting along any better with the guys at work?"

He just gave a noncommittal shrug and knew from the flash in her gaze that she understood.

"We'll always be on the outside, won't we?" she asked, as she walked around to the front of the store.

"I don't know," he told her. "Maybe, yet maybe it doesn't matter."

"Yeah, I've been trying to get myself to that point," she shared. "I'm not there yet."

He chuckled. "Not sure any of us are." He looked around at her store. "Do you have to do anything here?"

"No, just make sure the security system is on and grab my to-go cup and my purse."

"Good. How long do you need at the funeral home?"

She pondered that. "Maybe half an hour."

"Even better," he said. "Then how about we go for dinner afterward?"

She stopped, looked at him, and then asked in a teasing voice, "So, is this a date?"

He chuckled. "I'm okay to call it a date, if you are."

"I think I am." She smiled. "Give me a second." She dashed into the back room, while he waited out front. She came back out with her purse and her lidded coffee cup in hand. "I would call to make sure that my father wasn't there, but a part of me says I'd be better off to just sneak in downstairs, take care of the projects I have to deal with, then come back out, hopefully without seeing *anybody*."

"Sounds good to me," he said.

She looked at their vehicles and asked, "Am I driving?"

"Nope, I am."

"Don't you have more work to do?"

"I've already done quite a few hours of it already. I've got searches being done as we speak, and I've got a bunch of information that I'm waiting for. I was hoping to snag a meal in the meantime because it doesn't seem that I'll be getting any downtime tonight."

"Right, that makes sense."

"Yep, and, while there's a case happening, I pretty much have to grab a little food and sleep whenever I can."

"Got it," she murmured. "Let's go then."

Once they got to the funeral home, she quickly headed downstairs and let herself in, smiling when she realized that, once again, the place was completely empty. She wondered how they were even handling the business as it was. As she worked, Hanson dealt with emails and phone calls while he waited.

She walked over to him and announced, "Okay, I'm ready. Let's go eat!"

He hopped to his feet. "Good timing. I'm pretty sure my stomach wouldn't last much longer."

She smiled and nodded. "A good burger joint is around the corner."

"I can do that." He looked around the funeral home. "It's pretty quiet when they shut it down, isn't it?"

"It's very quiet when they shut it down, unless somebody, like me, is working in the basement."

"I guess you're just not scared of the dark or the dead, are you?"

"Not anymore. When I was a child, I was, but, after I started to get comfortable with this work, I realized that not only is there nothing to be afraid of in the dark but that the dead are far more harmless than the living."

"Can't argue with you there," he stated and led the way to the burger joint.

CHAPTER 18

TASMIN LET HERSELF back into her shop and stopped for a moment to stretch before she got busy. Hanson had dropped her off and headed back to his office. He didn't like anything about her sleeping on the floor at her shop, but it was all she had at the moment, so he wouldn't argue with it. She planned to get a bunch more paperwork done in the meantime, unaccustomed to having free hours in the evening.

As she walked into the back, she put on the teakettle, choosing tea rather than coffee, and heard a weird buzz. She turned to look around, but nothing was there, except that odd sense that she wasn't alone.

She stopped, looked around again, and called out softly, "Hello?"

Immediately Nanny asked, "So, what did you eat for dinner this time?"

She smiled. "I had a burger."

The other woman sniffed. "Hardly the healthiest choice."

"No, but it's better than not eating at all," Tasmin argued.

"Maybe."

"How was everything while I was gone?"

Only silence came.

Of course Tasmin understood that but didn't like it a whole lot. She was hoping that one day these ghosts would tell her something useful, but it rarely happened. As a matter of fact, she couldn't think of a single point in time when one had.

As she waited for the teakettle to boil, she wandered around her place, thinking about Hanson's suggestion that she leave town. What would she do? In theory, she could still do the same work, but people here knew her, knew what she did, which was both good and bad. At least she didn't have to explain it to people. But knowing that the funeral home wouldn't ever be hers, was she okay to be the bigger person and not have that come between her and her sister, or would Tasmin have to put a stop to it?

When the teakettle boiled, she quickly made a cup of tea, then walked over to her workbench. Just as she sat down, her phone rang. It was her sister, Lorelei. "Hey, Lorelei. What's up?"

She asked, "Have you been in the shop tonight?"

"I'm in my shop right now, if that's what you mean."

"No, like downstairs here."

"Sure. I was there a bit ago before dinner. Why?"

There was another silence. "Did you leave the door open?"

"No, of course not," she said, "I locked it up, like I always do."

"Are you sure?" her sister asked.

"Yes, I'm sure. Why would you ask?"

"Because it's open, and I don't know why."

"What are you doing there at this time of night?"

"I'm not there, but the cops just called me," she said.

"What?"

"Yeah, and I don't know what I'm supposed to say to them, except that you were the last one in or out, and I presume you left it unlocked."

"Why were they called?"

"A passerby supposedly," she replied, her voice doubtful.

"Okay, that doesn't sound very possible."

"I'm not sure either way," her sister said.

Tasmin asked again, "So you are not at the funeral home right now?"

"God no, you know I won't go there at nighttime."

"So, what? So you want me to go check to make sure everything's okay?"

"Yeah, that would be perfect, thanks." And, with that, her sister rang off, not giving Tasmin a chance to say anything.

She pinched the bridge of her nose and muttered, "Shit."

Ignoring her hot cup of tea, she locked up, walked out to her car, and raced to the funeral home, heading around to the back. Sure enough, the door was open. As in wide open. No cops were around; there was nothing to see. Frowning, she walked down into the lower levels and did a full search. She felt the hairs on the back of her neck rising, but absolutely nothing was amiss that she could see here. It made no sense at all.

She had definitely locked up, and she knew it because she had Hanson right there, reminding her. This made no sense, so who the hell had been here? As she wandered through, she checked to make sure her pieces were safe, and thankfully they were. Of course they weren't exactly out on display because of the way that they were being preserved, so nobody would know they were even here anyway. And considering the recent break-ins and drive-by shootings, that made her feel somewhat better. But, at the same time, it was all a little too bizarre.

She phoned Hanson, and, when he answered, he sounded distracted. "What's up?"

"I'm back at the funeral home," she explained. "My sister phoned and said that the cops had contacted her about a potential break-in."

"What? Really?"

"Yeah, but I don't see any cops here, and there isn't any—I mean, yes, the door was unlocked and opened, which is already weird, and I don't know what to think of that, but I'm here now, and the place is empty."

"I'm on my way," he snapped. "Don't do anything."

"I wasn't planning on it, but I would like to know why no cops are here, and, if they were here and left, who was it and what did they see?"

"I'll see if I can find the report, but I'm on the way to you now."

"You don't have to come," she said, walking toward the downstairs entrance. "I'm just leaving. However, I'll lock up again and try to figure out just what happened."

"And nobody's there?" Hanson asked. "No sign of *anybody* there?"

"No, nothing." She headed over to the stairs and added, "I've locked the other rooms, and I'm just heading to the stairs to go outside."

He swore at that. "You could just wait for somebody to come along and help, you know?"

"I don't know what you could do. Besides, this is the thing that I always had to do anyway."

After a moment of silence, he asked, "What do you mean?"

"I mean, we had an incident, a series of incidents, where the doors were always opening and closing, even though they were locked."

"Such as ghosts?"

"You know nobody here will listen to that talk," she replied, with a note of laughter.

"Maybe not, but considering all the weird things going on right now, I'm not comfortable with you being there alone right now."

"You might not be comfortable with it, but this has been my life for a very long time. So it's not exactly something I'll stop doing," she explained. "And, speaking of which, I'm now outside, and I'm locking up the door." With that done, she said, "There, okay? Did you hear that *click*?"

"Yes, is that the door lock?"

"It is, and now I'm walking over to my car."

"Okay, but I won't relax until you get into that car."

"Even if I get in the car, that's still not exactly a free pass home."

"Ah, jeez, don't say it that way. Remember all these drive-by shootings."

"Hey, I didn't mean it that way," she clarified. "I just don't want to start freaking out when this is something I've been doing all my life."

"And I get that, but I haven't been, and it's not my life right now that I'm worried about."

"I'm not particularly worried about mine right now," she murmured. "As far as I'm concerned, everything's good."

All of a sudden there was a loud *crack*, followed by silence.

He cried out, "What was that?"

She looked around and muttered, "I'm not sure."

"Are you in your vehicle?"

"Just about," she said, picking up the pace. "Okay, it's just up ahead." She quickly unlocked it with the button on her keypad, then jumped inside. "Now I'm inside." And she slammed the door shut, but it wouldn't lock. "And it's not locking."

"Why not?"

Then she heard a voice in the back seat.

"Shit," she cried out, just as a hand slapped over her face, and she knew no more.

∼

HANSON DROPPED EVERYTHING and raced out to his vehicle, screaming into the phone, "What's going on? What's going on? Are you there?"

When a *click* sounded in his ear, he knew something even worse had just happened. He bolted out of the parking lot and raced toward the funeral home. It was the longest ten minutes of his life, and, when he got there, he pulled into the parking lot and parked diagonally behind her vehicle. As he raced around, he noted the driver's side door was open, and her purse was on the seat, but there was no sign of her.

He swore, spinning around in a circle, looking to see if she'd been dragged off somewhere. Thankfully he'd called for backup as he drove, so, just as he turned around, a black-and-white pulled in. He quickly identified himself and explained what happened.

As he phoned for additional backup, the first two officers started a full search around the perimeter. He raced to check the door to the building she had just locked, and, sure enough, it was unlocked now. Feeling the hairs rising on the back of his neck once again, he opened it, running inside and down the stairs.

He didn't know if they had any security system going off or how anybody had even known that this door was open because this door could not be casually seen from the outside. Being a basement door, it was below ground level. Somebody had to park in the parking lot and come onto the property and around to this door in order to see if anybody had opened it.

As far as he was concerned, that meant one thing. ... It was all a setup to get her here. He raced down the stairs through the double doors and froze. Tasmin was strapped to the embalming table, at each of her ankles and her wrists. She was slowly turning her head from side to side. He raced up and quickly worked on releasing the straps. "Hey, are you okay? Are you okay?"

He called out to the cops who were outside searching, screaming at them to come down. One immediately popped into the door, took one look, and raced to his side.

"Check the rest of the building," Hanson yelled. "I've got her, but we need an ambulance."

At that, he pulled out his phone, and the cop took off. Calling in for an ambulance, he stayed at her side, gently waking her up.

When she opened her eyes and stared at him, he murmured, "Easy, don't move."

She blinked hard and then asked, "Why not?"

He winced. "Because you won't feel very well."

She groaned, closed her eyes, and winced. "What happened?"

"Last I knew, you were on the phone with me, when you got into your car. Then you shrieked, and everything went quiet. I don't know if you're ready to open your eyes and to move, but you need to understand where you are right now."

She opened her eyes, gazed around the room, and back to him in a jerk. "Good God, I'm in the embalming room."

He nodded slowly. "Yeah, and you were strapped down on one of your own gurneys," he added.

She slowly sat up and took a look, her face paling. "Jesus. What's going on?"

"That's the question I'd like you to answer," he said, his voice harsh. "I don't know what game somebody is playing at here, but this is an image I don't want to see ever again."

She looked over at him. "Yeah, you and me both," she replied, with feeling. "I don't know. I remember talking to you on the phone, and then—" She closed her eyes, as if trying to remember something. "Something was slapped over my face. Something smelly."

He nodded. "Seems somebody drugged you."

"And what? Picked me up and brought me down here?"

"The door was unlocked again," he told her.

She sucked in her breath. "I locked it. I locked it," she repeated. "You heard it, remember?"

"Oh, I believe you. I'm just not sure what's going on here."

She slowly sat up, kicked her legs off the side, then, using the metal table and his arm for support, she slid to the floor. "I can't say I feel all that great," she muttered, her tone turning wheezy. He caught her just as she fell, and she gazed up at him. "Oh, wow."

"I've got an ambulance on the way," he said. "Just relax."

She shook her head. "I'm not sure it's that easy."

"It is that easy," he replied.

He scooped her up into his arms and carried her outside into the fresh air. "Now that you're out here, just try to breathe, slow and steady, try to take some deep breaths and clear your head."

She obeyed, and he heard the reassuring gulping of fresh air, as she tried to exchange the oxygen in her lungs. "I don't know what that was all about," she muttered. "What the hell is going on here? None of this had anything to do with me before."

"What do you mean *before*?"

She looked up at him and blinked. "I don't know. I'm not sure what I'm saying."

"We'll have a talk about it, as soon as we get your head clear," Hanson declared. "Obviously something's going on here, and I'm not exactly sure what, but I'll find out."

CHAPTER 19

ALMOST IN SLOW motion Tasmin surfaced, her body very slow to respond, as if she were coming out of very deep, sleep. Almost instantly, she heard a voice at her side.

"Take it easy, and don't move too quickly. You've been hurt."

She opened her eyes, stared around the room, and, sure enough, there was Hanson.

"Hey," she whispered. "Wow, I don't know what they gave me, but, man, I'm still so groggy."

"And you're likely to be that way for a little while," noted another brisker voice at her side.

She shifted her gaze ever-so-slightly to look at a man in a white coat. She asked, "Are you the doctor?"

"I am. I'm disappointed you don't recognize me."

She frowned at that but felt instant relief when she saw the white-coated man leave. She turned to Hanson. "Where am I?"

At that, Hanson replied, "I hate to say it, but we're at Bellevue."

Her gaze opened wide, and she stared at him in horror.

He nodded.

"What happened?"

"The ambulance transporting you to the main hospital was redirected here," he explained, his voice hard. "And believe me. I've had a hell of a fight ever since, trying to get you proper treatment."

"What time is it? How long have I been here?" she asked.

"It's late in the evening."

She swallowed and reached out a hand. He responded, clasping it gently. "Get me out of here," she said, her own voice hard.

"I'm working on it," he reassured her. "I'm not sure how my orders to get you to the main hospital were countermanded, but it appears that someone didn't worry too much about paperwork."

She blinked several times, but all she could think about was her overwhelming fear of this place. "I have to get out of here, Hanson. Now."

He gripped her hand and in a very low tone said, "You need to get control of yourself. I know why you're feeling the panic, and I get it. I'm trying to find a legal way to stop this, but the bottom line is, if they think you're panicking unnecessarily, they'll sedate you. Once they start that, I won't have as much recourse because they'll present you as unstable."

She swallowed hard several times but definitely understood what he was saying. She nodded. "As long as you don't leave me. Really. Please don't leave me."

"I'm not going anywhere," he declared, then looked around. "The doctor is gone for the moment, but he'll be back."

"How do I get away from him?" she asked, her voice harsh. She looked down and gasped. "I'm naked under this hospital gown."

"It seems to be one of the first things they do, isn't it?"

Hanson agreed.

"Yes, they immediately try to make you uncomfortable and feel like a victim."

He nodded, then didn't say anything, as he glanced around. "I don't know how much of this is connected," he said, but then he stopped and walked over to the window.

"Are we on the first floor?" she asked.

"We are. Why?"

"Good. Can you open the window?" she asked.

He stared at her. "Really?"

"Oh yeah, you don't understand. They will never let me out of here."

He shook his head. "I don't understand."

"No, but he's doing all kinds of testing, and believe me. Now that Dr. Bellevue knows that I'm back here again, it'll be absolutely brutal."

"What kind of testing?" he asked, his voice hard.

"Abilities," she whispered in a hoarse voice. "Believe me. You do not want to be here either."

He felt the immediate fear encroaching in his throat too. He looked at the window, tried to open it, and shook his head. She got up, threw back the covers, and grabbed onto the side of the bed, even as the room swayed around her.

"Take it easy," he warned, rushing to her side.

"Hell no," she muttered. "You don't understand."

"No, but I'm starting to," he added. "We need to get you out of here, and we need to get you out fast."

"Yeah? However, unless you've got another way to get me out of here, the only way is through that front door."

"And you won't get out the front door without clothes."

"I know. Any chance of getting my clothes?"

He opened all the cupboards but found no sign of any.

"See if you can find me a nurse's outfit, scrubs, something, even lost and found. Steal something, anything you can," she suggested. "Please."

"I have to leave you for that."

"Go ahead. I'll use the bathroom and see if I can come up with a solution to this. But if you see anybody come in here, you run back. If nothing else, you arrest me for whatever charge you think you need to arrest me for, but you get me out of here."

He gave her a startled look, and then he booked it.

∽

HANSON HEADED DOWN the main walkway, to reception, and there he asked for her clothes.

The receptionist looked at him, then shook her head. "She can't leave, not until she gets clearance from the doctor," she explained.

"That's not happening," he declared calmly. "She's my prisoner. I'm a detective." He pulled out his badge.

She startled and mumbled, "What?"

"Yes, and right now I want to know why she was brought here in the first place. I'm getting her back again, one way or another. So you get me her damn clothes, or I'll bring the law down on this place and do a full assessment as to what's going on here."

"What are you talking about?" she asked. "We didn't do anything illegal."

"Yes, you did," he snapped. "And believe me. I'll get to the bottom of it. You can count on that. She's being detained without her permission, after I ordered her to be sent to a hospital for treatment for her injuries after being attacked. No way in hell you're getting away with keeping her here."

The other woman protested, but he shot her a look and demanded, "Clothes. Now."

She subsided and started punching buttons on the phone.

He walked over, put his hand over the phone. "That doctor will be up on his own charges very quickly," he declared in as pissed-off of a voice as he could muster. "So you just make sure you decide which side of this you'll be on. That woman was detained without her rights being honored and directly against police orders, so you think fast and decide where you stand in all this."

She swallowed and looked at him, then he nodded.

"Make the right decision."

She got up, walked to a series of lockers, and pulled out a bag with Tasmin's personal belongings in it.

"Good. Now I'll walk her past here, and we'll go right out that door. Do you hear me?"

She nodded slowly. "He won't like it."

"No, he won't, but he's also threatened and attacked her, and now he's infringed on her personal freedoms against her will and interfered in a police action. Believe me. We'll have an awful lot to say about that."

Snatching the bag from her hand, Hanson asked, "What's your name?"

She swallowed.

He repeated, "Your name?"

She gave it to him. Susan Miller was possibly her correct name. He didn't know at this point, but he wanted something to come back on her with.

"Remember. If you don't know my name yet, you'll definitely know it after today." His tone was hard, as he slapped his card down in front of her, so she could see his detective status. She almost looked relieved when she did.

"Yeah, I'm not lying, but you can sure as hell bet an awful lot of shit is going on in this place that's not legal."

She looked up fearfully, and he turned to look behind him, heard doors slamming shut. He turned and walked back over to the room where Tasmin was. The room appeared empty, until he called out. She opened the bathroom door, and he handed over her clothes. "Hurry up. Time is of the essence."

She didn't waste a moment, dropping her hospital gown and quickly dressing in front of him, rather than take an extra moment to disappear behind the door. As soon as she was dressed, she walked beside him.

He wrapped his arm around her and said, "We're going straight out that front door, do you hear me?"

She nodded. "You realize that, if you weren't here with me, no way I'd be getting out of here, right?"

"Yeah, I'm starting to realize that. It's pissing me off more and more."

"Yeah, well, if anybody gets on your wrong side, it'd be nice to know somebody was there to help bail you out."

"And, if we get further into trouble, we'll have to get Stefan's help, but, for now, let's get you out of this place."

As they walked to the front door, she looked over at the nurse, who even now hid behind the counter. "Why is she hiding?"

"So she doesn't have to admit that she saw us," Hanson guessed. "I've already terrorized her into letting us out of here."

"Good, I didn't do anything to merit this."

"No, and you don't have to put up with this shit."

At the front door, he pushed it wide open, and she quickly raced through. As it snapped behind him, he could hear her take a deep break of relief. "Can we get out of here right away?"

"Yeah, we're going to my car right there."

As they headed toward the car, a shout came from behind them. He walked her to the car and let her in. As he turned around, the doctor raced to catch up with them. He pulled out his shield and held it up in the doctor's face, when he got there.

"She's coming with me," Hanson stated, his tone as hard as rock. "And, if you ever bother her again, you better have court orders and lawfully filed papers giving you the right, and even then you'll have to come through me."

"No, no, you don't understand," the doctor wailed. "She needs to be here."

"She does not. Not only does she *not* need to be here, she's no longer allowed to be under your care. Do you hear me?"

"You have no right to take her from me," he cried out, almost in tears, stamping his feet.

"Did you have anything to do with the way she was brought here?"

He stopped, as if trying to figure out how he should answer.

At that, Hanson glared at him. "If I find out that you did, I'll shut down this place faster than you can turn around."

"No, no, no, of course I didn't. I don't know what you're talking about."

At that, Hanson snorted. "I don't believe you, you lying piece of shit."

"No, you don't understand."

"No, I don't understand. Why was that ambulance redirected here, when she needed proper medical attention from being attacked?"

"But she wasn't attacked," the doctor argued, with a bright smile on his face. "See? That's what I mean. She needs to be here because she makes all this shit up."

At that Hanson stared at him and took one step forward.

The doctor immediately backed up.

Hanson grabbed his phone and brought up a photograph. "She did not make it up. I'm the one who was there, along with four other cops. I'm the one who found her tied up in the basement of that funeral home. This is evidence," he said, moving his phone closer to the doctor's face. "So unless you're planning on charging me with being unstable, I highly suggest you back that fat ass of yours right up again and let me out of here. I will be opening a full investigation into what happened and how you managed to redirect the ambulance. When I get to the bottom of it, you better hope that I like the answers. Otherwise there'll be hell to pay."

And, with that, he pulled open his driver's side door, hopped in, turned on the engine, and backed up. The doctor stared at him in shock, then pulled out his phone and start making phone calls.

"I wish I knew who he was calling," she muttered.

"Who do you think he's calling?"

"I don't know, but somebody's playing games with my life, and I really don't appreciate it." He drove silently for a while. "Where are we going?" she asked him.

"To my place," he muttered.

"Oh." She sank back. "Any particular reason why?"

"Yeah, because otherwise I won't get any sleep tonight,

worrying about where you are and who'll attack you next," he snapped.

She chuckled. "I'm not saying no, and I have to admit that I appreciate the fact that you're concerned. Waking up in *that* scary place is not an experience I want to go through ever again."

"Are you kidding? I can't imagine anyone ever wanting to see the inside of that place again."

"No, it's definitely hell on earth to be there, and, as you can tell, everybody is pretty well traumatized by him."

"Yeah, you're not kidding. How is that even allowed?"

"I don't know that anything is allowed, but he pretty well runs the show."

"But who arranged for that ambulance to be redirected?"

"I presume it was probably him," she guessed. "I don't know who else would have. I was sitting here, trying to think about that."

"It's not tonight's issue," he declared. "At least not at the moment. Let's get you home, get some sleep, and get this night over with. I want to make sure your head is okay, and now I'm a little worried about sending you anywhere in an ambulance."

"Ya think? I didn't really think ambulances were something I needed to be terrified of, but apparently I do."

He pulled into his parking spot at the apartment, hopped out, and then said, "I get that you think of this town as your home, but have you really considered all the crap that happens to you here?"

"I know, and, every time something like this happens, I have to rethink it. I mean, I have connections. I thought I had friends, but I'm starting to wonder if what I really have is mostly enemies."

"Not to mention the fact that your family is definitely on the weird side too." He led the way to his apartment, and, as he unlocked it, he nudged her forward in front of him.

She yawned, as she headed inside. "I can't keep taking your bed though. You need to sleep too."

"I do. I didn't get any last night," he muttered. "And this is just even more insane."

"I know, and I can't have you babysitting me all the time. You've got a job to do, and so do I."

"Yeah, it's starting to become a problem."

"What, me?" she asked, turning to look at him.

He shook his head and smiled. "Not you, as in you're the problem. Just that I keep thinking about you, where are you, and if you're okay," he shared.

She shook her head. "You don't have to worry about me. You know that, right?"

He stared at her, one eyebrow raised.

She flushed. "Yeah, okay, I'm grateful for your help, but I don't want you to ruin your life or your job because of my life being a mess."

"Wouldn't it be nice to think we could compartmentalize our emotions so easily," he stated, "but I've never found a way to do it. Have you?"

She winced. "No, I guess not."

"Right. So why don't we just shelve this conversation for the night. It's late, and you're still under the effects of whatever they used on you. So let's get you to bed, and I'll crash and try and get some sleep, before I get called out on another job."

"Right, the drive-by shootings."

"Right. All affecting your friends and people associated with the industry."

"And that sucks too." She rolled over, twisting up on the bed. "This is a huge bed. Just get in here beside me."

He hesitated.

She looked over at him and shook her head. "Look. Even if you did have any amorous ideas, I'm not in any condition to do anything but lie here and piss you off," she admitted. "So, don't even think about it. Let's both get some sleep for a change."

"Didn't you sleep last night?" he asked in a conversational tone.

She blinked at him. "I don't remember. Obviously the drugs are affecting me more than I thought."

He nodded. "I'll go grab a shower. You sleep, but take off a layer at least. Otherwise you won't sleep well."

∽

AS SOON AS Hanson disappeared into the shower, Tasmin got up, stripped off her bra and pants, put on her T-shirt again, and just curled up under the covers. She could hope that she would sleep as easily as she wanted to, but every time she closed her eyes, she kept seeing the damn Bellevue doctor.

It bothered her a lot that she had ended up there and that, even now, he was still trying to get her back to that place. It made no sense, except that he obviously felt she had some abilities that he wanted to tap into. And who would have told him? Who in their right mind would have let some psycho like that even know about it?

And, of course, the only person who came to mind was her father. He'd been the one to arrange the psychiatric testing in the first place. She hated to think that he might have set this all into play, but how could she not think about it?

So many things were going wrong in her world right now—and in Hanson's too, if she thought about it. For the first time she wondered if any of it could be connected. Was somebody targeting her because of him? Was somebody targeting him because of her? Was any of this related in some way to Pinch's customers? That theory just broke her heart. To think that other people were dying for somebody's sick motivation was enough to keep Tasmin wide awake as she lay here, listening to Hanson shower.

When he came back out and saw her still awake, he noted, "You're supposed to be asleep."

"I hoped I would be," she muttered, "but I kept thinking about connections."

He had a towel wrapped around his hips, but that was all he wore. He smelled masculine, with a wonderful aftershave scent that made her nose tingle.

"I don't know what you've used for an aftershave, but it smells really good."

He shrugged. "Just a fresh-scented one."

"I like it," she said.

"When you say, *connections*," he began, reverting to the previous subject of this conversation, "what did you mean?"

"Just the connections between you and me, as to whether I have anything to do with the troubles in your world or if you have anything to do with the troubles in mine. Or whether either of us has anything to do with the troubles in Pinch's world."

He pondered that, as he grabbed a pair of boxers, which he quickly slipped on, completely comfortable in front of her, as he tossed the towel up over the open door. He walked into the kitchen, presumably to check on the locks and the windows. Then he came back and stretched out beside her on the bed.

"I don't know," he admitted. "I've been wondering the same thing. I just don't see how. Everything is so disjointed. It doesn't mean that it's not related. I don't understand how or why it could or would be all connected, but I have to wonder. And honestly, having it be connected isn't any more farfetched than having all this stuff happening randomly without a connection."

"I know, right?" Tasmin sighed. "It's hard not to see a connection here, even if it's only because we're all having such trouble. And yet yours is work, Pinch's is clients, and me, well, hell, it's my personal life," she noted.

"So that's your creative side, your career, *and* your personal life. What's that? The trifecta of the world. The only other thing would be a relationship," he added.

"In that case, our relationship would come into that too," she said, rolling over to look at him.

He nodded. "I don't know if it works for you to close your eyes and to ask to have answers when you wake up," he mentioned, "but, if it does, I highly suggest you do that. And, if I'm not here when you wake up in the morning, it's because I've been called out on another job."

"I hope it won't be another drive-by," she muttered. "We're getting way too many of those."

"Yep, we sure are," he mumbled, as his voice started to drift away softly.

"You sleep," she said. "Just rest. We'll get to the bottom of this somehow." She patted his back. "Now it's time for you to sleep."

He smiled, linking his fingers with hers, and he drifted deeper and deeper, as she watched. And, just like that, he was under, his breathing deep, heavy, rhythmical, right before her eyes.

"I don't know how you did that," she muttered to herself, "but I think I'm jealous."

Resolutely she closed her eyes and finally joined him in sleep.

∽

HANSON WOKE TO his phone ringing. He reached over, took it off the charger, and grumbled a response. It was the dispatcher.

"You've got another drive-by shooting," she said, her voice almost tart, as if blaming him for it.

He groaned, as he got out of bed. "Give me the address." He turned to look where Tasmin slept soundly beside him.

Noting the address, he replied, "Contact Mark."

"Already have," she confirmed. "He's the one who told me to call you."

He laughed at that. "Good enough." He dressed quickly, grabbed his keys, and, with one last look at Tasmin, let himself out of the apartment and locked it behind him. The last thing he wanted was to have her disturbed by somebody coming in after her. The fact that somebody already did in the first place was enough to shake him up. He knew it would be a long time before he got rid of the nightmare of the ambulance completely redirected to a place he had not expected.

And, once he'd realized what had happened, he'd managed to get there at the same time and had stuck with her the whole way. He'd been looking for documentation to show where and how the ambulance drivers had been directed there, since they both looked at him blankly and reported that's what their orders had been. Now it would be a chase to figure out how and why.

But it needed to happen because somehow somebody was after her, and Hanson had to put a stop to it. Otherwise there would be no peace for either of them. And, with that, he drove to the scene of the crime. As he got out of his car, it was still early in the morning, not quite 4:30 a.m., and that bothered him. This wasn't exactly the time of day you would expect to have a drive-by shooting.

The cops were keeping people behind the crime scene tape. Even this early in the morning, a few had gathered here and were observing the nightmare. Hanson walked up to one of the cops and asked, "Do we have a time frame?"

"Yeah, just about forty minutes ago now," he replied. "I'm one of the witnesses."

Hanson raised an eyebrow at him.

The cop nodded and pointed to the little gas station store on the corner. "I was going in there to get a coffee and a few snacks," he explained, patting his very ample girth. "When I came out and got to my vehicle, I saw it all happen."

"Do we know who the victim is?"

"A young woman just getting off work at the same store," he replied. "She can't be more than twenty-one."

"Damn," Hanson muttered. "And there's just the one victim?"

"Yes, just one."

Hanson shook his head at that. "And that breaks the MO too."

The cop frowned at him.

Hanson explained, "The other recent drive-by shootings have all been in pairs."

"I don't know if he's breaking MO or not, but this asshole needs to be stopped. That's Jenny, Jenny Cleavers. She's just a kid, and she won't even have a life now and can't grow up, for crying out loud," he muttered. "What the hell is this world coming to? If it had been five minutes later, it could have been me," he added, staring down at the body.

"You don't fit the profile in this case," Hanson argued, "but who knows about the next one." He stepped forward, rearranged the angle of the poor woman, so he could take a better look at the woman's face. As he waited for the coroner to come, Hanson quickly snapped a photo. Just as he did, he heard the vehicles arrive.

The coroner took one look at him and glared. "Another drive-by?"

He nodded. "Yeah, another one." Hanson studied the photo he took. "This one's just a kid."

"They were all just kids," the coroner replied in disgust. "Even the mother was young."

As the coroner bent down to take a closer look, he noted, "Single bullet to the chest."

Hanson asked, "You know what I really need to know?"

"What?" the coroner asked, looking back at him.

"Does she have any tattoos?"

"You think it's connected?" the coroner asked, his brows furrowing.

"Three others all are, and we're checking into the rest. So, yes, I think it's connected."

The coroner did a quick check and then lifted up her shirt on her back. "That would be a yes on this one."

Hanson noted a fairly fresh tattoo because it was still red and not fully healed. "Crap," he said, sitting back on his heels, as he looked at it. He quickly took a photo of it. "I might even know the artist. I'll check it out. Let me know anything as soon as you can."

"Not a whole lot to tell you right now."

"I know," Hanson muttered.

"Cause of death, gunshot to the chest. TOD, about an hour ago. I've already got an ID," the coroner stated.

"I'm on it."

And with that, Hanson hopped to his feet and headed down to Pinch's shop. He didn't know if Pinch was the same as Tasmin and lived on the premises, but, as far as Hanson was concerned for everybody else, the night was already over.

CHAPTER 20

TASMIN WOKE WITH a start. She sat up and looked around, but Hanson's side of the bed was empty. She knew instinctively that the apartment was vacant as well. She threw back the covers and padded to the living room and double-checked just to confirm it. She quickly found the coffeepot and put on some coffee, not even considering whether it was something she should do or not. She figured that, by now, they were well past that point.

She sent him a quick text to let him know she was awake. She quickly jumped in the shower and came out to find her phone ringing. She snatched it off the bed. "Hey," she greeted Hanson. "What's going on?"

"I got called out for another drive-by," he said, weariness in his voice.

She winced. "Oh God, please not another one of Pinch's clients."

"I was at his shop early this morning and got him out of bed. Unfortunately it was."

She collapsed on the bed, tears welling in the corners of her eyes. "Jesus, what is going on?"

"I won't be getting any more sleep until I get that sorted out," he declared, the fatigue evident in his voice.

"Did you get any sleep last night?"

"A bit," he said.

She didn't even know what to say. "Dear God, somehow we have to stop this from happening."

"Don't I know it."

"I'm just making coffee." Then she stopped. "I guess I should be asking you if that's okay."

He snorted. "Make your coffee. We're pretty-well past all that, right? Do you remember that your car is still at the funeral home after last night?"

"Crap," she muttered. "That's all right. I'll see if I can catch a ride."

He grimaced. "Look. I'm really not all that sure about you going back there."

"Yeah, I'm not either, but I have a job that I need to go work on, two of them, and I can't leave them there for other people to destroy or to toss out or whatever they might do. I really have to be protective of these pieces, until they are finished and in the hands of the families."

"As you should be," he agreed. "I understand how they must be, as it's a part of their friend, their daughter, but we also need to talk to your sister about what she got for a report from the police last night, then try and figure out how that creepy doctor managed to get you redirected to his place."

"I know. I'm more than a little worried about heading back there myself, but, if it's just my family, I feel better about it."

"I would think you should be more worried," he stated, "because you don't necessarily want to assume this, but your father could be right in the middle of it."

"Possibly, but the last time I spoke with him, he wasn't very … contained," she replied, for lack of a better word.

"I know. That's one of the reasons I'm bringing it up.

Sorry, but I have to go."

"Yeah, that's fine. Talk to you in a bit."

She hung up, got dressed, poured herself a cup of coffee, and rummaged in his fridge, enjoying the feeling of being in an actual apartment and away from the mess that her life had become. She hadn't even mentioned anything to her family about that and presumed they thought she was living somewhere other than at the shop. But the shop was all she had, and even now she was wondering about Hanson's suggestion to leave. She just didn't know where she would go or how she'd make a living or if she would just do the same damn thing and start over again. What would it cost her to pull up stakes and leave?

She pondered that, as she made herself a couple pieces of toast, figuring that since she'd already been taking advantage of his place and his generosity, a couple pieces of toast wouldn't hurt. And, with some food in her stomach and the coffee gone, she let herself out of the apartment, locking it behind her, and headed down to the street. Phoning for an Uber, she headed to the funeral home.

When she got there, she checked over her car, relieved to find that it was still there and doing fine, then let herself into the basement of the funeral home, where she checked on her work. One of the pieces was more or less ready, and she wanted to bring it with her, so she loaded that into the car. The other piece would be a little while yet. It was bigger, thicker, so it needed more time. She'd switched out the chemicals and stretched it. With that done, she escaped from the place.

It was also weird that it was already nine o'clock, and nobody was here. Not sure what she was supposed to do about that, yet realizing it wasn't her headache nor her job anymore, she headed to her own shop and let herself in. As she walked in, there was an odd sense of let-down, as if realizing for the first time just how badly her lifestyle appeared to anybody on the outside.

Seeing it clearly for the first time, all her protests that she was doing fine fell on deaf ears, even hers. It was foolish. She was living out of her damn shop. If she put the time and money into the loft, then maybe it would make sense to be here, but was it worth the time and money to do it now and to rebuild what she had here? Or was it better to just cut her losses and leave? Not that there was all that much to cut.

Where she was based geographically didn't necessarily matter for her job. She would just fly, if need be, or pay to have the organic material flown, as with any organ donation. They were time-sensitive and had to be kept at a specific temperature, but they could be flown all across the country.

Opening up her shop, she turned the sign around, then pulled out her phone and checked her voicemail messages. She went through them first, listening to them all. With that done, she answered a few and then went to the back room and started to work on the piece she had brought back with her. She took several photographs of how she thought she should lay it out, then quickly sent it off to the clients. When the phone rang a bit later, it was the mother of the tattooed decedent, and she was in tears.

"Oh my gosh," she said, "that's so beautiful."

"I'm glad you think so," Tasmin replied, with relief. "It can be quite hard for people to see this."

"No, not at all. It's a piece of my daughter, and I get to keep it forever. To me, it's absolutely gorgeous."

"Good, I'm so glad. I wanted to discuss your preference on the color of the backing."

She hesitated, and they went over a few of the options. "Look. I'll set it up with black, and I'll set it up with this soft gray, which I think would match the gray tones in the background, and I'll send you photos of both." With that, she hung up the phone and headed off to get started.

By the time she had the photos taken and sent off, she realized the toast from Hanson's kitchen had been a long time ago. Quickly she placed an order for a couple big sandwiches and was soon back on the phone again, with the same client. By the time all the details were done, they'd arranged for the shipping date and a final payment. Then Tasmin got to work to get it all set up.

Tasmin still had quite a lot to do in order to make sure it was preserved correctly behind sealed glass, so that the air wouldn't get to it. Though, by now, the skin was absolutely nothing resembling skin but more like parchment paper. She set up the framework, laid it down gently on the soft gray matting, and secured it in place. Working with the glass, she was so intent on her work that she didn't hear anybody coming in, until her sister spoke from right behind her. She burst to her feet and twirled around in shock.

Her sister frowned at her. "Good God, are you ever jumpy."

Tasmin held a hand to her chest and closed her eyes for a moment, trying to get her heart rate and breathing back down. "God, you scared me."

"Well *sorr-rry*," her sister muttered, glaring at her. "I just came by to see if you were okay."

She looked at her and then nodded. "I'm fine. How's the funeral home?"

She shrugged. "Mom opened up this morning, so hopefully it's fine. I'm heading there now."

"How is Mom?"

"If you would talk to her, she would probably be a whole lot better."

Tasmin stared at her sister. "I don't know what that is supposed to mean. We *do* talk, and you know it."

"Yeah, but not lately. It seems I'm the only who has to handle all the family drama." She gave her sister a half smile.

"Not a bad idea that you *do* handle it," Tasmin stated, "considering it's something I had to handle for an awful long time on my own."

"Oh, cut the crap," Lorelei said, with an eye roll. "Just because you're five years older."

"Exactly. Maybe you should think about that. I'm five years older and have had five years more crap to deal with than you have." Then she turned back to her work. "Now, if you don't mind, I have to get this ready. I've got a courier coming."

"If you say so." Then Lorelei noted, "You don't seem to be at all bothered if Mom and Dad get a divorce."

"My concern is if Dad is stable enough for it," Tasmin replied, turning to look at her sister. "But seriously, Mom's been using that against me for well over a decade now."

Her sister stared at her. "You're serious, aren't you?"

"Very serious. She used to tell me all the time that, if I didn't do something, that would be the reason she packed up and left. You get very dulled to that threat after a while."

"It's new to me," Lorelei stated defiantly.

"I'm glad to hear that. It's nice to think that she didn't use that on you all the time because it does wear one down."

"I'm not sure I believe you." Lorelei stared at her sister steadily and then shrugged.

"And that's your prerogative. I'm not playing that game

anymore either."

Her sister frowned. "What do you mean? What game?"

"Whether you believe me or not, I have to do what I need to do in order to protect myself. Sometimes the BS that comes from you three is more than I care to handle."

At that, her sister flushed. "Look. Dad's been quite difficult."

"Yeah, he sure has," Tasmin agreed. "And so is Mom sometimes."

"She loves you, you know?"

"That would be a nice thought," Tasmin stated, "but I'm not so sure I really believe it. At least not anymore."

"What? You think love is temporary?"

"It's definitely temporary in some cases," Tasmin declared, frowning at her sister. "And, in their case, I'm never quite clear on what they're up to."

"I get that, I guess," Lorelei admitted. "Dad has certainly been more upset than usual."

"Any idea why?" Tasmin asked curiously.

"No, I'm not at all sure what he's upset about, but he's thinking you need to go get tested again."

She stiffened and glared at a sister.

Immediately Lorelei held up a hand. "Hey, I'm not agreeing. I'm just warning you."

"Yeah, thanks for that," she snapped, staring at her sister, wondering if she should ask Lorelei about the phone call last night. "Do you know what time the cops called you last night?"

She shook her head. "No." And then she yawned. "Look. I have to go. I need to go make sure everything is okay."

"Go, you do that. As I mentioned, I've got something

here to finish."

With that, her sister left.

At least Tasmin thought she had left. Hearing odd sounds, she turned and headed back out to the front of the store, but nothing was there, at least nothing that she could identify.

She frowned at that, turned, looked around again, and called out, "Anybody here?"

Hearing something faint and thinking it might be upstairs, she hesitantly made her way to the loft stairs and stared up.

"Anybody there?" she cried out softly again.

What really worried her was that the ghosts were absent. As in, she saw no sign of any of them. She stared up at the loft, and her instincts kicked in. Whatever the hell was up there was not good, and, if she were smart, she'd go in the opposite direction. After last night's Bellevue event, she really should get the hell out of here and call for help, before whatever the hell was up there came after her.

And, with that, she turned and booked it out the front door to the street.

∽

HANSON STARED AT Pinch. "Anything else you can tell me? Also I'll need to cross-reference everybody who was in your store when Jenny Cleavers was here."

Pinch stared at him wildly. "I can't tell you who all was in here every day," he whined. "If you would tell me ahead of time that this person was about to get murdered, maybe I would take better notice of who's here, but, because of that, I can't," he cried out in frustration.

Hanson stared at him and then gave a clipped nod.

"Look. I get that, but, at the moment, this case is obviously related to you and whatever is going on here. So, when was she here last?"

"Just yesterday." Pinch frowned. "You were here yesterday too." He pointed a finger at him. "How many people do you remember?"

At that, Hanson had to agree that it was a problem. Nobody else was in the shop yet, and he already had photocopies of the records of all their clients. Soon he would start phoning everybody to see if they had any idea who else might have been in the shop at the time.

"Cameras?" he asked Pinch.

"Yes!" Pinch exclaimed, staring at him. "We just put them in two nights ago." He walked to the back. "I'm not even really sure how to use the system yet."

Hanson followed him. "Let's get back there to yesterday's feed right now and take a look."

Pinch brought them up, and, sure enough, there were at least enough cameras to cover everybody who had been there the previous day.

"Now what we need to do," Hanson repeated, "is cross-reference everybody here to the previous days."

Pinch sat down hard on the chair. "It's just too unbelievable to think that I'm being targeted."

"Who else would be targeted in such a situation as this?"

Pinch stared at him and shook his head. "I have no idea. I … I don't know why anybody would." Then he stopped. "I had a horrible thought earlier, but it was just too horrible. So I didn't want to even voice it."

"At this point in time, all of it's horrible," Hanson stated. "So let's hear it. Go ahead."

"It just that everybody who's involved or has been murdered …" He hesitated, and then said in a rush, "We all discussed the fact that they were interested, if they died, in preserving their tattoos."

At that, Hanson froze. "Seriously?"

"Yes." Pinch looked over at him and bit his bottom lip. "That just sounded so wrong, and it didn't even make sense, but now that we're talking about similarities, I have to wonder."

"Have to wonder what?" Hanson asked cautiously.

"If somebody isn't trying to drum up business for Tasmin."

"Or trying to close your business and Tasmin's." Hanson stared at him. "Either way, you're right. That is a horrible thought."

"I know. I know, and I'm not saying that's what I'm thinking," he cried out. "But now that I have spoken it out loud …"

"It's hard not to think about, isn't it?" Hanson finished his thought for him.

Pinch nodded slowly, sinking back and looking at him. "I mean, I've known that girl for years, and she's had nothing but trouble from that family of hers. I wouldn't wish this on her at all."

At that, a woman called out from the doorway. "I'm really glad to hear you're not deliberately putting that out there to make it seem as if I'm doing this," Tasmin said, as she walked in the doorway.

Pinch stared at her. "I didn't mean it that way," he added in a rush.

"Good." Her tone was brisk and yet hard at the same time. "Because there's another aspect to this too."

"What's that?" Hanson asked, as he eyed her carefully.

She didn't appear to be too affected by last night, but something was obviously bothering her.

"Everybody who may have been here may have had something to do with a conversation in favor of preserving the tattoos," she noted. "But did you ever think that maybe it goes a little more personal than that?"

"How much more personal can you get?" Pinch cried out, staring at her. He shook his head. "Such as what?"

"Such as the fact that maybe someone wants *your* artwork preserved."

CHAPTER 21

TASMIN STARED AT her friend, knowing it would be a hard pill for Pinch to swallow, but, since he'd managed to turn the tables by creating a theory about how this was good for her business, she did feel justified in bringing up the fact that it could just as easily be about his business. And, right before her eyes, Pinch aged a decade.

She walked closer and sat down in front of him. "Talk to me," she said. "What's going on?"

He shook his head. "I have no idea," he whispered, but tears were in his eyes, and she knew that he knew more than he was saying.

"Is somebody trying to preserve your artwork?" she pressed.

"I don't know," he muttered. "Just the thought of it is enough to make me throw up."

"Yeah, that's about how I feel at the thought of somebody doing it so I had more business. Yet most everybody in my world would rather see me shut down and *not* succeed."

Pinch stared at her for a long moment, before he shook his head and asked, "Why would they want that?"

"My father absolutely detests what I'm doing. My sister wants me to work exclusively for the funeral home, and my mother just wants to bail. So there's basically no end of headaches in my world right now. None of it has to do with anybody wanting me to succeed."

"But that's BS," he cried out, staring at her. "What you're doing is a valuable service."

"I want to think so, but you also know as well as I do that it freaks out a lot of people. Including you sometimes."

Instantly he nodded. "I know. We've had quite the conversations about it. But the good news is that most people in my industry are quite positive about the concept."

"It's not them who you need to worry about. It's the people who they leave behind. They might leave their tattoos in a will to somebody, but it doesn't mean that somebody wants it," she explained. "What I'm seeing is that an awful lot of people are grossed out by the concept. Some have been very appreciative, particularly the one I finished today. She's absolutely over the moon to have a piece of her daughter back and because it looks so good. It doesn't even look like skin, and certainly not as if I just lopped a piece off her daughter." She pulled out her phone and brought up the picture that she had taken and held it up for him.

Immediately Pinch whistled. "Good God, that almost looks better than how it did on her."

"Right?" Tasmin murmured, as she stared at it. She looked over at Hanson, who came over and studied the photo.

He held out a hand. "May I see it closer?"

"Sure. It's also sitting over at my place, waiting for the courier."

"Speaking of which," Pinch began. "any reason why you're here?"

She nodded grimly. "Yeah, I thought an intruder might be at my place."

At that, Hanson stiffened and stared at her in shock.

She nodded. "Up in the loft. So, rather than go investigate, considering what's recently happened, I just booked it."

"Damn," Pinch muttered.

Hanson returned her phone. "Stay here with Pinch. Did you lock up the store?" he asked, as he walked out to the front.

She shook her head. "Honestly, I didn't even think about it. I just ran."

With that, Hanson turned and raced down the sidewalk.

She sank down beside Pinch. "Jesus Christ, Pinch, what the hell's going on in our world?"

The saddest look came to his eyes, and he shook his head. "I don't know," he muttered. "If they aren't trying to drum up business for you, is it really possible that somebody is trying to preserve my art?"

"I don't know. Or is it a case of somebody trying to destroy it, yet somehow I'm interrupting and preserving it? I just don't know. We can start to get all kinds of mixed-up motives here."

"Seems they are all mixed up," he noted. "And it sucks. All of it sucks."

"I'm right there with you on that," Tasmin agreed.

"And now you think you have somebody in your shop?"

She nodded. "I really don't know what was going on up there, but all kinds of noises weren't making me happy. So believe me, I didn't stick around."

"Yeah, I would think not," he muttered.

She looked around. "Where's Puggs?"

"He's at home. He's pretty upset. He came in this morning early, but the detective was here. When he found out what happened, he turned around, tears in his eyes, and just walked out."

"He's such a gentle soul," she murmured. "Something like this will devastate him."

"Yeah, he was pretty upset with the latest death," Pinch noted.

"And he doesn't know anything about who might be doing this?"

Pinch looked at her. "Why would he? Do you really think he knows something?"

"I'm not sure," she murmured. "I guess it was just a question, just wondering." She shrugged. "Like everything else right now, we have to explore every possibility. If he happened to know anything about it or thought he might, it would be good if we could ask him."

"You're welcome to ask Puggs whatever you like," Pinch explained, "but I can tell you right now the answer will be no. He doesn't get involved, but he's always been kind of sweet on the girls around here."

"Ah." Tasmin winced at that. "Then I'm doubly sorry for him."

"Puggs has always been here, kind of a silent background personality."

"And a big favorite with all your customers."

"He was a bigger favorite than even I understood," Pinch admitted. "And maybe it's a good thing that something like this happens. It kind of shakes us up and makes us realize who our friends are—and who they aren't, in a way."

"I guess." Tasmin sighed. "Yet it's kind of sad."

"It's all sad." He bolted to his feet, pulling at his hair. "What's going on is absolute insanity. I just don't get it. I don't understand, and I don't like it."

She waited till his outburst was over, then nodded. "Do you have any coffee?"

"Why? Don't you have any at home?"

Such a wry look was on his face that she had to laugh. "Yes, but I was just thinking it might help *you*."

"Sure, go put on a pot of coffee." He waved his arm in that general direction. "I probably have enough business to pay for at least a pot or two."

She stopped in her tracks. "That's another aspect we didn't discuss."

"What's that?"

"I mean, we're talking about preserving your art, but what about destroying your business?"

He blanched. "Yeah, I thought of that one earlier, but again I don't have any clue why someone would do this, or who would even want to. It just doesn't make any sense to me who hates me that much."

She walked into the back and put on coffee, knowing a full pot was back at her place, but she wasn't heading there anytime soon. Yet she couldn't just sit here either. With the pot dripping, she heard the door open and headed out, expecting to see Hanson, but it was another one of the tattoo artists.

With Pinch now talking with some of his artists, Tasmin tried to keep out of his business, knowing that this would be an ongoing thing all day, as everybody came in and found out what had happened. A tattoo artist, who she thought was named Kit, looked over at her, as if looking for acknowledgment.

Tasmin just nodded.

Kit shook her head, looked over at Pinch, and said, "I think I'll go home then."

"Don't you have appointments?" Pinch asked.

"Yeah. I guess I do at that. Let's take a look." She walked

over to the schedule and muttered, "Once the news filters out …"

"I don't know," Pinch said, staring out at the window, a forlorn look on his face. "It'll either make business go nuts, or it'll kill us."

"Right. Weren't you talking about heading back to California?"

He looked at Kit, then shrugged. "I was considering heading back to California."

"Really?" Tasmin asked him. "I thought you didn't like it there."

"I initially left because of several problems, and I ended up here because this was home. But, at some point in time, this no longer seems to be home. Honestly, it's leaving a very ugly taste in my mouth."

"What about your sister?"

"I don't know," he said, raising both hands. "I don't know what the hell to do about any of it."

Just then the bell on the door jangled again. All three of them turned to look, and there was his sister.

"Hey, Rosie," he said, with an affectionate smile. "How you doing?"

"I'm fine," she replied in that gentle voice of hers.

Rosie was recovering from a severe accident, that resulted in some brain trauma, but she was a sweetheart. She was very high functioning, whatever the problem was. Tasmin had never really asked for any details, but it was obvious that she was special in many ways. "Hi, Rosie," she said cheerfully.

Rosie looked at her, and her face broke into a big grin. "Tasmin." Then her voice lowered. "Did you guys hear?"

At that, Pinch nodded. "Yeah, we heard."

She stared at him. "Isn't it awful?" she asked.

"It sure is," Pinch agreed.

She just nodded, then beamed. "I smell coffee."

"I just put a pot on," Tasmin replied, with a wry look. "I was taking advantage of his generosity."

At that Pinch laughed. "Come on. It's a pot of coffee. You've brought me plenty of business."

"And ditto," Tasmin said in return. "This is just a big mess. That's what it is."

Kit looked at her and nodded. "It's beyond a mess. It's threatening our livelihood."

"I know. Mine too," Tasmin pointed out.

At that, Kit frowned at her. "You're the one who preserves the tattoos, aren't you?"

"I am," Tasmin confirmed, surprised that Kit didn't know who she was. But then why would she? It's not as if Tasmin visited Pinch at his shop all that often. They usually spoke by phone.

Kit continued. "There's some talk that you're doing this on purpose to get the business."

"That talk would be just that ... *talk*," Tasmin declared, sensing a turn in the conversation to sheer aggression as Kit needed an outlet, somebody to blame. She looked over at Pinch, who stared at Kit as if she were a bomb about to explode.

Deciding it was time to leave, even if it meant foregoing the coffee, Tasmin got to her feet and looked over at Pinch. "I'll head on out."

He looked at her with relief on his face. "Thank you," he murmured.

"Yeah, I know," she muttered. Then she headed out again.

"Hey, wait," Pinch hollered. "You can't go. What about the cop?"

"Yeah, if he comes back, tell him I'm already gone."

With that, she walked out, knowing that staying would just make things uglier. That was just the tip of what would happen now, as people tried to work their way through all this to figure out who was to blame. Because that was human nature. Everybody needed somebody to blame. Even when nobody was right in front of them, they would pick the closest target. It didn't matter whether it was fair or not. That's just the way life worked. And, with that, she turned and resolutely headed back to her business.

∼

HANSON HAD NO problem getting into the store; after all, Tasmin had left the door wide open. Hanson made a quick search on the ground floor and then raced to the stairs. He stopped and cocked his head to listen. But absolutely nothing was up there. As he stared at the darkness, he realized shadows were separating all around.

Feeling that inner knowing, he slipped up the stairs and stood at the top to survey the loft. He found no sign of a physical body, no intruder per se, but definitely something was odd about the energy.

"Hello?" he whispered into the darkness.

No response came, but the shadows shifted and moved, undulating toward him. He stood his ground, watching the shadows, looking for any sign of what they were doing, at what insanity had brought them here.

He calmly spoke to them. "I don't know who you are or what you're doing, but you need to leave now."

One of the shadows shifted enough that it became slightly opaque, as if changing form of some kind.

He stared at it in curiosity, having seen all kinds of things over the past year, but none showing him anything such as this. And an explanation, although it would be nice, hadn't been forthcoming at any point in time up until now, so he couldn't imagine it would be any different this time. He tried to sort out what he was feeling and what he was seeing.

Suddenly he sensed Stefan in the background. "What do I do with this?" he asked Stefan.

Try to get an entity behind it.

Stefan's voice came through Hanson's head, strong and clear.

See if you can identify who it is, Stefan instructed, *what it is, what they want.*

"They're not talking."

That's because you're using your vocal cords, Stefan replied. *Use energy to talk to them. You'll get further that way.*

Not exactly sure was he was doing, and feeling like a fool, Hanson closed his eyes and sent out a message. *What do you want?*

Freedom.

The answer slammed back into his head, he jerked backward in surprise. He opened his eyes and stared at the shadows that even now were surging. "Stefan? Did you hear that?"

I did, he said, his voice calm. *And I can't say that I'm surprised.*

"What, that the ghosts want freedom?" Hanson asked. "What the hell does that even mean?"

They're looking to live again. They're looking to get out of this space that's locked down, that they can't change. They don't realize that it's their own feelings, negativity, and possessiveness keeping them tethered here. That's the reason they can't leave. So they're looking to blame the people around them. To use them as a reason, an excuse, for them to get out of here, without too much effort.

"And yet," Hanson noted, "it takes effort. It takes a lot of effort."

But it may not look that way to them, Stefan murmured in Hanson's head. *Try to talk to them again.*

"Will that do any good? It's obviously stronger than I thought."

I'm not sure it's even an it, Stefan muttered. *I'm here, just watching, trying to get a sense of what's going on, so the more you can communicate with that energy, the better.*

"Says you," he muttered. He shifted so that he was leaning back against the pony wall that stopped him from falling over the loft to the floor below, then spoke quietly to the entity in his mind. *There is no life for you here. You need to go home.*

The entity roared, as if it had no power, no ability to do any more than that.

Hanson nodded, trying hard to stay in control himself, and let it speak. *You know that you can't live again. You know that your time here is over and that you're supposed to go home to wherever that is.*

Can't came the hard voice.

Why can't you?

There was an odd sense of a struggle, as if more than one person were involved, where one person wanted to speak, while the other was trying to stop them. It was a weird thing to get the sense of a war happening on another level, something that Hanson had never even contemplated.

Finally deciding to shake this up a bit, Hanson shared via his thoughts, *I can see more than one of you are here. Let me talk to the other one.*

No came the same voice. *You can't.*

Well, I'm going to, he snapped. Hating the fact that, even in the ethers, somebody was trying to stop him from finding out what he needed to know. He spoke to the other entity. *Speak up. What is it you want? What are you here for?*

To help her came the voice. *She needs help.*

He stiffened at that. *Tasmin?*

Yes. And then the voice started to fade away, as if the relief of finally being heard took more energy than they could handle.

I know she's in trouble, Hanson shared. *Somebody is trying to lock her up.*

Yes. And, at that, she sighed a faint sigh but one of relief. *Help her.*

I'd like to, but we're not sure what's going on.

At that, the other spirit seemed to jump into the fray in front of her and added, *Freedom.*

Yes, you mentioned that before. Hanson turned his attention to the other energy, which even now was almost tethered in place.

Are you tied to the storefront? he asked in sudden enlightenment.

But when the *No* came back instantly, he groaned. *I don't understand any of this. I don't know why you're haunting her or haunting this place.*

Not haunting. Freedom.

Got it. You want your freedom, but you won't get it here, he snapped.

Yes, I will.

At that, Hanson sensed the same internal war between the two spirits going on again. "Stefan, you got anything to add to this? We're not getting anywhere."

But the fact that Hanson wasn't getting anywhere also allowed him to detach a bit emotionally, so he could see this for what it was, almost like prisoners tied to a spot, desperate to move but unable to. They were fighting, their energy wiggling and twisting about, as if they wanted to get at him but couldn't. And then he wondered. "Stefan, are you stopping them from coming forward?"

Stefan replied, *I'm not, but somebody is.*

Confused, Hanson tried to get clarity, but then another roar came from one energy, as it took another surge toward him. He instinctively shrunk back, and the entity laughed.

Fear is good. And, with that, the spirit disappeared.

Shaken, Hanson stood at the top of the loft and whispered, "Stefan?"

Yeah, I'm here. I don't know what that was though.

"Great," Hanson muttered. "Since when are ghosts like this even a thing?"

They've always been a thing. It's just that the world doesn't want to know about it.

Hanson gave a bitter laugh. "Hey, I don't even want to know about it."

And yet, Stefan pointed out in a quiet voice, *you've been chosen.*

"Chosen? I don't like sound of that," Hanson stated, his voice rising in alarm.

No, I'm sure you don't, but, for whatever reason, when you came back from that shooting after you died, you came back with the ability to communicate. And when you felt as if you came back with something, I'm wondering if that something isn't what's there. It's not tethered to Tasmin or to this place, but maybe it's tethered to you.

"But, in that case, it's not really tethered," Hanson noted abruptly. "I left. I'm coming and going. It's not. It's here."

But you don't know that, Stefan added. *For all you know, you left something here, and it's attached to that.*

Hanson thought about that for a moment. "I've come here a couple times over the last few days. ... And I did bring a tape measure. It was my brother's. I keep it as a memento as he used it all the time before he was killed in a car accident. I like to think it's a connection to him. he was the protective kind of guy. I miss him."

Where is it? Stefan asked urgently.

"It's, ... it's here in the loft," Hanson replied. "Did you know she's sleeping here, on the floor? That she has no place to live, so she's staying on a stupid bedroll downstairs in her workshop. I was going to convert the loft at least to sleeping quarters."

No, Stefan said abruptly, *don't do it.*

Hanson paused in the act of looking around for his tape measure. "Why?"

Something is going on in her world, and she definitely needs more protection than that. Your brother's tape measure is involved.

"Yes, but that kind of protection won't exactly come from nowhere," Hanson argued. "Being here won't be any different than being where I am."

Yes, it will. As long as you are with her, she will have some level of protection.

"Whoa, whoa, whoa, hang on a minute," Hanson said. "I can't even tell her what's going on, so how the hell am I supposed to protect her?"

I don't know, Stefan admitted, *but you're connected in some way, and you need to figure that out before it's too late.* And, with that, Stefan disappeared from Hanson's mind.

Hanson turned around, wondering what had happened to the tape measure, his mind already twisting on the messages that Stefan had left churning away in his head, trying to figure out just what he meant, since none of it made sense. It was all too convoluted and too crazy to make sense.

When he heard a voice downstairs, he looked over the railing to see Tasmin walking in the door, calling out for him.

"I'm up here," he yelled.

She looked at him and came running. "Was somebody here?" When he hesitated, she looked at him, frowning. "What aren't you telling me?"

"I won't say that someone was here," he murmured. "Let's just say that some*thing* was here."

"Oh, crap," she muttered.

He tried to explain what had just happened, but she kept staring at him and shaking her head, as if to refute it.

Finally he gently held her head, stopped it from shaking, and said, "Listen. This is important. Whatever's going on, Stefan says we're connected somehow. Also, whatever this is, the one ghost said you were in trouble."

She nodded. "I wonder if that was my grandmother."

He stared at her.

"Is it possible?" she asked.

"I don't talk to ghosts, so I wouldn't know," he replied, with a note of humor.

"It sounds to me that you did talk to ghosts today," she rebutted, with a cheeky grin in his direction. "I just don't understand what Grandma's got to do with any of this."

"Maybe it's because, from her perspective, you're in trouble. Maybe she saw whatever was happening yesterday with the psych ward."

Tasmin winced at that and shuddered. "That is possible, and my grandmother is not the kind to ever want that to happen. My father tried to get her committed a decade or two ago." She pondered that. "I don't remember how long ago or any details. I heard something about it from her."

"What?" Hanson frowned. "Really?"

"Yes." She nodded. "And it was hard, really hard. Just the thought of him trying to do that to his own mother."

"Do you know why?"

"Well, she thought it was because he wanted the business. My grandfather had just passed away, and the business had gone to her, not my dad."

Hanson stared at her in shock. "Would he really do something like that for the business? Particularly when he doesn't have anything to do with it now?"

"He doesn't now because he's so unstable," she murmured. "I don't know what will happen if he and my mother do divorce. I would have thought their marriage would have blown up in their faces already," she murmured. "But so far they've held it together long enough to not have it happen."

"That's not always a good thing," Hanson noted hesitantly.

"No, you're right. Delaying a divorce when the marriage is no good isn't always a good thing, and, in this case, I would say that no good could come of it. But definitely something weird is going on with my family that he seems to think is an avenue to get money."

"Are you sure it was your dad?"

"My grandmother was sure it was him back then," she stated. "Do I really know? Of course not."

"Come on. Let's get downstairs. You're starting to shiver."

She looked at her hands and winced. "Right? I hadn't even realized that."

"It seems to be a side effect of all this energy work."

"And trying to keep it quiet, so nobody else knows."

He nodded at that. "That's the hard part, isn't it? When we start talking to invisible people, the other people immediately think we're crazy."

"Yes, especially my family."

"And we still have to talk to them about all this too," he muttered.

"*Great.*"

"Come on downstairs first." Then he nudged her so that she went down the loft stairs carefully in front of him.

By the time they got down to the bottom, the front door opened and a woman tried to get inside. In a panic, she caught herself in the door because she hadn't opened it wide enough.

When she finally made it in, she called out at the top of her voice, "Tasmin! Tasmin!"

"I'm here," she replied, looking at her sister. "What's going on?"

"It's Mom. There's no sign of her, and she didn't open the store this morning."

Tasmin stopped, thought about it, and then nodded. "When I was there earlier, I thought it was odd that nobody had opened it yet."

"Why didn't you say something earlier?" Lorelei snapped.

"I didn't think of it. Plus it was early, and honestly you were heading up there anyway. Did you check to see if she was at home?"

"Yes, and I didn't find her at home either." She turned and looked around almost wildly, as if someone would give her the answer she was desperately looking for.

"Did you phone her?" Tasmin asked.

Yes, of course I phoned her," she stated in disgust. "I'm not a complete idiot. Can you try to come up with something useful for a change?" She turned, recognized Hanson, then frowned. "Problems at my sister's store again?"

"More problems, yes," he clarified. "When did you last speak to your mother?"

"Last night," she uttered, almost absentmindedly, "but she never *doesn't* open the store."

"Not until now, but maybe this is the first time. Tasmin mentioned that a divorce was potentially in the offing. Do you think it's possible that she's left?"

"She told me that she wouldn't leave without telling me, so she wouldn't have. I mean, if nothing else, my mother loves me." At that, she flushed and looked over at Tasmin. "And, yes, probably more than she loves my sister."

Tasmin snorted at that. "No doubt about that. It's always been that way."

"You had Grandma's love, and I had Mom's love."

"And your father's?" Hanson asked them.

They turned, looked at him, and both shook their heads.

"No, not much of that to go around," Lorelei admitted.

"And where is your father now?"

"I don't know," Lorelei snapped. "I thought he would be at the house, working in his own shop, doing something."

"What work does he do there?"

"He does woodwork," Tasmin replied. "It's kind of a therapy for him."

"And is he any good at it?" Hanson asked.

"Yeah, he's very good," Tasmin stated. "Why?"

Hanson shrugged. "I guess, if he wanted to, he could have helped you fix up the loft."

"*If he wanted to* being the operative phrase," Tasmin noted in a wry tone. "Remember. This is my father. The man who tried to get me committed and threatened to kill me with a knife."

"Right." Hanson turned to Lorelei. "The cop who called you to say that the basement door was open, who was it?"

She stared at him. "I don't know. How am I supposed to know that? You're the one who can get a record of the report."

"There is no record of the report," he said immediately.

She stared at him in shock. "What?"

Tasmin turned and looked at him too. "What?"

He nodded. "There was no report because no *cop* reported the basement door being open. I wondered about the witness seeing anything because, when I was there, absolutely no way could anybody—such as a neighbor or someone driving by—have seen that door, since its clear around the back and out of sight, below ground level."

"I wondered that myself." Tasmin turned toward her sister. "Unless you made it up."

Lorelei flushed and shook her head in a hard panic. "I did not do that. Jesus, what do you think I am?"

Tasmin just stared at her intently.

Lorelei flushed darker. "You really think I would do that?" she asked, but the hurt in her voice rang true.

Tasmin relaxed slightly. "I guess it depends how much

you're under Mom's influence."

"You mean, Dad's influence," she snapped. "And the answer to that is I'm not. He needs to be committed himself."

"I wouldn't say that out loud," Tasmin warned her. "You know how he'll react to that. The same way he reacted to Grandma about it. He turned the tables and tried to get her put away."

"What the hell is it with this family? That every one of you deals with your problems this way?" Hanson asked at Tasmin's side. "That's just wrong."

Tasmin snorted. "It all comes down to money. It all comes down to the business." Tasmin looked at her sister. "See? That's one thing that I guess I need to find out for sure here. You say that the business isn't doing very well."

"No, it isn't," she said. "I barely have enough to pay the bills."

Tasmin nodded at that, not seeing any sign of duplicity in her sister's voice or expression, then added, "You do realize that it's always been a very successful and lucrative business."

"Sure it was, until the economy tanked, and this stupid virus took over everything. Then the business came too hard, too fast, and nobody could pay."

"Grandma hasn't been there for a long time," Tasmin noted.

"No, she hasn't been there for six months, but that's it. In the meantime she did a lot of burials that she didn't charge anybody for," Lorelei argued crossly.

At that, Tasmin frowned at her sister. "Grandma has been dead for *one year*, Lorelei. And she always carefully balanced the charity cases with those who could pay, in order to keep the business in good order."

"Well, she didn't pass that magic on to me or to Mom apparently," Lorelei argued, "because, ever since she's been gone, there just hasn't been any money."

Tasmin didn't know what to say to that. She turned to Hanson, with one eyebrow raised.

He shrugged. "Honestly, I don't understand why the business would be suffering at all," he said, facing Lorelei. "So, I guess maybe you need to come up with a better explanation than that."

"She doesn't get any explanation," Lorelei snapped, glaring at him. "And neither do you. It's got nothing to do with your case. It has nothing to do with anything, so you keep your big fat mouth shut."

It came across as such an odd thing from Lorelei that Tasmin stared at her in shock. Her sister at least had the grace to look ashamed.

"Look. You think that I failed as the person responsible for the business, particularly when it was given to me," Lorelei explained, "but honestly, I'm trying."

"I get that you're trying," Tasmin noted, "but did you ever consider that the reason you aren't succeeding is something other than the fact that you might have been doing something wrong?"

Lorelei shook her head. "You're not even making sense."

"Let me see the books, and I'll figure it out," Tasmin muttered.

Her sister stared at her, and then she shoved her fists into her jean pockets. "You'll just laugh at me."

"Did they not show you how to keep the books?"

She shook her head. "I mean, I'd seen a bit of it, but nothing like what I'm doing now. It's just too insane to try and even figure out where the money's going."

"There's only one place for money to go. So it's either staying in the account or you're paying it out in bills."

"But it's not though," Lorelei complained. "Big chunks are paid out in automatic payments, and I don't know where it's going. Plus the amount has changed."

"And you haven't asked?"

"Asked who?" she demanded, staring at her sister in fear. "Who am I supposed to ask? Who's behind this? It's happened since Grandma died."

Tasmin stared at Lorelei, and Hanson spoke up. "Seems time to visit the bank and maybe the lawyer."

Lorelei nodded. "I was wondering about doing that. When I mentioned it to Mom, she got really angry about it all. She said that it would be some more BS that Grandma set up to try and stiff us."

Tasmin shook her head. "She's been gone for a year and the business is continuing to run as it always has, so nothing could have been changed, at least not that much." She looked over at Hanson. "Right?"

"The easiest way to find out is to go to the bank. And, considering everything else that's going on, I highly suggest we get to the bottom of it, just in case it's connected.'

"How could it be connected to anything with you?" Lorelei cried out in horror. "That would imply that some of these murders are connected, and no way that has anything to do with us."

"So prove it," Tasmin declared in a voice of bravado that Hanson was surprised to hear from her. "Let's go to the bank and figure out what's happening to the business because, honest to God, you should be making money hand over fist right now. Especially since you haven't even been paying for the bulk of the work."

"Well, I'm not making a cent," Lorelei stated. "I can't even pay the bills this month."

And, with that, she turned and walked out the door.

CHAPTER 22

TASMIN RACED AFTER her sister. "Look. I know you're embarrassed, and you think you've done something wrong, but let's find out what's really going on, so we can fix it, before you lose the company."

"I feel as if I already lost it or as if I shouldn't have had it in the first place. It seems everything's bad luck over there right now. I didn't even want the damn thing."

"I know you didn't," Tasmin agreed, "which is also why it was very hard on me when Dad supposedly gave it to you."

Lorelei shook her head. "I don't understand that either. He must really hate you."

"No, he's afraid of me," she corrected. "Afraid that whatever it is that I see will reveal something that he did."

"What do you mean?"

She lowered her voice. "I'm afraid he might have had something to do with Grandpa's death. And, if I follow that even further, I'm afraid he had something to do with Grandma's death."

Lorelei stared at her in horror. "Oh, no, no, please don't say that."

"Why not?" she asked, staring at her sister defiantly.

"No, I don't want to think of our parents being murderers."

At that, she tilted her head. "*Parents?*"

Lorelei flushed, closed her eyes, and took several deep breaths. She heard noises at the door behind her, as Hanson stood in the doorway, listening. "Look. I don't know anything for sure," Lorelei added. "I just heard a conversation before Grandma died. They were pretty upset that she was still alive and still controlling the funds they thought should be theirs."

"Oh," Tasmin snapped, "so the money she earned from the business she developed all on her own, with her own hard work and sacrifice? *That's* the money they felt should have been theirs?"

Lorelei had the grace to flush at least, but she nodded. "I didn't say I had the conversation with them. It's a conversation I overheard them having."

"Right, so go on," Tasmin muttered. "Let's hear the rest of it."

"They went into their room at that time, and I didn't hear anything else," she replied. "But things went from bad to worse, and Grandma died not very long afterward."

"And, at the time, you suspected they might have had something to do with it?" Hanson asked.

"No, I didn't," Lorelei snapped. "I really still don't. I don't even want to think somebody would even contemplate such a thing," she said. "Nobody wants to think of their family in that light."

"And yet how can you not, after hearing something like that?" Hanson told her.

She looked at him, fear in her eyes, and she slowly nodded and didn't say anything.

Hanson added, "It still doesn't explain why these murders would be connected."

"They aren't connected," Lorelei replied. "They can't be.

It has to be completely separate. There's no way." And if she repeated it enough, it's obvious she hoped she would finally convince herself of it.

It wasn't working on Tasmin. She motioned at her sister. "Come on. We're going to the bank right now."

"Why?" Lorelei asked defiantly.

"Because we need to figure out what's going on and fast. You're in the will. I'm in the will, and we do have copies of Grandma's death certificate, so we need to find out what's happening."

"Fine." Lorelei rubbed her hands along her arms, as if cold. Then she turned to Hanson. "What do I do about my mother?"

"I'll take a look," he said, "and see what we can do, but she's an adult, and she hasn't been missing for very long."

"No, that's true," she murmured. Still, she looked at him and asked, "Would you check out the funeral home?"

His eyebrows went up ever-so-slowly, and he nodded. "That I can do, but I'm going to the bank with you guys first."

"Why?" Lorelei asked.

"Because I don't want Tasmin out of my sight right now," he muttered.

She looked from one to the other, bewildered. At that, Tasmin explained what had happened the day before.

Lorelei gasped in horror, her eyes widening, and absolutely nothing was artificial about it.

Feeling more convinced that her sister probably didn't knowingly have anything to do with her abduction to Bellevue, Tasmin nodded. "So that's where my world's at right now. I get attacked, and then somebody takes me in an ambulance to the psychiatric hospital again. So, you tell me.

How many family members would be very happy to see me locked in a padded room again?"

Lorelei's face turned pale gray. "I didn't have anything to do with it," she cried out. "You know that, right? God, I hated that place the one time I went to visit you. I couldn't stand it. I was getting claustrophobic in there myself."

"Yeah, well, try being the one who is naked and locked up," Tasmin spat. She looked over at Hanson. "Come on. Let's lock up the shop and go to the bank. Hopefully we can get the facts on at least one problem. That place should not be hurting for money, so we need to get to the bottom of whoever is getting these withdrawals and fast."

By the time they got to the bank and got access to the bank manager, the two sisters sat down, with Hanson in the background, having identified himself to give the visit a little more officiality.

"I can certainly take a look at any automatic payments," the manager said, "but you really should talk to your parents."

"And why is that?" Lorelei asked.

"Because they're the ones who still control everything."

"And yet the business is mine," Lorelei declared.

He turned to her and asked, "Do you have proof of that?"

She frowned. "Dad told me that it was mine, and I signed a bunch of papers."

"But did he file them? Were they properly recorded? Was it done as a sale or a bequest, or did he just get started, then didn't get any further?"

Lorelei shrugged. "I have no idea. Why?"

The manager didn't say anything, but he brought up the accounts and explained, "Look. I'll print off the activity over the last three months."

"We need to go back farther," Tasmin stated, "so we can compare things from before and after Grandma's death."

He nodded, changed the settings, then sent the documents to the printer. He got up, walked over, and returned with a sheaf of papers, which he handed to them. Tasmin grabbed them, and, instead of looking at the most recent ones, she went back to the three months before Grandma died.

With everybody looking, they quickly went through the payments, and then, after Grandma's death, payments that had been $2,000 a month had suddenly jumped to $20,000 a month.

Tasmin whistled. "So from a two to a twenty, with one click of a finger, and somebody has taken thousands from the account over this last year."

Lorelei looked at her in shock, turned to the bank manager, and asked, "Who is getting these payments?"

He said, "It's an automatic withdrawal that was set up during your grandmother's time."

"No," Tasmin corrected. "It was originally set up at during Grandma's time, but, after her death, somebody multiplied that figure by ten."

He flushed as he looked at it and admitted, "I don't know who authorized this. Just a minute."

Then he got up and spoke to someone out in the front. With that, one of the tellers came back with him, and they went over some of the codes that had been used.

He sat back down and reported, "Someone within the company, one of the signing officers, authorized us to multiply that figure from $2,000 to $20,000."

Tasmin sat back, with a knowing smile, and said, "And

let me guess. That money's going into my mother's bank account, right?"

He flushed, but he slowly nodded. "Yes. That's exactly where it's going."

Lorelei looked at her sister in horror. "How did you know?"

"She's bleeding the company dry so she can leave Dad," Tasmin explained. "That's why you're broke. That's why you don't have any money to pay the bills. Mom's taken it all. To the tune of $20,000 a month."

As they went through the documents, Tasmin studied the numbers again and stated, "And here, as of yesterday, the latest figure that just came out was $50,000. And look at the balance you have left." She pointed out to Lorelei how less than $4,000 was left in the account.

"Oh my God," Lorelei exclaimed. "So they give me a company and then take all the assets?"

"No, they took all your *liquid* assets, the cash out of the bank account," Tasmin noted. "Presumably you have deeds to the actual building itself, all the equipment, and the actual funeral business, which is an intangible asset," she added. "Such as your client list, the reputation that you have, the service that you've been providing for the last decade, based on Grandma's work. But what we don't know is whether they gave you anything else or not. For that, we'll have to go to the lawyer." She looked over at the bank manager. "Can you stop any other withdrawals?"

He asked, "Do you have signing authority?"

Tasmin looked at him and said, "You tell me."

He went to the account, looked it up, and asked, "Are you Tasmin?"

"I am," she stated.

"Then you do have signing authority."

"Can you reverse that last $50,000 payment? It's just going out now, right?"

"It is." He went into the computer and quickly entered several lines and then nodded. "I can reverse it."

"Do so, and please move that $50,000 to open up a new business account," she stated, "so that it's available for the funeral home, so it can pay its own bills. Both my sister and I get signing authority on that account, and then please make sure that no other money goes to my mother from the original account."

"She also has signing authority," he warned.

"Yeah, this is temporary," she stated.

"You can put a freeze on that account," Hanson shared, stepping forward. "We could set that up."

The bank manager looked at him in relief. "Don't suppose you want to give me something legal to do that with, do you?"

"We'll be picking her up on the suspicion of murder," he stated in a hard tone.

The bank manager paled and quickly worked on the computer again.

Lorelei stared at him in shock. "Please tell me that you don't mean that."

But Hanson's gaze remained hard.

Tasmin shrugged. "I'm not sure what's going on. Let's go see the lawyer first. We've got to find out what the situation actually is and get control of whatever we can." With that, she grabbed her sister by the arm, got up, and led her from the bank. As they stepped outside, the wind had picked up a bit, hitting them directly in their faces.

Lorelei stopped, pulled her lightweight jacket together

around her neck, and asked in barely a whisper, "Now what?"

Tasmin considered her sister and realized that a good share of her sister's world was crumbling down. Their mom had systematically been gutting the company financially and had left Lorelei to struggle with the shortfalls this whole time. Other staff came in and helped out, plus they had all their suppliers to pay as well. As far as her mom doing what she'd done, it was such a betrayal, and who even knew how much worse she had done.

"We have to understand that Dad may not have any knowledge of any of this," Tasmin noted. "So again, we need to get to the bottom of where things stand, which means the lawyer next. Then we go talk to our parents."

"*Great*," Lorelei whispered.

"You also need to expect that Mom will be pissed, really pissed, when she finds out that $50K is not landing in her bank account, plus that she has been frozen out."

Lorelei nodded. "Not as pissed as I am though," she whispered. "They make this big deal about giving me a business, then completely steal everything out from under it. Don't they have any decency?"

Tasmin didn't say anything because, as far as she was concerned, they did not. The business had been given to Tasmin by her grandmother, and she had no idea how her father had managed to pass it on to Lorelei. For all Tasmin knew, it was all verbal, and that's why they needed the lawyer. She looked over at Hanson. "Are you coming?"

He was torn, she could see it.

She nodded. "Look. You have important cases to go deal with. I promise that we'll go see the lawyer, and I'll fill you in afterward."

He hesitated. "You'll call me if you need me?"

"I will." And then, surprising them both, she reached up and kissed him gently on the lips. "Go on. Figure out whatever the hell's going on in your world, while we try to straighten out ours."

⁓

AS MUCH AS Hanson wanted to see the lawyer with them, he also needed to get back to the office and to keep functioning on everything else he had going on. As he walked into the office to sit down at his desk, his phone rang. "Hey, Pinch. What did you find?"

"I just talked to Puggs, and he told me that the same guy was hanging around the shop yesterday and the day before."

"Does he have a name?"

"Yeah, his name was—" Pinch called out, "Hey, Puggs, what was that name again?" He came back on a moment later to Hanson on the phone. "Eric Sparken. At least that's the name he knows him by."

"And he's a regular?"

"Yeah, once I figured out who he was talking about, by looking at the camera feed. He's been a regular, and he's been asking a lot about the process of trying to preserve tattoos."

"Okay, that's great, thanks. I'll swing by and talk to Eric. I also wanted to ask for a list of any enemies you might have."

Pinch sucked in his breath. "Wow, I would have thought none, up until these murders," he shared. "Now I'll have to think about it."

"Do that," Hanson said, "and do it fast."

Pinch sighed so loudly that Hanson heard it clearly over

the phone. "You're worried we'll have another one tonight, aren't you?"

"I hope not, but obviously it's possible."

"You know Tasmin's family, right? You said you did. Do you know anything about the father?"

"A little. It seems the whole family is messed up. Even the grandmother, depending on who you talk to. Yet everybody tells me that she had a heart of gold."

"She did, if you were in trouble, but, if you were doing okay, she was a hard-ass," he shared, but there was affection in his voice.

"And you never held it against her?"

"No, she was good people, and you always knew where you stood with her. She didn't like shysters, or anything like that, but, if you were honest and upfront, then she was there for you."

"Right. That gels with what I've heard." Hanson made some quick notes on his notepad.

"She was good people," Pinch stated. "Now the mother, I never could get a bead on her. I avoided her because she always gave me the creeps."

"In what way?"

"She seemed fake," he said. "I guess that's the easiest way to say it. She just never really came across as being the real deal."

"I'm not even sure what the real deal is with people anymore," Hanson admitted, with a laugh.

"Right? You and me both. But I can tell you that she always had that fake makeup, that fake laugh."

"Got it. And the father?"

"The only times I met him, he was on a fire-and-brimstone roll, practicing his minister thing. But considering he thought what I was doing was desecrating the human body and that I should be shot for it, I didn't stick around very much."

"That is honestly a fascinating insight into his character too," Hanson noted.

"Everybody's entitled to their own religious beliefs," Pinch stated, "but I've never been one of those guys who shared what I believe out in public. I don't want to be embarrassed or humiliated or have my sins blasted in front of some judgmental community. Her father's been working on getting his license, but he's just someone I was always happy to avoid. The fact that he owned a funeral home always seemed like an ideal scenario in a way, just because he does a funeral service and helps the souls across, at least that was our impression. But he sure pounded into the rest of us that were still alive."

"Interesting," Hanson muttered. "Any idea how they were money-wise?"

"As far as I knew, they were fine," Pinch said. "There never appeared to be anything lacking in their world when I was around, but I was a kid, so what would I know? It seemed the grandmother handled most of that. It was really shitty when they didn't give Tasmin the business though."

"Yeah, what do you know about that?"

"The grandmother herself even told me that it would go to Tasmin, and that everything was set up. All the legal documents were done, and it was going to her. But then, when I talked to Tasmin, she said her father took control of things, and they had given it to her sister, which is something that made no sense at all. They decided that Tasmin was too unstable or something."

"But the grandmother didn't decide that, the father

did?"

"Apparently, but the father was messed-up. He was focused on one thing, ... raising money for his church and the programs he was setting up. So, if you were donating money to that end, he would have done anything. And, if you weren't a part of that, you were a sinner, heading straight to hell."

"Seriously?"

"Oh yeah, very seriously." Pinch snorted. "But his beliefs are what were really scary. We're talking religious evangelical to the absolute tenth degree. I mean, if anybody would murder people, it would be him."

"But why would he though?" Hanson asked. "I get that whole feeling of wanting to blame the people we don't like or who scare us, but what reason would he have for killing someone?"

"I don't know, maybe because they dared to get tattoos. Maybe it's as simple as that. He hated tattoos and what they represented in his mind, which was an insult against God—so much so that he used to come into my shop to rant and rave about it. At one point in time I told him to get out or I would call the cops, and he didn't come back again, which was a good thing. Afterward I did call the cops and talked to them about it, so maybe somebody went and talked to him privately. I don't know, but, yeah, he's, ... he's a loose screw."

"So, he makes a great bad guy."

At that, Pinch asked, "What do you mean by that?"

"Nothing, I was just talking to myself," Hanson muttered. "Anyway, thanks for the info, and send me a list when you get a minute. And I mean, like, today."

"Great, so 'when I get a minute' is on your time frame,

not mine."

"Yep, absolutely," he declared. "Remember? We're bound to have another body tonight, if we don't figure it out very soon."

"What about all these vehicles the shooter drives?"

"They're all stolen," Hanson shared. "He's picking small gray or silver cars, and he steals them, then leaves them parked a few blocks away, clean as a whistle, no evidence to be found."

"Shit, man. And, of course, nobody ever reports them stolen, not until the next day."

"Exactly," Hanson confirmed, "so he's got an anonymous getaway vehicle, and he's gone."

"But how is he finding all these cars?" Pinch asked.

"We're trying to figure that out. There's a lot of small gray four-door cars, sure, but it's really not that common of a car that he could just drive down some street and find one whenever he wanted."

Then Pinch frowned. "Unless it's one of those models where they had recalls on some of the locks and or the ignitions or something."

"I don't even think they need to be that specific," Hanson stated. "There are so many easy ways to jerry-rig a vehicle these days to get it started, particularly if it's an older model, which all of these are."

"So, a bit of a car buff maybe."

"Yep, that's what we figure, but, even then, as much as I hate to say it, all that information is available on the internet, so he really wouldn't need to be a car buff at all."

"Man, sometimes I hate the internet," Pinch muttered.

"Yeah, for every good thing, there's a bad one," Hanson said. "We just have to figure out how to handle the information in a positive way. And you know there's no way for that. For every person who wants something, another is screaming about their rights being axed."

Pinch almost laughed at that. "Good point. Anyway, I'll start writing down some names."

"Yeah, you do that, preferably before somebody else dies." With that, Hanson hung up.

Silence filled the room. He turned to see Mark and John staring at him. "What's the matter? Did you get anywhere on that last drive-by?"

"We're getting somewhere," Mark said.

"Have you guys got something?" Hanson asked Mark. In fact, Hanson wouldn't put it past Mark and John to *not* update him.

They shook their heads. "No, but we really need to get this shit together."

Hanson raised an eyebrow. "So, *now* you're concerned?"

John flushed, but Hanson didn't know whether it was from anger or embarrassment.

"Look. That last kid, I knew her," John stated.

"Oh, I see, so now you want to work on the case," Hanson said in disgust. "Now that it's personal to you."

At that, the captain stepped forward. "Look. I don't give a shit about what problems you're having working together. This is top priority, so everybody is on this case, and no other case matters. You get this drive-by shit solved, and you solve it now, do you hear me?" he barked into the room.

The other detectives nodded.

Hanson turned to look at Mark and John again, now that the captain was gone, and again asked, "Have you guys got anything to go on?"

"Seemed you're the one who was handling this," John

replied, with resentment in his voice.

"Somebody had to," Hanson snapped, immediately tossing it right back at him.

Mark stepped forward and suggested, "Look. Let's combine what we have for information and see where we can go from here because the captain's right. This has got to stop."

John didn't say anything to that.

"So," Hanson began, "let me give you a bit of a recap. Every night they're stealing a similar vehicle, the same vehicle or at least the same approximate look. We've had a couple different makes and models, but they're always small gray or silver four-door cars, always stolen, always left a few blocks away, always out of camera range, and, so far, nobody has seen very much, although we do have a cop who saw the Jenny Cleavers's shooting, and we have that witness sketch from earlier."

"Right," Mark noted. "I know that cop. He's a good guy, and he's pretty shook up, but he couldn't tell us very much either."

"And neither did he go after the guy," Hanson noted, "which is something I don't quite understand."

"No," Mark corrected, "the cop told me that he did, but the shooter was already too far ahead. And we found the vehicle not very long after that. At least the black-and-whites did," he corrected. "So we got that far at least. The cop stayed at the crime scene, while everybody else went looking, once he realized the shooter had already taken off. He'd raced over to the girl at first."

Hanson nodded at that. It made sense, considering that the victims come first, but she was already dead and gone, and they'd lost their one chance to track down this asshole.

Mark asked Hanson, "Have you talked to the tattoo artist?"

"Multiple times. He's putting together a list of people who either hate him, want to shut him down, or the opposite, fans who would want to ensure that his art was preserved."

At that came more silence in the room.

"What?" Hanson asked the guys, then nodded. "At every scene, at least one of the victims is connected to Pinch, the artist, and to Tasmin, who preserves the tattoos. There's been a lot of conversation in the tattoo shop recently about the preservation of these high-quality tattoos."

"So, we're looking at her then, are we?" Mark asked.

"No, we're not looking at her," Hanson stated patiently. "At least not beyond the fact that we're looking at everything. But there's also the angle that it could be somebody trying to preserve the work of the tattoo artist."

At that, the detectives sat back and shook their heads.

"That's just sick," Mark said.

"This is a sick world. Mowing down people like this is sick, no matter the reason behind it," Hanson snapped, glaring at them. "And, if it is connected to Tasmin's work, then that is possible. I've already got her taking a look at who would want to either build up her business or try and tear it down."

"But the tattoos were put in a public space."

"Two of them were, yes. We recovered the two pieces that were stolen from Tasmin's shop and put in public places, but whether that was to ridicule or to gross out the public or to make them more aware of this art form, we don't know," Hanson stated.

"Has it had an effect on her business?"

He pondered that. "I haven't directly asked her that, but

enough time has gone by that she may be able to answer that by now."

"I suggest you do," Mark replied. "Besides, you're the one who's closest to her, aren't you?"

"Closer than you guys definitely," he said, his tone flat, and his gaze even flatter. "But if you're suggesting that there's anything inappropriate between us, there isn't. But there could be someday, maybe, if this case ever gets solved. But, in the meantime, it's not solved, and she's got a hell of a lot of problems of her own right now."

"In what way?"

He hesitated, then told them about what had happened to her, the attack at the funeral home. He included the part about the cop who supposedly called Lorelei and the fact that there was no record of a cop phoning. He also shared the fact that she'd been found tied up and drugged at the mortuary and how the ambulance had been rerouted to the sanatorium. They just stared at him, wordless. He nodded. "As I said, she's got some problems of her own."

"Jesus, so who is it that's making it up then, her?"

He stared at them. "So, in case I didn't make this clear, I, along with several other backup cops, in the funeral home—where she had been kidnapped from her car, drugged, unconscious—and strapped to the gurney, ready to be embalmed alive." he snapped, his voice rising. "And that has nothing, as far as I can tell, to do with these drive-by shootings, though I've been trying hard to find a connection, if there is one."

They just stared at him, as if unsure where to go with it.

Hanson sighed. "I think what happened to her was likely orchestrated by her father."

At that, John snapped his fingers. "Oh my God, that's

Father Baker, isn't it?"

"Is he ordained or something now?" Hanson asked.

"I don't know," John admitted, "but that's what he insists on being called. He is a fire-and-brimstone preacher man."

Mark closed his eyes. "That man is freaking scary. Is that who she is?"

Hanson nodded. "That's her father. And the funeral home is the family business."

At that, the others just stared.

Again Hanson nodded.

"The funeral home where she was found strapped down?" Mark asked.

"Yes, the funeral home where she was strapped in."

"Did you look at the straps to make sure that she couldn't have done that herself because I'm pretty sure I've heard rumors that she had to be locked up before."

"She was committed to Bellevue Hospital for examination at her father's orders because she believes in tattoos, and tattoos are something her father will not tolerate."

At that, they all stared back at him.

"Which is why I've been trying really hard to see if there is any connection to this drive-by situation because tattoos are running amok through all of it."

"Oh my God," John said. "That's just …" And then he was at a loss for words.

Nodding at that, Hanson said, "Exactly. However, if they're connected somehow, maybe we can solve two issues at once."

"I still think she could have done it herself," Mark repeated in a low voice to John.

Hanson looked over at him. "Well then, you should

know that I did look at the straps and buckles, and there is no way she could have put them on herself. And she certainly couldn't have put tension on all four of them, one on each of her feet, one on each of her hands. Think about it."

Mark studied him for a long moment, then reluctantly agreed. "If you say so."

Hanson stood and slammed his hand down on the desk. "Look. I don't need this shit. We've got a lot of cases here, and your aggravation and prejudice is really starting to be a pain in my ass. So either shut up and get to work, or get the hell off my case and leave me alone to figure this out on my own because obviously this is my problem, not yours."

And, with that, a dead silence filled the room. As he sat back down at his desk and reached for his phone, he found the captain standing there, staring at him.

The captain turned, looked at the rest of the men, and asked in a silky soft voice, "Anybody got anything to add to that?"

They immediately shook their heads.

"In that case, you will each step up and deal with this case immediately. Do I have to explain this a second time?" He shook his head. "Believe me. Although I've got budget constraints, if one of you won't be pulling your weight, I'm quite happy to kick you out the door. It saves us money to have people who actually do the job."

At that comment came some startled looks, as if they'd finally realized just how serious the captain was and that their jobs could be in jeopardy. Immediately everybody looked busy.

"And I don't mean just look busy. Do your damn jobs." Then the captain looked over at Hanson and said, "My office, now."

Hanson nodded, picked up his pen and notepad, then followed him.

He pointed at the chair in his office. "Take a seat."

Hanson sat down and said, "The only thing I have to say right now is that every minute you keep me in here is a minute I can't be on the damn case."

"And I appreciate that. Look. I'm sorry that they found out about your psych eval. As far as I can see, there was absolutely no need for it, and it shouldn't have happened in the first place."

"Look. I got shot, and I came out of surgery, talking all kinds of weird things," he explained. "I didn't blame my department at all for it. But, unless you were there, you just didn't understand what happened. And these guys, they don't know, and they don't care, but I'm just about at the end of my rope with their bullshit. I could really use a hand with this case, and I'm not getting it."

"That stops right now," the captain said.

At that, Hanson nodded. "I'm not one to bitch, but I'd just as soon leave the department myself after this," he snapped, as he got up.

The captain stopped and waved him back down again. "Hang on a minute. I know you're new here, and things have not exactly been easy."

"I don't give a shit about easy, but I expect to get the job done and not have my own team sabotage me."

At that, the captain flushed. "Right. Is there anything I can do?"

"Yeah," Hanson said. "We've got all kinds of shit going on here right now. I don't know if you heard the last part of that conversation, but supposedly there was a police call to Lorelei's phone, saying that the funeral home had an open door and seemed to be broken into," he explained. "I can't find a record of that call at all, and I can't get a subpoena for Lorelei's phone without some reasonable excuse."

"And this relates to the drive-by case how?'

"Outside of tattoos, I'm not sure it does." But then he quickly explained what had happened.

"And this is that same preacher man, right?"

"Yes, and that's the funeral home place and the family is in a big mess right now, so I don't know whether there's some twisted idea about saving these souls or something else is going on."

The captain shook his head, picked up the phone, and said, "It doesn't matter what it is. We need to get to the bottom of it. Sometimes ruling things out can be just as important as finding things. I'll get the warrant for the phone calls, and you get out there on the streets and find this asshole."

"We've already got the car for the last one. Forensics is going over it, but, if it's true to form, there won't be anything," Hanson shared. "I've already mapped things out, and I needed the map printed, but apparently we don't have anything to accommodate something that big. So I've been printing off small maps to get the crime scene locations marked on there and figure out a circle, so we have a targeted area."

The captain finished his call and stood. "Come over here."

Hanson walked into another conference room, where the captain pointed at the huge city map on the wall, exactly what Hanson had been looking for.

"Mark the crime scenes on here." With that, the captain turned and glared back at the office, shaking his head.

Hanson figured somebody was supposed to have shared this with him. He immediately walked over and started putting stickpins in at the locations of each of the murder victims from the drive-by shootings. He'd done it efficiently, before he stepped back and noted that he had a beautiful circle mapped out. And then, picking up two other pins, he put in Tasmin's shop and the tattoo parlor. Then with a completely different-colored pin, he put in the funeral home. All of it was within the same circle. He stepped back and looked at it.

The captain nodded. "You've definitely got a targeted area. The fact that they're all in the circle is suspicious."

"It is and it isn't," Hanson replied, "because this is where we're at, a smallish town. So it's quite logical that they would all be within a relatively narrow radius of each other, but this? ... This is a little too close for comfort."

"And, once again, what we have is information but no answers."

"Yeah, but we're getting there." When Hanson stepped back again and looked at it, he said, "All of it must be connected. It's too bizarre for it not to be."

"Yeah, but until we know how there's a connection, it doesn't help us."

"We'll take what we can get right now." He asked the captain, "Did you get approved for the phone call list?"

He nodded and held up his phone. "Just came through."

"I'll go check that first," Hanson said.

"You said it was a cop."

"I said a cop made the call, or at least Lorelei thought it was a cop. I don't know if there was a cop, or even a call for that matter, and I need to. It's one thing if Lorelei made up the whole thing or if someone coerced her into doing it. It's a whole other kettle of fish if she got a call or if there was a cop."

"And if there was?"

"Then we could have a bigger problem," he stated, turning and looking at the captain. "How well do you know your force?"

He shook his head. "How well does anybody know a force in a mess like this?" he muttered. "Obviously not as well as I would like."

Hanson nodded at that. "Let's hope I don't find any calls that connect to them."

And it didn't take long for him to go through the list. He found the one at the right time frame, quickly dialed it, and when a voice answered, Hanson said, "Identify yourself."

There was a snort on the other end, and somebody said, "I don't know who the hell you are, buckaroo, but that don't work for me."

"Maybe not, but I've already got a track down on your number here," he replied, "so you'd better identify who you are."

"What do you mean who am I?" he said. "I'm Puggs."

"Puggs, as in you work for Pinch?"

"Yeah, I do. Why?"

"Because you made a phone call to Lorelei Baker, saying that the funeral home door was open and that it looked like a break-in."

Puggs sucked in his breath. "I might have made that call."

"And did you represent yourself as a cop?"

"I figured she wouldn't listen to me if I didn't say something like that," Puggs explained. "Man, am I in trouble for that now? Jesus, you try to do a favor for your neighbor and look what the hell happens," he muttered.

"How did you know the door was open?"

He hesitated.

"Come on, Puggs. You're already in pretty deep, so you better tell me."

"I walked past it," he said. "I've always been a fan of that place."

"A fan?"

"Look. I'm not some creeper. I'm not some weirdo who likes funeral homes or anything," he shared. "But I was really close to the old lady who was there. Every once in a while I used to stop by to make sure she was okay, and it's a habit."

"A habit. And does Tasmin know that you do that?"

"I don't know whether she does or not," he said. "Why?"

"She works a lot of nights there, and last night, after you made that phone call, Lorelei called Tasmin to check on the funeral home. I raced up there to find Tasmin unconscious and strapped onto an embalming table, pushed up against the sink, as if ready to be embalmed alive."

"Oh Christ," Puggs cried out. "No, no, no, I wouldn't do that," he cried out.

"Yeah, well, Puggs, you haven't convinced me. So get your ass down here, where I can ask you some more questions face-to-face, or I'll get your ass hauled in here by a squad car immediately."

As he finished speaking, he already heard only a dial tone on the other end of the phone.

CHAPTER 23

AT THE LAWYER'S office, the two sisters stood in front of the reception desk, and Tasmin spoke up. "Hi, Clara. We need to see him, please."

Clara looked up and frowned. "You didn't make an appointment."

"No, we didn't, but we've suddenly discovered some big issues to deal with, and, since they could be time sensitive, we need to talk with him right now," Lorelei stated.

At that, Clara stared at the two of them. "Well now, let me see if he's free." She quickly picked up the phone and gently explained the situation.

Tasmin heard Pete's voice coming through the phone, saying, "Send them in, send them in." At that, she turned and walked over to the door, her sister on her heels, and headed inside.

Pete stood and reached out a hand. "I haven't seen you two girls in a few years now," he said. "What's going on?"

Tasmin stood in front of him and said, "We've got problems."

"Yeah?" he asked cautiously. "Sit down and tell me about it."

She looked over at her sister and asked, "You want to start?"

But Lorelei just shook her head. "This is your deal. You

do this."

So, Tasmin started with the bank accounts, her mother threatening to divorce her father, the money that was rapidly disappearing out of the business, then asked for clarification on who had actual rights to the business and what the current status was because the sisters hadn't been clearly informed about any of it.

He stared at them. "Hang on a minute. What do you mean, you haven't been informed?'

"Just what I said, we haven't been informed."

"I mean, I did a reading of the will."

At that, Lorelei muttered, "Oh great."

Tasmin turned and looked at her. "What do you mean?"

"I was there for the reading of the will, but you weren't."

"And why was I not at the reading of the will?"

"Because you were sick," the lawyer replied in confusion. "Your parents okayed it, and I sent home a copy of the will for you."

She stared at him. "The fact was, I wasn't sick, but my father had me institutionalized for a psych evaluation," she stated, her tone bitter. "Against my will by the way."

He flushed. "I did hear something about that."

"I'm fine, you know. It's my father's way of dealing with his objection to the supposedly horrendous thing that I deal with in my business, plus the fact that I actually like tattoos, which is—in his mind of course—a blasphemous insult to God."

At that, Pete's face turned blustery red.

"Look. We're not here to tear down my father or anybody else," Tasmin snapped, "but I want to see a copy of that will, which, for the record, I have never seen."

He stared at her, then quickly walked over to the filing

cabinet and brought it out. He looked over at Lorelei. "You were here, weren't you?"

"Yes, I was, but I didn't really pay any attention."

He just stared at her, nonplussed.

Tasmin turned to her sister. "Meaning that you didn't pay any attention or that you just let Mom tell you what was in it?" Tasmin shook her head, beyond frustrated.

"I was having a fight with my boyfriend at the time, if you remember," she stated.

"No, I don't really because I had problems of my own, trying to avoid being locked away for the rest of my life. Oh good God, Lorelei, are you telling me that you were texting him the whole time instead of listening to what the will said?"

"Maybe," she muttered. "I didn't really expect there to be anything in the will for me, or about me, but Mom told me that I needed to be here, so I was, but I wasn't very happy about it. And, as it turned out, it was a waste of time because I wasn't mentioned, was I?"

Pete shrugged. "You were mentioned but not in any great financial way."

Tasmin took the will from his hand, quickly flipped through it, and there it was—the business was hers. She dropped it in front of him.

"So, if the business is mine," she asked Pete, "how is it that it was not turned over to me? How is it that my parents are stealing money from the company, and that it was all supposedly turned over to Lorelei?"

Pete blinked at her several times, and then turned and looked at Lorelei.

She shrugged. "Apparently they gave it to me."

He shook his head. "It's not theirs to give."

"That was my understanding," Tasmin declared, staring at him. "And you're the lawyer who's supposed to be keeping all this BS straight, so what's your take on it, and how much are you getting paid for sitting back and staying quiet?"

"Hey, hey, hey," he protested. "I didn't know any of this was going on, and you didn't come to me."

"That's because I was told that I got cut out of the will," she snapped. "Do you think my parents haven't made that very clear?"

He obviously didn't know what to say. "It's still in probate."

"Okay, and, in that case, the business was supposed to function as normal, correct?"

"Yes, and you had signing authority to run the business," Pete pointed out. "I assumed that because you weren't available—" Then he flushed.

"Because my father was trying to find me incompetent, while violating my legal rights. You do realize I haven't granted power of attorney to anyone?"

"They are your parents," he stated, staring at her. "They have power of attorney over you."

"No, they do not," she declared. "I'm thirty fricking years old, and I have my own lawyer, thank you."

At that, he paled. "Oh my God, what have I done?"

"You'll find yourself in legal jeopardy in two seconds flat if you don't explain exactly what you've done and how you plan to fix it. Not to mention my mother has been stealing $20K a month since my grandmother passed away."

He started to shake, literally, right in front of her. She looked over at her sister, and her sister glared at him.

"So, I gather I'm not getting the business," Lorelei said.

"I don't know what to say," Pete stammered, "but obviously there's been a great misunderstanding."

"Yeah? And what is that misunderstanding, Pete?" Tasmin asked. "The fact that I'm actually of sound mind and have been all along? You do realize that what you've done here has gone completely against everything that my grandmother stood for and identified in her Last Will and Testament, which she entrusted you to oversee."

He flushed. "I did check with your parents several times and followed their wishes."

"And yet it wasn't their business."

"But you were not—" And then he stopped again.

"I was then and remain now of absolutely sound mind. This was just a con, the same damn thing as always. It's all about money. We've only just discovered that my mother has helped herself to a good deal of money from the business, like $216,000, from the business bank account, to the point that my sister hasn't even been able to pay the vendors," Tasmin explained, her voice rising in fury. "This all makes me very worried about your competency."

"But—"

"I'm not through. Believe me. I will have my lawyers checking into this immediately, but, in the meantime, I want that money back from my mother, and I want my business as it was intended to be, when it was handed over," she snapped. "And I don't know what the hell is going on with my father, but you can bet that'll be another legal challenge that I am more than fully prepared to meet."

He just stared at her, almost glassy-eyed, as if finally realizing what had happened. "I had no idea something like this was going on."

"Yet how could you not?" she asked, staring at him.

He brightened and turned to his files and pulled out a

document. "Here, this is how."

She looked at it and found it was literally a document declaring that she was not of sound mind and that all the paperwork and money would be under the control of her parents.

"This isn't even a legal document," she said in disgust, "but thanks for this. Now I know with certainty that you're totally okay turning a blind eye to the actual legal ramifications of stealing from one of your clients." She looked at the document and shook her head. "This isn't even Dad's doing this. This is Mom's doing." She turned to face her sister, holding up the document for Lorelei to see.

"So," Lorelei whined, "Mom gave the company to me, but, in the meantime, she was picking it completely clean, so that I didn't even have anything to inherit either?"

At that, Tasmin broke into a bitter laugh. "Yeah, that's about the size of it. However, it wasn't yours in the first place. I've got so many years and hours, hours that both Grandmother and I counted into this estate. And, by the way, the money that you were supposed to get is the money Mom is stealing as well."

"What are you talking about?" Lorelei asked.

"The will, which apparently you were too busy texting to bother to listen to, said you were supposed to receive $50,000 when you turned twenty-five and another $50,000 when probate was completed."

"What?" she asked in outrage. She turned and looked at the lawyer. "What happened to that?"

"At the time you weren't twenty-five," Pete said, "and your mother took charge of it."

The two of them just glared at him.

He flushed. "Wow. I've known your mother a very long

time, so I had absolutely no reason to doubt her."

"Yeah? How about now that we know that she's been stealing money from the company?" Tasmin asked him.

"But why would she do that?" he fretted.

"Because she's finally divorcing my father," she snapped. "And you gave her the means to do so."

∽

HANSON HAD JUST gotten off the phone, getting updates from Tasmin, still shaking his head. The two sisters were about to go track down the mother and have it out with her. In the meantime, Tasmin had apparently contacted her own lawyer, and a legal feud was building that would be of epic proportions. As far as Hanson was concerned, Tasmin had done absolutely nothing wrong. It all went back to the document that her father and the creepy psychiatrist had concocted together to give it a very thinly veiled legal standing. But it wasn't one that would stand up in court. It was literally, as she'd said, all about greed.

When his phone rang, it was the front desk. "Somebody's here to see you."

He got up and walked out to the front, where Puggs stood, turning his hat around in his hand. Motioning him inside, Hanson took Puggs down to one of the interview rooms. "Now you need to talk and tell me all of it."

Puggs glared at him. "It isn't what you think," he said.

"Maybe you could explain that a bit more."

He shook his head. "Only if you won't record me."

"And why is that?"

"Because I don't want anybody thinking I'm crazy."

Slowly Hanson sank back into a chair, studied him, and asked, "Has this got to do with ghosts or something?"

Nodding eagerly, Puggs was wide-eyed. "Yeah, it does. That's why I can't have it go on the record."

"I get it." Hanson pinched the bridge of his nose. "For the moment, you tell me. I'll record it, but I won't—No, let's just talk for a moment."

"Good, just talk," Puggs repeated, "because, if you'll record, I ain't saying nothing."

"Okay, now that we're just talking, what the hell is going on?"

"Her grandmother came to me in ghost form," he began.

He stared carefully at Puggs, this man who looked like his face had been beaten up recently. Remembering the description from one of the first witnesses, Hanson wondered if Puggs was the drive-by shooter. "What do you mean?"

"She told me that Tasmin was in trouble, getting ripped off, and somebody needed to look after her."

Considering what Hanson had just heard on the phone, that made sense. "And how were you looking after her?"

"She wasn't—did you know she wasn't even sleeping anywhere but on the floor in that shop?" he asked in disgust.

"And how did you find that out?"

"Because I came there one day and asked her if she had any coffee. When she sent me into the back to go pour a cup, I saw her bedroll there." He stared at the cop in disgust. "She just had a bag of clothes. That's all she had, and her grandmother was screaming at me to do something. What am I supposed to do?" he asked. "I mean, I didn't do anything, but I was supposed to look after her somehow. I knew she would go up to the funeral home at night. Still, I couldn't figure out, especially if she was working up there all that time, why she had no money to get a place. I figured that maybe, because of what the doctors were saying, that maybe she really was crazy and needed help."

Hanson nodded slowly. "And what kind of help were you trying to give her?"

"I wasn't really trying to give her any help. I was just trying to keep an eye on her and to make sure that she was okay. Things were getting kind of crazy, and then all these drive-by shootings started, and her grandmother just wouldn't leave me alone."

"What was she saying?"

"The same thing over and over, that Tasmin needed help, she needed help. But I'd tell her that there wasn't anything I could do, that I didn't know how to help her. And she'd say I'd have to go, go, go, so I'd get up and I'd go. Next thing I know, I'd find myself wandering around town, wondering what the hell I was doing."

"Whereabouts were you wandering around town?"

"Always different places," he muttered, scrubbing his head. "I didn't even understand what the hell was going on. Then I started to lock myself in, and then I ended up sleepwalking my way out on the other side of town anyway. I took Ubers back home again."

"Ah, shit," Hanson muttered, staring at him.

"What? What's the matter?"

"You're our shooter."

He looked at him and shook his head. "No way, man. I don't do guns. I hate guns."

"Yeah, how come?"

"Because of what happened to my family," he said. "Years ago, they were shot in a break-in."

"Really?" But now Hanson's suspicion was fully and truly aroused. "That's what you say."

"No, it's true," he said, looking at him. "And I don't do guns because of that. You can talk to Pinch. You can talk to anybody."

"I will." As he questioned Puggs on the nights of all the drive-by shootings, every night he found himself out wandering around town. Of course at that point, Hanson was even more suspicious. "Crap, crap, crap," he muttered, as he took notes upon notes. "So you have no alibis, and you found yourself out in every one of these locations on the nights of the shootings, and you're telling me flat-out that you didn't do it."

But now Puggs stared at him with fear in his eyes. "I didn't do it, man. I did not do it."

"Okay," Hanson said cautiously. "You know how it looks though, right?"

"Yeah, I know how it looks. Talk to Pinch. He knows me. He knows my family history."

"I will talk to Pinch, but I need you to stay here for now."

"No, I have to go to work. I have to go to work."

"Why is that?"

"Well, for one, Rose needs me," he said. "I look after her, make arrangements to ensure she's okay," he replied, "and Pinch depends on me."

"It could be that Pinch needs to find somebody else to depend on over all this," Hanson suggested, "because we must get to the bottom of this, and I want you to stay in jail here overnight."

"Why?"

"If we get another drive-by shooting, and you're here, we'll know it's not you."

Puggs opened his mouth and then slammed it shut, and

he slowly nodded. "Fine, but it's not me. I can tell you right now it's not me. And I have to go to work."

"I hear you," Hanson stated, "but I am not so sure about letting you go to work right now. Let me go talk to Pinch."

With that, he got up and sent one of the detectives to get Puggs a bottle of water and to keep him comfortable, then Hanson started making phone calls. When he reached Pinch on the phone, he explained, "Hey, I got Puggs in here. Apparently he's a sleepwalker."

"Ah, shit," Pinch groaned. "Man, that kid just can't catch a break."

"You want to tell me about his history?"

"His father came home and shot his sister and his mother. He also shot Puggs but didn't kill him. It got pretty ugly there for a while, but he survived, on the streets after foster care, but he was different afterward. He's always been super protective, always the one person who would go to bat for the underdog. He's just an all-round nice guy. He would never hurt a fly."

Hanson interrupted, "Except for the fact that he woke up miles away from home and just a few blocks from every one of these damn drive-by shootings, every single night we've had one." Hanson sighed. "And Puggs has got absolutely no recollection of anything happening during that time."

There was shocked silence on the other end, and then Pinch swore. "No way he'd do that, man, no way. He loved that last victim, like, he loved her. He was even going to talk to her about going out with him."

Hanson tried to imagine the twenty-one-year-old and a beaten-up, bruised, and broken old street fighter together, but he knew love put a whole different spin on things. So it wasn't for him to judge that pairing. But he wished he had the young woman alive to ask. "I'll have to talk to her family about that to see if there was any relationship between them."

"You do that," Pinch said. "I'm telling you, man, no way Puggs would have done this. You have to understand that he's a gentle soul, and, after everything with his family, he absolutely detests guns. Now he might have followed the guy and tried to stop these killings. That I could see," Pinch admitted, "but no way he would have been responsible for it. Sleepwalking or no."

Long after he hung up the phone, Hanson sat here, staring off in the distance, trying to figure out this crap. Something didn't make any sense to him.

He picked up the phone and dialed Stefan. Afraid that somebody would hear when Stefan answered, Hanson said, "I'm stepping outside, so I can talk a little privately."

"Good enough. What's the matter?"

"I'm just trying to figure out how much ghosts can have an effect on other people."

"They can do all kinds of shit unfortunately," Stefan replied.

Hanson explained about the drive-by shootings and Puggs waking up streets away from home, but not very far from all these killings.

"It's possible, but, if that's his innate personality, a ghost cannot force him to do something completely abhorrent to his nature. If it's not part of his belief system or if it's something he's completely against, a ghost cannot force him to get past that feeling and make him kill anyway."

"Interesting, so based on what I've told you, what do you think?"

"Based on what you've told me, I would say he's quite possibly not the shooter, but that doesn't mean that it couldn't be some kind of a possession issue."

"Possession? Oh, shit, I won't like this, will I?"

"I just don't know what to tell you, but the fact of the matter is, he could be possessed at the time or could be racing behind this killer. He could even be showing up just in time to be a great patsy for this but not necessarily be the killer."

"Yeah, I won't like any of this. Of course this is all superficial, and—outside of the fact that I had him not very far away on every one of these locations with no alibi—it'll be an even bigger problem."

"It's hard to convict on something like this too," Stefan shared apologetically. "Just think about trying to bring this evidence to court."

"There's just no way," Hanson noted.

"No, there isn't," Stefan confirmed. "What is quite likely is that somebody who's close to him could be doing this to him, because he's either somebody they can manipulate or somebody they don't like and can't manipulate."

"Can't manipulate?"

"Or they're manipulating in order to get him into trouble because they can't get what they really want from him."

"Oh Jesus. Why the hell is none of this straightforward?"

"None of it is ever straightforward," Stefan told him, with half a smile. "But, as you'll see over time, it's quite worth it." And, with that, he hung up.

Hanson stood here outside the police station for a long moment, trying to get his head wrapped around this. As he headed back into the station, a woman raced by, and he realized it was Pinch's sister. She was ahead of him, bolting into the main reception area. He stepped back slightly and called Pinch. "Your sister's here. Did you know that?"

"Christ," Pinch said. "What else can go wrong? I'll be right there. She probably heard that Puggs was there. She's very close to him. She'll throw a hissy fit over this. As far as she's concerned, he can do no wrong."

"Right," Hanson noted, "but I haven't charged him with anything. However, I am detaining him."

"Yeah, *great*," Pinch muttered. "I'll be there in ten."

With that, Hanson walked in to find Rose at the front desk, trying to see Puggs. Hanson walked right past her.

She called out, "Hey, I know you."

He turned and raised an eyebrow, and asked, "Do I know you?"

She frowned. "You were at my brother's tattoo parlor."

He nodded. "Yes, that's right. You're Pinch's sister, right?"

She beamed. "I'm doing the family memoirs."

"Right, that should be interesting reading."

"It is. I just don't have enough information, but I'm getting there."

"What do you mean that you're getting there?"

She just gave him an oddly vacant smile, and he tried to remind himself that she was different—damaged, but different—and still she was beautiful, very angelic looking. Behind him he heard a series of horrible shouts and then gunfire. He immediately bolted down the hallway.

Rose called down the hallway, "It's too late."

He froze, turned, and stared at her, the pieces slowly tumbling into place. But it was too far out there for his mind to grasp all the nuances. The tableau in from of him stood as if locked in time. As if in some weird way she had stopped time. At least for the three men in her vicinity.

If stopping time were possible.

Rose stood beside one of the cops, who had just come in from where Puggs had been waiting, plus Mark was there. He was looking over at John, and the two of them had their guns out—but weren't moving—while Rose smiled, saying, "It's really too late."

"What did you do?" Hanson asked her, taking a half step toward her, wondering just what all she'd done. His gaze darted from one man to another.

"Puggs couldn't live after this, could he?"

"Of course he could, and he should," Hanson snapped. "All he was trying to do was protect you."

"I couldn't let him continue to protect me when he didn't love me, and he made it clear that he loved Jenny, not me."

Hanson stared at her, wondering if it were really that simple.

"So, you had Puggs do all those drive-by shootings because he loved the last victim?"

Rose blinked at him. "Oh, it doesn't sound very good when you put it that way, does it?"

"No, it doesn't." Hanson's gaze was intense, as he suddenly looked at the cop who stood with his gun pointed at John and Mark.

Such an odd look was on Mark's face, as if he were struggling to free himself. Hanson had no inner knowledge of anything going on with the other two men. Including the one positioned to shoot.

"And what have you got these guys in, some kind of a hypnotic trance?"

"Kind of." She waved a hand in the general direction of

the men. "I can reach out and grab people inside their minds and make them do things." She giggled. "It's pretty fun."

"Oh, that's bullshit," John snapped at her side, as if finally regaining control, and pissed at having lost it in the first place. "You're nothing but a fucking loony bin."

She looked over at him, and, with an ease that shook Hanson to the core, she seemed to reach into John's brain and rattle it. He shook violently on the spot and then collapsed to the ground, still riddled with tremors.

Rose looked back at Hanson, and her face lit up. "See?"

"I do see. That's a pretty neat trick," he said cautiously. What the hell was he to do against this shit? How could anyone stop her? Unless they had similar skills.

"Yep, it sure is," Rose declared. "It makes life easier when I can get people to do what I want because it's really not very nice when they don't do what I want. It makes me very angry."

At this point Pinch had arrived. In time to hear her last statement. Rose didn't see him, but Pinch stood frozen, hearing those chilling words coming out of Rose's mouth. A cop nearby was making sure Pinch didn't do anything stupid here.

Hanson asked Rose, "And did you have anything against all those drive-by victims, or was it just the fact that your brother was very involved with them?"

"No, I needed them," she stated earnestly. "You have to understand that they were necessary sacrifices."

"Necessary sacrifices?"

She nodded and beamed. Mark was staring at her, like he was ready to shoot her dead. Hanson hoped they didn't until they got answers, yet Hanson was afraid that shooting her would be the only way to stop this. At least he hoped it would ... "And what were they necessary victims for?"

"The book I'm doing, of course," she stated simply, as if he should have understood. "I'm doing memoirs, but how can you do his life in art history, if there isn't any art to memorialize. People have to be dead for that to happen."

Pinch slapped a hand to his mouth, trying not to make any noise. The cop moved him silently away from the door and any backward glance by his sister.

"But you could have just taken pictures of the tattoos, right?" Hanson asked.

"I could have, but everything's in the past, and it's not in the past until they're actually dead."

"Whoa, whoa, whoa, what do you mean?"

"I'm doing a *memorial*." She shook her head and explained again, as if Hanson were simple and just wasn't getting it. "That means everything has to be in the past."

"Right, but it's usually the artist who's done and gone."

"That was next," she declared, with a bright smile. "After all this was over, that would be next."

Pinch looked ghostly white.

"So, you would kill your own brother so you could finish the book?" Hanson asked, side-eyeing Pinch.

"Yes, exactly." She beamed at him. "See? It's not that hard to figure this out," she said in such an encouraging tone of voice, as if urging Hanson to try harder.

Behind him, Hanson heard the door open, then watched with horror as Tasmin walked in. Tasmin immediately froze and took in the scene going on around her.

Rose turned, looked at Tasmin, and beamed. "Hey, Tasmin. Come on in."

She walked in cautiously. "Rose, what's going on?"

The cop who had the gun facing John still hadn't

moved, as if he were completely frozen. As was Mark. John's tremors had stopped. Hanson feared he was dead. Whatever Rose had done appeared to be fatal.

"I was just explaining to your friend here why all those people had to die," Rose told Tasmin.

Hanson replied before Tasmin could. "The earlier ones I don't understand at all, although I think maybe I understand Jenny." Hanson deliberately tried to draw Rose's attention back to him and to leave Tasmin a way out.

"Yes, well, Jenny had to go right from the beginning, plus the other people—once I realized what a good idea this was. I mean, Jenny wasn't even going to get a tattoo."

"Until you convinced her, I suppose," Hanson suggested cautiously.

"Exactly." She gave a clipped nod. "And Puggs helped with that. And she loved Puggs, and Puggs loved her, and it was disgusting," Rose declared in a vicious tone. "Puggs was mine."

"So, that's why Jenny had to go," Hanson stated, with sudden understanding.

"That's why she had to go, and that's why Puggs had to go, like go-go. There was just no other way for it. I couldn't tolerate that kind of betrayal. But I would use him to get the job done in the meantime," she admitted, with a beaming smile.

"And what did you do just now?"

"Oh, I had him take a gun from one of the cops and shoot him, as if trying to escape. But, of course, I made sure he didn't do a good job, so the cop could turn around and defend himself, and now Puggs is dead." She gave a royal wave of her hand.

"And that doesn't bother you?" Tasmin asked quietly. "I

thought you loved him."

She looked at Tasmin, frowning. "Yes, it does bother me." She gave a dismissive shrug. "However, I won't think about it right now."

"No, of course not," Tasmin stated, "because then you would have to accept responsibility for your actions."

"I *am* responsible for my actions," she snapped. "Puggs betrayed me, so he's responsible for the repercussions of his actions."

"You are responsible for what he did to the others though, aren't you?" Tasmin pressed.

"Sure, in a way." Rose smiled dreamily. "It's not as if he would have done that on his own."

"No, of course not, because Puggs was all about looking after people, the way he looked after you all this time," Tasmin murmured gently, as she walked a couple steps forward.

By now cops were all around, and everyone had a gun raised at Rose, as they listened to the horror story coming out in her angelic voice. Most at the end of the hallway, as close as anyone dared.

Pinch was frozen, maybe in shock.

Hanson knew there would be one million questions, no matter how it ended. This was beyond what most could comprehend. He just wished Tasmin hadn't shown up.

"What did you do to the cop on the floor?" Tasmin motioned to John.

"He didn't believe that I could shake somebody's brain." Rose shrugged. "It's really not that hard. But when I jump inside, if I can get them to do what I want them to do, then I don't have to shake them."

"Have you killed very many people?" Mark asked, finally

getting control of his body, his voice hoarse.

"Plenty," she declared, "but only the ones who pissed me off, not that you would ever recognize who they were. I mean, there was that homeless guy, who was gross, and he touched my pant leg. Pinch was with me at the time, and the guy suddenly had a seizure." She gave her brother a beatific smile. "Not my fault it killed him."

"But of course it killed him," Tasmin stated, "and you were the one responsible."

Hanson glared at Tasmin, wishing she would quit confronting Rose. This could end so badly.

Rose shrugged. "Maybe it's my fault, a little bit, but it's not my problem."

"Not your problem?" Mark cried out in rage. "You just killed my partner."

She looked down at John on the floor. "He's not dead, but he'll wish he was. He's kind of, you know." And then she made a circling motion alongside her head. "He'll be looney tunes now." And then she laughed. "Hey, Tasmin, you understand all about that, don't you?"

"I understand other people who seem to think I'm like that." She looked over at Hanson, then back at Rose. "Did you have anything to do with my father's instability?"

"He's really crazy. He's one of those guys who you can just go into that playground in his head and put suggestions in there, and he runs with it."

She nodded. "Yeah, and I gather that's why he's really strange all of a sudden. Did you decide that was just another thing you should try?"

"Once we started—it was really your grandmother's fault, you know that."

Tasmin sighed. "And here I thought my grandmother

was a beautiful woman."

"She was, and she did an awful lot to keep me in control." Rose's smile widened. "She used to talk to me all the time about how I needed to only use my abilities for good. Not to collect other damaged souls—which is seriously easy to do by the way…" she shrugged, "So, it's her fault really."

"How is it her fault?" Tasmin cried out in outrage. Collect? Damaged souls? Like what an army of entities? That didn't bear thinking about.

"She died," Rose stated. "And, once she died, I mean, there was nobody to look after me."

"She didn't die on her own though, did she?"

"Nope, she didn't, but she didn't know that. Your father killed her." Rose giggled. "I didn't even have to do anything with him. He did that all on his own. Yet I think it did something to him. It slowly destroyed whatever sanity was inside him. You're the sanest of the lot, Tasmin, if truth be told. But watching everybody play games around you, that was scary, and the guardians you collected … How? I don't get it. Even Hanson's brother was out there keeping your place safe—well as much as he could." She laughed mockingly. "But look at you? You're doing fine now," she said cheerfully.

"Can you manipulate anybody?" Hanson asked.

"Lots of people but not everybody. I tried to get inside your mind." She turned and glared at him. "But I can't. I can't get inside Tasmin's either. I don't understand."

"We have guards up, for one," Tasmin explained, with a note of humor. "My grandmother taught me that."

"Right, back to your grandmother again. See? I've really missed her," Rose added in a forlorn tone of voice. "If she hadn't died, none of this would have happened. Your grandmother was keeping me well and truly comfortable. And, of course, what you don't realize is that you were doing it too."

"I was doing some things with her," Tasmin noted cautiously.

"Yeah, you didn't get any of the notes that she left you because I didn't leave them around long enough for you to get them. Because, whatever she was doing, I figured I'd be better off without her doing it. So all those notes that she supposedly left you that you've been looking for and couldn't find were the notes and the instructions about how to keep me under control. It's only now I realize how much smoother and happier my life was with her around."

"That's too big for me to control," Tasmin shared in astonishment. "That's way too much to put on me."

"That's what I thought too, so you're welcome."

"But you didn't kill her?" Tasmin asked, with a note of fear.

"I told you. Your father did that, and that's also why he's kind of loopy right now. I think your grandma did something at the time, and he just, … well, he won't be normal ever again. Sorry about that."

Tasmin nodded. "I feel better knowing that somebody who absolutely loved her didn't try to kill her."

"Not me, not Puggs. We all loved her. She was beautiful, and she was the only person who made any sense in my crazy world," Rose muttered.

"And I'm sorry you've had such a hard time of it," Tasmin said, stepping closer and reaching out a hand.

"Nobody touches me. You know that," she whispered, as she looked down at Tasmin's hand a whisper away from her arm.

"Except my grandmother."

At that, Rose smiled, and a tear came to her eye, shocking Hanson. How the hell did this even work? Her moods were mercurial, yet something odd was happening with Tasmin. Worried, he could only watch their interaction with wariness.

"She was beautiful," Tasmin repeated. "She was beautiful inside and out. And she could touch you like you didn't realize anybody could."

"That's true." Rose looked over at Tasmin. "Did she show you how to do it?"

"I don't think so. I've never tried before."

"Well, don't," Rose snapped. "Otherwise I'll have to kill you too."

Tasmin just smiled and closed her hand around Rose's arm. "Do you really think you can?"

"Absolutely I can." Rose's smile turned mean. "Ready to find out?"

CHAPTER 24

IT FELT LIKE a fist coming through Tasmin's brain, rattling the contents inside her head. Instincts and training kicked in. Tasmin immediately followed her grandmother's rules, grabbed that hand, snapped it back at the wrist, and tossed it back out again.

Rose collapsed to the floor, screaming in agony. But it wasn't enough. Rose opened her eyes, and naked hatred glared at Tasmin.

With the tiniest movement as Rose ever-so-slightly started to close her eyes, Tasmin realized what would happen next—and reacted first. She drove her fist right into Rose's brain, grabbed it, and rattled it hard.

Giving Rose a taste of her own medicine.

Rose stiffened, stared at her, and then, in a shocking movement, fell flat onto the floor, completely unconscious.

At that, Hanson raced forward and bent down beside the fallen woman. He checked for a pulse, then looked up at Tasmin. "She's still alive. Does that mean she's still dangerous?" he asked urgently, as the other men slowly approached, weapons drawn, as if that were the proper defense in this war.

"She's alive, but ... I don't know where her brain function is," Tasmin whispered. "Yet we must ensure that she can't do that anymore."

Hanson nodded. "Yeah, you're not kidding. That needs to never happen again."

The captain raced up behind them. "I don't know what the hell that was, but she doesn't get back up again."

Everybody surrounded their group, the captain barking orders everywhere. "Make sure she ends up in Bellevue. She's incredibly dangerous. And get those damn ambulances in here. We have injuries, people. Move."

Organized chaos took over. Hanson led Tasmin to lean against a hallway out of the way but where she could still see what was going on.

Watching the men take care of things, they, for the most part, ignored her. Tasmin wondered if everybody would treat her differently now. Hanson, who'd been called over to speak with the captain, walked back to her, wrapped her up in his arms, and pulled her close. She whispered, "Is she out of the building?"

"She is now," he confirmed. "I watched them load her into the ambulance." He added, "Can she heal from whatever you did? Enough to play those killing games again? Even a little bit? If so, we need to find a way to stop her."

As if hearing that same question, Stefan stepped into her mind. *In this case, we must ensure that she can't come back in the form she was before.*

She whispered to Stefan, "Then you do it. I'm not even sure how."

He slowly added, *Honestly I think you already did. The stem between the two parts of the brain has been separated. Energy is there, but it's aimless. No control. No direction. No intention behind it.* He heaved a sigh of relief. *We don't need to do anything more. Good job.* And, with that, he was gone.

She looked up at Hanson, and he crushed her in his arms and whispered, "Thank God that's over."

CHAPTER 25

TASMIN LOOKED UP at the building and blinked. "I didn't even realize we were coming back to your place." Then another yawn escaped, and she muttered, "And honestly I really don't care right now."

He chuckled. "I think we have a few things to talk about."

"If you're planning on talking, that won't go down so well. I'm tired, worn out, and my head is killing me."

"I recognize that," he murmured. "Come on. Let's get you upstairs."

"What will the captain do about all this?"

"Honestly I think he's got the biggest headache of his life right now, trying to figure out what to do, who gets charged, and how. The bottom line of it all is how could he possibly convict anybody on this? Thankfully that's not your problem or mine. I did suggest that maybe he contact Stefan about it. He recognized the name but wasn't at all sure for the reasoning behind calling him. When I explained that this is something he's had to work with over the last multiple decades in terms of convicting killers like this, he might want to get some advice as to what was culpable and not."

"I can't imagine him thinking very highly about the suggestion."

"I think at the moment he's pretty shell-shocked and not

at all sure where to go. He definitely needs to talk to somebody who knows more than the captain does about these matters. He also has to explain what happened to John to the brass and to John's family."

"Good on him if he does it."

Hanson led the way to the front of the apartment building, unlocked the door, and nudged her inward toward the stairs. "Stairs or elevator?" he muttered to her.

She yawned again.

"Elevator it is."

She chuckled. "I'm not that tired."

"Yes, you are. You can barely stay awake."

"I think it's the energy," she muttered, "from whatever the hell that woman was doing."

"Do you remember any of it, all of it?"

"As I try to remember what happened," she explained, "a lot more is coming into place, and it's beginning to make a whole lot more sense."

He looked at her, startled.

She shrugged. "Remember? She knew my grandmother. And being around my grandmother meant that I was exposed to an awful lot of stuff very early on."

"I never really expected something like this though," he admitted. "Rose was pretty adamant about not having killed your grandmother, but do you believe her?"

"I don't know. Maybe. My father has deteriorated rapidly, and I wouldn't be at all surprised if that wasn't the end result of murdering my grandmother. It would make me very sad to think that she was cut down in the prime of her life like that."

"Prime?" he repeated, with a wry look. "Most people wouldn't think an eighty-year-old was in her prime."

"You didn't know my grandmother," Tasmin declared, with a wry look in his direction. "She was a force. You don't see many like her anymore."

When the elevator doors opened, he led the way to his apartment. Unlocking it, he helped her inside. "Do you want to crash on the bed or the couch?"

"Couch will be fine." She yawned again.

"I don't know about that," he muttered. "You're pretty-damn tired."

She sighed. "I don't even know how much of it is sleepy-tired versus just exhausted from everything that happened."

"With good reason. I mean, think about it. In all that you've been through, just so much is wrong with this, with everything in your world."

"So much wrong," she murmured. "And it's frustrating because you know shit was going down that you can't do anything about, but you just don't know how to make it right."

"You can't blame yourself for your grandmother's death."

"And how do I even come to terms with that?" she asked, looking at him.

As they sat down on the couch, he pulled her into his arms. "Just relax for a bit."

She chuckled but turned into his embrace and snuggled up close. He put his feet up atop the coffee table, and she stretched out even more in his arms.

"What will we do about this?" she muttered after a moment.

He didn't even answer. She shifted so she could look up at him, and his eyes were closed, his chest rising in a rhythmic motion.

"Have you gone to sleep?" she asked, reaching out and lightly smacking his arm.

"Ouch." He chuckled. "And, besides, I was just resting my eyes."

"*Uh-huh*. How is it you can just do that, zap out, and not have any trouble sleeping?"

"Practice?" he replied, with a questioning tone.

"Maybe, but, if that's what it takes, I need to figure out how to do that."

"You're doing just fine. You know that, right?"

"It doesn't feel like it, not when I know what's going on with my mom."

"Your mom, your dad, your grandmother. It's a lot to process."

"I know. And, at the heart of it all, I'm not sure how my sister will handle it."

"And how will she handle the fact that your father killed your grandmother?"

"In a way she might be okay with that."

Startled, he stared at her. Tasmin shrugged. "You have to understand. My grandmother and I were close, but maybe my grandmother wasn't exactly the person I always thought that she was. And I'm not at all sure that everybody else loved her the way I did."

"Ah," he said gently. "From what I'm hearing, maybe not."

"And yet everybody had so much good to say about her that I'm … confused."

"You have every right to be confused, and nothing has to be solved right anyway."

"Are you sure?" she asked. "It seems as if we got only so many answers."

"And the other answers will come," he said. "We got the big ones, and that's the real issue. We still have a lot of things to settle up, not the least of which is your grandmother's will, the lawyers, the funeral home business, your mom's stealing, all of that."

"I know," she whispered.

As they snuggled here, her phone rang.

She groaned. "I don't even think I want to answer that." But she reached for her phone and looked at the screen. "*Great*, it's my sister."

"And she might need you right now."

"What she needs and what I need are two different things." But she answered it. "Lorelei, what's up?"

Her voice was shaky as she replied, "Mom's gone."

"Of course she is. She probably saw the writing on the wall and booked it."

"Yeah, guess who she booked it with?"

"The lawyer," Tasmin replied.

There was a moment of shocked silence on the other end of the phone. "How did you know?"

"Because it's the only way this would ever come off. The lawyer had to be crooked and involved." She looked over at Hanson, who nodded gently.

"They won't get far," Hanson said.

"How do you know?" Lorelei cried out. "They could have been gone for hours."

"I don't think so. We've had a rough day, I admit, but I'm pretty sure the cops are on it." At that, Hanson added, "I put out an APB for her earlier. I don't know how far they're planning on getting, but—"

"She took a lot of money from the company," Lorelei said. "I still can't believe she did that."

"I believe it," Tasmin stated. "She was getting desperate and wanted out. Dad was getting so much worse. By the way, we also got accusations today that Dad may have killed Grandma." There was silence and then Tasmin said, "You already suspected that though, didn't you?"

"I wondered," Lorelei replied. "Mom mentioned something once that made me question it, and you already heard about the conversation that I overheard between them."

"I suspect Dad will be picked up pretty soon too."

At that, her sister started to cry.

"It'll be all right," Tasmin said gently.

"How can you say that?" she murmured. "Man, I hated the damn business, and believe me. I'm certainly glad it's not mine, but the layers of betrayal, the deceit. I can't even believe it."

Tasmin winced at that. She'd had a lot more years dealing with the family dysfunction than her sister had. "For that I'm sorry," Tasmin told Lorelei. "I don't know whether you want to work in the business or not, but you can if you want."

"No, I don't. It always creeped me out. I hated being upstairs, knowing dead people were downstairs. I hated being downstairs, knowing bodies were there."

"Which is why I was so surprised that they gave you the business."

"And now we find out they only gave me the business because I'm too stupid to know anything about it or to challenge anything, so they could rip me off, and I wouldn't even know."

There wasn't anything Tasmin could say to that because unfortunately it was quite possibly true. "Decide what you want to do now," Tasmin suggested, "and I'll help you make it happen."

At that, her sister hesitated. "You mean, you'd help me financially?"

"Of course. Obviously we have to figure out how to get the money back because of our dear mother and the lawyer thievery. So I don't know exactly how much money there'll be for a while."

"You need to go to the funeral home and sort it out," Lorelei said in exasperation, "because I never could make those figures match up."

"How bad is it?"

"Oh, it's bad," Lorelei admitted, "so I hope you've got some money saved that you can pay the vendors with. Otherwise they'll be pissed at you, and you'll be in real deep trouble."

"*Great*, thanks for the heads-up." Tasmin could already feel a headache coming on.

"Look. I'll head out and visit some friends for a while," Lorelei said.

"Which friends?"

"Hey, you're not my mom."

"No, but it's been a pretty rough couple days, and I'd like to not have to worry about you as well."

"Fine, that makes sense. I'll just go to Rosanne's place, down the coast a bit."

"Okay, you do that. Relax. We'll figure this out."

"Right," she muttered. And, with that, her sister hung up.

Tasmin slowly put her phone on the coffee table.

"I guess that's a pretty rough one for her, isn't it?" Hanson asked.

"Yeah, it's been pretty rough on all of us. It goes along

with a father who's losing it, plus a mother who had already decided to walk away and was just looking for somebody to help make it happen." Tasmin shook her head at that. "You know the funeral home business is a cash cow, right?"

He stared at her.

She nodded. "It makes money hand over fist, at least it used to. What they did in the meantime to drive it into the ground so quickly, I can't even imagine," she muttered.

"But you'll fix it," he stated confidently.

She smiled. "Yeah, I will."

"And your grandmother, do you think she's at ease right now?"

At that, she caught movement in the living room, then smiled, pointed it out, and suggested, "Why don't we ask her. Grandma, are you okay now?"

Her grandmother shimmered in front of her. "I am now. I couldn't let her go off like that."

"You left notes apparently."

"Yes. They're in the home. Your mom got a hold of everything and locked it up. I don't know where."

"We'll find them. Obviously it was about Rose."

"It was about Rose. It was about a lot of things including …" Grandma mentioned something garbled.

At that, Tasmin turned and looked at Hanson. "Did you hear what she said?"

"Yeah, something about bank accounts."

She nodded. "That would make sense too. Grandma, did you leave all that bank account information somewhere?"

Then came a light laugh, which started to fade, along with the spirit form.

Tasmin bolted to her feet. "Wait."

But there was no waiting, as her grandmother was disappearing in front of her. She felt the tears in the back of her eyes and her throat. "Goodbye, Grandma," she whispered gently.

She felt a hug wrapping around her, then, just like that, Grandma was gone. She turned to see Hanson standing behind her, his arms open. She stepped into them and burrowed deep. "I really loved her," she whispered.

"That was good because she loved you too," he noted gently. "Obviously she was the safe place in a life caught up in a storm."

She nodded at that. "And it was just so insane with my father."

"We have a lot of things to sort out with him, not the least of which is a full investigation into that psychiatric hospital and the treatment you were put through."

"Good. Tear it to the ground," she muttered.

"Maybe. I need to find some people to give me a hand with that."

"Maybe Dr. Maddy. She mentioned something about helping me that time."

"Yep, not a problem. We'll get her on board, if she's willing. Other than that, we'll figure it out together."

"Does that mean you'll stay?"

He shrugged. "Does that mean you'll stay?" he asked in a teasing voice.

She searched his gaze. "I will if you will."

"If you are, I am," he vowed.

She grinned, slipped her arms around his chest, and laid her head against his heart. "I didn't expect this."

"And maybe that's why it happened," he guessed, his arms gently stroking up and down her back. "I think sometimes, when we're not expecting it, good things happen.

Yet, when we're out there, trying hard to find good things, it's almost like our energy or our desperation chases it away."

She pondered that, looked up at him, and nodded. "I was pretty desperate for quite a while," she murmured. "As far as I'm concerned, I asked for help, and help came. I just didn't recognize the form when it came," she noted, with a chuckle.

"Hopefully you're not disappointed."

"With you? Never," she murmured. "I'm hungry."

He rolled his eyes at that. "Of course you're hungry. I need a shower, and, if we order food first, by the time we have a chance to settle down, have a shower, and get changed, it should be here."

She pondered that for a moment and nodded. "Not a bad idea." She looked around at his apartment. "Do you want to stay here?"

He frowned at her. "I don't want to stay in your loft if I don't have to, although I think we should build out the loft."

"Or move the entire business to the funeral home," she suggested. "Lots of empty offices are there."

He stared at her. "That would make a whole lot more sense, wouldn't it?"

She nodded. "It absolutely would."

"Sounds good to me," he noted, "but I can't say that sleeping at the funeral home will be at the top of my list."

"I don't know. There's a certain peacefulness to it."

"In what way?" he asked.

She shrugged. "I've just always felt at home there."

"Even after being locked up? And who the hell was responsible for that anyway?"

She pondered that. "I suspect that, when we find my mom, she'd be the first person to ask, either her or my father. I can see my father doing it and leaving me, not wanting to ever touch me again and dirty his hands anymore, but making sure I was there already trussed-up and ready for Bellevue."

"Which is just beyond the pale," he muttered.

"But those are answers that we can sort out later," she murmured. "I'm pretty sure it's bound to be either one of them, if not both."

"What takeout do you want? There's a really good Greek place around the corner."

She looked at him with interest. "Go ahead and order, and I'll jump into the shower first."

He rolled his eyes at that. "Don't you take all the hot water."

"No, I won't." She laughed, as she raced toward his bedroom.

There she stripped off her clothes and crawled into the hot water. It was so tempting to just stand here and have the heat wash all over her, and it reminded her of how exhausted she really was. She yawned several times, but she managed to scrub down. By the time she figured she'd used up more than her share of water, she was about to turn it off when she found him stepping in behind her.

She burst out laughing. "I guess that saves on wastage, doesn't it?"

He just nodded and grinned, then grabbed the bar of soap and asked, "Are you done?"

"I am. You want me to get out so you have room?"

"No." He handed her the bar of soap. "But you can make yourself useful."

Surprised and yet charmed, she had him turn around and proceeded to scrub down his whole back. He was a big man, and an awful lot of real estate was involved that needed a good scrub. By the time she was done, he turned obediently, and she smiled to see the erection between them.

He shrugged. "Hard to contain myself in this case," he muttered. "Naked woman in a shower." He gave her a sloppy grin. "Kind of perfect."

"It depends what you mean by perfect," she added, as she went to work on his chest. "I mean, beds are kind of perfect."

"Those are perfect too." He smiled. "Yet there's nothing wrong with a shower."

"I don't know. I think it's one of those things that people talk about being great but it isn't actually all that great," she explained.

"Have you ever tried it?" he challenged.

"Nope," she muttered. "I think my brain always convinced me to opt for the bed."

With that he swooped down, snatched her up, and planted her gently against the tiles, then nudged up to her, his erection pressing intimately against her.

She wiggled. "That part is really nice."

He smiled, his hand sliding all the way down her body to each of her butt cheeks, where he lifted her gently a bit higher and positioned himself right at the heart of her.

"No foreplay this way though," she murmured, as she kissed him.

But when he didn't move, she started to twist even more against him. "You know something? Foreplay's overrated."

He chuckled. "No, it's sure not, but all that soapy scrubbing was doing it for me. I was hoping it was doing it for you too."

"If you don't do something soon," she threatened,

"you'll find out how I feel about all this teasing."

His hand lifted her chin, and he kissed her, gently at first and then harder and harder, as passion overtook the two of them. Before she realized it, she was panting in his embrace, her arms looped over his neck.

"You damn well better do something about this now," she complained.

"Yeah, and what will you do if I don't?" he teased.

She reached a hand down between them, her fingers encircling him, and he let out a growl. "Yeah," she muttered. "Two of us can play that game."

He entered her in one fell swoop, making her gasp, her head relaxing against the tiles, the water washing all over them. And then, when he started to move, her world went to pieces again and again and then again.

By the time he slowed, his breathing raspy, as he held her pinned against the wall, he whispered, "So, what do you think about showers now?"

"God, they're death machines." But then she gave him an impudent grin. "And I've never died quite so nicely before."

He burst out laughing, turned off the water, and only then did she realize the heat was gone from the water, and it was down to a tepid temperature.

He slowly separated from her and said, "With any luck, dinner should be here soon."

Her eyes widened, then she nodded. "In that case, let's go."

And he helped her get out and across the tiles, so she wouldn't slip on the wet floor. He tossed her a towel and then followed her out.

"You know," she said, shaking her head. "I really never … I never expected this."

"I know. We mentioned it once before."

"It just feels like, when it's right, it's right, and you slip into this mode, unsure of how or when it ever happened. I don't know where you were before, but it seems you've always been here as a part of me," she murmured.

"I won't say that I've been there all this time, but I certainly haven't been holding back," he admitted, reaching out with a comb and gently untangling her hair.

She waited, letting him take care of her, and then he wrapped her hair up in a towel and squeezed off most of the moisture.

With that done, he noted, "We really do need to get you some clothes."

"I know. I'm constantly wearing yesterday's clothes, and it's starting to get pretty disgusting."

He walked over to his dresser and pulled out a big T-shirt and handed it to her.

She grinned, tossed it on, and it came down well below her hips.

He stood in the bedroom and glanced at her, a smile twitching at his lips. "My clothes have never looked so nice. You know that, right?"

She smiled and walked past him, her chipmunk cheeks bunching the T-shirt as she walked, and she added a little extra sashay to it as she moved past him. "Why is it that I seem to end up with no clothes on when I'm around you?" she asked. "Not that I'm complaining, mind you."

Just then the doorbell rang.

She raced to the door, and he yelled, "Wait."

She stopped, turned to him, and nodded. "Right, we still have to be careful until everybody's picked up, *huh?*"

"Exactly."

But she looked through the door peephole, and it was the delivery guy.

He quickly paid for the food, brought it into the living room, sat down, and asked, "You okay to eat here?"

"I'm okay to eat anywhere. I want to eat, and then I want to sleep for a week."

"And yet ..."

"I know, and yet I can't. I have my own jobs. Plus now I need to go take care of the funeral home."

"It's got to be tough for your sister to know that they gave it to her intentionally, knowing she wouldn't know the difference when they stole from her and that they could do it easily."

She nodded. "That's on her though. That's not on me, and I know a whole lot more about the detailed workings of that place than either of my parents understood because I ran it with my grandmother."

"Seriously?"

She nodded. "Yes. Everything from the financing to collections to picking up caskets and dealing with the vendors. Seriously, it was my place right from the beginning. I just need to make sure that my sister knows there'll be something for her too. Whatever that means, whatever she decides to do," Tasmin said, "I'll be there to help her."

He reached over a hand, and she placed hers in it. He nodded. "I hear that."

She squeezed his fingers and whispered, "And you'll stick around close, right?"

"I will, unless you got a problem with that."

"No, but you'll have to get more comfortable with the funeral home."

He winced and then shrugged. "I guess considering what you and I see …"

"Exactly, and just think. Now we can help more ghosts go home."

He stopped and stared, and she nodded.

"Yep, you better believe that's what Grandma was doing. And so was I. I suspect that's why everybody has gone so crazy around here lately. Probably an awful lot of ghosts are hanging around since Grandma went and since I got kicked out. So they don't know quite how to head home again, without her there to guide them."

"Is that what you'll do?"

"Absolutely. You don't have a problem with that, do you?"

He quirked his lips at her. "If I do, we'll work through it."

"Good, because I'm not letting you go. I've been through too much, and you're part of my life now, whether you like it or not."

At that, he burst out laughing, handed her a plateful of food, and said, "You'll need to keep up your strength."

"And why is that?" she asked, looking at him curiously, as she accepted her meal.

"Because being part of your life means an awful lot of shower time."

At that, she blinked, then got his meaning and burst out laughing. "And I'm totally okay with that. A bit of loving goes a long way."

"And a lot of loving …" he began.

She leaned over, kissed him on the lips, and added, "Goes even further. Thank you for joining my life."

He stared at her in surprise, and then a slow grin crossed

his face. "Isn't that the other way around?"

"It can be any way you want it to be," she said. "I just felt the need to say that." Then she picked up her fork and started eating.

Life had not been nearly this brilliant in a very long time. A whole new chapter of her life was beginning, and she couldn't wait.

This concludes Book 23 of Psychic Visions: Inked Forever.
Read a sneak peek from Insanity: Psychic Visions, Book 24

Insanity: Psychic Visions (Book #24)

Dr. Cresswell Simmons, a dream worker, is passionate about traumatized psychics and works in a psychiatric hospital to find those she can help. Six months ago, she barely survived a traumatic experience with a patient. Now on the cusp of returning to work and dreading every minute of it, she's asked to step back into the same case that almost destroyed her. She desperately wants to say no, but an eight-year-old boy's life is at stake.

Gray Burnett had worked on the original case, watching the devastation that had hurt Cressy. When asked to help her retrieve the information they need, he agrees—but more to protect her and the little boy than following orders. When her return to work is less than joyful, he wonders at the undercurrents in the hospital, as jealousy, admin disputes, even Board of Director members dominate the investigation and not in a good way.

Cressy is used to a world that doesn't understand her work, but she needs Gray to open up and to see what's going on around them. It's the only way they will survive, as the case takes a bizarre turn that shocks even her …

CRESSWELL SIMMONS BLINKED in the darkness, the drum of the phone beside her slow and insistent. She groaned as she reached out a hand. She checked the number on the caller ID and whispered, "Maddy?"

"Sorry," Maddy muttered. "I forgot what time it was."

"Or what time zone it was. Where are you?"

"I'm in England right now."

"Great, that's nice for you. I'm in Maine. Remember?"

"I know. I'm just …"

"You just what?"

"I'm in trouble."

At that, Cresswell bolted upright.

"What kind of trouble? Do I need to call Drew? Grant? What's going on?"

Maddy's laughter rolled free through the phone. "No, not that kind of trouble. I need help, very specialized help."

"Oh no, not again." Cresswell moaned.

"Unfortunately you're the only one I know who can do something about this."

"And you know how it hurts me to do it," she muttered.

"And yet you're getting better at it," Maddy added encouragingly.

"At least you hope I am."

"We've certainly saved a lot of people," Maddy noted,

"so I don't really want to think of this as being something that we can't do more of."

"Because it's not you going into these crazy minds and trying to figure out how to straighten them up and decide who is sane and who is not."

"I know. This one's ..."

"Special?" Cresswell asked. "You say that every time. You do know that, right?" She pushed herself up against the headboard and rubbed the sleep from her eyes. Looking around the room in the dim light, she checked the alarm clock. "It's five in the morning," she muttered.

"Yep, I know. I know, and I'm sorry."

"It's fine. Who am I going after, and what's going on?"

Maddy began, "It's a male."

"That's a change," she noted, with a yawn. "Won't make a damn bit of difference, you know? I still might not get in."

"You might not be able to, but Stefan has had some luck with him, and I've had just enough luck to realize that he's there."

"And, if he's there, why isn't he coming out?"

"Now this is the part that gets dicey."

"*Uh-oh*, don't tell me this is another dangerous one. You know I don't like those."

"I know you don't, but this is a boy. He's only twelve years old, and his mind is still at the point where we can do something with it."

"Where is he?"

"He's in Bishop's Sanatorium," Maddy stated.

Cresswell hated that, absolutely hated it whenever it involved a sanatorium. Especially that one—her home away from home—when she'd been working at least. "And who'll get me out when I get locked in there?"

"I'm really hoping you will get in and get out without any trouble."

"You're hoping for that, but you're not sure that it'll happen, are you?"

"I can't be sure. You know that. It's dicey, but both Stefan and I think that the boy's in there and that he's hiding."

"And why is he hiding?" she asked. "You need to give me some background."

"His family was murdered. By a *family annihilator*, as the FBI profilers call it," Maddy explained, her voice low.

"Great, and I suppose you found this one through Grant."

"I heard about him from Grant, and Grant gave me all the background history on the boy. Which is already rough enough."

"Are you sure the child even wants to come back out?"

"I don't think he knows he has a choice. I think he's hiding because he believes the annihilator is still coming after him."

"Was the annihilator caught?"

"Yes," Maddy confirmed. "He's been locked up, and this little boy needs to know that it's safe to come back out to reality."

"*Great*. Okay, well, you make it sound easy enough, but, if it were easy, you would have done it already."

At that, she sighed. "No, I … It's never that easy, is it?"

"No, it sure isn't."

"He's had some testing done, and basically he's nonviolent, but he's withdrawn, disassociated from society. One of his doctors has been working with him and saw obvious signs of stressors, where slight noises make him jump. All kinds of stuff are going on in there."

"Right, of course there is," Cresswell agreed. "And how is it you think I'll get him out?"

"I need you to go in there. I need you to go into his head and tell him it's okay."

"Again, if it were that easy, you would have done it already. So what's the trick?"

"The trick is, he's not listening," Dr. Maddy shared. "As far as he's concerned, the wrong person was caught, and so he doesn't believe us."

Cresswell pondered that for a moment. "Okay. And you think it's all part of his delusion?"

"Yes, I do. Grant does. Everybody does. We have a confession from the killer, so the boy should be free and clear. Yet he doesn't want to come out. I think he's just so caught up in his own psychopathy that he can't get out."

"Fine, I'll try," Cresswell stated, "but, even if I can talk to him, that's no guarantee that he'll want to come out. You know it's safe in there."

"It is safe," Maddy acknowledged, "which is why he's there. I just need you to try."

"Is there something else that is special about this one?"

"There's always something special, but yes. He has a grandmother who's desperate to have him come back to her. The poor grandmother lost everybody, and now it's just this little boy and an aunt. We want to give him a chance at life."

"How long ago did this happen?"

"Four months."

Cresswell winced at that. "Just enough time for him to settle in there."

"I know, and that's why it'll take somebody special, like you."

"Yeah, you know that the sympathy and flattery stuff

really doesn't work on me."

At that, Dr. Maddy laughed. "I know, but will you try?"

"Yeah, I'll try. I also want the name of the FBI agent assigned to the case."

"Why is that?"

"Because I need to know what this boy went through and what he's built for a retreat, a shelter in his own head, so I can make him realize the world outside of that shelter is also safe."

"I can give you his name," Maddy replied, "but—"

"Oh, don't tell me. He's a nonbeliever, I suppose."

"Yeah, he is. He knows that Drew's married to me and that we have both worked with FBI Agent Grant Summers before, but, as far as this other agent is concerned, it's all BS."

"And is that because he's also very gifted and he's ignoring it or because he only sees black-and-white?"

"I've only met him one time, and I would tend to say he only sees black-and-white, but I don't really know," Maddy admitted. "That's up to you to sort out."

"You never make it easy, do you?"

"It's not me," she replied. "I'm a pushover for kids. ... Last time we talked, so were you."

"That's a low blow," Cresswell growled into the phone.

"No, you're right. It is. I'm just ... I need you to go in after him."

"I told you that I would," Cresswell repeated, "but I'm not going in unprepared. And you know what happens if I open up that line."

"I know. I do. Stefan will help. I'll be there, and, on this end, if you contact that FBI agent, we can make sure that nothing else happens."

"Yeah, but once we open the doors to crazy, crazy comes out," Cresswell declared.

"And, when we open the doors to somebody who's hiding," Maddy added, "joy, laughter, and love can come out again. Let's give this little boy a chance."

"Fine," Cresswell said, "but I'm calling the agent in the morning."

"You don't have to. He'll be there in an hour." And, with that, Maddy started to hang up.

"What's his name?" Cresswell cried out.

Maddy's voice rang out loud and clear. "His name is Gray, and you met him last time. He was there." Then Maddy hung up, leaving Cresswell to stare down at the phone in dismay.

She also hadn't asked for the name of the boy, but she knew the file would be coming. All the files would be. It's also why there would be an FBI agent attached, whether she asked for it or not. Obviously a whole lot more was going on in this case than Maddy had let on. Especially if the FBI would be at her door in an hour.

With that, she threw back the covers and headed for the shower. In spite of herself, she was intrigued. And a little scared. The last time she'd been caught up in one of Maddy's cases, Maddy had damn-near died. Cresswell really wasn't about to sign up for another one of those again.

Yet, as she stepped into the bathroom and stared into the mirror, she shook her head. "Seems you did it anyway, fool." Then she got in and turned on the water.

Find Book 24 here!
To find out more visit Dale Mayer's website.
https://geni.us/DMSInsanity

Simon Says...: Kate Morgan (Book #1)

Welcome to a new thriller series from *USA Today* Best-Selling Author Dale Mayer. Set in Vancouver, BC, the team of Detective Kate Morgan and Simon St. Laurant, an unwilling psychic, marries all the elements of Dale's work that you've come to love, plus so much more.

Detective Kate Morgan, newly promoted to the Vancouver PD Homicide Department, stands for the victims in her world. She was once a victim herself, just as her mother had been a victim, and then her brother—an unsolved missing child's case—was yet another victim. She can't stand those who take advantage of others, and the worst ones are those who prey on the hopes of desperate people to line their own pockets.

So, when she finds a connection between more than a half-dozen cold cases to a current case, where a child's life hangs in the balance, Kate would make a deal with the devil himself to find the culprit and to save the child.

Simon St. Laurant's grandmother had the Sight and had warned him that, once he used it, he could never walk away. Until now, her caution had made it easy to avoid that first step. But, when nightmares of his own past are triggered, Simon can't stand back and watch child after child be abused. Not without offering his help to those chasing the monsters.

Even if it means dealing with the cranky and critical Detective Kate Morgan …

Find Simon Says… Hide here!

To find out more visit Dale Mayer's website.

https://geni.us/DMSSHideUniversal

Author's Note

Thank you for reading Inked Forever: Psychic Visions, Book 23! If you enjoyed the book, please take a moment and leave a short review.

Dear reader,

I love to hear from readers, and you can contact me at my website: www.dalemayer.com or at my Facebook author page. To be informed of new releases and special offers, sign up for my newsletter or follow me on BookBub. And if you are interested in joining Dale Mayer's Reader Group, here is the Facebook sign up page.
http://geni.us/DaleMayerFBGroup

Cheers,
Dale Mayer

About the Author

Dale Mayer is a *USA Today* best-selling author, best known for her SEALs military romances, her Psychic Visions series, and her Lovely Lethal Garden cozy series. Her contemporary romances are raw and full of passion and emotion (Broken But … Mending, Hathaway House series). Her thrillers will keep you guessing (Kate Morgan, By Death series), and her romantic comedies will keep you giggling (*It's a Dog's Life*, a stand-alone novella; and the Broken Protocols series, starring Charming Marvin, the cat).

Dale honors the stories that come to her—and some of them are crazy, break all the rules and cross multiple genres!

To go with her fiction, she also writes nonfiction in many different fields, with books available on résumé writing, companion gardening, and the US mortgage system. All her books are available in print and ebook format.

Connect with Dale Mayer Online

Dale's Website – www.dalemayer.com
Twitter – @DaleMayer
Facebook Page – geni.us/DaleMayerFBFanPage
Facebook Group – geni.us/DaleMayerFBGroup
BookBub – geni.us/DaleMayerBookbub
Instagram – geni.us/DaleMayerInstagram
Goodreads – geni.us/DaleMayerGoodreads
Newsletter – geni.us/DaleNews

Also by Dale Mayer

Published Adult Books:

Shadow Recon
Magnus, Book 1
Rogan, Book 2
Egan, Book 3
Barret, Book 4

Bullard's Battle
Ryland's Reach, Book 1
Cain's Cross, Book 2
Eton's Escape, Book 3
Garret's Gambit, Book 4
Kano's Keep, Book 5
Fallon's Flaw, Book 6
Quinn's Quest, Book 7
Bullard's Beauty, Book 8
Bullard's Best, Book 9
Bullard's Battle, Books 1–2
Bullard's Battle, Books 3–4
Bullard's Battle, Books 5–6
Bullard's Battle, Books 7–8

Terkel's Team
Damon's Deal, Book 1
Wade's War, Book 2
Gage's Goal, Book 3
Calum's Contact, Book 4
Rick's Road, Book 5
Scott's Summit, Book 6
Brody's Beast, Book 7
Terkel's Twist, Book 8
Terkel's Triumph, Book 9

Terk's Guardians
Radar, Book 1

Kate Morgan
Simon Says… Hide, Book 1
Simon Says… Jump, Book 2
Simon Says… Ride, Book 3
Simon Says… Scream, Book 4
Simon Says… Run, Book 5
Simon Says… Walk, Book 6
Simon Says… Forgive, Book 7

Hathaway House
Aaron, Book 1
Brock, Book 2
Cole, Book 3
Denton, Book 4
Elliot, Book 5

Finn, Book 6
Gregory, Book 7
Heath, Book 8
Iain, Book 9
Jaden, Book 10
Keith, Book 11
Lance, Book 12
Melissa, Book 13
Nash, Book 14
Owen, Book 15
Percy, Book 16
Quinton, Book 17
Ryatt, Book 18
Spencer, Book 19
Timothy, Book 20
Hathaway House, Books 1–3
Hathaway House, Books 4–6
Hathaway House, Books 7–9

The K9 Files
Ethan, Book 1
Pierce, Book 2
Zane, Book 3
Blaze, Book 4
Lucas, Book 5
Parker, Book 6
Carter, Book 7
Weston, Book 8
Greyson, Book 9

Rowan, Book 10
Caleb, Book 11
Kurt, Book 12
Tucker, Book 13
Harley, Book 14
Kyron, Book 15
Jenner, Book 16
Rhys, Book 17
Landon, Book 18
Harper, Book 19
Kascius, Book 20
Declan, Book 21
The K9 Files, Books 1–2
The K9 Files, Books 3–4
The K9 Files, Books 5–6
The K9 Files, Books 7–8
The K9 Files, Books 9–10
The K9 Files, Books 11–12

Lovely Lethal Gardens

Arsenic in the Azaleas, Book 1
Bones in the Begonias, Book 2
Corpse in the Carnations, Book 3
Daggers in the Dahlias, Book 4
Evidence in the Echinacea, Book 5
Footprints in the Ferns, Book 6
Gun in the Gardenias, Book 7
Handcuffs in the Heather, Book 8
Ice Pick in the Ivy, Book 9

Jewels in the Juniper, Book 10
Killer in the Kiwis, Book 11
Lifeless in the Lilies, Book 12
Murder in the Marigolds, Book 13
Nabbed in the Nasturtiums, Book 14
Offed in the Orchids, Book 15
Poison in the Pansies, Book 16
Quarry in the Quince, Book 17
Revenge in the Roses, Book 18
Silenced in the Sunflowers, Book 19
Toes up in the Tulips, Book 20
Uzi in the Urn, Book 21
Victim in the Violets, Book 22
Lovely Lethal Gardens, Books 1–2
Lovely Lethal Gardens, Books 3–4
Lovely Lethal Gardens, Books 5–6
Lovely Lethal Gardens, Books 7–8
Lovely Lethal Gardens, Books 9–10

Psychic Visions Series
Tuesday's Child
Hide 'n Go Seek
Maddy's Floor
Garden of Sorrow
Knock Knock...
Rare Find
Eyes to the Soul
Now You See Her
Shattered

Into the Abyss
Seeds of Malice
Eye of the Falcon
Itsy-Bitsy Spider
Unmasked
Deep Beneath
From the Ashes
Stroke of Death
Ice Maiden
Snap, Crackle…
What If…
Talking Bones
String of Tears
Inked Forever
Insanity
Psychic Visions Books 1–3
Psychic Visions Books 4–6
Psychic Visions Books 7–9

By Death Series
Touched by Death
Haunted by Death
Chilled by Death
By Death Books 1–3

Broken Protocols – Romantic Comedy Series
Cat's Meow
Cat's Pajamas
Cat's Cradle

Cat's Claus
Broken Protocols 1-4

Broken and... Mending
Skin
Scars
Scales (of Justice)
Broken but... Mending 1-3

Glory
Genesis
Tori
Celeste
Glory Trilogy

Biker Blues
Morgan: Biker Blues, Volume 1
Cash: Biker Blues, Volume 2

SEALs of Honor
Mason: SEALs of Honor, Book 1
Hawk: SEALs of Honor, Book 2
Dane: SEALs of Honor, Book 3
Swede: SEALs of Honor, Book 4
Shadow: SEALs of Honor, Book 5
Cooper: SEALs of Honor, Book 6
Markus: SEALs of Honor, Book 7
Evan: SEALs of Honor, Book 8
Mason's Wish: SEALs of Honor, Book 9
Chase: SEALs of Honor, Book 10

Brett: SEALs of Honor, Book 11
Devlin: SEALs of Honor, Book 12
Easton: SEALs of Honor, Book 13
Ryder: SEALs of Honor, Book 14
Macklin: SEALs of Honor, Book 15
Corey: SEALs of Honor, Book 16
Warrick: SEALs of Honor, Book 17
Tanner: SEALs of Honor, Book 18
Jackson: SEALs of Honor, Book 19
Kanen: SEALs of Honor, Book 20
Nelson: SEALs of Honor, Book 21
Taylor: SEALs of Honor, Book 22
Colton: SEALs of Honor, Book 23
Troy: SEALs of Honor, Book 24
Axel: SEALs of Honor, Book 25
Baylor: SEALs of Honor, Book 26
Hudson: SEALs of Honor, Book 27
Lachlan: SEALs of Honor, Book 28
Paxton: SEALs of Honor, Book 29
Bronson: SEALs of Honor, Book 30
Hale: SEALs of Honor, Book 31
SEALs of Honor, Books 1–3
SEALs of Honor, Books 4–6
SEALs of Honor, Books 7–10
SEALs of Honor, Books 11–13
SEALs of Honor, Books 14–16
SEALs of Honor, Books 17–19
SEALs of Honor, Books 20–22
SEALs of Honor, Books 23–25

Heroes for Hire

Levi's Legend: Heroes for Hire, Book 1
Stone's Surrender: Heroes for Hire, Book 2
Merk's Mistake: Heroes for Hire, Book 3
Rhodes's Reward: Heroes for Hire, Book 4
Flynn's Firecracker: Heroes for Hire, Book 5
Logan's Light: Heroes for Hire, Book 6
Harrison's Heart: Heroes for Hire, Book 7
Saul's Sweetheart: Heroes for Hire, Book 8
Dakota's Delight: Heroes for Hire, Book 9
Tyson's Treasure: Heroes for Hire, Book 10
Jace's Jewel: Heroes for Hire, Book 11
Rory's Rose: Heroes for Hire, Book 12
Brandon's Bliss: Heroes for Hire, Book 13
Liam's Lily: Heroes for Hire, Book 14
North's Nikki: Heroes for Hire, Book 15
Anders's Angel: Heroes for Hire, Book 16
Reyes's Raina: Heroes for Hire, Book 17
Dezi's Diamond: Heroes for Hire, Book 18
Vince's Vixen: Heroes for Hire, Book 19
Ice's Icing: Heroes for Hire, Book 20
Johan's Joy: Heroes for Hire, Book 21
Galen's Gemma: Heroes for Hire, Book 22
Zack's Zest: Heroes for Hire, Book 23
Bonaparte's Belle: Heroes for Hire, Book 24
Noah's Nemesis: Heroes for Hire, Book 25
Tomas's Trials: Heroes for Hire, Book 26
Carson's Choice: Heroes for Hire, Book 27

Dante's Decision: Heroes for Hire, Book 28
Steve's Solace: Heroes for Hire, Book 29
Heroes for Hire, Books 1–3
Heroes for Hire, Books 4–6
Heroes for Hire, Books 7–9
Heroes for Hire, Books 10–12
Heroes for Hire, Books 13–15
Heroes for Hire, Books 16–18
Heroes for Hire, Books 19–21
Heroes for Hire, Books 22–24

SEALs of Steel
Badger: SEALs of Steel, Book 1
Erick: SEALs of Steel, Book 2
Cade: SEALs of Steel, Book 3
Talon: SEALs of Steel, Book 4
Laszlo: SEALs of Steel, Book 5
Geir: SEALs of Steel, Book 6
Jager: SEALs of Steel, Book 7
The Final Reveal: SEALs of Steel, Book 8
SEALs of Steel, Books 1–4
SEALs of Steel, Books 5–8
SEALs of Steel, Books 1–8

The Mavericks
Kerrick, Book 1
Griffin, Book 2
Jax, Book 3
Beau, Book 4

Asher, Book 5
Ryker, Book 6
Miles, Book 7
Nico, Book 8
Keane, Book 9
Lennox, Book 10
Gavin, Book 11
Shane, Book 12
Diesel, Book 13
Jerricho, Book 14
Killian, Book 15
Hatch, Book 16
Corbin, Book 17
Aiden, Book 18
The Mavericks, Books 1–2
The Mavericks, Books 3–4
The Mavericks, Books 5–6
The Mavericks, Books 7–8
The Mavericks, Books 9–10
The Mavericks, Books 11–12

Standalone Novellas
It's a Dog's Life
Riana's Revenge
Second Chances

Published Young Adult Books:

Family Blood Ties Series

Vampire in Denial

Vampire in Distress

Vampire in Design

Vampire in Deceit

Vampire in Defiance

Vampire in Conflict

Vampire in Chaos

Vampire in Crisis

Vampire in Control

Vampire in Charge

Family Blood Ties Set 1–3

Family Blood Ties Set 1–5

Family Blood Ties Set 4–6

Family Blood Ties Set 7–9

Sian's Solution, A Family Blood Ties Series Prequel Novelette

Design series

Dangerous Designs

Deadly Designs

Darkest Designs

Design Series Trilogy

Standalone

In Cassie's Corner

Gem Stone (a Gemma Stone Mystery)

Time Thieves

Published Non-Fiction Books:

Career Essentials
Career Essentials: The Résumé
Career Essentials: The Cover Letter
Career Essentials: The Interview
Career Essentials: 3 in 1

Printed in Great Britain
by Amazon